DEMENTED: DESTINED DERANGEMENT

The Demented Trilogy: Book the First

Zifeara Nightshade

Cover designed by 33-ko

This book is a work of fiction. Names, characters, places, and incidents either are products of the author's imagination or are used fictitiously. Any resemblance to actual persons, living or dead, events, or locales is entirely coincidental.

Zifeara Nightshade
Visit my website at https://dementedseries.wordpress.com

Printed in the United States of America

First Printing: March 2019

ISBN-13 978-1-0959261-8-5

CONTENTS

DEDICATION

I have a lot of people to dedicate this book to, but the most important are my encouraging mother Karen and my loving husband Logan.
A giant friendly 'fuck you' to Siena, my self-proclaimed wife and best friend of way too long that made me start writing in the first place. I love you, you gremlin.
*Lastly, I'd like to give two flippant middle fingers to a former friend I had a massive falling out with; because of the chaos you threw me into, **my** characters gained a life of their own and I wrote them how they should be.*
We survived.

ACKNOWLEDGEMENTS

In all seriousness, Siena Moreno was there for me during some of the hardest times in my life and I cannot thank her enough. She has been the truest friend I've ever had and after 12 years, I can say she still makes me laugh like a hyena over wording missteps and accidental innuendos. I sincerely hope she and I never change.

My mother and I have had some rocky times, but I love her with all my heart; even enough to base the actual devil off of. My own mom may be far preferable, but she gave me some damn good writing material. Thanks, mum~

My husband believed I could pull this off and without him, this book wouldn't exist. I'm so lucky to have found someone that truly loves me and believes I can make things work if I just set my mind to it, so Logan, thank you.

Most importantly: MY AMAZING BETA TEAM! This spectacular group of friends has been so supportive and has given me amazing suggestions. They've been with me through late-night giggles and mid-editing crisis, through misunderstandings and preemptive correcting, through too many silly drawings to count. Without them, this could have been a trainwreck. So to Eleiren Bowen, Amy Willhite, Jacqueline Heinze, Gemma Collins, Luke Hendricks, and Meagan Poetschlag, thank you all from the bottom of my heart. I hope you'll put up with me into the next book and even throughout the series.

PROLOGUE

In the beginning, the barren cosmos stretched endlessly, drifting with aimless abandon. The first collision of galaxies sparked life in the scattered stardust, spawning two entities. The beings observed each other, uncertain of their purpose though compelled to remain together. With not much else to do aside from experimenting with the stars surrounding them, they found they each had a talent for creation. Their abilities to alter the flow of time or manufacture new forms of life from nothing amazed them and they wasted not a moment more. Together they created new planets and stars, each full of wondrous lifeforms and endless possibilities. However, as time soldiered on, they came to want more beings akin to themselves and together created two children.

The new children toyed with the stars and galaxies so carefully put in place by their parents, displacing centuries of hard work as children do. The parents decided their children needed a toy of their own, one to be shared so as to strengthen the bond between siblings. This new toy was a planet, one of many biomes and much water. A planet named Marien.

While Marien was full of unique plants and had several varied climates, it was devoid of moving entities. This they gave to their children to fill with whatever creatures they could conjure. They also gave their children names; to their son they gave the name Dios and to their daughter the name Satan, to which she pouted and claimed it wasn't grand enough. The parents passed each other a look and thought, asking her what sounded better to her. The child deliberated a moment and replied "Lucifer," and her parents conceded.

"Now dears," Mother Nature cooed, "this world is for you *both* and so you must strike a balance between what you choose to populate it with. No one of you may control more of the planet than the other at any given time. I also want you to realize no life is unending. Each thing you place down there has a soul, and each soul you must keep track of. Run along darlings."

Dios, being eager to begin work, claimed the top bunk for himself and rested upon the clouds, leaving Lucifer to nestle under the ground amongst the brimstone and fire. As specially tasked by their father, Lucifer began by creating a being to claim the souls of those who eventually die so the creatures didn't linger, and new souls had a chance to experience the world. This creature she called Mortis, and to everything that saw him, he adopted a different form.

While Dios began creating lovely creatures with flowing manes and sturdy bodies, Lucifer watched, planning and improving upon his creatures. For every pair of antlers, she added vicious claws to drag them down. Every set of swift legs she modified into lean muscle to out sprint them. Every pair of alert, perked ears brought padded paws to sneak behind them. For each set of wary eyes, a sleek pelt to hide the monster in the plants the peaceful creatures ate. Dios was getting rather sick of all this, and went crying to his Mother Nature.

"Mother, Lucifer is making these horrible monsters that keep eating my beings!"

Mother Nature looked down upon their world and smiled. "Dear, your sister is doing exactly as I asked; keeping your world in balance. Without all those things she's making, your animals would consume my garden. Now, why don't you build something together?"

Dios sulked back to Marien and visited his sister to tell her he'd been told to play nice. Unwillingly, they sat down to make something they both liked.

"I'm sick of four legs. Let's try two," Lucifer suggested.

"Well okay," Dios replied, "let's also try less fur for once. Like on elephants. They look good without it."

Lucifer made a face. "Ugh, elephants are one of the grossest things you've made yet! Can we at least not make the skin rock hard?"

Dios sighed and smoothed the skin of their creature. He then made it smaller and gave it proportionate limbs to its strange, bipedal body. Lucifer squinted at it and arranged the organs around so it could eat whatever it felt like.

"I feel this one should be... smarter than the others if you're going to let it eat whatever it can put in its mouth," Dios commented and they both agreed.

Next Lucifer added a few patches of hair here and there, giggling at how naked it looked. She also added a tail, which Dios quickly removed.

"All your things have tails! Let's just give it better balance."

Lucifer pouted but didn't argue for once. "What do we even call the ugly thing?" she asked.

"Hmmm, I like duggles. That sounds right," he proclaimed.

Lucifer gave him a withering look and said "Listen, that may be an even dumber name for a thing than when you called that freakin' bird thing a chicken. If you took off its tail, I get to stop you from naming it something terrible. How about..." she seemed to give this way more thought than it deserved before finishing her sentence, "...human. That sounds way better."

Dios rolled his eyes and gave her a "yeah, whatever" look since he wanted to start on a new creature for the ocean and they placed humans on Marien. Lucifer, on the other hand, thought humans could be improved, and without telling a soul added tails and ears and all her favorite parts of her creatures to them, creating demons as we know them. Dios saw this and once again went running to his Mother.

"Mom," he whined, "she's doing that thing again! That thing where she's being evil!"

Mother Nature looked down to see the humans and demons doing battle, resulting in terrible bloodshed on both sides. What Dios chose to overlook, however, was that in some places, the demons and humans coexisted, and often even bred to create strange new hybrids.

"Now dear, you can't just look at the bad side of what your sister does. Look at how they're getting along! Sure, some of the demons are killing the humans, but how is that different from your animals? They eat each other all the time. Why don't you make a fun human yourself and you'll feel better." And with that she shooed him off.

Mother Nature turned to Father Time and giggled, "Isn't it funny, they've created humans on Marien just like we did on Earth. I wonder if their humans will turn out like ours..."

Father Time also gave a hearty laugh and replied, "Well they do seem to share ideas with each other. Who knows, maybe they can communicate somehow and they don't even know it. Let's see how similar they become once they have technology worked out."

Slightly irritated with how unconcerned his mother was by his sister's monsters, Dios went home to ponder what he would make. Seeing one of the demons that was clearly part bird, he had a wonderful idea. He took a human, gave it the gorgeous wings of a white dove, the stunning blonde hair of a champagne stallion, and the irrevocable will to crush evil and bring mercy to the suffering humans. Dios called this creation an angel, but decided this first one was special and deserved its own name.

"I'll call you... Gideon, I think. And I'll make more of you so you can sweep through the world and keep my sister's beasts more at bay."

Just as he was about to create a second one of these creatures, he heard an awful commotion down below; humans screaming and the unmistakable roar of fire, the sickening crunch of bone fracturing, and a new sound he couldn't place but reminded him of the crack of thunder. Before he could make out what it was, his father appeared, halting time itself and whisking the new abomination away to his sister's realm to give her a good scolding for going too far.

Since Lucifer was very good at getting what she wanted, she persuaded her parents to let her keep the terror, on the condition she restrained it in some way. Lucifer was sent to her room to think about a solution to this before she was allowed to create any more. What she decided on was a vessel.

She took her favorite animals and piled them on to one demon. The body of a human, the wit and ears of the fox, the claws and pelt of the black leopard, the fluff on the tail and fangs of the wolf. *And why the heck not, Lucifer thought, let's not restrict her to one set of animals, the ability to change her appearance as she wished. It does look like a she, doesn't it?*

Lucifer added a mystifying voice to lure in her creature's prey, shaped her body better than most human females to throw the others off, and gave her the composure to fake her way through any lie. She left her devoid of emotions that would weigh her down. This was what she would encase her greatest terror in. This new demon, her new daughter, which she would name Zifeara. It had fear right in the name. Lucifer felt that something was missing, however. She pondered it for quite a while before she knew what was bothering her.

"This new one is different from the others. I feel as though I'll be greatly upset when she dies..." Lucifer thought to herself, "That is... *if* she dies."

At that moment, Lucifer hatched a cunning, awful plan. She went to see her father who, busy man as he was, always made time for his children.

"Father," Lucifer began, "has anyone ever just, not died?" Father Time cast a sideways look at his only girl.

"Well no dear," he began, "that's why we had you create your, what did you call that thing? Mortis? Since he collects souls, all runs as it should."

"But Father, things are living longer and longer now," Lucifer reasoned in her most persuasive voice. "Mortis has much less to do now that there is longer between collectings. Can't I have a way to give me more work? I hate sitting around doing nothing... I know! What if I deal with all the," Lucifer held up her hands and made quotes in the air, "bad souls, and you let old fuddy duddy up there do the good souls?"

Father Time considered his daughter's words while stroking his never-ending beard. "I suppose that makes sense. What do you *really* want, girl?"

Lucifer gave a wide, slightly disturbing grin. "Oh, not much, Father. It's just that, to speed up our work, I thought of something to do with my best monster!"

Time gave a concerned look but let her continue.

"I made it a vessel," Lucifer explained, "and once every full moon, it gets loose for a night and scatters as many souls, good *and* bad, as unbiasedly as it can. It doesn't care who or what it kills, but as soon as the first rays of sun hit it, it returns to its prison. The vessel itself has a purpose, of course."

Father Time raised an eyebrow for her to elaborate.

"The vessel is for when those crafty mortals figure out how to hide their souls from us. I know they will, they get smarter every day. My vessel will free the souls that Mortis can't get to because they've avoided a normal death. She's the clean up crew."

Her father nodded, as this sounded unusually reasonable for his daughter, and was about to tell her as much when she cut him off.

"There's just one thing I really want, Father."

Father Time sighed and asked what it was. Lucifer replied "I don't think this system will work if Mortis and the vessel can die. Grant them immortality and this system is flawless. Besides... I've grown very attached to this vessel. I've named her and she feels like my pride and joy, like Dios and I surely feel to you!"

Lucifer knew exactly how to pull her father's strings. He consented, but only if her brother's favorite toy got to be immortal as well. This was agreed upon, and Father Time created six vials of a strange liquid that would capture the soul of whatever drank it and seal it away in the vial for eternity. One for Gideon, one for Mortis, one for the vessel, and three more because Time liked to be prepared.

With their new creations let loose upon Marien, this is where the real story begins. My story, in fact. My name is Zifeara Mortis Nightshade and inside me lives the most evil, ruthless, and downright demented creature known to this world. Goody.

CHAPTER 1

When Karma Comes Calling

The night was dark out in the frozen north woods. The new moon was high and the stars lent very little light to the snow scattered over the thick pines. A small cabin had a fire going, smoke spiraling out of the brick chimney.

A man made his way slowly across the porch. He looked gaunt, worn from a long journey. The man was average, at least for the time, fit from a life of adversity. He was guarding a very important secret; he had discovered a way to make himself immortal. In order to craft the draught, he needed special ingredients only found in a far-off land by the ocean. He just had to get to the coast to find the components he needed, and he was safe.

Something is following me. Has been for weeks. I can feel it. His long, dark hair swayed with the midnight breeze and he shivered slightly. The man held his katana tightly by his side, scanning the trees around his lodge, a fearful gleam in his coal black eyes. He seemed content with his sweep, confident whatever haunted his steps was still too far off, but he was quite mistaken. As he headed back in, something shifted imperceptibly in a tree far off to the left of the cabin. Something biding its time in the cold.

Late that night as the man's fire died down and he nodded off, the shape in the tree stirred again. It unfolded itself from the still ball it had been curled in. An owl nearby began to fuss, but a low growl quickly hushed it as the cat-like shape slunk down the tree in near perfect silence.

The large snow leopard crept through the wintery powder to the back of the cabin, its movement muffled by the thick fur between the pads of its paws. As it reached the window at the rear, it slowly stretched itself up to the sill to look in. The man was asleep now, propped up in the corner nearest the fireplace having clearly succumbed to exhaustion while trying to watch both the door and window. Excellent.

The large cat shifted its form and grew smaller, turning into a tiny black moth which fluttered up to the roof and down the chimney. The moth landed lightly on the man's shoulder, not stirring him in the slightest. The insect rapidly shifted into an abnormally large black wolf with its jaws around the man's throat.

Woken with a start but unable to scream, the man choked as he flailed wildly for his precious sword. The wolf crunched down swiftly, crushing his windpipe and severing the carotid artery. Releasing the doomed man, the wolf watched as he struggled to breathe, the thought of defending himself gone as he tried to stop his life force from seeping into the soft wood of the floor. Finally, the lack of oxygen and blood loss took its toll and the man expired.

A black mist formed in the corner of the room. A gaunt man took shape as the mist itself settled like a cloak around his shoulders. He was in his early twenties at best, with pitch black hair that was neatly trimmed to ear length but clearly unmanageable on top. His narrow eyes were a color implying blindness but were much too alert for that to be the truth. As his thin face turned to his lupine companion, the beast shifted again into a more human shape.

A lithe but shapely woman stood over the dead man, tail swishing behind her. The dying light of the fire revealed that her long, sable hair had the faint spots of a black leopard, but her ears were large and pointed, like those of a fox. Her tail looked feline as well, save for the thickness and shape of the fur as it neared the end in a broad, rust-colored tuft reminiscent of the wolf she'd been moments ago. Her large, indigo eyes glanced toward the man in the corner, the right side of her mouth pulling upwards in a smug grin.

"He's all yours, brother," she told him, licking the blood from her lips.

He returned her smile, though less enthusiastically, and moved over the new corpse. He held his hand out and slowly, a swirling red orb seeped through the dead man's chest and lightly placed itself in the cloaked man's waiting palm. Tucking the orb into a silvery drawstring pouch at his side, the young man shot the woman a look. "Jeez, Zifeara, going for a new record lately? That poor bastard had no idea you were on him 'til he was already half dead."

Flicking her hair, Zifeara gave a wave of her hand. "Well, you know me, Mortis. Always the efficient soldier. I don't suppose you have time to catch up for a bit? I haven't seen you in ages since my work's been slow this month."

With a sigh, he shook his head. "Wish I could, hun, but I gotta get back to the present. Death is moving forward even if the past is changing. Makes me wish Grampa was as consistent as he thinks he is with his bloody timeline. I only stopped in at all because I had about half a second to say hello and see that you looked well. See ya later, sis." And with that and a smile, he vanished back into the fog he had appeared in.

Zifeara sighed and moved over to the fireplace. She couldn't say she didn't miss her brother sometimes. He was calming and pleasant to talk to. Snapping her fingers, she conjured a ball of brilliant red flame which she tossed atop the extinguished cinders and turned to leave, shifting once more into the massive black wolf. As soon as she stepped off the porch, the once quaint little cabin burst into intense flames. Soon, the only trace that anything was ever there at all was the pile of ash and the oddly large paw prints in the snow.

CHAPTER 2

With Friends Like These, No Wonder I'm Mental

Zifeara exhaled loudly as the hot water ran through her freshly cleaned hair and over her aching shoulders. Sitting cramped in a tree for nine hours really made her appreciate showers. Truthfully though, Zifeara loved the modern era. As much fun as time jumping was, she always felt most at home here where she could take full advantage of the luxuries of modern life, especially running water and electronics. They were the best things about this time.

Well, maybe not the *best* things, exactly. Zifeara smiled as she thought about where she was going tonight, and with whom. She finally had a night to herself and had told her best friend as much. A knock at her bathroom door snapped her from her thoughts.

"Madam," said an elderly male voice from the doorway, "Master Fang is here and waiting for you downstairs."

Zifeara frowned. "Damn, I was in here longer than I thought. Then again, he *is* always early, so probably not entirely my fault. Thank you, Graham. Let him know I'll be a while yet and get him something to drink. If that little shit rolls his eyes at you, I give you permission to tell him to shut up and go sit in the game room. He's too old to be sassing you still."

The older gentleman chuckled at the lilt of teasing in her tone. "Very good, Madam. I'll make sure he's comfortable."

Leaving Zifeara to hurry with her shower and dress herself up for the evening, Graham Bergham made his way slowly down the wide staircase leading out of her large top-floor room and to the foyer to inform their guest he'd be waiting a while. The butler wasn't as old as he looked; in fact, he was only fifty-three, but a hard youth had aged him an extra ten years. His slicked-back, grey hair complimented the broom-like mustache decorating his upper lip. Two curled ram's horns wrapped from the top of his hairline down and around his petite furry ears. His small tail flicked to and fro as he descended. Graham was an average ram hybrid. Thankfully he hadn't inherited his father's cloven hooves. He couldn't imagine how much the marble floors here would trouble him should he not have had human legs.

A tall man stood in the grand, marble foyer and turned long before Graham reached the bottom of the staircase. He huffed, blowing wild, raven-black hair out of his ruby red eyes. He was starting to fidget, crossing and uncrossing his long arms, only serving to highlight how awkwardly he was holding his lanky frame. Fang Nightstalker looked like a really tall geek. And he was.

"Sir, Zifeara has requested that you be patient as she lost track of time and will be a while," Graham announced as he reached the bottom of the stairs.

Fang rolled his eyes and was about to say something, but the old man cut him off. "She also said if you rolled your eyes, I was to tell you to 'Shut up and go sit in the game room'. May I get you a beverage to occupy your silenced mouth?"

Fang snapped his mouth shut, his oversized canines loudly clicking together. He appeared angry for a moment, but then laughed. "She knows me too damn well. Ah, whatever, I *am* almost half an hour early. Yeah, what kind of tea you got, Graham?" Before the old man could reply, he waved his hand. "Actually, just surprise me - I think Zia's got the newest Dino Destructor on her GameWizard, and I've been dying to try it." With that, he whisked himself through the archway to his left, leaving the smiling butler to head to the kitchen for tea.

Graham did truly like Fang; he'd known him since he was just a boy. He was ever amazed by how completely oblivious Zifeara was to the depth of Fang's affection towards her, even if she was created without love as a standard emotion. He had seen her come a long way in that regard since she'd hired him thirty-four years ago, but he'd never say anything about it. Even though Zifeara was good to him and treated him as an equal, it wasn't his place to give his opinion where it wasn't requested. Unlike someone else he knew...

A nearby crash prompted him to hustle through the double doors leading to the spacious, modern kitchen where he was greeted by a myriad of pans strewn across the floor. Standing in the middle of the mess was a sheepish-looking pixie of a girl, her large white wings tucked tightly at her sides.

"I'm sorry, Graham. I hit the pot rack again..."

Graham sighed. "Confound it, Lola, for once keep track of your wings. Doves are supposed to be graceful, not a bother to the poor old goats who have to look after them!"

Her brow furrowed and wings drooped further. "But Graham, I just get so excited when I'm baking! The brownies just went into the oven. It'll be a while, but do you want a cookie in the meantime? Gasp, does Fang want a cookie? I heard him come in and I made some fresh ones this morning!"

"I was just about to make him some tea, so you can try and force your confections on him when you take it in. Just be careful not to drop it all. And pick up these pots," Graham said, almost as much to himself as to her.

The young girl smiled and began to clear up her mess while the butler got the tea going.

Lola Darner was a cheerful girl of only seventeen with wings as white as fresh snow. She, as well as her older friend Graham, were two of Zifeara's rescues. Zifeara had this strange habit of finding all her help in good people down on their luck, which was kind of weird for someone with Zifeara's history if you asked Lola.

When she mentioned it out loud, Graham shushed her and told her it wasn't her place to say such things, but she didn't see the big deal. Zifeara had never gotten mad at her for anything in the two years she had worked here, much less even seemed offended by anything Lola said. Regardless, she was glad to have quite literally bumped into someone as nice as Zifeara as soon as she had gotten off the bus. She had run away from home because her father was an abusive bastard whose new wife was a druggie.

Graham interrupted her angry thoughts. "Lola? Are you alright girl? You look upset."

Lola jumped a little but quickly smiled. "Yeah, I'm good, just thinking a little too hard about unimportant stuff. Tea ready?"

Graham nodded and handed her a tray with a tea set and a plate of cookies on it.

"Aww, Fang doesn't get the good tea set?" she asked, nodding at the lovely white and red striped set on the tray.

"Well, first of all, the good set is reserved for formal events and fancy dinners; and secondly, I wouldn't give you the good set unless we tacked training wheels to you first. You'd be so excited by handling the good set you'd trip and drop it, probably right on Master Fang, as you did with the other set. Thank the gods Zifeara hated that one," Graham replied with a slightly annoyed tone.

Lola pouted but took Fang his tea. She was *extra careful* to hold the tray with as much grace as she could muster. Fang always made her nervous and far clumsier than she ever was. He was super cute, and an absolute sweetheart as well, though she knew exactly how out of her league he was. He was actually a little more than twice her age but being immortal and nineteen forever meant you looked it. She had met other guys, but none of them were like him, not even close. She could hope that he'd stop drooling over Zifeara someday. He was smart- he had to eventually figure out that Zifeara just wasn't into him and try to find himself a real girlfriend, right? She was willing to wait- Fang was worth it.

After much careful balancing, she finally reached the game room to the sounds of muted roaring and much stomping about. Fang was playing some game with dinosaurs and was currently stabbing at a big ugly thing with horns on its head that was trying to ram him. He cursed quietly to himself when he failed to dodge and got trampled. Lola had been holding her breath when she peeked around the corner and finally exhaled.

Something rustled about in Fang's hair and he paused the game as he turned to look at her. "Oh hey, Lola. Got tea for me?"

She quickly gave a cheerful "Yup!" and moved to set the tray on the end table to his right. "The brownies aren't done yet, but I baked cookies this morning, so there's a plate of those, too. You better try them because Graham is being an old codger and won't even humor me," she told him, not making direct eye contact.

Fang immediately picked up a cookie, glancing it over before shoving the entire thing in his mouth.

Lola stared at him wide-eyed and blushing as he chewed before a giggle escaped her.

His mouth was full, but she could still make out what he said. "Lola, you know I love your cookies. They're always good. Except for the salt incident. That was pretty bad, but still not the worst food I've ever put in my mouth."

After swallowing, he unpaused his game and was instantly flattened by the thing from earlier. "Ah, shit, see? Your baking made me forget I was being murdered by a giant *ugly lizard rhino*," he griped as the death screen appeared and he put the controller down. Taking a sip of his tea, his hair shifted around again, and he looked toward the upstairs bedroom.

"Sounds like Zia's almost done."

Lola finally realized why he looked so different tonight and lowered her tone of voice to almost a whisper. "Fang, where are your headphones? I don't think I've ever seen you not wearing them before. Am I being too loud for you?" she asked apprehensively.

He smiled. "Nah, I left 'em in the car so they could charge before I really need them. I accidentally fell asleep with them on last night, so they're just a little dead."

[1]Lola went to say something else to him, but he shifted his focus behind her and his eyes widened. She hadn't even heard Zifeara come down the stairs just outside the room. Turning around, the dove was almost upset; Zifeara always looked good but jeez, could she just not try for once? She had natural-looking waves in her usually straight hair, had some crazy acid-green eyeshadow on and was sporting black lipstick. The red, plaid miniskirt and black, short-sleeved top with rainbow ravens flying across it over what looked like a blood splatter hugged her every curve. Her ridiculous boots were covered with enough zippers for about a dozen jackets. She looked like a goth model.

Lola realized she officially didn't exist to Fang anymore, especially since Zifeara looked like she really wanted all of his attention tonight. She huffed and sadly wandered back to the kitchen.

Zifeara swept through the archway to the game room and jumped on Fang all in one swift motion. She hadn't seen him in so long, if she had to breathe, she wouldn't have been able to with how tight their hug was. As soon as he put her down, he all but yelled at her.

"Hairy *hell*, woman, where have you been? It's been, like, two months since you've been here! You better not have found some medieval hunk to run away with or I'm gonna have to kick his ass."

Zifeara laughed, minding her volume for him while rolling her eyes and lightly pushing on his chest. "C'mon, you know me better than that. I don't have the time or patience for some random sexy schlup with pretty hair, and tight abs, and gorgeous eyes, and-"

Fang stopped Zifeara by putting a hand over her mouth and glared at her. "I *am* going to have to kick some dude's ass, aren't I?"

She just snickered and removed his hand, keeping hold of it and leading him toward the door so they could go. Usually, Fang found it cute when she teased him, but in the last few years it had become less funny, especially on nights like tonight when she looked hot as hell.

---

[1] "Sugar" - Robin Shultz

CHAPTER 3

There are Eyes Under Here Somewhere

As Zifeara led him down her front steps, Fang almost pushed the random guy thing further. He was about ninety-eight percent sure she was just screwing with him, but that other two percent was murder. He let it go as she reached his car.

She paused, confused for a moment; his doors were proximity triggered and usually opened for her at this distance.

Fang smirked as she turned to look at him and ask if he had really bothered to lock his car in her driveway. "Ask D1g1t to open it for you," he told her.

She raised an eyebrow at him but did as he said. "D1g1t, open the door, please." She sounded dubious, but she knew better than to completely doubt him by now.

"Digit, digit!" exclaimed a high-pitched, robotic voice from the hood of the car as the front doors swung upwards.

"You're kidding, you wired D1g1t to your freaking car too? What can't you do with computers, man?"

Fang's smile only grew wider, his mouth pulling up to his left, and wagged his eyebrows at her as he walked around to get in.

Once comfortably seated, he clapped his hands. "D1g1t, we're going to The Trench tonight. Let's go!"

The car roared to life, hovering off the ground by about a foot and zooming down the path out of Zifeara's twelve-acre plot of land.

"So how long did it take you to get D1g1t in here? A hot minute, or was it actually hard?" Zifeara teased him.

"Oh no, it was pretty easy. Since lord knows I can't drive a regular car, this thing is so automated it has a ton of computers in it already. I just had to put a copy of D1g1t's hard drive in one of the extra slots in here and figure out some programming hiccups."

Fang was a rather rare type of demon, and as a result, he had some quirks to him. Vampyratu were true vampires; creatures with a craving for blood and the physical equipment to stalk their prey in the dead of night. What they lacked in eyesight and strength, they made up for in their excellent hearing and ability to influence other creatures. These hideous beasts could sneak right up on a human, intimidating them into silence while their lifeforce was drained, and leaving little trace they were ever there past puncture wounds in the victim.

While modern-day Vampyratu were at least much more attractive than their feral counterparts of yesteryear, Fang drew the short end of the stick when it came to other inherited traits. He couldn't see much further than an arm's length away, he'd scared a lot of other kids in his early years before he knew *why*, and he still had incredibly long ears. They measured around three inches each and he could swivel them nearly ninety degrees in any direction. He'd been self-conscious of his ears ever since he was a kid and hiding them was the main reason for his wild mess of hair.

Now that they were in the car, he could reclaim his favorite piece of technology. Reaching into the middle console, he unplugged what looked like large, red headphones without the connecting band to keep them on. He held them up to the bases of his unique ears, easing hair out of the way and ensuring the very specifically shaped slots in them lined up properly. As he pushed a button on either side of the earpieces, a ring around the middle of each one began to glow faintly, and a whirring sound softly suggested the machinery inside was calibrating them. A quiet hiss of escaping air signaled the pressure lock activating, and he spun a dial on either side of the outside rim, adjusting the level of volume at which he perceived sound.

The future made some pretty awesome stuff, but these headphones were how Fang was able to get by day to day. Normal sounds that most people were okay with were excruciatingly loud to him; a regular person's inside voice sounded like screaming most of the time. In fact, Lola had been basically shouting at him earlier before she realized he wasn't wearing his headphones, but that poor girl was shy enough without him making her feel bad. Besides, she brought him cookies. Really good cookies.

"All ready to go?" Zifeara asked him.

"You bet your ass I am. It's been a while since I've seen Sara, too. Tonight should be fun," Fang replied, an eager smile on his face.

The car sped them off to the bustling metropolis of New Tinning; the biggest nightlife hotspot for at least 300 miles. With skyscrapers holding impressive penthouses, a vast harbor to launch party yachts, and hundreds of cramped alleyways to peddle all manner of illegal substances, it was no wonder this place turned mental as soon as the sun fell below the horizon.

Fang and Zifeara talked of the latest nonsense in their lives as they were stuck in traffic, laughing and gasping at their different forms of drama like two schoolgirls. It took them almost forty-five minutes to get to their friend's nightclub, a marine-themed place located inside of a huge glass dome. The Trench was an aquarium for general admission during the day, but by night they opened up the spacious, underground portion of the building. Themed as a deep ocean trench, the club came complete with more soundproof tanks holding strange and mysterious wildlife from deep beneath the waves. The highlight of The Trench, however, was the large, tube-shaped aquarium which held a very different type of fish; their DJ.

Sara was a shark demon. While able to breathe air, she preferred to be submerged as much as possible since too much air made her scales itch. Designed to accommodate her need to be underwater, her show featured an entirely waterproof soundboard. Just thinking about that thing made Fang drool sometimes.

Sara was pretty cute too, with a thin, lean build, pale, blue-grey skin, alert yellow eyes, and a pixie cut. Unfortunately, the only thing that wasn't cute about her was her smile. There wasn't much you could do for a great white's terrifying set of teeth-especially since they were serrated and came in two rows.

15

Her long, split tail swished behind her as she spun in her tank. It was pierced in several places and sported a myriad of pirate-themed jewelry pieces. Fang liked Sara a lot; she was a bitch but in an awesome way. He had even considered asking her out before, but something about her drove him crazy, though he never could figure out what it was. Still, she was probably his best friend aside from Zifeara, and Zifeara didn't count. She had her own category as far as Fang was concerned.[2]

They were immediately granted entry to the club since all the bouncers could spot Fang from a mile away and knew Sara would be mad if they gave him even a hint of trouble. They got right up near the tank so that Sara would spot him the next time she looked up. With her trademark, toothy grin, Sara put the music on autoplay and hauled herself out of her tank to say hello.

Yelling over the music, Fang was greeted by his friend with a wet hug.

"Hey Sara, how you been? Sorry I haven't been in for a while; we did some work on the SoundCave this month."

She smiled, horrific teeth glinting in the light from the overhead strobe. "Oh sweet, I have to come see that! I'm off on Tuesdays now, so you'll have to show me around before you open." She nodded toward Zifeara. "I see someone's back from the dead!"

Zifeara grinned and began yelling a conversation of her own.

As far as Fang could tell, she and Sara liked each other, but to be fair, one of Zifeara's specialties was being nice to people she didn't actually care for. Hell if he'd ever ask either one of them about it though; their amicable relations were good enough for him.

Sara elbowed him in the ribs and brought him back to attention. "Hey, I know Zifeara's been gone a while, so I'm gonna go play some extra hard music and let you two have fun." She passed him a slip of laminated paper with her name signed in jagged lettering at the bottom. "Hand this to Shayne, he's running the bar tonight. He'll set you both up with whatever you want, all night. Try not to get too wasted too fast!"

With a mischievous wink, Sara made her way back to her booth, flopping back into her tank with a solid splash.

Zifeara and Fang moved over to the bar area to get their first round of drinks before they went to dance. The fun thing about fire demons like Zifeara was that alcohol combusted once it hit their stomachs, serving the same purpose as giving a young chipmunk a hefty dose of speed. She'd be bouncing off the walls and unfocused for hours after only a few shots.

Instead, fire demons got drunk off what was essentially synthetic flavored mercury, with true elemental mercury tending to be the insanely high-priced, rich-people-only top shelf stuff. Zifeara always took one hit of real, straight up mercury, but usually only when she was coming down off her first round of intoxication.

Fang was, amusingly enough, a fan of foofy, brightly colored drinks in between rounds of stag blood based Bloody Marys laced with tequila. It was an interesting set of concoctions but true to her word, the bartender took Sara's card and kept offering to get them more of whatever they wanted.

After they had a few drinks and were loosened up for the evening, the pair spent several hours letting all their stress out, dancing to the excellent set the shark-girl had promised. Fang couldn't help sometimes pretending to move, but instead watching the way the lights reflected off the leopard spots in Zifeara's hair or allowing

---

[2] "Let's Go" - Joe Ghost

himself to be mesmerized at the way she swung her hips in perfect time with her favorite songs. He was getting worse at keeping his composure around her the drunker he got.

Even though he never let himself get drunk enough to experience a total lack of control, it was slowly becoming harder to hide how he really felt about her. Every time he thought about trying to bring it up, someone got in the way, the mood wasn't right, something exploded, or he simply chickened out. Yeah, an explosion did derail his attempt once and he *still* couldn't believe it, even after two years. *Oh shit, she realized I was staring like a gormless moron.*[3]

Raising an eyebrow, Zifeara motioned for him to follow her as she made her way through throngs of people back to the bar. He watched the bartender pour her what had to be the real stuff. Twice. This *was* going to be a fun night, maybe even *the* night. Aw hell, he didn't know if he could do this without something to shut his reasonable brain up.

Fang asked for two shots of a murky liquid and slammed both of them. This awful crap was alcoholic snake's blood, basically the most potent but miserable alcohol a vampire could ingest. As long as he didn't taste it, he could keep it down, and he'd need that liquid bad judgement to keep up with Zifeara on that much mercury.

They stayed and partied hard, their drunken bodies moving loosely like the water around them until The Trench closed for the night, only a few hours before the sun came up. It was a handy thing that Fang had a fully automatic car because by the end of the night they were lucky they still knew what it looked like. On the ride home, they laughed way too much, and too loudly, remembering silly looking people they had seen and a dude thinking another dude was a woman and getting decked for it.

When they finally reached Zifeara's house, they both made their way upstairs to get some pajamas and crash. Fang always had spare clothes here since he would stay at her place whenever she did. He was looking forward to cuddling up to his best friend for the night. They still slept together and had ever since he was a child with nightmares. To them, it was only seeking comfort in the presence of someone they trusted more than anyone else. At least, it used to be until Fang started his crush; now it was more a battle of self-control, cowardice, and willpower.

They both grabbed their clothes and turned away from each other to change. Fang had a t-shirt and some flannel pajama pants with a leaf pattern on them and Zifeara had a fluffy pajama set with all sorts of black cats on them.

Even her pajamas are adorable... Fang tried to put that thought out of his mind as she pulled her hair up and out of the way before running a hand over her face, using her fire to burn her makeup off.

She tilted her head at him slightly and closed the gap between them to stand right in front of him. Fang's heart started beating insanely fast and he knew he had to be blushing at least a little. He was positive he'd gotten drunk enough that he was one breeze short of an open book and he hoped she was far enough gone to not notice the start of his physical meltdown. Zifeara reached toward his face and he almost lost his cool and told her every emotion he had kept secret for the past three years right then and there. When she put her hands over his headphones and pushed the buttons to take them off, he flinched, but she didn't seem to notice.

"You don't want these to die again. You'll forget to charge them before breakfast, I just know you will," she said softly with a slightly lopsided, tipsy smile.

---

[3] "Jetfuel" - Joel Fletcher and Uberjak'd

She placed them on her dresser on the other side of the room and Fang finally exhaled and shook his head. Crisis averted, at least for tonight. Tonight was absolutely not the night; they'd both had too much to drink and anything he'd try to say to her would come out sounding less romantic and more idiotic.

They piled into Zifeara's king-sized bed and buried themselves in blankets, quickly falling into a drunken, happy sleep.

The next thing Fang knew, he opened his eyes and daylight filtered through the windows in heavy beams. The light was way too bright to be any time before noon. Looking down, Zifeara was snuggled up to his chest, talking in her sleep.

"Mrrmm, mmm, Fang..."

She totally just said my name. Huh, that was new. Wonder what exactly she could be dreaming about. He dare say it sounded good. Her eyes fluttered open and she groggily looked up at him. Something seemed off about her, but he couldn't tell what. He must have just been fuzzy from the massive hangover he had. Damn snake blood... He should really stop trying to drink that stuff.

"I just had the weirdest dream," she told him.

"Yeah, what was it about? Anything fun?"

"Well sort of, I think. You were there and we were at Sara's when you just..." She trailed off and stared strangely, almost *curiously* at him for a moment.

He had no idea what the hell possessed him at that moment, but the look in her eyes made him lose all his reservations like magic. He leaned down slowly, nearly laughing at the way her eyes widened further and further the closer he drew. With only a breath between their lips, it was exceptionally easy to forget why he had waited so long to do this and even easier to remember how much he loved the vast depths the intense purples of her eyes seemed to contain. Finally closing that gap somehow felt like the greatest thing he'd ever accomplished.

"Mrf! Mmm..." Zifeara was clearly surprised, but grabbed onto the front of his shirt and pulled herself closer.

He wrapped his arms around her and ran his hands down her back, almost all the way to the base of her tail. He inhaled sharply as she used her tongue to encourage him to open his mouth, clearly impatient to explore this new possibility. He couldn't have been further from complaining if he tried. This was far better than he had even thought possible, but after a moment he felt sort of a weird falling sensation, like his heart had dropped into his stomach.

Fang shot straight up in the bed, panting lightly like he had been jogging and tried to look around the briefly unfamiliar room. The light was coming in through the window, but it wasn't as bright as it had been a minute ago. Based on the intense pounding in his head, he was awake this time. He glanced over and there she was, turned away from him and lightly snoring. Shit. That's what had been wrong- she wasn't *real*. He was having the best dream ever and he had tried to stop himself from getting too into it.

Now a little depressed, he got up to fetch some water from the bathroom sink. Trying to push his hair out of his eyes to at least somewhat discern where the cup Zifeara always kept on the counter had moved to was like trying to part a dense jungle with a butter knife instead of a machete. He must have slept on his face at some point because this was just ridiculous.

He looked up into the mirror to see how bad the damage was. "Look at you, you idiot," he said quietly to himself, "it's been almost four years and you still suck at this. It's only getting worse too. You were ready to take this *way* further than just telling her how you feel last night if she let you, weren't you?"

Still not able to locate the stupid glass, he cupped his hands to drink. As he reached for the towel, he found the cup and it found its way to the floor, shattering into pieces. *Shit.* He heard a muffled growl coming from the bedroom and was a touch scared to go see what it was she had turned into this time. Peeking around the corner, he saw that the crash had only sort of woken Zifeara up; activating her, as he called it, 'oh crap there's danger, I better look scary' reflex.

Sitting atop her bed was a tiger, much larger than physically possible, snarling at the room in general while trying to scan the entirety of it for the threat. With its unfocused eyes and unbalanced posture, it was one wasted tiger.

"Zia, it's me, I made that sound," Fang said softly as he slowly moved around the corner, "Sorry, I knocked a cup off your counter. Go back to bed."

She turned quickly, stared at him, blinked sluggishly a few times while what he had said sank in, and circled on the bed before huffing back down. He smiled a little and went to clean up the remnants of the cup.

And she almost heard you talking to yourself. He climbed back into bed, now sans-tiger, and pressed his back against Zifeara's.

I'll do it next time. I'll prepare for it and just get it over with so I can calm down. I just need a definite yes or shut up and I'll probably not be suicidal. Unless she hates me. Damn it, now I'll never get back to sleep... he thought as he drifted back off.

CHAPTER 4

Memories and Exposition

After a late lunch, some video games, and an unwilling goodbye, Fang made his way home. Zifeara had more work to do and needed to get back to a different time. She had promised him she'd return in a week, but that pretty much never happened. She could claim work was slow all she wanted to, but she had been gone for longer periods of time lately.

Sighing and looking out of the car window at the blur of colors moving by his short-sighted eyes, he recognized the particular blend of shapes his car was passing. Jonnan Park was the largest piece of nature left in the whole city, and where he had spent a good eightish months of his life. It had been the worst time he could remember.

Fang had two siblings, his brother and sister, twins Morrow and Melody. They were tiny versions of himself, but more proportional than he was, with shorter ears and smaller fangs. Melody had beautiful goldenrod eyes like their mother, whereas Morrow's were a deep mahogany color like their father's. They were only a year younger than him, but they were impressively smart and very quick learners. At barely three, they could read all their baby books and could hold a simple conversation for a good few minutes before they were distracted by any number of things. They did, however, have trouble saying his first name, Mortichai, so instead of shortening it they just called him Fang since his teeth were so much bigger than theirs.

He didn't mind really, and even his mother began affectionately calling him Fang, so he just went with it. Even though his siblings were essentially the same person at this age, Fang felt a stronger affection for his sister. He loved his brother, sure, but something about Melody compelled him to take extra good care of her. Maybe it was just an older brother thing.

Regardless, Fang was an exemplary big brother, so much so that his mother left him to take care of the twins when she went off to work one of her jobs. Fang wasn't sure how many she had, but he remembered she was gone for a long time most days. She always left them pre-made lunches, since Fang could only work the microwave, and gave them each a kiss before telling them to play nice and heading out the door.

Sometimes Fang's father was there, but he always told them not to bother him and either went off to his room or placed himself in front of the TV. It was always trouble when he went to his room. Fang didn't understand what he did in there until he was older, but his father always came out in a state that if he even so much as *saw* one of his children he'd launch into a fit and throw things.

Therefore, when Fang saw his father make for his parents bedroom, he shuffled himself and his siblings into their room, locked the door, and began a game of build a fort and pretended to be knights, or dinosaurs, or both. His mother would come home, knock on the door to be let in, play with them, make dinner, then ready them for bed. This routine held true for quite a while until a few months after Fang's fourth birthday.

On that particular day, his mother didn't go to work, meaning she could spend the whole glorious day with them, and everything was wonderful. Wonderful, until his father came home that evening. He stormed in through the door yelling, his voice slurred almost beyond comprehension, and Fang's mother quickly shooed them not only to their room but the closet which they almost never played in. She told Fang to keep his siblings close and quiet and that she'd be back as soon as she dealt with whatever his father's problem was. He did as his mother said until his sensitive ears heard something distinctly different from the fights they always had.

This was a sound Fang would remember for the rest of his life as the sound of bone fracturing and giving way- a sound he would only ever hear twice more as he grew up.

This very specific noise came from the kitchen now, shortly followed by his father breaking into their room, searching for them. Fang kept his hands over his sibling's mouths, trying to keep them still as his mother had asked. When his father stomped back out, Fang knew they had to move. He felt it, and though he didn't know what instinct was yet, it was telling him to *run*. He told his brother and sister to be the quietest ever and slowly led them by their tiny hands from the closet and down the hall to the front door, not stopping even for a second.

Everything went exactly to plan until his sister screamed. She must have been frightened by something in the kitchen, but by the time Fang turned to see what the danger was, their escape was obstructed by the hulking form of their father. Since Melody was on the proper side of the door for such a maneuver, he yanked it open and flung her through it while attempting to swing his brother around him to do the same. Unfortunately, he wasn't fast enough, and his father grabbed them both. Fang thought quickly and sank his trademark teeth into the hand holding the front of his shirt, causing his father to curse and throw him into the nearest wall.

Fang couldn't see well at the best of times, but this was worse by far than turning out all the lights for bed. He could hear his brother screaming and tried to get to him, but his legs weren't moving the way he wanted them to. By the time he got up and was stable enough to do anything, he couldn't hear Morrow anymore. Panic and survival instinct took complete control when he realized the wall he hit was right next to the open door and he stumble-ran through it to quickly find his sister.

Listening intently, he caught the sound of her crying in a bush. He could also hear other people around, coming closer to the scene he'd fled, causing him to panic further. He grabbed Melody and ran. He couldn't let them get her too. He'd been taught to avoid strangers like the plague and that was exactly what he was going to do.

He dragged her through foliage, this way and that, making sure to keep them both out of sight. Fang could feel his heart struggling to keep up with such a strenuous pace; he wasn't used to running so much and prayed to anything that would listen that he wouldn't have to try to carry his sister too. He didn't give any thought to where they would go- *could* go- until he couldn't take another step. They had ended up in the park their mother took them to sometimes, underneath the biggest tree there.

They stopped to catch their breath and it finally sank in. It hit Fang first; they were alone with no one to turn to, very little idea of how to survive on their own, and a complete distrust of other sentients. It didn't take long before they both broke down crying. Fang promised his sister between sobs that he'd take care of her, that he wasn't going to let anything happen to her. He felt empty, knowing that his mother wouldn't be coming to pick them up this time, nor would she have Morrow with her. All he had was Melody, and he'd figure something out. His mother had always told him he was a smart kid; now he had to be.

¤ ¤ ¤

The day Melody left was a bittersweet one. There was a boy she always played with when he came to the park; some sort of lizard demon with big, yellow eyes, just like hers, and he dropped by to see her one day. She and Fang were living in the park, in the giant tree where they had first stopped. He tried to keep this fact under wraps in case it got them into any trouble, but one or two people knew. It might not have been the best idea, but Fang was only four, so he did what he thought was best for the two of them. A lot of fruit trees grew in Jonnan Park and at all seasons at least one type of fruit was available. It wasn't much, but it kept them going. There was a sweet old man who sold hot dogs and gave them each a free one every Friday. Fang was also getting better at hunting squirrels and catching fish from the lake.

Always one to stay positive, Fang was convinced things weren't that bad, considering. Melody had a friend. He could keep them both alive and the weather was almost always warm in New Tinning. Almost. Fang was starting to think about what they'd do when winter hit in about five months. Winter didn't last very long, but it sometimes made the nights cold enough for snow. He momentarily pushed the thought out of his mind to tell Melody to be careful as she and Jinto, her new best friend, wandered off to play on the swings.

Unbeknownst to Fang, Jinto's parents had planned to meet them since he had accidentally let it slip that his little friend *lived* in the park. Jinto was adopted too, and they asked Melody if she'd like to come live with them. Her little eyes watered up. She'd love having a family and a house again, and they were very nice people, but she told them she'd have to think about it and ran off before they could stop her. She returned to Fang and told him what happened.

He asked if they knew about him and she shook her head. He smiled at her and told her to go with them, not to worry about him. He didn't think they'd be as welcoming to him as they would a cute little girl. Besides, just in case he was a deal breaker, Fang didn't want to ruin what could be his last chance to take care of his sister.

He had watched the family for a while and was fairly certain they were not only nice enough, but they had a lot of money. Melody could finally have a good life. She cried and told him she didn't want to leave him, but he insisted that she be brave and go; she'd see him every time they came to the park. He promised that no matter what, he'd still be around.

After he got her to stop crying, he sent her off to her new home. She gave a final wave, and Fang was happy for her as he hid his own tears. Maybe the same thing would happen to him. He doubted it though- he wasn't cute. In fact, he was downright scary to most other kids he'd met. It would take someone crazy to want him.

¤ ¤ ¤

Winter sucked about as much as Fang thought it would. The days grew shorter and colder and there was less sunlight to provide any warmth. Most nights, the dew on the grass froze and there would be a light layer of snow on the ground come morning. Less fruit grew and the fish were sluggish and hid deep within the pond which was now far too cold to enter. Fang was used to not often having more than one meal a day, but now that he needed body heat to stay alive, getting enough food in his skinny little frame was becoming impossible.

He hated to think about his situation, since it tempted him into crying like a baby, but this night he gave in. He missed his siblings and his mom. He missed the warmth of a bed and the feeling of falling asleep full. He was so angry at his stupid father for taking his life away from him. He hoped whatever happened to him was just as awful if not worse than what his son was going through.

Then he thought of something better to calm himself down. Melody was warm and full. She had a bed, a family, and was happy. And she hadn't forgotten him. He'd seen her just the other day and she had brought him as much food as she could cram in her new lunch pail, then made Jinto give up some of his as well. Fang smiled thinking of how tightly she already had her new brother wrapped around her finger, just like she always had him. He lied to her and told her he was still doing great so she wouldn't worry.

Just as he had settled, he heard someone coming. *At this time of night?* He sat, curled in as tight of a ball as he could on his favorite branch, a blanket he had found draped over him. Looking down, he listened intently and waited for the intruder to come into view.

It was a woman, tall and slim, with a light coat on, holding a cup from the coffee place down the street. She had large ears, so Fang tried to be very quiet. He hoped she would just carry on through the park like most people did at this hour. Much to his dismay, she didn't. She sat right at the bottom of his tree and drank her coffee, quietly humming to herself and enjoying the night. She pulled a paper bag out of her pocket and reached into it for something.

Curiosity won out over fear, and as Fang tried to see what she had, he accidentally shifted a little too far. The movement caused a tiny piece of bark to dislodge and make some noise on its way down before lightly crunching in the snow below. The woman froze and her ears pivoted around, alert for another sound. She stood up and looked about, listening carefully as she realized that she might not be alone.

Fang tried to make himself as small and invisible as possible, but to no avail. She finally glanced up and spotted him, his large red eyes faintly shimmering from beneath his blanket. She seemed surprised, but not afraid.

"Hey there. What are you, little one?"

Fang didn't know why in the world he wasn't scared of being spotted, but the woman's voice relaxed him somehow. It was gentle and hushed, not too hard on his ears. She smiled and reached into the bag again, pulling out a giant cookie.

"Hungry?" She shook the treat a little. "If you come down here, I'll share with you."

Fang's mouth watered. He was hungry and he hadn't had anything sweet in forever. He slowly peeked his head out of the blanket as the woman sat back down and resumed sipping her coffee, not looking at him.

She had hoped he'd come out if she pretended to just hang out and not make eye contact. She'd heard about a feral kid in the park from the coffee shop owner and curiosity had gotten the better of her. She planned to take him to an orphanage if she could catch him, by force or otherwise since it was getting too cold out here. Compassion was a fairly new, but somewhat strong, feeling to her.

Fang slowly crept down the tree, on the side opposite the woman and slunk around it.

The twitch of her ears meant she must have heard him come up on her left and she broke the cookie in two. "Here. When you finish, I'd like to know your name," she said softly, offering him the bigger half of the treat.

He hesitantly took it, nibbling cautiously, ready to run if she tried anything, but she just sat there, eating her half and enjoying her drink. He had eaten his whole half when he began to feel an odd sense of trust for this woman. Even at such a young age, Fang knew she was very pretty. Her eyes were big and a beautiful shade of purple. He swore he could almost feel a warmth coming off her even though her coat was too light for the weather.

"Fang," he said without thinking.

Crap. He hadn't meant to say anything at all to her. At least he didn't tell her his actual name. She seemed relaxed enough, but the way she didn't turn her head when she met his stare set him even more on edge.

"Nice to meet you, Fang. My name is Zifeara. How old are you?"

Now that she was looking at him, Fang was properly scared. Those indigo eyes froze him to the spot. He wanted to stay there next to her when he should have wanted to run until his lungs hurt.

"F-four. A-almost five, I guess..." Fang told her.

Never losing that cool smile, she eyed him like a predator. He didn't miss the soft sound of her scenting the air. "I hear you've been doing pretty well for an almost five-year-old. A few people told me you've been here quite a while. Definitely a feat for a juvenile Vampyratu."

Now Fang's head was screaming at him- *run, you stupid idiot*. Not a single muscle moved. If his vocabulary were larger, he'd say this woman was bewitching. He nodded, unsure of what she had just called him but lost in the unfathomable depth to that one shade of purple. He almost hadn't noticed her move a hand from her cup toward him, but he caught it before she could touch him, finally taking a step back.

"You don't look like your clothes are very warm. I happen to be a fire demon and can do something about that." As she spoke, a ball of red flame took shape in her hand. "Here, take it. It won't burn you, I promise."

Still transfixed, he held his hands out so that she could drop it into them. The sphere warmed his whole body, making it feel like summer again.

Fang shot her a confused look. He didn't understand what she was doing. Why she was being so... *nice*. "Why are you here? What do you want with me?"

Zifeara seemed a little taken aback by his forward question, but as she stared into his wide, suspicious eyes, she said the last thing he would have expected. "I want to take you home."

The boy dropped the fire and it fizzled out in the light layer of snow on the ground.

"W- you what?" he asked in a meek voice.

Her smile widened, adding a softness to her gaze. Fang's better judgement was gone. He'd been too badly off for too long and this was the sort of thing he dreamed of, though not the family he pictured. The odd sense of trust that had been growing was good enough for him right now. The woman stood up and held out her hand, looking at him expectantly. He placed his smaller hand in hers, his mind made up to simply accept whatever happened to him. He was done living in a tree. Whatever awaited him now, with Zifeara, would have to be better than this. Right?[4]

¤ ¤ ¤

Snapping out of his reminiscent haze, Fang requested D1g1t take a detour on the way home. The car obliged and they headed in a new direction; all the way to the northern outskirts of town. Arriving at his destination, Fang got out of the car with a huff, looking up at the building looming before him. The massive, grey structure looked as miserable as the vibe it put out, as if it were the dullest place known to man. He'd let this wait for too long and was ready to get it over with.

He walked into the main reception area and asked the rather rude, disinterested secretary at the front desk to see one man in particular. She told him to go sit down and fill out a form. Fang did as she asked, contemplating what some of the questions could possibly be for and wondering if certain answers meant they wouldn't let him in. Form completed, the woman at the desk took it, gave it a once-over, and handed Fang a clip-on badge with the word 'visitor' printed in bold, red letters on it. She then hit a button to open the large door to the right and off Fang went, going down long corridors and nodding to staff until he came to another, well-guarded metal door. The men around it stopped him to inspect his badge and escort him to his visitee.

After moving down cell after cell of inmates, they finally reached the area of New Tinning Penitentiary where those convicted of more serious crimes were kept; Delta Ward. The specific cell they stopped in front of was an average one; fire-resistant bars, reinforced concrete, bare necessities inside, and a small, sliding plaque holder on the right of the door which read 'Kayne Nightstalker.'

His father sat on the edge of his bed, doing nothing in particular, not even turning as the guard told Fang he had only to call him back to be let back out of the ward. Fang stared at the gaunt, prison-worn figure who looked so intimidating in his memory- now reduced to a sobered alcoholic inside the shell of a man with nothing left to look forward to.

"Who are you and what do you want, kid?"

"How long are you in for?" he asked the inmate.

"Feh," Kayne spat, "about a hundred and two years left. Folks don't take killing kids lightly around here."

Fang could feel decades of rage building inside him and his composure sinking like a ship rapidly taking on water. "I always wondered why you did it. I read about your case once and they said you never gave any motive. Why in the gracious hell would you kill the wife who worked more jobs than she should have just to take care of your useless ass, along with three kids? Same reason you said, 'Fuck it I'll kill those little bastards too'?"

At that, Kayne finally looked at Fang. He got up from the bed and came to stand at the bars, staring with an intensely confused look on his face. "Who the fuck are you?"

Fang glared at him hard for a moment before letting a huge, unnerving grin spread across his face, baring his large canines and all the malice from the last thirty-two years. "Take a guess, old man. Think real hard through all those dead brain cells."

Kayne grew white in the face and took a faltering step backwards. "You can't be. They never found my fucking kids. They died on the streets."

---

[4] "Ho Hey" - The Lumineers

Fang's grin faded. "No Dad, we didn't. Melody and I are doing fantastically well, actually. She has an adorable son and a loving husband. She's got an orchestra performance coming up, first seat cello in fact, and I just did some renovations to *my* nightclub. We both ended up rich and successful after you ruined our lives. I was just thinking about it today and figured it was finally time to come rub some salt and lemon juice in your eyes over your happy, well-off progeny."

Kayne sat back down to compose himself for a moment before he began a slow, rattling laugh that quickly got louder. "You want to know what happened? Fine. Your stupid mother and I got married because her parents owed me a debt and they were so damn poor they had to arrange the wedding to get me to drop it.

I didn't even *like* Aria- never did, she was just there out of obligation. Then she had you little shits when I didn't want a single one of you, much less three. She always spent all her damn money that was meant for me on you brats and that was what happened that day.

I went out for a drink and I hadn't been there very long when the barkeep cut me off because your stupid mother didn't put the money she should have on my card. She fucking *spent it* on you little bastards. So I fucking brained her. Harder than I meant to, yeah, but she deserved it."

Fang was lucky he had left the personal weapons he kept in case of emergencies in the car or the guards would have arrested him for shooting a man's balls off.

"You really were going to kill us all weren't you, you fucking prick?" There was no hint of composure left in Fang's voice anymore and it grated across his teeth. He was pissed and he wished he could do something about it besides glare through the bars at an inmate who would die incarcerated.

Kayne gave a sick, crooked smile. "You're lucky you were fast. You had some sharp fucking teeth for such a little shit." He held up his hand to show that he still had two rounded scars from where Fang had bitten him so long ago.

"You're lucky I wasn't older," Fang retorted as he turned and walked away, curiosity fully satisfied for a good lifetime. He was going to go home and play a game about shooting people or setting them on fire or something. It wouldn't make him feel much better, but it would keep him from figuring out how to break into the prison to kidnap that asshole and sell him into some form of abusive slavery.

CHAPTER 5

Remembering Old Friends and Making New Ones

Zifeara made her way into the kitchen, asking for a huge meal to be prepared for the night. She hated to lie to Fang about having to leave, but she just wanted a night to herself after spending so long at work. Tracking a guy through the snow for a week was tiring and a girl needed her time. She settled in with some videogames and a ton of food, eating and playing long into the night. She didn't need to sleep so long as she had fuel for her system- a fun perk of being immortal. Eventually, she decided she did want at least a nap before she had to go, so she lay down to rest.

The strange thing about the way Zifeara slept was sometimes she had dreams like normal people, but other times one of her countless memories played out like a movie in her head. She had been told at an early age that memories were stored in the soul as opposed to the brain, but since most souls have a timer, they move memories around and drop a few. Becoming an immortal means you not only gain an unlimited space for general memories, but a photographic and eidetic memory as well, enabling Fang to play so many instruments and Zifeara to know so many languages.

This night was a memory-dream night. She had just taken Fang to his first day of school. He'd lived with her for a while, so he knew that she'd often be gone for work, but that Graham would take good care of him. She didn't want to miss his first day of school though- that was special. She had made it very clear to Fang early on that she could never replace his mom and that she didn't want to; she was just a good friend that he was living with now. Still, this was the first time Fang would be truly back in normal society and she wanted to be there for him. As she waved him on, the dream warped to her waving to an older Fang as she was picking him up. He must have been about eight, and he looked upset.

"Zia, Ash and those other jerks won't leave me alone. They aren't scared of me for some reason and they always try to take the money you give me for extra snacks after school," he told her.

A sly smile spread across her face. "We'll see about that. Where do they bother you?"

Zifeara giggled in her sleep. She remembered this day fondly. She didn't abuse her powers as a shifter *that* much, but sometimes...

The bullies had cornered Fang behind the equipment shed for PE where it would be a while before anyone saw them.

"C'mon weirdo, give it to us. You can't take all of us at once," the hawk boy named Ash said as he sneered at Fang.

"Or what? You can't hit me, or you'll be in trouble. What do you think you can do to take it, Beaky?" Fang retorted.

Zifeara was already watching him as a cat in a nearby tree, just to see what was going on, and Fang's young wit made her grin. It was always so cute when he'd get that little edge of developing sass. The other boys crowded in on Fang, clearly meaning to hold him and take it.

Showtime. As she jumped down and shifted back to her normal form, Fang's bullies didn't hear her, but he saw her and smiled.

"What do you little *cretins* think you're doing to my boy?" Zifeara snarled from behind the group, and they all spun around, no longer confident with the appearance of an adult.

"We- we're playing a game. Zombies," Ash said quickly, "Fang's the survivor but he lost. So we're eating him."

Zifeara raised an eyebrow. Eaten huh? She could work with that. "Okay, let's play a new game. Fang, come here, I'll need you for this."

As Fang moved to her side, she lifted him onto her shoulders, smirking at the annoyed looking boys. "We're going to play dinosaurs. Fang is the Beastmaster, I'm the raptor, and all you little snacks better start running."

Ash opened his mouth to say something but as he did, Zifeara shifted into an actual Utahraptor, at least a good three feet taller than the largest child there and stared him right in the eye. A small squeak escaped the boy's mouth before she roared at him, exposing every single one of her teeth and sending them all screaming and running for their lives. Satisfied they'd learned who they were dealing with and accepting that she would probably have to placate the PTA later, Zifeara hopped the fence, Fang laughing as he bounced on her back. She carried him the entire way home like that and he never had any more trouble from those boys again.

Later that night he had come into her room. He couldn't fall asleep for some reason, so he asked her to sing[5] to him. She considered this their special song; it had become his favorite ever since she'd brought him home, likely due to how much it reminded him of how much his life had turned around.

The dream shifted again and he was much taller, likely a teenager. Actually, he looked just the same as he always did, which made it hard to tell which memory it was at first.

"Zifeara? I know what I want for my birthday," he said quietly after she had stopped singing.

Ah, now she knew when this was.[6]

"Yeah? It better be crazy, you're gonna be eighteen this year," she replied.

"It is. I want to be immortal, like you."

Zifeara looked up at him, very unprepared to have this conversation. She could feel his heart softly beating in his chest, his long body curled around her like always since he had grown taller than her. The past year had been strange due to his growth spurt;

---

[5] "Learn To Be Lonely" - Andrew Lloyd Webber and Charles Hart
[6] "Hate Me" - Eurielle

he gained eight whole inches on her seemingly overnight. He wasn't a little boy anymore, literally or figuratively.

"Oh, honey, no you don't. You can never have a normal life and there's no going back once you turn. I'm going to see everyone I know and like die someday, new things will become old and useless, civilizations come and go- Fang, I can never have a family. Being immortal sucks just as much as it's cool. Besides, I wanted a lot of things when I was actually your age that seem like the worst ideas ever now."

Fang returned the stare and answered in a very serious tone, "But that's exactly *why* I want it. You shouldn't have to be alone. You've saved my life Zifeara... It's yours."

Zifeara remembered what an odd feeling she had as he said that; as if her ribcage was rapidly shrinking, but not the organs it contained. She knew it wasn't, but reasoning with herself that such a thing wasn't possible without actively trying didn't make it stop. She wanted to get up, go downstairs, and try to decipher what was happening to her. Instead her eyes teared up and she was quiet for a moment as he gazed pleadingly at her. *No one ever chose her like this.*

Finally, when the tears receded and she felt almost normal again, Zifeara sighed. "Listen, I didn't want to say anything because it's a big surprise, but I already got you your birthday present. This is a staggeringly important decision to make, so I'll tell you what. I want you to think very hard about this for the next year. If you still want this, I'll see what I can do, and *if* I can pull it off, that's what I'll get you next year. Keep in mind that's one *massive* if. Deal?"

Fang briefly considered this before agreeing. In the end, Zifeara was glad her mother pulled some strings and she could steal a vial of immortality from her grandfather. She didn't know what she would do without Fang now. In fact, whenever she thought too long about him lately, she got a weird feeling she didn't recognize, as though her internal fire had somehow managed to start melting her organs or like something alive had worked its way into her stomach. Not only that, but she had no other emotion to compare it to. It was strange, but she wasn't sure if it was bad or not.

¤ ¤ ¤

Zifeara was back in a bygone era, where technology wasn't a word yet and the most interesting new invention was forming new metals into better swords. At least for the humans, anyway. This was a time when demons ran amok, doing as they pleased since a vast majority of them were far stronger than humans. Today she was tracking leads on a necromancer, highly frowned upon by the rules of time and dead things staying dead, in a small village called Otano, known for its excellent sake.

Around sunset, she made her way to the town inn to secure lodging for the night. She'd had enough of sleeping in trees for the time being. As she followed the upstairs hallway to her room, a young man came quickly around the corner and ran right into her with a soft grunt.

"Hey, sorry, I-" He faltered as he caught Zifeara by the arm to stop her from falling over, eyes widening as he got a good look at her.

The guy was about her height, lean and fit, slightly tanned from the sun, and had stunning green eyes that boasted a ring of gold around his slit pupils. His bright orange and black striped hair was cut short on all sides except over his left eye where it hung over his face. If she was honest, he was really cute. He was a tiger for sure, but he also had large, lavender-brown ears on his head, similar to a bat.

29

"I- I'm Aun. I was just about to head out to the tavern, and I guess I was in a bit of a rush. You okay?"

Zifeara was pretty used to awed sputtering as most men's first reaction to her. It was what she was built for, after all. She could use that. She nodded, smoothing the front of her shirt. "Yeah, no worries. I was lost in thought, so I didn't hear you coming either."

Though he was undeniably attractive, Zifeara thought it was rather odd for the boy to have bat blood in him; tigers were a proud race in this time period, who only bred with their own kind to keep their bloodline pure.

"I'm Zifeara, by the way. You actually might be able to help me; I'm here because I'm looking for someone. There's a necromancer around these parts and the sooner I find him, the sooner I can go home. Heard anything?"

"Nah, I've only been here a day myself, not for anything important. Someone at the tavern might know something though if you want to head down with me?"

The tavern was going to be her first stop for information anyway, but she was pretty sure this town had to relocate it after a fire last year. "Yeah, let me get into my room real quick and I'll be set. I don't know where it is, so that'd be helpful, thanks."

Leaning against the wall, he could not believe how ridiculously smooth that went. He'd thought he was out of practice talking to ladies, but damn, that was good.

Zifeara continued to her room, making sure it was satisfactory, then followed Aun down to the town pub. He was clearly trying his luck with her and she led him on as much as she felt was necessary before she knew if she would need him for something. More often than not, it was the smart choice to have more cards to play, even if you didn't know what said cards *did*.

The place was busy for the size of the population, and in the corner there was a man playing a lute for coins. Aun went to grab them both some signature sake while Zifeara started chatting up the locals, trying to get any information on her target.

"Yeah, I know who you're talking about," one man finally said. "Bastard lives up in the hills to the south of town, near the cemetery so he can get plenty of help. No one is brave enough to go deal with him though. He basically has access to an army."

Great, just what she needed. Her last kill was so easy, too. All she had to do was tire him out and chase him down, but this time she was going to have to do *real* work.

She was about to ask more questions when the ground began shaking. As the tremors steadily became more intense, a loud screech from outside prompted the townspeople to flood out the door to see what was amiss. Zifeara caught sight of Aun and moved toward him, grabbing his sleeve so as not to get separated. Ah, this might be exactly what she kept him for; someone who may be able to handle themselves in a fight. He was the only demon she'd seen here.

Once outside, the source of the commotion became clear; a sizable gelatinous beast had come from the nearby forest to hunt for food, and human was on the menu. Thinking she may still need these people for information, she decided helping them get rid of this giant pest would be the most prudent course of action.

"How good are you at fighting large monsters, tiger boy?"

Aun looked at her like she was crazy. "Uh, fine. Why do you want to fight this thing? Could we not just get out of here?"

Zifeara rolled her eyes and jumped to the top of the nearest building, forming a good-sized spear of fire and aiming for one of its prominent, jelly eyes. She only had about fifteen to choose from. As she threw it, however, the monster turned, taking the spear more where a nose should have been. That really pissed it off. Zifeara jumped, dodging its crushing blow to the roof and shifted into a hawk-sized dragon to hover above its head. The good news was, slime creatures were not thrilled about fire. Letting loose a few jets from her mouth was slowly starting to melt the creature down.

Aun sighed and grabbed a bit of fragmented wood to try to do as Zifeara had and take out an eye. Why did the hottest girl he'd ever seen have to be a crazy shifter? Launching his piece of wood, Aun managed to get it right next to one of the slime's furthest left eyes, causing it to roar and thrash about while Zifeara continued to whittle away at it. If he could keep it from hitting at her, she might do all the hard work.

Now that the slime was angry with Aun, it slammed its arm down again to try to flatten the sharp-thing-throwing pest. While he did dodge the initial attack, the slime swiped its arm sideways, catching the tiger by surprise and absorbing him into its mass. Though he struggled to get out, Aun was stuck and quickly running out of air as the slime sucked him into what he hoped wasn't a stomach.

Well, this wasn't how I wanted my night to go at all, he thought sarcastically. *Guess I'll have to get myself out of this one.* Aun rapidly changed shape, turning into a large bear with sickle-like claws, proving to be too heavy for the slime as he fell and slashed his way through the monster.

Slimes not being particularly brave creatures, it decided to find an easy meal elsewhere without all this clawing and fire and began beating a hasty retreat back to the forest minus an arm and some torso.

Aun changed back, standing annoyed amid the rubble of the destroyed house where he had landed. It would take him forever to get all this gunk out of his hair.

Returning to her normal form as she landed beside a slime-covered tiger, Zifeara scowled. "Well, that was a waste of time. I've had slimes half its size fight me to the death. What a bitch."

Aun gave her a cautious once over. "So you're a shifter too, huh?"

Zifeara seemed rather unconcerned, brushing some dust off her black pants. "Yeah, so what? Is that uncommon around here?"

"Well yeah, actually," Aun replied, "so it's kind of nice to meet another one of us out here. This is what I really look like. You?"

She understood his curiosity. It wasn't as though she'd never met a shifter that preferred to look less like themselves. Either way, Aun had just worn out his usefulness. "Yep, this is me. At least that thing didn't smash the inn. Now then, I'm going to try to get some sleep as I have a necromancer to track down tomorrow. Nice meeting you, Aun!"

And just like that Zifeara started off down the street like nothing had happened.

Aun stared after her before blinking quickly and heading the same way. "Hey, we're staying in the same inn, remember? How are you so calm about all this nonsense? It's not every night you fight off a monster attacking a town, is it?"

Zifeara offered him a weary look. "Man, I wish it weren't. Listen, I'm not a 'friends' kind of girl, so thanks for the help but I'm good now. You don't need to hang around with me after we get back." She brought two fingers to her forehead and gave a small salute, picking up her pace.

Aun raised an eyebrow as he easily held her gait. "Well I'm not a friends kinda guy either, but that's never stopped me from going home with a girl before. In fact, I think it's helped."

Zifeara stopped to turn around and provide a 'what the hell is that supposed to mean' kind of glare.

"Look," Aun began, "I wasn't entirely honest when I told you I didn't have a reason to be here earlier. I'm trying to locate a particular gemstone that's very important to my clan. It was stolen from our temple about two weeks ago. I might... be a little not great at this. All I've figured out so far is that the necromancer might at least be involved. Can we call it good for a little while and help each other out on this? I don't know why *you* want the necromancer, but getting him could help me find what I need, so can I just talk to him before you do whatever form of murder it sounds like he's in for?"

Zifeara narrowed her eyes as she thought about how inconvenienced she'd be; other people could only slow her down. And yet... the more she looked into those stunning puppy dog eyes, the more she felt her resolve weakening. This kid made her feel... something.

"Fine, but either be helpful or stay out of my way. I'm asking a few more questions tomorrow before I head out for the mountain that guy at the bar mentioned, so if you want to come, you better be there when I leave. Got it?"

Aun agreed and the two continued to the inn to wait for morning.

Great, Aun thought to himself. *She's gorgeous, a shifter, a fire demon, and some kind of assassin. You really know how to pick your girls, you idiot. She may still be worth it though...*

He didn't know if it was just hormones kicking in, but Aun was getting this feeling that he had to follow Zifeara; like he had to help her. Help her do what, he only had a vague idea, but he could swear he knew her already and just hadn't seen her in a very long time. Like the kind of person you were childhood friends with and then bump into many years later. Maybe some cosmic force was trying to tell him something. Or maybe he was just a horny nineteen year old who had finally gotten a taste of freedom from his stupid family.

CHAPTER 6

Work Could Be Worse

Zifeara didn't think she'd enjoy company on a mission, but having Aun tag along wasn't as bad as she'd feared. He was charming in an odd way and easy to converse with, even if it was about trivial matters such as how much that village sucked despite being famous for its sake. She was surprised to find that he made her laugh frequently and his easygoing attitude sat well with her. While on their way to the mountain the necromancer supposedly inhabited, she asked about where he had come from and Aun informed her about his tiger clan and how he came to have such odd ears.

He was the third child in his family, with his sister, Tava, being the oldest at twenty-six, and his brother just before him at twenty-three. His siblings were, realistically, only half-siblings as their mother passed shortly after his brother Saiga had turned two, during an attack by a rival clan. The raid came in the middle of the night and she had died a valiant death protecting her children. Devastated by the loss of his love, Aun's father, Rozhar, head of Clan Thunderfang, began taking long sulks in the forest around their land, doubling as patrol duty in case they were attacked again.

One night many years later, he came across a bewitching bat demon whose name he never mentioned and made a grave tiger faux pas to allay his loneliness. Thinking nothing of the encounter, he never saw her again. Months later while on his rounds he came across a crying infant with tiger-striped hair in the same spot he'd seen her last. At first, he didn't think the baby could possibly be his, but Aun had his father's eyes and elemental affinity for producing electricity, as all members of his clan did. He was taken home and raised, bastard child or not.

Aun loved Tava dearly, but Saiga not so much. Saiga never saw him as a brother, or even as an equal since he was supposed to succeed his father as head the clan, and Aun was a huge step away from purity of breed. His father trained him much more ardently since he was so out of place and had sent Aun to find their stolen gem in order to improve his reputation among the members of their clan.

So here he was, looking for some magical rock that he didn't care about for people who didn't care about him, maybe finding a better life for himself and having some fun on the way.

Zifeara rather admired Aun's carefree outlook regarding what an outsider he was to his clan since she sometimes wished she could be normal for more than a night at a time and accidentally told him as much.

"What is it that makes you a freak then?" He looked her up and down, a slight tilt to his head.

Zifeara stopped walking to consider whether the truth was a better answer or not. Aun raised an eyebrow and she sighed.

"Well, let's put this simply. I'm employed by someone extremely powerful to take out people who do certain things and being employed thusly gives me some perks, which are a blessing and a curse. I'm very hard to kill but have exchanged certain freedoms for this power. Does that sort of make sense?"

Aun raised an eyebrow. "So, you're a badass because you have a cool job?"

She smirked. "Yeah, that's a flattering way to look at it. I don't really like talking about it in too much detail if it's all the same to you."

He shrugged and carried on, "Where are you from, though? That's not super job related, is it?"

As Zifeara continued towards the mountain, she made a noise that denoted she was iffy on the subject.

Aun sighed. "Ooookay, so what kind of stuff do you like? Fun, food, books, whatever?"

She thought a moment before responding. "Uhm, well, I have a friend I go out with a lot and we like to dance. I eat as often as I can to sustain shifts for longer periods of time, so food is a magical thing for me and good cooking is hard to find around here. I like to hunt too, so there's that."

"And you're a fire demon," he added, changing his pace to be right beside her on the trail.

Zifeara nodded. "There is also that. Which is pretty fun to be honest; there's a lot you can do with fire, especially once you learn to get creative with it." A mischievous grin took over her face, thinking back of some of the craziest things she'd used her fire for over the years. "Hey, I think that's our mountain, Aun."

Pointing to a peak off to their right, the mountain in question looked heavily overgrown with trees, as if it were rarely visited. A mass of ravens was circling a particular spot in the forest, cawing like mad.

Zifeara looked at Aun and gave a wicked smile. "I think I have a faster way of getting over there."

Turning into a raven, Zifeara circled overhead, waiting for him to join her.

"Aw man, this is gonna suck." Aun sighed as he, too, shifted into a raven and followed Zifeara off to the scene of whatever commotion had the mountain birds so excited.

Joining their circle and looking down, the pair hadn't expected to find the necromancer this easily. The balding, gaunt, twig of a man nearly had a sign over his head that read 'up to no good'. He could have at least waited until nighttime to be creepy and dig up a dead body, but there he was, shooing ravens off his new friend. The two pseudoravens landed in a nearby tree and exchanged looks. They could easily just wait for the necromancer to take his buddy home, then they could get the jump on him, which sounded like as good a plan as any. Too bad it was only about two o'clock in the afternoon and it looked like their guy was starting a pile of bodies to mass resurrect. This could take a while.

¤ ¤ ¤

Fang was coming home from an early dinner with a friend in the present. His nightclub was situated in an inconspicuous alley off one of the main roads of New Tinning, mostly due to its restrictive access. Fang was odd like that; he liked to let certain people in to keep the club more friendly and had devised a rather unorthodox system to do so. Technology being what it was, most people did everything with their phones. Some even had them implanted into their bodies to make things easier and prevent themselves from losing them.

Fang's system relied on an app he'd developed, allowing entry to his club via the brick-camouflaged, automated, steel door that served as the one and only entrance into the SoundCave. The app was only available to download by invitation, so he alone selected who was allowed to enter and who could only hope to be a guest and maybe earn their own invitation. Fang socialized with his patrons often to determine this, and he had to admit it was fun. He'd made friends and even hired staff this way. All he had to do was use a slightly illegal piece of software he had on his phone to target and hack another's and he could force-install the app. The next time the person turned on their phone, it gave them a nice introduction to what it was and the option to uninstall it or get directions to the club. Surprisingly, it drew a lot of business and added an aura of mystique to the SoundCave.

As he approached the entrance, the door opened for Fang immediately, recognizing his phone as it did all the staff he employed. Heading down a set of stairs, he entered the main area of the club. The huge building had black walls covered in splatters of blacklight activated paint. The multicolored, swirl-patterned, tile floor turned to hardwood only under the bar to the far right of the entrance. In the middle of the spacious dance floor sat his booth and sound system. Since Fang's headphones allowed him to alter his perception of sound, they enabled him to become a very well-known DJ in New Tinning, mainly by how he chose to play his music. He turned his headphones down to the point that he barely heard what he was spinning at all, but instead felt it through his club's speakers which he had placed right under his feet. It was easier to play music well when it *felt* good.

Smiling to himself, Fang stepped up to an unremarkable section of wall and said, "D1g1t, I'm home."

The wall did nothing for a moment before a panel slid upwards to reveal another set of stairs. Fang followed them as they turned a corner farther down and led into his entryway, directly under the SoundCave. His house wasn't huge like Zifeara's, but it was still extremely spacious, and Fang had lived there since his eighteenth birthday when she had given him the club. She'd let him decorate it however he wanted and had provided the funds to do so on the condition that once he started producing a profit, he'd reimburse her, which he had done long ago.

In fact, Zifeara still technically owned the SoundCave, and his official position was 'Head Manager', which was a fancy way of saying he did whatever he wanted. He also assigned himself the roles of head technician, event coordinator, staffing director and, most importantly, DJ. Zifeara really just managed income, paid salaries, listened to Fang plead for an advance for some sweet tech, and had fun with him when she had the time. All in all, they had awesome jobs.

A series of well-timed beeps told Fang that D1g1t had welcomed him home and had started his kettle so he could make tea. D1g1t was an AI Fang had been working on for years that he'd managed to wire the entire SoundCave to, his house included. He'd even made it a physical body out of an old rounded display and parts from a hoverboard, just to make it feel like a proper companion. The little guy floated around his house, offering advice while he worked on things, and generally making the place feel less empty. All it could say was its own name, but it could communicate in Morse code so that most of the time only he could tell what it was saying.

After relaxing a while and having some dessert, Fang prepared himself for work and went back upstairs to make sure all the equipment was working properly. While checking the lighting, he heard the main door open, signaling his first staff member arriving.

A hulking figure emerged, barely fitting his broad shoulders through the doorway. The man was only a few inches taller than Fang, but with all his muscle, outweighed him by a solid 150 pounds. He was pale, bald, and had several visible scars.

"Well, you're a bit early tonight, Vhans. To what do I owe the pleasure?" Fang asked.

The man sighed and fiddled with his large fingers. "Being honest, is no pleasure I am here. I must ask a favor."

Fang had known Vhans for several years, since he had emigrated from the Arroll region looking for a job to support his growing family, and had never once had him ask for anything. In the Arroll region, things were less relaxed than in Queylinth; there, they looked out for their own and prided themselves on not owing anyone a thing.

"Mortichai, is my only daughter's birthday next week and I want to get her something special. Carolynn is to be thirteen years and she has always wanted a chongit. She was excited to be in country where they are born. Could maybe you give Einrit bonus early this year? I am aware Einrit has passed only months ago, however... I have almost enough myself, but... not quite. You are always more than generous at Einrit and I am betting it will be enough. I am hating to ask, but wife insisted."

Vhans looked rather embarrassed, but Fang smiled. Chongits were coveted pets, something like a cross between a chinchilla and a corgi; long and slender but with crazy soft fur, a broad muzzle, floppy rabbit-like ears, and a cotton tail. While their Einrit bonus was usually mildly fantastic at eight percent of their annual earnings, if Vhans wanted a chongit, he must have been saving here and there to get one by now. Fang paid his employees well, but not *that* bloody well, since a purebred chongit could be at least 6,000 Qan. That was 375 hours of work for a pet at Vhans' wage. Fang grabbed his business wallet and wrote Vhans an extra special Einrit check.

"Here Vhans, you've been here almost as long as I have, and you've always done an awesome job. If you get a purebred chongit they live way longer, so just promise to get a good one."

As Fang handed him the check and turned to go back to his work, Vhans grabbed his shoulder to stop him. "M- Mortichai. I- I cannot accept this. It is far too much. I- I couldn't begin to repay you for this."

Fang swatted his hand off and grinned like a madman. "Dude, it's cool. I don't expect you to. You've always gone above and beyond in your job, and hell, you bring me your wife's cooking sometimes. You've knitted me a sweater. You and I are friends, and I look after my friends. We've had an amazing few years and I can more than afford it. My only condition is that you let me come over after you've had it for a while so I can play with the fuzzball, alright?"

Vhans opened his mouth as though he were about to continue to protest, but Fang raised his eyebrows in the I'm-your-boss-don't-you-question-me kind of way he did every so often, and Vhans shook his head.

"Hell, we might even name after you." He gave up and went to clock himself in for the night.

Fang returned to his booth and continued his systems check, thinking on how he might as well spoil his friend's children since he'd never have any of his own. Zifeara hated kids. Not that she could even produce any since her anatomy didn't include ovaries or a uterus, but still. Like she'd ever have his kids even if she could...

Snapping out of his inappropriate line of thought and seeing that everything was in working order, Fang checked his phone for the time. Almost time to open. Seeing that Vhans was at his usual place just beside the entryway, Fang adjusted his headphones for the night, deafening himself to his passion to improve its strength.

Vhans turned, saying something to a young man who rushed down the stairs, across the floor and vaulted over the bar. Mavrik Reed, Fang's favorite barman, was never on time. He looked a bit disheveled, his rusty hair combed to the side and his suit still a little big for him. He was young, too young to actually work in a bar, but he had some serious talent.

Fang had found the stoat-boy in a restaurant working as a busboy, offhandedly mixing sodas together in his spare time, but clearly practicing a barkeep's flair. When asked where he learned to do that, Mavrik had answered that his uncle had taught him about his job, and Mavrik thought it was pretty sweet and wanted to learn. Fang offered him a job at the SoundCave and convinced Mavrik that he could pull some strings to get the underaged kid in. The legal drinking age in the Queylinth region was nineteen and Mavrik was almost eighteen now, but it had been close to three years since he started at the SoundCave. In fact, he only worked part-time since he still had to go to school.

Most days Fang loved Mavrik. He was a cocky little shit who had a joke or sarcastic remark about everything, and it was fun having someone so much younger around. Fang had been immortal for seventeen years, but he didn't feel as though he'd changed much. Screwing around with Mavrik always made him feel like he was nineteen again.

Mavrik dipped his head sheepishly and said something directed at him, but Fang pointed at his headphones to signal he was beyond caring as he climbed up onto his rig to start it up for the night's soundtrack. Tonight, Fang had some things in the set that didn't require too much work since he was always distracted after he and Zifeara had gone out. He constantly wished he could spend more time with her, but they both had very different jobs in entirely different times and she had told him before that he was lucky to be born in such a peaceful year.

It was true; Fang was not well-built for a combat-oriented era. Zifeara had taught him how to fight with just about anything as a weapon, and she had even bought him a set of matching pistols made specifically for him that put out less noise but were still very powerful. His biggest problem was, as per usual, his eyesight. Contacts bothered him and hurt after a short time. His vision was so terrible that the surgery to fix it could make it all worse, and glasses had to be about an inch thick to do anything at all. Plus, he looked terrible in them.

To use his pistols, he had gotten very good at guessing where to aim based on the blurs he could see, but it took too long to defend himself in a do-or-die scenario. Zifeara had run drills with him to test this and every time, no matter what animal she was, she always had him down before he could land a meaningful shot. Granted, she had been doing this exact same thing as a career for the past several *thousand* years, but still.

As the night went on, Fang took a break to socialize with a few of his favorite patrons and found that one of them had a piece of tech he had never seen before. The man wore what looked like some sort of jewelry that looped over his ear and had a solid metal seashell on the side where his earlobe would be. When he pushed the inside of the shell to show it off, a holographic display appeared in front of his eyes. He claimed the display helped him see one-hundred times farther than he normally could.

Plus, it could connect to his phone and alert him to various new messages and whatnot. He could even hide the display while it was still up so that it was sort of like having contact lenses in. Fang asked him a few dozen questions before returning to his rig to take it off autoplay and get back to work. He had found his perfect solution. He was going on vacation.

CHAPTER 7

Some People Shouldn't Have Important Jobs

As the sun had just finished setting, the necromancer finally began to raise his dead friends. Zifeara and Aun had been talking as ravens in a tree for hours since there wasn't much else to do with the time and Zifeara was genuinely surprised at how much she was enjoying herself. The nine hour wait on her last hunt was murder, but the past five had gone by rather quickly with someone to hang out with. That, and Aun had turned out to be a pretty cool guy. He was so much so that Zifeara had begun to wonder if she had been friends with whoever last embodied Aun's soul. She was so at ease with him she must have known and liked him at some point in the past.

As it would happen, one of Zifeara's more unique talents was that she never forgot a soul; she could look into someone's eyes and if she had met their last life, she would be able to see them in her mind's eye just as clearly as she had when she'd known them. She had done this to Fang before and while she could clearly see who he used to be... she couldn't remember the man. The more she tried, the more frustrated she got. Eventually she just gave up and figured that something, someday, would jog her memory, but she wasn't about to lose sleep over it; Fang was Fang now, and that was all that mattered.

As the procession of new zombies shuffled forward toward the necromancer's hideout, the two birds mobilized, along with the real ravens looking for a bite, and followed. The cave was tucked further up the mountain and frankly wasn't hidden at all; hoards of zombies just milled around outside, carrying simple things back to the cave for supplies. When the new crew arrived, the necromancer instructed them to do as the others were and make themselves useful. Nodding in satisfaction, he sauntered into his lair, and Zifeara and Aun perched themselves nearby.

"We need a way to take out the zombies without alerting the necromancer. Any ideas?" Zifeara cawed.

Aun thought a second. "If we created a commotion, how many zombies do you think would go see what it is? I mean, they are pretty freakin' stupid."

Zifeara squawked in approval. "Sounds like as good a plan as any. You get their attention and I'll subdue the necromancer."

Aun looked a tad concerned; at least, as concerned as a bird could. "You do mean subdue until I can ask him where my clan's gem is, right? You remember our deal?"

"Come on, Aun, of course I do. It was only yesterday, and besides, a deal is a deal. Anything to make my life easier. See ya in a bit," and off she flew to a tree closer to the mouth of the cave.

Aun just shook his head and flew into the throng of zombies, cawing like mad to get their attention. As the majority of the zombies lurched after him into the forest, Zifeara shifted into a salamander and made her way into the cave, past the few remaining troops. After following a couple of bends and curves of the cave, she found the heart of his operation. If this was his entire army, she was surprised this guy had managed to raid Aun's clan. He had so few zombies around, he didn't look like he could take out the village they had stayed at last night, much less a band of highly-trained lightning tigers.

As she turned a corner, she wished she hadn't thought anything at all. She should have known better than to insult karma by now. The large chamber she arrived in was packed wall to wall with the undead, the necromancer stood on a large rock at the head of his minions.

"My rotting friends, the time has come for us to make our way to the capital city. We shall amass three times our current numbers on the way, ensuring an easy victory over the unsuspecting bureaucrats who pollute that cesspool. We shall convert the city to a new home for us all and expand into a mighty empire. What say you, friends?"

The zombies gave a collective, disinterested grunt, but the necromancer seemed satisfied. He shuffled off to a side branch of the cave as the salamander on the ceiling trailed him. He had a whole bedroom set up for himself and he laid down for the night. Perfect.

Zifeara situated herself over him and shifted back to her regular form, landing solidly with her hand around his throat. "Good evening. I'm in need of some information and once I get it, I'll be on my way. Oh wait, I have an acquaintance who has a question or two as well. So friendo, how exactly are you bringing the poor dead bastards back to life?"

The necromancer made a few choking and sputtering noises before spitting an answer. "Like I would tell you anything! I know who you are, Torvak warned me about you! He said you would come for me at some point. You'll never get into his fortress to get that gem back! I don't care what the tigers told you, Terravak is impenetrable!"

Zifeara raised an eyebrow and grinned. "You mean the fortress city of Terravak, in the Vorlith region, on Kartak Island, on the other side of the planet? That I've been into many, many times and even saw constructed from the ground up? That one? Thank you my dear, I don't believe I need you anymore. Ta!"

She started putting pressure on the man's windpipe, but he quickly pleaded with her for his life. "No wait I- I could help you! I can tell you what Torvak wants with the Lightning Crystal! Just don't take my power gem! It's all I have... "

Looking at the stone hanging from a length of cord around his neck, Zifeara wondered if this job was just getting too easy, or if she was just in a period of time where people were really this stupid. "Alright, what does he want with it? I haven't got all day, so you better make this quick."

The necromancer sighed with relief, as if he were sure he was off the hook. "Torvak can use it to make himself immortal. He needs that one and is collecting a few other rare gemstones to use in a new ritual. He has enough of a following to never have to do his own dirty work again, so he simply has to sit back and rule his forces for eternity. It's a brilliant plan and he gave me this stone in exchange for the Lightning Crystal!"

"Hmm. Fascinating. Thank you for the information."

As Zifeara ripped the necromancer's head off and tossed it to the other side of the room in one fluid motion, she thought about how very long it would take her to *get* to the city of Terravak. Nabbing the gem from the new corpse and crushing it underfoot, she sighed. She'd have to tell Fang she'd be gone for longer than she ever had before, and he would not be happy about it.

Picking her way through the re-dead corpses lining the floor after being released from the necromancer's control, she met Aun at the head of the cave.

He immediately noticed she had blood on her hands - and zombies didn't bleed. "Damn it, Zifeara, I thought we had a deal! It sure doesn't look like I can talk to the necromancer now! Here I was, thinking you were cool and you-"

"He blurted out exactly where your gem was and who has it without me even asking him. It looks like we both need to head to Terravak." She had been given centuries to perfect her deadpan tone and it wasn't lacking.

Looking a tad embarrassed, Aun stammered, "Oh, uhm, thanks. I, uh, I guess I thought you'd let me ask the questions and get my answers myself. Sorry..."

Zifeara gave him a rather smug look before huffing lightly. "There's something I need to take care of before I set out, so I guess I'll see you around, Aun. It was nice having the company for a bit."

He looked quite unhappy at the prospect of her leaving, and Zifeara almost felt bad, but he spoke up. "Hey, I've... never been outside of this region before. I kind of have no idea how to actually *get* to Terravak... Do you think I could come with you? Besides, if this guy is really a threat, it doesn't hurt to have some back up, right? That, and I don't want to lose track of my gem after you ice this guy- one of his minions could take it or something. Better safe than sorry?"

Zifeara perked up a little since the journey would be long and boring by herself. She'd never had a companion for this before. "Hmm, I don't know, Terravak is on the other side of the world from here, and Torvak has a head start on us. Think you can make it the several months it'll take us to get there? We may have to do some odd jobs on the way, too."

Aun grinned in an adorably mischievous way. "It's about time I had some fun for once, I'd be glad to go. When do we leave?"

Zifeara subconsciously mirrored his smile. "Give me a full day to do what I need to. Then we'll be on our way, alright?"

Aun nodded. "Sure. I'll head back to town, so you can just grab me from the inn when we're ready to go. At least then if you show up at night we'll have a place to stay and we can head out first thing in the morning. See you soon, Zifeara."

As Aun turned back into a raven to fly back to the village, Zifeara found herself in a strangely good mood. *Oh, I look forward to it. I finally have something challenging to do and get to bring someone I kinda like along. Now I just need to deal with my mother... and Fang...*

¤ ¤ ¤

Hell had what was basically a never-ending library for souls; walls of shelves stretching out of sight in vault-like rooms where the souls were sorted by purity and awaited the day they could inhabit a new body. It was business as usual - sorted souls floated as if on an invisible conveyor belt before filing into their designated resting spots. Once they reached their slot on a shelf, they idled patiently until they would be dispatched again into the world.

Souls came in different colors which reflected how good of a being they had been in life, with most determining their colors as they moved through life. In Hell, they only dealt with four of the eight possible soul colors; red, purple, blue, and black. Respectively, these were animal or neutral souls, the slightly evil souls whose owners may have had some blood on their hands, the truly evil souls who have done terrible and inexcusable things for their own personal gain, and the souls who were the worst of the worst and had few to no redeeming qualities. Black was a rarity, as was gold on Dios' end of the spectrum, but they did exist and were highly prized by their deity of favor.

When she was created, Zifeara's soul was as black as it got, but she liked to think it had since turned blue. She didn't know though; she had never actually seen her own soul more than once. Lucifer kept it in her room, which Zifeara was forbidden to enter, along with Fang's soul.

As Zifeara made her way to her mother's office, past the souls moving swiftly around her, she could hear Lucifer barking orders at her servants. The demons she had created to serve her were mindless imps in varying sizes and colors, bound to Hell with no will of their own. Zifeara was glad she at least had free will since the imps always looked bored. Hell was kind of lame if you spent too long here; nothing but racks of souls, her mother's house and private, expansive garden of horrors, and the workshop where her mother played with and tweaked her creatures to combat Dios and his things.

For many thousands of years, he and Lucifer had a bet on that every 400 years they would see how many souls each of them had collected... because they were siblings and had to fight over everything. Whoever had a decisive lead by 1,000,000 souls would get to reign over Marien for a hundred years. The problem was they were almost always fairly matched, but lately, Lucifer was pulling ahead a little. With any luck, in about 230 more years she would control the planet and bring about the apocalypse she had always wanted.

As Zifeara stepped into the office, her mother caught sight of her and smiled.

"Zifeara, love, what brings you in here today? You never come for a visit unless you want something. That's my girl!"

Lucifer preferred to take on a more human form as opposed to the massive demon she truly was, simply because she always maintained it was so old school to look insanely menacing. It was far scarier to appear somewhat normal and be the master of the Underworld than to look the part. Currently, she looked more like how people imagined a school principal; sharp features and strict demeanor, long, ginger hair pulled up in a bun, red skin, business suit, but with two long crooked horns sprouting from her forehead. Her narrow, gold eyes shimmered as though they contained fire.

Zifeara hugged her mother and replied, "Actually, I have something that may interest you."

"Oh? What happened this time? You know I watch you when I can, but I've been busy lately since there's that fantastic sickness going on in Farrowlith right now."

Her mother quickly turned to tell the imps to sort her souls for a moment, something she never left them with for an extended period simply because she loved choosing which souls to store and which to send back right away. It gave her an ounce of joy to send the most warped souls back into the fray so soon- just ruining her brother's day that much more quickly. But with Zifeara here, she could afford a break.

"Well, Mother," Zifeara began, "the necromancer you sent me after told me of one called Torvak who is currently collecting things for a ritual to create immortality for himself. I know we usually just clean up the mess, but this guy sounds crazy powerful, and I'd like to get to him before he gets his immortality so that it'll be easier to take him down. I can still do jobs along the way, but I would really like to start the journey to Terravak as soon as possible to try to nip this in the bud. He sounds like a pain in the ass."

Lucifer smiled widely, baring all her far-too-sharp teeth. "Oh, Zifeara, you do make me so proud. Such initiative. Go ahead dear, I know Torvak's soul and he is a nasty one. I had so hoped he would do more for us before we had to kill him, but maybe next time, yes? Do what you feel you need to, you have my full support. Speaking of support, how is Fang? I watched him the other night and he seemed *well*."

Lucifer could look in on people's lives at will, which was how she found those susceptible to making deals with her, but she treated it more like television than a tool for her trade. She spied on Zifeara and Fang especially since they were her two privately kept souls.

Zifeara offhandedly laughed. "He's the same as he always is, and I'm heading to his place right after this to tell him I'll be gone for a while. It may take as long as six months to get to Terravak depending on what I run into on the way there, and I feel bad about leaving him. He gave me enough shit for being gone two months last time, but there's nothing I can do about it. So I'm spending tonight and part of tomorrow with him before I go."

Lucifer gave a wry smile that Zifeara had learned to dread. "Oh, are you now? You know, you've grown quite attached to that boy lately. I don't blame you, so have I, but still."

Zifeara hated that tone. She didn't want to admit she probably started blushing even as she voiced her indignance. "Mother! You know Fang is my best friend. He and · I have never been anything else! Besides, I raised Fang- he's essentially family. It's only natural for me to be attached to someone I've known and practically lived with for almost thirty-two years. He's the only person I've ever genuinely never gotten tired of spending time with."

Lucifer shook her head and laughed loudly. "I know, I know, I rarely get to tease you anymore since you never visit unless summoned. Go spend time with your boy toy and have fun."

As Zifeara rolled her eyes and turned to leave, she yelled over her shoulder, "I've told you exactly 2,487 times now not to call him that! This is why I never visit!"

Lucifer chuckled and headed down the hallway, into her house to freshen up a bit while she was taking a break anyway. As she opened the door and stepped into her bedroom, closing it behind her, she glanced at the two vials on her decorative dresser. In the flasks, two distinct wisps swirled. One vial had a black tag hanging from its neck and the other a red tag. The black read 'Zifeara' and the other 'Mortichai'.

The consistency of a soul was hard to describe; while they were shaped as what could most definitely be called a 'wisp', they were oddly fluid in the way they moved. The souls in the vials would have resembled little lava lamps if they didn't retain their shapes as well as they did. As they pulsated, tiny flecks drifted upwards from the main mass as embers did from a flame.

Fang's soul shone a bright silver, one of the purest level of souls a mortal could possess, while Zifeara's had two colors; a light blue which only reflected the color of the beast writhing within her, and oddly enough an indigo color around that. Lucifer had watched its color change over the years and honestly... she was more surprised than angry. Zifeara shouldn't have been able to defy her programming and attain emotions, much less a *conscience* as she had. Once Fang had come along it only got worse, pushing her color just that last shade further from blue to purple.

Lucifer leaned over the dresser, turning Fang's vial onto its side and rolling it across the surface. When she'd bought the boy's soul, the strange sound emanating from her bedroom was a tad annoying at first, but now it was more of a curiosity. The soft hum rose and fell in volume directly proportional to the distance between the two souls, its yearning call indicative of the bond they shared. She always knew when Fang and Zifeara were together, because then his soul would *sing*; humming escalating to a wide variety of noises that wove together in an ever-changing aria.

It was rare for souls to do this; to bond so strongly that one could not exist without the other, but it wasn't unheard of. It *was* excessively odd that such a pure soul had chosen to bond to the harbinger of ultimate evil, but the world worked in mysterious ways and Lucifer couldn't break that bond without killing both of them.

"Oh, my dear girl... he's changed you in ways you don't even realize."

¤ ¤ ¤

Arriving in the present era while the SoundCave was just opening, Zifeara spent some time getting herself cleaned up and making sure her house was still in order. She also reminded herself to grab her cell phone on the way out so she could get into the club with no hassle. She never called Fang to let her in while he was working because he'd never hear it anyway, therefore he programmed the door to always open for her just like any other staff member, so long as she had her phone on her.

[7]She could tell Fang was having a pretty good night based on what he was playing. When he was in a good mood, he played harder songs and he'd only been at it for about three hours so far. Smiling as she made her way to the bottom of the flight of stairs, she greeted Vhans with a hug.

"Zifeara! Has been forever since seeing you last! To what do we owe the honor? You want I get Fang for you?" he thundered over the music.

---

[7] "The Munsta" - SCNDL

Zifeara politely declined, "That's okay hun, I'll wait until he stops for his break. He'll likely only be an hour. When he comes to check in with you, just tell him I'm hanging out with Mavrik. I haven't seen him in even longer than I have you."

Vhans nodded and Zifeara went to take a seat at the bar. After not five minutes of laughing and having Mavrik flirt with her as he always did, Zifeara felt a hand on her back. She turned to tell whatever loser didn't know who he was about to mess with to shove off, but it was Fang. Zifeara was sure it would have taken Fang longer to take his break tonight.

"How- you couldn't have seen me come in, could you?"

Fang grinned that giddy, lopsided grin of his. "Not exactly. I have something to show you though. C'mon," and with that, he grabbed her hand and led her to the door down to his house.

Standing in the entryway in front of the living room, Fang pushed a new button on his headphones and a holographic display materialized in front of his eyes.

CHAPTER 8

Babysitting Those Who Love You

A bsolutely not." Zifeara scowled. She was starting to flick her tail nervously; this was a *terrible* idea.

Fang had just shown her his cool new gadget and demonstrated how well it helped him see by lobbing a paperclip into a cup sitting on his coffee table from all the way across the room.

"But Zia, I just-"

"No Fang, you are *not* coming with me. Not only do you have a responsibility to the SoundCave, but the world I work in would literally tear you apart every chance it gets. Getting ripped apart isn't *fun*. You'll live of course, but it hurts like hell and your body has to put itself back together afterwards. Not to mention, I haven't trained you in enough survival and combat techniques for you to be okay on your own in a dangerous world. If you really want to come that badly, I can start training you better every chance I get, and in a few years you may be-"

"Zifeara!"

She flinched and looked up as Fang had quite forcefully cut her off.

"I'm thirty-six years old and I've never done anything exciting before. I've never been outside of Queylinth and in fact, the furthest I've been from New Tinning is going to Salvage for the SpinOff every year. That's only a few hours away by plane! Besides, I've already planned out exactly what to do with the Cave in the meantime, and I'm more than ready for this. Please, I just want to spend more time with you. I hate it when you leave me here by myself. Don't you miss me when you're gone?"

He looked like he was about to cry, and as much as she was pretty sure he was doing this just to soften her up, it was working. She ran a hand over her face.

"Fang, that's not fair, of course I do," Zifeara started, "I just... I don't want anything to happen to you. This wouldn't be like some kind of vacation. The creatures of a bygone era are gone for a reason. Some of them are awful abominations that were eradicated because they were a threat to civilized society. All they know is murder and destruction. You've been through enough, I don't want to put you through what I *know* will happen- not *you*. I don't want you to have to know what getting a hole in your chest or losing a leg feels like. I want you to keep doing what you love and having fun with your friends. I want to keep you *safe*."

Fang could feel his ears attempt to droop despite the constraint of his headphones, taken aback by how worried Zifeara looked by mentioning the possibility of him getting hurt. He almost felt bad for wanting to go. If it meant being around her more however, Fang had to guilt her into taking him with her. This was the only way he'd finally get up the nerve to tell Zifeara the *other* reason he wanted to spend more time together...

"Zia, I understand your concerns, but I don't care if I get hurt. I'll be fine. I just hate you being gone for so long by yourself and this time it's not going to happen. I'm immortal for exactly one reason and I *need this*. How long were you planning to be off for?"

Zifeara fixed her gaze to the floor, pinched the bridge of her nose, and sighed heavily. He was being a little shit and he knew damn well she was weak for him playing his abandonment card.

Fang narrowed his eyes and used his business tone. That kind of I'm-not-playing-around tone he rarely dared address her with. "Zifeara? How long?"

She gave him a withering look, throwing her hands in the air. "Well, Terravak is only on *the other side of the planet* with no means of quick transportation. Adding in the time it would take to do Mother's other odd jobs on the way, I can't imagine it taking any longer than... oh, maybe six months."

Fang grabbed Zifeara by her shoulders and shook her lightly, now no longer using his inside voice. "*You were going to leave me for six **months**?*! Are you *insane*? It's a good thing I got this thing when I did. Like *hell* I'm letting you leave without me! Six months- what the fuck... I'm coming and that's final. Okay, what kind of things do I need to pack? Obviously I'm bringing my pistols, but what else?"

Zifeara shook her head. She'd never seen him so fired up about something, and honestly, she was done arguing. He'd eventually either admit she was right or adapt.

"Really, you won't need that much. We can always come back here and grab stuff when absolutely necessary, so just pick a few things you think you can't be without and I'll throw them in my bag. Now come on, you have to get back to work and get things settled for leaving. We don't set out until tomorrow night," she said turning to head back up to the club.

Fang followed close behind, but he couldn't focus on work for the rest of the night, not after being told he could shadow Zifeara on her adventures. He could finally spend time with her and hopefully work up the nerve to get the fat, shining elephant out of the room.

Zifeara didn't stay for long. She went back home to grab a few things she'd need now that her plus one was plus *two*. Since Fang was coming along, she didn't think she had to stick around while he was working, but she'd be back later to spend the night.

Fang continued to play and let Vhans know the next chance he got that he would be leaving as planned. The moment the Cave was closed for the night, Fang shut his rig down and raced towards his home to prepare for the best time of his life. He could finally be there for Zifeara in a way she actually *needed* him. He damn near tripped on Mavrik, who at 5'4" was more of a speed bump at Fang's size.

"And where are you going in such a hurry, huh? Were you even going to say goodbye or anything? Speaking of goodbye, is Zifeara coming back? 'Cause if she is, I wanted to at *least* say goodbye to her too. Do you know what kind of flowers she likes?"

Mavrik would not shut up. That last part however, caught Fang's attention.

"Excuse me? Why in the world would you bring her flowers? The hell are you on about?"

Mavrik grinned. "Hey, I'm almost eighteen now, I'm officially a man. Men like women for the most part, and Zifeara is the hottest babe I've ever seen. If she's gonna be gone a while, I gotta make a good impression so she might miss me. Duh. You've had girlfriends before, right? You should know how this works by now."

Fang almost slapped the smug-ass smile right off the kid's cocky face. "Mavrik, shut the fuck up. You should be ashamed of yourself, talking about her that way. Not only is Zifeara *your boss*, but she's about 9,982 years too old for you. Show some respect for once in your life."

Mavrik scoffed and rolled his eyes. "Fang, she's immortal, age gap doesn't matter when all you do is accumulate years. By your logic, she's 9,964 years too old for *you*. And technically she's your boss too. Besides, she doesn't tell me to shut up whenever I talk to her. She laughs at all my jokes, and even really liked the stuffed cat I brought her before she left last time."

Okay, now he was starting to get pissed. *"You did what now?* When the hell did you give her that? How... how long have you been doing this?"

Mavrik's grin had faded and now he was scowling. "Fang, what the hell? I've been drooling over Zifeara since I got here. A year ago, I started kicking my game up to try to get her to go out with me since I was practically old enough. I haven't asked Zifeara to dinner quite yet, but I'm working on her. Are you *that* freakin' blind? That woman is gorgeous. How have *you* of all people not been trying to get in on that? She-"

That time Fang lost any self-control he had left. He smacked Mavrik right upside the head. It wasn't nearly as hard as it could be, but it definitely got the message across.

Vhans had come over to ask Fang a question, but he wasn't fast enough to stop him. He did, however, grab Mavrik in a bear hug just in case the boy had one of his famous 'rabid' fits. He had had a few scuffles with rude patrons that rivaled an actual weasel in ferocity. Vhans honestly didn't know which was scarier; Fang being mad enough to hit the kid, or Mavrik being so calm in his arms.

From his position now at eye level with Fang, Mavrik shook his head slightly to relieve his dizziness and his smirk returned. "Oh, I get it. That *is* why you're upset. You haven't told her that you want her too."

Fang practically snarled at the stoat. "Mavrik, I'm giving all your shifts to Hawke for the next two weeks. Get out of my club."

Now Mavrik was mad. He struggled to be put down, but he was held fast. "What?! You can't just-"

"Like hell I can't. You aren't a man until you start acting like one. I expect that when you are allowed back in here, you tell Zifeara what you just said and you apologize for it. *No one* talks about her like she's some dumb, giggling girl while I'm around. Now get out." And with that, Fang resumed his walk to his home and pulled out his phone to dial his senior bartender.

Hawke Baker had been the head bartender at the SoundCave for several years. She had been working at some sleazy bar when she had gone to the Cave to see what it was like right after opening night. Fang had sent out invitations at random to get the club going and she had happened to receive one. The problem with Hawke was that she was a doe and she *hated* when people decided to point out how strange it was to be a doe named hawk. Fang told her he didn't care if she told people to piss off when they got obnoxious with her and that had been the selling point for accepting the job at the Cave.

Vhans carried his young friend to the door and shoved him out, per Fang's order. "Sorry Mavrik, Fang is right. Zifeara is boss, but she is also ancient being. She is far smarter than anyone you meet before. My thinking is she humor you. You are young, Mavrik. You are good *kid*. She like you and do not want to upset you. Think on the shame your actions bring upon you and on why you have upset Fang. Goodnight."

Vhans closed the door and made his way back downstairs to hear Fang confirming with Hawke that she'd like to put in extra hours.

Hanging up the phone, Fang sighed and looked to his large companion. "Vhans, was that uncalled for? Like, really uncalled for?"

Vhans paused a moment then replied, "Well, in a way yes. Mavrik is still a child, and much needs to grow. He does not ever listen, so he may have needed that. On other hand, Mavrik is a child and you did just lose your temper and hit a child. You may be letting this thing with Zifeara get you, yes? While on trip, you need to do something with yourself. Do something with *her*. Straighten life out, yeah?"

Fang felt heavy and now rather sheepish about losing his cool. He knew Vhans was right. "Yeah. Yeah, I know. That's really why I'm going to be gone for so long. At some point during this trip, I'm going to find that perfect time to tell her and get it over with. Keep an eye on things while I'm out; don't let anyone else do anything stupid."

Vhans nodded and began cleaning up while Fang went downstairs and gathered a couple of things. Leaving them all on the couch in his living room, he wasted as much time as he could trying to get the next night to come a quickly as possible. Nothing held his attention for more than an hour at a time. He gave up and took a nap when it was close enough to sunset, later waking up to... something. He had this feeling that someone was here that shouldn't be.

He sat up in time to see D1g1t float into the room yelling about someone coming into the club. Zifeara must have arrived. But why did he wake up if it was just her? He had a bad feeling about this. Getting up and climbing his stairs, Fang opened the door to the SoundCave. Standing there in a very historical style of clothing Fang had only ever seen in books was Zifeara, looking at him with curiosity. She wore a black, loose-fitting, pleated shirt and matching pants with flames embroidered on the bottom of the legs and ends of the sleeves.

Apparently, he was giving her a weird look because she tilted her head slightly and said, "What? Did you think we were going to the very far past in modern clothing? Before you start some shit, I have a set for you too."

"Zia, are you wearing men's clothes right now?" Fang asked, barely managing to stifle a laugh.

Huffing almost indignantly, Zifeara rolled her eyes as she very often did. "Fang, have you ever seen a kimono and how much frickin' work goes into putting one of those things on? It takes, like, three people to dress a geisha. Not to mention how impossible it is to fight in that. I'll take pants. Now would you take your damn silks and get dressed? It was a test of my amazing determination to find these in your freakish size."

That last bit she said with a smirk, so he knew she was teasing him, as always. She never meant it in a harmful way and in fact, Zifeara went to great lengths to make sure he never felt out of place because of how tall he was. Whenever they hung out, she shifted herself to be about 6'1" so he didn't have to look so far down at her all the time. Truthfully, Fang couldn't remember how tall she really was; he'd only ever seen her as tall as she needed to be for him.

"Alright, alright, give them here. Did- did you get me a kung-fu uniform?" Zifeara had handed him some very nice silks, all black with red trim and a sash to match.

"So what if I did? I figured it would be easier for you to move. Unless you'd like a kimono? They make manly kimonos." She gave a mischievous grin, "Actually, I'd love to see *you* in a skirt. I'm getting you a kimono when we get there."

Fang felt his cheeks redden slightly. "Shut up," he grumbled at her. "Let me go change. All of my stuff is on the couch."

Truth be told, wearing a skirt would not be the worst thing in the world- it was the weird, ancient, rag-style underwear he pictured having to wear under it that made him uncomfortable. Which led to worse thoughts. What was Zifeara wearing right now? Did they even have bras back then or did she not care to be *that* accurate? It didn't *look* like she had-

Being distracted by inappropriate thoughts for the second time that night, Fang walked right into the wall next to his stairway. Zifeara laughing him all the way down the stairs was not a good start to his first epic adventure. Whatever.

The drawstring pants and wrap-around top fit way better than he thought they would and were pretty comfortable too. Finished, he returned to his living room to find his things packed away in Zifeara's bag and her playing with something idly while she waited.

"Watcha got, rabbit?" He had fallen into the habit of asking her that question, likely due to one of his favorite kid's books, "*The Rabbit and the Raven.*" The Raven often asked the Rabbit what he had because the Raven was a hoarder and always wanted whatever cool thing the Rabbit had found at the time. And the bird was a bit of an asshole now that Fang really thought about it.

Zifeara turned and smiled. "My ticket to time."

She held out a small, light blue, plumb bob shaped crystal that reflected light like a prism. Before Fang could get close to touching it, she dropped it. With a clink and a whooshing sound, a gateway the same color as the stone pulled itself into existence from seemingly nowhere and stood open, humming softly.

"Hurry up, it only stays open for about twenty seconds so that not just anyone can get through."

Fang hustled through and found himself standing in a dirt alley in a town with wood and straw buildings. As he gawked at what he could see, he could practically feel his blood boil with anticipation. Half of a few houses looked smashed in, and the building he was next to was the only two-story structure that wasn't a barn for as far as his new gadget let him see. Everything was so old and technologically lame. And it was super dark. And he was here with Zifeara. Everything was *awesome.*

¤ ¤ ¤

Climbing the stairs to their room at the inn, Fang looked forward to finally being alone with Zifeara with nothing but time to talk. He hadn't really been listening to what she was saying to him as they neared their designated room because he had a montage of pure bliss running through his head.

A few key words snapped him back to attention- "there's just one more thing I forgot to tell you."

"Huh? Sorry Zia, I kind of spaced out for a second; taking in all the time difference and whatever. What did you forget to mention?"

Fang reached for the sliding screen of their resting place for the night, but didn't get a chance to even touch it. The screen slid open to reveal some guy with bright orange hair and massive ears leaning on the doorway, clearly not expecting all six-odd feet of Fang. The kid was staring at him like he was some kind of alien. Shit, this guy looked like the very definition of sexy schlup.

"Zifearaaa? I thought you said this was *our* room?" Fang looked back to her, but what he saw didn't make him happy.

Zifeara was short. Maybe only an inch or two shorter than this guy and instead of answering, she looked around him at this new person.

"Hey, Aun. This is Fang, my best friend. He put up a rather annoying and convincing guilt trip that he should come with us and would be helpful on this endeavor, so here we are."

Aun looked Fang up and down, then very dryly said, "Great. The more the merrier, right? Farrah, you're really fuckin' tall. Like, freakishly so. Where is this guy from?"

This time Fang spoke before Zifeara had a chance. "I, my small, stripey cat, am from the future, where being tall is quite normal for a lot of races. You're short." He hadn't quite managed to mask his disdain.

Aun scowled while Zifeara shook her head and pushed him out of the way so she could get into the room.

She flopped down on the nearest bed and mumbled, "C'mon you two. You can be friends in the morning. I'm going to bed."

Aun quickly leapt across half the room to claim the other bed, beaming smugly. "Sorry Scarecrow, you'll have to sleep on the floor. This one's mine."

Fang raised an eyebrow and gave an unconcerned smirk. Oh, this kid was in for some disheartening revelations. "I don't know what you're talking about." He calmly walked over to Zifeara's bed of choice and laid down, arms behind his head, legs crossed. "I always sleep next to Zia on sleepovers. We're perfectly okay sharing."

Aun pouted and his ears flattened. "Zia? What kind of-"

"Hey, only Fang gets to call me that," Zifeara interjected, "You do, and I cover you in spiders while you sleep."

Aun laughed, seemingly surrendering for the night. "Alright, alright, whatever. Don't get your little lute so high strung. I'll have to think of something else to call you then."

"How about her bloody name?" Fang was already very done with everyone hitting on Zifeara tonight. He'd gone from Mavrik to this asshole in no time flat. This was shaping up to be less of a dream vacation and more of a game of Don't-Kill-The-Cat.

Zifeara sighed before it turned into a strangled noise of frustration. "Fang, do not make me regret bringing you along. Aun, shut up. Go to sleep you two. I'm waking you up by becoming a rooster and screaming as loudly as possible."

Fang was put out at first but then gave Aun a very deliberate look as he did what he usually did at bedtime and cuddled up to Zifeara, her head by his chest, his head over hers.

Aun's ears didn't come out of being flat against his skull until he actually fell asleep. This was going to be hard work for him; this skinny bastard already had a head start on Zifeara and it didn't feel like he was going to give that up easily. What the dark wonder didn't have, however, was his tiger-like ferocity at getting what he wanted, and most importantly, his feline charm. Aun would have this girl off of Fang in a month. Tops.

CHAPTER 9

A Horse, Of Course

The nice thing about immortality was how much more streamlined life became. Lack of sleep never bothered Fang as long as he was well-fed, and this morning, he woke up just as Zifeara did. Even though he was hungry, he was full of energy and mostly ready to go. He was still a little drowsy, but functional due to the adrenaline of starting a new adventure. Aun, on the other hand, was still out.

Fang was not thrilled to discover Aun to be what he liked to call a 'beautiful sleeper'; he looked innocent as a kitten and not a hair on his head was out of place. What an asshole.

Fang got up and stretched. "Zia, what's for breakfast. I'm starving."

She yawned, exposing her sharp canines and curved her back to stretch as most house cats did. He was immediately *much* more awake. Aun had heard them talking and stirred. Opening his eyes, he looked far more alert than either of them. Must be a cat thing.

"Yeah, Zifeara, what *is* for breakfast? We have plenty of options out in the woods if you'd like to join me for a warm-up hunt."

Zifeara nodded approvingly. "Ready, set, go pussycat!"

She quickly shifted to a small black cat and jumped straight over Aun and out their window, which conveniently had a tree outside. Before Fang could protest being left behind, Aun became an orange tabby of about the same size and bounded out after her. Well shit. As Fang poked his head out, he watched the two cats grow into their wilder counterparts while racing each other to the expansive woods to the right of the town. He heaved a sigh and made his way downstairs and out to the woods himself.

Fang had just barely gotten there when he heard a familiar voice approaching.

"No fair! How the hell did you find that so quickly? You got stupidly lucky!"

That sounded like the new cretin. Zifeara was laughing heavily as she dragged a small boar by the hind legs out towards where Fang was standing, Aun sulking behind her.

"Hey, hun. I caught us breakfast in record time. You're going to *love* wild game from this era; New Tinning has nothing like this."

He looked at the dead animal and his stomach reminded him he was, in fact, hungry. "Neat. So how do we cook it?"

Zifeara raised an eyebrow. "Sweetie, do you not remember that I'm a fantastic fire demon? I can have this done in about thirty seconds. I figured you'd want the best part first, though."

Right. In this time, blood came straight from the dead, still warm carcass.

Aun shifted on his feet impatiently. "Please tell me he can't have all of it? I'm part bat too, you know. No playing favorites."

Zifeara cocked an ear and put a hand on her hip, shifting the dead weight. "Please. You get this all the time. Fang's never had boar. I doubt he can take all of it, but you'll have to wait your turn."

Zifeara set the pig down, seated herself by its head, and motioned with a finger for Fang to join her.

He sat beside her and she began to explain. "Okay, the hard part is drinking without bowls. I'm going to cut it here and you'll have to quickly put your mouth over the cut to get the blood."

Fang shot her a slightly disgusted look and Aun rolled his eyes.

"Oh, come on man, it's just a pig. You're going to touch it with your mouth when you eat it anyway." He shook his head and muttered, "Putting your blood in bowls."

This kid was getting on his nerves and it was only day 1.5.

Zifeara sliced into the boar's neck with one of her claws, and Fang quickly did as instructed. The outside of the boar was just as gross as he'd thought it would be, but the blood was delicious. What he could only describe as a haze started to overcome him, and something almost primal took over his body as the taste of the still warm blood crashed over his tongue and numbed his senses. He lost track of how long he drank, but at some point, Zifeara shook him softly to make him let go and backed him away from the carcass to let Aun have his share.

"You okay, Fang? I honestly don't think I've ever seen you drink that much at once. You must have drained a solid two-thirds of that body..."

Fang did feel a little dizzy from not pacing himself, but he smiled as he wiped residual blood from his mouth. "Yeah, that was amazing. I can't wait to taste it cooked though, the skin tasted like mud and sweat."

Zifeara giggled and claimed that did tend to happen as Aun drained the rest of the blood. "Yeah, most wild game does at first. Once cooked, I bet you'll think the meat is one of the best things you've ever eaten. I can't wait to have you taste some of the animals that are extinct in our time."

Aun paused his feast, blood still dripping from his chin, to glance back at them. "Alright, what are you on about? Last night, he said something about the future, and now you as well? You can't be serious. You're both just messing with me."

Zifeara grinned. "I'm afraid not. Remember what I said about my job yesterday?" Aun nodded and she continued, "Well, part of my job involves time travel. I'll explain it more while we're on our way, but let's eat and get going. Terravak isn't exactly a quick trip."

She moved Aun out of her way and inhaled deeply before exhaling a steady stream of fire over their catch. When she stopped, the boar sizzled loudly, and all the skin and fur had burned off.

"Well, that's *insanely* handy. I didn't know fire demons were that skilled at flash cooking," Aun remarked.

"When you've been around as long as I have, you get good at it. I've had plenty of practice at temperature control. You should see what I can do with just a few pounds of stone."

Zifeara grabbed hold of one of the rear legs and twisted, snapping it completely out of its socket and returning to sit next to Fang. He looked at her like she had just killed a puppy.

She caught his gaze of abject horror and turned a bit sheepish. "Oh, right. You probably don't remember what it looks like when I completely dismember something. In this world, I don't have to be reserved about my strength. Keep in mind, I did kill this with my bare teeth and claws a few minutes ago."

Fang *had* forgotten somewhat that Zifeara was, in all actuality, a nightmarish killing machine. In fact, he had only ever seen her kill a man that had broken into her house. Aside from that, Fang couldn't think of a single thing he'd seen her attack. They really did live in different worlds.

"That's why I love this time so much, honestly," she continued. "I can do whatever I want here. No one thinks it strange that I went hunting this morning or went for a run as three different animals. This period is awesome."

Aun looked dubious of all this different time talk, but he grabbed the head of their kill and tore it off much the same way Zifeara had. "Demons are strong here. Are they really no challenge to you where you're from?"

Zifeara thought about her answer a moment. "Well... not exactly. We live in an era of peace, so full on fights don't really break out like they used to. A few hundred years back though, there was a massive war that I may or may not have participated in."

"What? Since when do you fight in wars? You don't mean the Great Clash, do you?" Fang asked. He had never been told this story before. As far as he was aware, Zifeara preferred to stay out of major world conflicts for the sake of history doing its own thing.

"Well, I didn't really have much of a choice..."

She looked down and quietly filled her mouth with boar. Fang knew that look. That was the look Zifeara usually presented when talking about her dragon. She had told him a few things about it, but generally avoided the topic since she wanted nothing more than to pretend it didn't exist. Fang knew better than to press her, so he moved to get his own piece of breakfast. It was at about this time he realized he had no idea how Zifeara had dislocated that leg so easily.

As if reading his mind, she swallowed and said, "Up and back, hun. With legs, you have to sort of unscrew them from their sockets. Tearing meat is easy, tearing ligaments and cartilage is hard."

Fang wasn't thrilled about having to rip a dead animal apart, but it was something he'd clearly have to get used to. He grabbed the other hind leg tightly and did as Zifeara had said. It felt awful, but it sounded worse. Fang was too hungry to not eat though, so he sank his teeth into the meat, trying not to think too hard about having to eat this way from now on.

"Holy shit, this is awesome," he said with a mouth full of food.

Zifeara smiled through her own stuffed mouth. "I told you. You'll get used to having to kill it yourself. In fact, hunting your own food will help you practice for the real fights."

The three finished their food, putting some in Zifeara's bag for later and headed out of town, down the dirt road which led to the next major city.

"Alright," Aun ventured. "How do we get to Terravak, Zifeara?"

Still walking, she pulled a weathered map out of her bag and gave it a once over. "Well, most of the trip is over solid land, so at least that will be easy. The hard part will be getting across the ocean without him seeing us coming. We'll probably need to forge some paperwork and get a ride on one of the ferries. Until then, we'll be passing through the Akatama forest first, so at the next major city, I suggest we get horses. It'll save us the energy of moving ourselves since they should only need a few hours rest a day."

Aun's ears pointed themselves back at the mention of the forest and he made a face. "Do we have to go through the forest? Couldn't we go around at the same speed just by shifting?" Zifeara and Fang looked at each other and then back to Aun until he continued, pointing at a spot in the north of the forest. "Look, my clan lives at the far end of that forest here and I really don't care to say hi."

Zifeara thought about their route a moment and traced a line on her map with her index finger before replying, "Well, if we went through Rujik as opposed to Fumasha, that would put us far enough south to give clan Thunderfang a wide berth. Rujik is slightly larger so it would be easier to find some suitable steeds. It's the best I can do; the Akatama forest is the most peaceful and simple route to take so we're going through it."

Aun still seemed a little put out, but he merely grumbled his complaints and let it go.

In order to save some travel time, Aun and Zifeara had turned themselves into hefty deer and were moving at a rather brisk pace, Fang on Zifeara's back and Aun at the front should there be any trouble.

The long walk gave Fang the chance to ask about a million questions along the way.

"So, in this time what do people even fight with? Like, do they even know what guns are yet?" Fang asked while peacefully reclining along Zifeara's newly broadened spine.

He could feel her chuckle as she trotted onward, keeping pace with Aun. "No, they don't. They mostly use swords, polearms, chain weapons, that sort of thing. That's the only advantage you have in this time, boyo; fancy metal filled with gunpowder. Remember all that time I spent making you fight me with random crap from around the house?" He nodded and Zifeara continued, "Well that was preparation for what you'll have to do if ever you lose your guns in a real fight. Hopefully, it'll come in handy in this time, too."

After hours of explaining the new way of the old world to Fang, a bustling city began peeking into view past the scattered patches of trees and farms they had passed.

"Here we are, guys," Zifeara said, "Rujik is the last true city between us and the forest. It's rather fortunate Aun changed our course, actually; I had forgotten that this is the furthest out this way that you can still find an Arneir."

Aun glanced back over his shoulder. "No kidding? I didn't think they had those for miles near the forest."

Before Fang could ask, Zifeara explained, "Arneir horses are sort of like Clydesdales but are a hybrid of normal horses and a very special demon called an Errant; large elemental terra horses who usually live in dense forests and keep travelers from desecrating the land. Errants are extremely intelligent and can understand our language. They also cannot be tamed, so humans had to release regular horses into Errant forests and wait generations to attempt to domesticate the offspring." Shaking her shoulders slightly, she craned her neck back to nudge him. "Off you get, we'll walk from here."

Fang hopped down, and Aun and Zifeara changed back to their normal selves.

Once they made their way into the town, Zifeara asked the nearest street peddler where they could find an Arneir horse.

"Ah, you'll want to see Kanta. He lives on the farm just up the big hill there," the man selling leather replied, pointing to their destination, "You're in luck, Kanta has some new yearlings he's looking to sell I think."

Zifeara thanked him and the trio moved on.

"So, besides the obvious, what's so special about these hybrid horses?" Fang asked.

"Well, Arneirs can move onwards for long periods of time without stopping, sometimes even for days before needing rest. Since they're terra elementals, they can draw energy from the living beings around them, especially foliage. They're fantastic in forests, but you have to keep them focused or they'll be tempted to run away. Nature calls to them, just not as strongly as if they were a full Errant."

Fang felt he shouldn't be so surprised how much Zifeara knew, but he always was. She knew all of the world's history for the past 10,000 years and was living through it twice. She sometimes forgot things, but it was always only temporary, like her mind was searching an encyclopedia for the right page.

As they made their way to the farm, Aun yawned and strove to keep himself entertained. "Hey Zifeara, why *aren't* we just flying? If you're in such a hurry, it would surely be faster, right?"

Zifeara cast him a sideways glance and sighed. "Remember how I have a job to do? Well, my 'employer' provides me with my next tasks as they appear. It's entirely random. If we do fly and we go too fast, we may end up having to turn around and ultimately waste more time than we're saving. These jobs are extremely urgent and must be taken care of immediately. Torvak is still gathering the gems he needs, so that buys us some time, but it also means he isn't embedded in the number one slot in my priorities list. It allows me time to plan for his every move. In theory."

Aun blinked in understanding, but a sympathetic grin spread across his face. "You sound like you're going to be *tons* of fun on this trip. Do you ever stop to just enjoy yourself?"

Fang turned to look at Zifeara inquisitively as well, making her laugh. "Of course I do! Sometimes I have weeks off at a time to just move around as I please and find ways to get myself into trouble. In this day and age as well as the one Fang is from, there's always something to do. I'm planning on detouring to awesome spots that are well on our way since you two are sheltered toddlers compared to the shit I've seen. Have a little faith. I'm not boring, I swear. I've been alive too long to be lame."

While both boys gave her grief for referring to them as toddlers, they both knew she was closer to the side of 'exactly and entirely correct' to really put too much effort into it. Coming up on the farm, the three heard the neighing of horses and a gaunt, short man greeted them near the gate in the expansive fence. He came up to Aun's chest and had stiff, short black hair. His skin spoke of years toiling under the burning sun. This man looked like he had seen some stressful days and had a general air of grouchiness.

He did, however, lose his sour demeanor while welcoming them to the ranch. "Ho there! You lot travelers?"

Zifeara affirmed that they were and the man continued, "I expect you'll want some horses for the journey then. I'm Kanta, the owner of this ranch and you've come to the right place; I'm the only successful breeder of Arneir steeds for miles around. I'd be happy to show you to the barn if you've got the gold. These horses don't come cheap; five gold for a filly or mare, ten gold for a colt or stallion. We've got some of all ages right now, mostly yearlings though."

Aun hadn't considered the cost of horses and looked to Zifeara, but she simply smirked self assuredly at the short man. "Of course I didn't expect them to be inexpensive. We'll need three of them, so I'd like to see who you've got ready to ride today."

Kanta dipped his head, turned and waved them onward, leading the way to the sizable barn.

Once through the open door, Kanta pointed to two horses to the immediate left sharing a large stall. "These are the only two besides the black one not for sale right now. The other breeding pairs are out in the field currently, but any other horse in here I'm willing to sell you. Just let my farmhand Jin over there know which ones you want and he'll get some reins on 'em. Saddles will cost you extra though."

Zifeara thanked the man as he wandered his way back out of the barn. "Well, he was a charming human. Pick your horses, boys. We'll be needing them for several months, so find someone you like."

As the three spread out into the barn, talking to and petting the horses in their stalls, Zifeara evaluated the farmhand at the back of the barn. He almost looked like he was guarding a stall, watching them with curiosity. Zifeara went to go see what he had in there.

"H-hold up, miss. All the better horses are closer to the front," he said as she approached.

Zifeara looked past the young man to see a sizable colt, deep black with white speckling on his legs and muzzle, staring at her nervously with his large, yellow eyes. He was huge for such a young Arneir.

"What's the matter with him then? He looks exceptional," Zifeara asked.

The young man, Jin, shook his head and answered, "He's wild, miss. He ended up with too much Errant blood in him and won't let anyone ride him. It took me all morning to get this thing back in from the pasture, since he usually won't even let anyone touch him. We have much nicer horses, honest. Tomorrow we have a buyer coming in to take him away, but I don't think they want to tame him. It's been over a year since anyone has been able to do anything with him, so we have to get rid of him."

Looking back to the steed, Zifeara heard his voice. Along with her other abilities, talking to animals telepathically was one of them. Nearly all living animals felt what she was, and more often than not gave her their respect.

61

"Who... Who are you? Can you actually... understand me?"

Zifeara smiled and thought her reply back to the horse, "Sure can. I'm a normal demon but of great importance- that's about all you really need to know. My friends and I are looking to buy some horses to aid us in our long journey across the continent." He looked away, off into the corner as if in defiance, but Zifeara continued, "I know why you won't let them touch you. Your Errant blood calls for freedom, for the smell of the forest. You're too special to be handled by mortal hands."

The colt looked back up, staring Zifeara hard in the eye.

"I have a solution to your problem. Come tomorrow, they will sell you to someone who surely has nothing good in mind for you. Errant parts are highly valued, and full blood Errants are very difficult to catch. I only require your services for a short time."

Jin went to speak as it was odd for someone to just be staring at one of the horses, but Zifeara swiftly held a finger up to shush him and carried on her silent conversation. "Once we hit the coast on the other side of the continent, I promise to set you loose. The other two horses we're about to buy too, if you like. Then you can go wherever you want. All you have to do is let me ride you. Do as I ask for the next few months and you'll live to be free for the rest of your life. Do we have a deal?"

The horse was still a moment and then tossed his head in agreement.

Zifeara turned back to the poor confused worker. "If I can ride him, will you sell him to me?"

Jin looked confused, but ventured, "I- I guess, if Mr. Tayaki says it's okay but... what makes you think you can touch him, miss?"

"Open the stall," Zifeara commanded.

Intimidated and not willing to piss off a demon, Jin forgot his master's wishes and did as she asked. Zifeara backed up to move out of the way of the door and held her hand out, beckoning the horse to come to her. The young colt hesitated at first, but stepped forward until his muzzle rested under her outstretched fingers.

She smiled, not looking at the farm hand and instead silently praising her new friend. "Go get your master. I'm taking him."

While Jin ran back out to the farm to get Kanta, Zifeara, followed by her new companion, moved down the stable to see if the boys had chosen. Fang was the closest to her, stroking the neck of a beautiful black and white appaloosa filly, and Aun was closer to the entrance, talking to a golden palomino.

Kanta reentered the barn, face red and clearly angry. "What do you think you-" He stopped short, seeing the problem hybrid standing calmly by Zifeara's side, her hand resting on its neck and a gentle smile on her face. Fang and Aun also turned to look at him, clearly happy with their choices.

"Young lady, how in the name of Dios did you get him out of there?" Kanta asked astounded.

Zifeara patted the black horse's side. "I asked him nicely. He's not a bad steed. In fact, he's an amazing creature, you just don't know what to do with him. I'll give you twenty-five gold for just him. I'm sure that's more than you'd make off selling him for *parts*, isn't it?"

Kanta quickly glared at Jin for telling the visitors what he had planned to do with their untamable, but sighed and conceded. "Alright, but I will *not* take him back for any reason, you understand?"

Zifeara agreed and pulled open her pouch, producing thirty-five gold pieces and holding it out for Kanta to collect. As the owner stepped up to grab his payment, the large colt snorted maliciously at him, making the short man jump. He quickly grabbed the money and left, yelling at Jin to reign up the horses while Zifeara stifled a giggle. She and this horse were going to get along *great*.

Jin handed her a set of reins and her new mount dipped his head obligingly for her to put them on. With all the horses ready to go, Zifeara showed Fang how to properly mount his horse without a saddle and all three of them were off.

"We'll stay at the inn tonight and leave tomorrow. It's too late to start out for the forest since it took most of the day to walk here. What are you going to name them?" Zifeara asked her friends.

"Huh? What do you mean?" Aun tilted his head.

Fang rolled his eyes. "The horse, you idiot. Were you not planning on calling her something besides 'horse'?"

As they rode down to the town inn, Fang was the first to make his decision. "Treble. Mine's colors remind me of sheet music, so I think that's what I'll call her. What about yours, Zia?"

She looked down at her new friend, patting his neck as he snorted begrudgingly. "Orro Heme. He's so stubborn with all that Errant blood in him, so unmovable. Like obsidian. His name means 'Obsidian Heart' in Drakonic, so probably Heme for short. Aun, did you think of something for yours?"

He stared forward for a moment before he spoke. "Thrush. Her colors are similar to the thrushes that live in the trees around my clan, so it'll do."

The inn wasn't far from Kanta's ranch, and they arrived quickly. The large, hybrid horses took long strides, and all huddled together, hitched in the modest stable. The gang ate some of the boar Zifeara had saved from that morning and settled into their room, wasting no time drifting off for the night.

CHAPTER 10

At Least It's Not Customer Service

When Lucifer had a new job for her, Zifeara would see her mother in a dream, telling her everything she needed to know about her new mission and catching up on the goings on in her life. Tonight was one of those nights. Zifeara was in a tea house, people coming and going around her, indistinctly talking. By the looks of it, the sun had long set outside, and all the candles in the tea house lanterns had just been switched out. She was sitting on a fluffy, comfy pillow and a steaming pot of tea rested on the table next to her. It smelled wonderful.

As Zifeara poured a cup, something dripped from the ceiling onto the cushion across from her. It looked like tar but had a viscosity more akin to water. It dripped more rapidly, forming a puddle about the diameter of a beach ball before her mother slowly came up through the ooze, like an alligator surfacing in a swamp. Her mother always did have a flair for the dramatic.

Lucifer fully emerged from the puddle before opening her eyes to look across the table at her daughter. "Hello, Zifeara. How have things been? I see you made a new friend. I like the tiger stripes. They match your spots nicely. And he's almost as cute as Fang."

Zifeara rolled her eyes as she sipped her tea. "Hi, Mom. I'm going to ignore that last comment. Aun is coming with us to try to get to Torvak. We think he's collecting rare gemstones for his ritual, so at least we have time to go after him. One of those stones belongs to Aun's clan though, so he's been sent to get it back. Other than that, we got horses today to make the trip a little easier."

Lucifer's eyes glinted in the dim light of the tea house. "Coming with 'us'? Who else is going to Terravak with you? I saw you the other day and it looked like just the two of you."

Zifeara's eyes narrowed slightly. "I'm not thrilled about it, but... Fang is." Lucifer squealed with excitement, and Zifeara continued, "He's wanted to come with me for forever, but with his eyesight being what it is, I've always told him no. He got some new gadget that works to not only help him see way better but improve his aim, all while being hidden. He installed it in his headphones, so he can still wear those too. He one hundred percent guilted me into it, and I sort of regret giving in. I'm not happy about him being here, I just know something is going to go terribly wrong. He and Aun hate each other already for whatever reason, so now I have to babysit the both of them. I'm just hoping they get their shit together."

Lucifer giggled deviously. "You're worried about Fang. It's cute. He's never been outside his safe little bubble, has he? Look at it this way, at least this will prepare him for the Apocalypse so he can help you. I'll need the two of you to exterminate as many people still loyal to your uncle as you can, so at least he'll be hardened from the trip."

Zifeara sighed and looked into her tea. She thought about how much trouble Fang had even tearing the leg off a dead boar. She thought about his gorgeous silver soul. "I'm not going to make him do that, Mom. Just because he'll be stuck with me doesn't mean he has to *be* like me. I didn't want him to have to live my life. I don't want to ruin him."

Lucifer dropped her smile and any other pretense of a merry conversation. "Zifeara, you can't protect him forever. Someday he'll have to do something that drops his color. He's mine now- it will have to happen."

Zifeara didn't look up from her cup, but her features stiffened. She was going to keep him as pure as she could for as long as possible. She knew the elixir would very likely alter him over time, but she didn't want him to change *that* way.

Across the table, Lucifer scowled; her child was not only being defiant of her wishes, but was doing so quietly. If there was one thing she couldn't stand, it was secretly being told no. No one said no to Lucifer, Queen of Hell, without saying it to her face.

She dropped the subject, adopting an icy composure. "I suppose you know why I'm here. Hajikata. Woman of about eighty-seven, no living relatives, name is Shiiga. She isn't big news, but she has been using her magic to bring back dead family pets, children taken before their time, that sort of thing. Just enough to get her in trouble. I expect it won't be a problem. It's on your way. Get it taken care of."

Lucifer began to melt back into the same black ooze she appeared in, slowly seeping through the pillow she had been sitting on and disappearing entirely. Zifeara threw her cup across the room angrily, shattering it on the far wall. No one messed with her DJ. Not even the Queen herself. Zifeara would do everything she could to stop Fang from making those mistakes when the time came. She couldn't let him be entirely like her.

¤¤¤

Zifeara opened her eyes quickly but didn't stir. She could see nothing but impenetrable darkness. She was about to jump up when the blackness in front of her seemed to move, slowly and rhythmically. Then she realized she heard Fang, still asleep, breathing peacefully. She blinked in confusion a few times before understanding washed over her, followed by a sigh of relief. She had her face pressed to his chest; his silks were blocking out the moonlight pouring in from the window on the other side of the room. He was on the side of their bed closer to the window, so he towered over her like a wall. Fang had one arm draped over her shoulders and the other under the pillow beneath his head.

Zifeara relaxed further into him; everything was as it should be, and she had just been startled for a moment. That happened frequently when she woke up from talking to her mother since it was always disorienting to go from one place to another so quickly. She moved one of her arms from her side to wrap around Fang's waist, seeking his familiar brand of comfort, and he involuntarily squeezed her lightly. Zifeara smiled to herself. He made her feel better without even being awake. They really had been together for a long time. Although they were both light sleepers, simple movements like that didn't wake either of them, but one out-of-place noise and they were both up and armed. She closed her eyes again, listening to her friend's heartbeat and letting its steady thumping lull her back to sleep.

As soon as dawn broke over the rolling fields, all the nearby farmers emerged to go about their duties and earn their living for the day. Someone's rooster strutted his way out of his coop and began to crow loudly, heralding a new day of hard work.

Fang yawned, slowly coming to, the sunlight streaming in through the window annoying him into consciousness. He moved his arm over the other side of the bed to find it was worryingly vacant. Zifeara must be up already. He sat up and looked around, not finding his friend, but his gaze stopped on Aun instead. Damn it.

The sunlight filtering in played on the tiger's hair, making it gleam, and was reminiscent of fire in places. Sometimes Fang wished he were a shapeshifter too; having pitch black hair and being so plain could really get old sometimes. That, and he'd seen the way Zifeara looked at Aun every now and then. She thought Aun was attractive, he just knew it.

Getting up, Fang quietly walked around the tiger's bed to look out the window. He had intended to look at the sunrise since he was usually still asleep for it in his time. He ended up staring at the tree that was about thirty feet away. Zifeara was indeed awake, perched on a limb, also watching the sun climb over the horizon. The sunlight glinted off her, highlighting all the hidden spots in her hair and making her look as radiant as Fang had ever seen her. Maybe she was secretly adopted and was just a misunderstood angel. Maybe Lucifer stole her and corrupted her. Maybe she just didn't know any better and was forced into this life. Maybe he was actually a pink goblin.

He walked out of the inn and made his way over to the tree, which he then began to climb. He stopped at the limb just under Zifeara and sat, enjoying the early morning light. They were silent for a while, but he could feel the tension in her muscles and almost see the stress rolling off her in waves.

"What's up?"

"I have a job. Mom showed up last night and told me who it is next," Zifeara said quietly.

Fang looked up at her and her expression was grim. "What's the matter? I can't imagine killing people excites you, but you look unusually upset."

Zifeara returned his gaze, an emotion he couldn't quite pinpoint swirling behind her eyes. "You know, it used to. I used to think it was fantastic getting to just go around, doing anything I fancied, killing anyone I felt like. You looked at me wrong a few thousand years ago and I might have killed *you*. It loses its appeal. Sometimes, though, I get a job where... I feel like the rules are stupid. Like, I get why the person has to go, but it's too bad I can't give warnings or something. It's just death, that's it. No second chances."

Fang never knew Zifeara felt bad about doing what she did. It made sense, but he never really thought about how hard doing that sort of thing must be for her. "Well, I guess it's better than chaos. Without you, a lot of horrible people would still be out doing whatever they wanted and making everyone else miserable. The work you do is important, even if it has its bad points... right?"

Zifeara stared down at him, surprised for a moment before smiling softly. "I guess you're right. I don't think anyone has ever outright validated what I have to do before. Thank you."

Fang felt kind of upset and now a little concerned. "Zia, have you ever really talked about what you *do* with anyone else before? Surely anyone with sense can see how wrong things would be without you doing your job?"

Zifeara looked away and thought. After of few moments of staring she quietly replied. "There was one person I talked to about it. Quite some time ago now. He didn't call me a monster or a murderer. Even though I essentially am a murderer, assassins murder for a purpose, not because they want to. He at least understood that. He didn't say he approved like you just did though, so I don't know how well he understood, but he and I were friends. We..."

Zifeara trailed off and her eyes crinkled oddly.

Fang didn't know what to do; he had never seen her this upset while talking about someone she used to know. He had never once seen Zifeara Nightshade cry and he didn't think he was ready to handle the fallout.

"Zifeara?"

She snapped back to the present and shook her head. "I don't wanna talk about it. C'mon, now's the best time of day to go look for deer. I want to teach you how to hunt for yourself." With that, she dropped herself out of the tree and landed with a solid thud.

At least fall damage wasn't so bad when you were a demon, especially an immortal one. Fang climbed down and looked sheepishly at Zifeara. "I'm still kinda scared to just straight up jump. I don't know how to land."

She merely laughed and shook her head, "Okay, put that on the list of things to work on with you. Now, the first thing you need to know about hunting deer..."

¤ ¤ ¤

The early morning light filtered softly through the leaves, tinting everything a magical shade of orange. The buck was grazing, perfectly unaware of the danger he was in. The birds around him sang their merry tunes, carefree as always and announcing the bounty of life around them. As he raised his head, however, he felt something the other animals did not. There was a presence nearby and he didn't like it. Just as the deer moved to bolt, the bullet went straight through his neck, noise muffled by the design of Fang's futuristic weapon. The deer fell, wounded but alive. His powerful hooves pawed the dewy soil for purchase, finding none and only compounding his distress and confusion.

"You missed." Zifeara emerged from her hiding spot in a nearby tree first.

Fang popped up out of the shrub he'd been hidden in and cursed softly. "He moved just as I fired. What do we do?"

Zifeara looked apologetically at the deer. "You have to shoot him again. Put him to rest, quickly. He's still food and he won't recover from that."

Fang swallowed hard but he understood. He did this to the poor thing, he had to fix it. He aimed at the deer's skull and pulled the trigger again. This time was a bull's eye. The deer was dead and Fang looked to Zifeara, clearly upset.

She tried to be as sympathetic as she could under the circumstances. "It's how things are here. You kill to eat and survive. This just means you'll be more careful to get a clean kill next time. Learn from your mistakes. Don't fire unless you know you'll kill it right away; it's better to have it run off and have to find it again than to have it suffer. I could have dropped down on it if you'd let it go, but my kills are more natural. Either suffocation or a quick snap of the neck depending on what I'm shifted into and how big the prey is. You'll do better next time though. Sneaking up on herbivores is the hard part, and it seems to me that you're a natural in that regard."

Fang still felt a little glum, but this process wasn't as bad as he feared hunting would be. He thought he'd have felt guiltier over killing a peaceful animal, but providing for Zifeara made it somehow worth it. Even if this was the kind of quality time he was spending with her, it was still nice. He had a chance to show her that he could be more than just fun to hang out with. He was finally useful.

"What in the hell was that?!" The tiger strode out of the trees to their left and Aun shifted back to his normal self. "Seriously, what did you do to that deer?"

Zifeara rolled her eyes and her ears reflexively tilted backwards in annoyance. "Good morning Aun, I was wondering how long you were going to just follow us. That is called a gun. You'll invent it a few hundred years from now, but it won't be this good. Where Fang and I are from, these are pretty commonplace. It works by sending a small, pointed metal pellet through the air at high speeds using tiny explosions. Don't touch Fang's pistols, you may end up shooting yourself."

Fang glared at Aun. "Yeah, leave these alone. It would be such a *shame* if you got blood on them. Hard to clean out of the intricate machinery."

Aun made a face. "Whatever, Scarecrow. I don't need those to fight, I have pure strength and muscle, like a real man."

Fang was about to make a biting remark when Zifeara interrupted. "Do you two want breakfast or not? You keep griping at each other and I'm making Aun cook."

They both scowled at each other but sat down and shut up. Zifeara quickly roasted the deer after letting the two vampires have their fill of blood, and the three of them ate in relative silence.

Once they got back to town to retrieve their horses, the trio started the long journey through the Akatama forest. Orro Heme led the way, followed by Treble, then Thrush. It only took them a couple of hours to reach the perimeter, but once they did, the forest seemed to stretch on forever on either side of the path they were following. Fang looked at the ancient trees in awe, having never seen trees so old they were covered in moss and creeping vines. The forest quickly became thick, roots often snaking over the path. Orro Heme was looking around with a deep longing, changing his pace erratically and sometimes even coming to a stop. Each time he did, Zifeara gently stroked the side of his neck and the colt would correct himself and carry on, almost apologetically snorting each time.

At one point, Fang got bored and asked for Zifeara's bag. She undid the strap which held it to her sash and tossed it back to him, making Treble falter a little, but she quickly regained her composure, moving a bit faster to get closer to Heme. The forest seemed to be unsettling her for some reason. Thrush and Aun moved along in mutual relaxation, however, and Zifeara could see why he had picked the mare. She had a calmness to her and Aun was laid out on her back as a housecat, dozing in the shade the trees were providing.

Fang turned to recline along Treble's back, almost as if he were in a lounge chair and pet her side, comforting her and urging her to just follow Heme. He pulled his favorite acoustic guitar out of the bag, a black one with red trim, and began to strum it, playing nothing in particular at first. Then the strumming sounded sort of familiar to Zifeara, and Fang began to sing softly.[8] All three horses soon fell into step with the song, clearly enjoying the music. Zifeara, too, began to relax, laying herself out on her stomach along her colt's broad back and turning around to watch Fang's fingers as he played. When she had put all of Fang's stuff in her bag, she hadn't questioned him about bringing some of his instruments, but now she understood; he was bringing music for the road trip. Music always made traveling so much nicer and Fang had a voice she'd never tire of.

Once Fang had started singing though, Aun perked up and slowly lifted his head to glare. Fang caught the look and wagged his eyebrows, smirking, but continuing the song. Aun swiveled his ears to complete his sour face. He hadn't expected Fang to be good at singing, and he certainly didn't think he could play... whatever weird instrument he was holding. He looked around Fang's horse to see Zifeara completely relaxed, laid out backwards and listening to whatever the Beanpole was playing. He hated to admit it, but Fang's voice was very soothing, and it pissed Aun off. He knew he wasn't bad, but he definitely couldn't out-sing the Scarecrow. He was betting Fang was as weak as he looked, so the next time Aun got the chance, he'd have to get time with Zifeara by doing something Fang couldn't. He knew he could physically be the bigger man, he'd just have to find a way to go about it that did something for Zifeara. It always worked to get the girl eventually if past experience taught him anything.

Zifeara didn't seem to respond terribly well to flattery, so Aun would have to try a different approach. Maybe being friendly with her at first to get closer was the way to go. It would be hard not to do his usual routine of complement and charm, but she seemed more rough-and-tumble compared to other girls he'd fooled around with. She was different, and yet Aun felt like he knew what he had to do; he had to goof around with her, maybe try to go fishing or something. His instinct was telling him so, but he was positive he'd never met Zifeara before; he absolutely would have remembered a figure like that. So why did she seem so familiar?

Fang played several songs, pausing in between and strumming out whatever random melodies that came to mind, singing each one in turn. He even played a few songs Zifeara joined in on.

Aun thoroughly enjoyed hearing Zifeara sing. Sometimes she even lulled him to sleep, causing him to wake with a start when he hadn't realized he had drifted off. He just couldn't seem to stay awake during certain songs. He didn't realize it, but there were some Fang fell asleep in the middle of playing as well.

After about the fourth time he woke up, Aun finally thought to ask Zifeara what in the good name of the forest goddess she was doing. "Hey, Zifeara, what the hell is going on? I keep falling asleep. Are you...?"

---

[8] "The Girl" City and Color

Zifeara looked back to the cat and gave a lopsided smile. "Sorry, Aun. Sometimes I just kind of forget when Fang is playing. I happen to have the ability of Siren's song, just one of the many tools of my trade, I suppose. I can sing people to sleep or get them completely infatuated with me. I've lured a lot of my marks into getting close to me that way without having to expend a lot of energy doing so."

Fang chuckled a little as he plucked random notes. "Zia, I've fallen asleep a few times now too. Ease up, yeah? I know I'm good, but if you want me to keep playing, I have to be conscious for it."

They shared a brief laugh and Fang started to play something else they both sang to.[9] Before anyone knew it, night had arrived and Zifeara informed them they wouldn't be camping.

"Orro Heme told me none of them are tired yet, so we won't be stopping. Try to get some rest, but be careful not to fall off. We'll take a quick break in the morning then carry on."

The group passed the night without any trouble and did indeed stop in the morning to eat and get the Arneirs some water by a small stream. While everyone was washing up after breakfast, Aun saw his chance to test his theory.

"Zifeara, think fast!" He cupped his hands and threw water at her, hitting her quite squarely in the face and making her gasp and keep her mouth open for a moment.

Slowly all the water on Zifeara began turning into steam and she closed her mouth. She shifted larger and larger, turning into something that looked rather like a fat moose with an elephant trunk and no antlers. As she did so, the tip of her trunk dipped into the water and she inhaled. Aun quickly got up, but wasn't quite fast enough to get away. Zifeara lifted her snout and unleashed a heavy stream of water, like a firehose, knocking Aun over and drenching him head to toe. Fang was laughing hysterically by the time Zifeara had shifted back, and she gave Aun a 'that's what you get' kind of look. She seemed smug, so he knew she saw the humor in what he had just done. Bingo. This was the way to go for sure. Childishness seemed to be endearing, so he just had to be fun for a while. Aun shifted into a large dog to shake himself off and try to be mostly dry for Thrush's sake.

Once they had resumed their pace, Zifeara began telling the boys about their first detour. "Hajikata. It isn't much further from here. It's a small human settlement that produces almost everything its people need so that they can live this far into the forest. Their town is considered to be a marker of how far you are into these woods. Once we hit it, we'll be about a third of the way through."

"So why are we stopping here?" Aun asked.

---

[9] "Little Talks" Of Monsters and Men

Zifeara turned on her horse to look at him. "Work-related detour, we won't be there long. We should get in just after sunset. While you two take care of the Arneirs, I'll do what I have to, then we'll leave. Easy as that."

While Aun looked confused, Fang kept his expression neutral. He knew this was what Zifeara was bothered about yesterday and he didn't want to ask about this job if she didn't want to talk about it.

Sure enough, they got to the village about an hour after the sun had dipped below the tree line. She pointed the boys to the town well and instructed them to keep moving once they had watered the horses, guaranteeing them it would be no problem for her to catch up. Zifeara stroked Orro Heme's muzzle since he looked almost unsure of having to follow Fang, reassuring the colt that he would be okay with the others. She and this horse had bonded rather well in the few days she'd had him, mostly because he was still young and they conversed whenever Fang didn't feel like playing songs. Heme watched her go before turning to follow the new person Zifeara had handed his reins to.

Fang and Aun did as she asked, heading to the well and carrying on once the horses had their fill. They both seemed to agree that the easiest way to deal with each other was to completely ignore the other's presence as much as possible. The horses passed a few looks between themselves, feeling the tension smothering the peaceful good will from the morning. They knew they didn't want to be too involved with whatever feud was raging amongst their new owners.

Zifeara, on the other hand, made her way around as a small black cat, looking in windows, searching for the old woman she was after. One of the last houses she came to seemed promising. A grey-haired woman sat in a rocking chair by her roaring fireplace, sewing some ratty clothes. Zifeara scratched and meowed at the window, getting her attention. She was hoping the reputation this lady had meant she might not have to work to get into the house.

The elderly woman rose and opened the window, moving out of the way to allow the feline to enter if she wished. "Hello, kitty. Come to keep old Shiiga company tonight? In you get then."

That would do. Zifeara jumped inside and wandered around a bit as Shiiga closed the window and returned to her sewing. The cat caught sight of a cup of tea by the old woman and she knew exactly how to do the poor old lady in without hurting her too much. Zifeara shifted her teeth slightly in her mouth and began producing a toxin from a snake locally known as the Death Sleeper. She jumped up on Shiiga's lap and laid down, covertly placing her face near the tea. Opening her mouth, Zifeara quickly dipped her fangs in and released a good quantity of the toxin. Now it was all waiting and ensuring the job was done. Allowing herself to be stroked was far from the worst thing Zifeara had ever tolerated in the line of duty. She could be patient.

After petting her cat companion a while, Shiiga drained the rest of her tea and it wasn't long until she slowly drifted off to sleep for the last time. She may have really hated doing this job sometimes, but there were things she could do to make it easier for those she needed to eliminate.

There was no point hanging around now; Mortis only came for immortal souls if he had time to spare, so Zifeara wouldn't be seeing her brother. All other souls went to him, seeking out the man who could give them rest. She got up and stared at the old woman for a short while, thinking an apology before getting out by sidling up the chimney. Turning into an owl, Zifeara jumped off the roof and flew after her friends.

CHAPTER 11

Sleepwandering

T he horses walked almost tirelessly well into the next day, only requesting a break the following evening. Arneirs really were something; they had gotten the group almost the entire way through the forest in record time. While everyone settled down and enjoyed leftover deer, Fang realized he didn't know how they would be sleeping tonight. He was pretty damn sure Zifeara hadn't taken the time to put an entire bed in that bag of hers.

"Zia, where exactly are we sleeping? I mean, I know we're roughing it now, but you didn't really give me heads up on a tent or anything..."

Zifeara opened up her bag and took out two sleeping bag rolls; one looked rather large and the other somewhat smaller. "This forest is pretty peaceful, so sleeping on the ground won't really be a problem. In more dangerous areas it's far smarter to sleep either in a tree or a cave, whichever you have access to. These sleeping bags are lined with chongit fur," Zifeara said as she unrolled the large sleeping bag and held it out for Fang to feel, "so they're quite comfortable."

She tossed the smaller roll to Aun, but he looked at it dubiously. "Thanks, but I honestly prefer to sleep in a tree anyway. Makes me feel more at home out here."

Aun laid the bag roll on the ground and jumped up into the nearest large tree, stretching himself out into a leopard and settled in. Zifeara shrugged and crawled into her bag, unzipping it a little so Fang could join her. This sleeping bag was deceptively long and he had no trouble fitting himself in. It also had a built in squishy lump at the top to serve as a pillow, so even though they were on the ground, Zifeara and Fang were fairly comfortable.

The night passed quietly, the only disturbances being the horses readjusting themselves and Aun's leg periodically twitching as he dreamed. The past few nights he'd been having these dreams about someone else, though it was like he was seeing life through their eyes. The only things he'd been able to discern were that he was an archer, and he was pretty sure he was a wolf demon with long black hair, but things looked unfamiliar to him and he couldn't tell where exactly he lived. It was mountainous and there were pines everywhere and snow in places- somewhere Aun himself had never seen. It snowed in the Akatama forest nearly every winter, but these were not the trees and rocks surrounding him now. The other wolf demons he saw seemed familiar to him, but he didn't actually know anyone, even though they were doing things together and acting friendly. Any time someone said his name, it sounded mumbled through a mouthful of berries but they certainly weren't calling him Aun.

He just couldn't make out what they were calling him, but on this night in particular, he saw someone he knew. Or at least he thought he did. While going through this odd forest hunting with his bow, he thought he saw... Zifeara. He had barely caught the sly wink she shot his way before she darted behind a large tree. He ran to go catch her, but there was no indication she'd been there at all.

Aun woke suddenly, no longer in his leopard form and almost falling from his branch. Steadying himself, he glanced around. Fang and Zifeara were exactly where he'd last seen them, as were the horses. He ran a hand through his hair. It felt like his, but not like it did in the dream. He was himself. But who the hell was he dreaming about, and why now? He had never had these kinds of dreams before, but lately he was having one every night. He couldn't be sure it was Zifeara he'd glimpsed, but if it was, maybe his dream was trying to tell him something about her. Aun thought about it a while longer and decided to just go back to sleep. He figured he needed to have at least one more dream with Zifeara in it to understand what she had to do with anything.

The young tiger laid back out on the branch and stared up at the stars for a while, thinking on how once they left this forest -the only home he had ever known- there would be no going back. He'd be going with Fang, and more importantly Zifeara, wherever they led, getting into who knows what trouble and having a real adventure. He wanted this, right? Aun had always dreamed of leaving his clan and making it out into the world, but now that the opportunity presented itself, he realized he was a little nervous. He was only nineteen after all.

No way. Aun wasn't going to give up the chance to do what he wanted for once. That, and he was getting the stupid rock back for the good of the clan. Surely his father would understand that, even if it took a really long time. Screw his clan, he was going and that was that. He'd show them who was a fuck up now. He wasn't born a mistake, he was born to be different.

¤ ¤ ¤

The next day passed uneventfully, though the cloudy weather put everyone in a glum mood. Fang still sang his songs while taking in the unfamiliar scenery, but all of them had a darker and more somber theme than yesterday's.[10] Aun brooded over what his dreams could possibly mean. Zifeara quietly read something she had pulled out of her bag when she wasn't conversing silently with Heme.

All was still and uneventful until the heavy clouds fell away, revealing the last rays of dying light losing its battle against the inky darkness of night. The distance between trees slowly but steadily increased until they disappeared altogether, opening up into a grass prairie as far as the eye could see. The boys stopped what they were doing in order to dismount their horses and gawk at the unfamiliar sight. Heme stopped walking before the females did, which made Zifeara look up from her book and she smiled broadly to herself. Seeing her two companions share the same sense of wonder in something new to them was endearing. Neither of them had ever seen a prairie before since neither had ever been very far from their own homes. They also didn't seem to realize that they both wore the same expression on their faces.

Zifeara dismounted as well, deciding she needed to stretch her legs as it got truly dark out. She was starting to think her boys looked a little too *comfortable* out here with nothing to do. She shifted to her wolf form and broke into a run, intentionally bumping Aun as she did so. If he thought she was boring, she'd just have to prove him extremely wrong. Before he could glare at her, Aun watched Zifeara run ahead of him, then turn around, all 150 pounds of pure murder dipping her front paws and raising her tail; the universal dog symbol for 'come play with me'.

A wide smile worked its way across Aun's face. Oh, it was on, he *never* lost at tag. Turning into a large rust colored wolf, he sprinted off in pursuit, starting a race through the ever deepening stalks of grass to catch one another. Eventually though, the grass was too tall to see through, and tag became hide and seek. Aun crept quietly through the wall of stalks, scenting the ground to find his target; he could smell Zifeara, but she wasn't in the direction he'd thought she went. She also didn't smell like the same animal.

She had circled back to where the horses were. Back to where Fang had resigned himself to laying down and staring at a sky full of more stars than he had ever seen in his whole life. While he had his wide red eyes fixed on the heavens, the sharp indigo eyes of a predator were unwavering as they closed in on him. With a solid leap and a roar, Zifeara had pinned her friend flat before he could even react. Fang held his breath after sharply inhaling. He had completely forgotten about the rest of the world, lost in an entire galaxy he had never imagined to be so stunning.

He exhaled as he looked Zifeara in the eye, recognizing her distinct shade of purple and hearing a growly voice coming from the large panther sitting atop him, "You're dead."

---

[10] "Thistle and Weeds" – Mumford and Sons

Zifeara moved off and shifted back to herself. "You really need to work on your survival instincts. It's peaceful here now, but we're about to move on to the real stuff; big angry monsters who want to eat you. I'm going to start training you tomorrow."

Behind them, Aun emerged from the edge of the grass, turning himself back as well. "What the hell, Zifeara? How did you get all the way back here?"

She looked at Aun over her shoulder, throwing him a sly smile. "You could use some training too, apparently. It was too easy to sneak past you; I just had to throw a rock I rubbed my face on one way and then go the opposite direction."

Aun flushed a little, angry he'd been tricked so easily, but he still had some sass in him. "So teach me, oh great and powerful being. Teach me how to not track a rock."

Zifeara laughed and placed her hands on her hips. "Alright, training for you begins after you help me train Fang."

"*What!?*" both boys managed to exclaim at the same time.

"You heard me. It's far better to teach you how to deal with more than one enemy at once early on. If you can beat two of us, you can beat one of us. So we'll cycle when I'm coming at you and when we're *both* coming at you, Fang. You'll learn faster. Oh right, I almost forgot." Zifeara reached into her bag and pulled out clips for Fang's pistols. She held them out for him, and as Fang took them she elaborated, "These are full of paint. This way, instead of using blanks, you can accurately tell where you've hit us and work on your aim. Before, I was just seeing if you could come close to hitting me, now I'm training you how to kill me. This is where the real work starts, yes?"

Fang couldn't help himself. He switched his real clips for the paint ones, took very quick aim at Aun, and fired. Not expecting it in the least, Aun took the bullet point blank in the chest, right where his heart was.

Yelping and wiping furiously at the paint, Aun's ears went flat against his skull and his pupils constricted in momentary panic. "What the fuck, you skinny bastard?! What are you-"

Fang cut Aun off and gave his best deadpan, "Oh no, Zifeara. Aun is dead. I guess we have to leave him behind now."

Zifeara clutched her sides and began to laugh unusually hard, causing Aun to growl. He wasn't thrilled at being laughed at, but he supposed being in on the joke would be better than being the butt of it.

"Oh no. I'm dead. This means I'm going to haunt the shit out of you, Scarecrow. I'm going to steal every single one of your left socks, for forever."

Now it was Fang's turn. The annoyed expression he usually reserved for Aun softened and he snickered before busting out as well. Soon all three of them were giggling like they were actually getting along. Once they had recovered, they mounted their horses and began the trip through the plains, moving on to whatever awaited them on the other side.

CHAPTER 12

A Vast Expanse of Memory

The worst part of a road trip is getting bored and having nothing to do but stare endlessly at the scenery, especially scenery that consists of grass and more grass, until you fall asleep from lack of brain activity. The best part of a road trip is being bored with your friends, making up stupid games and being generally idiotic together. Zifeara had never had this sort of company on her many trips, so this was by far the best time she'd ever had chasing after a madman.

"Okay, okay, never have I ever... had a one night stand."

Aun cursed and put his fourth finger up. That move from Fang had put the tiger one away from losing the game. Both boys did stop and stare at Zifeara for a moment though. She hadn't put a finger up.

"Okay, no fair lying, Zifeara. We both know Fang is going to win this one," Aun said.

She had three fingers up and Fang only had one, but Zifeara looked insulted, "I'm not lying, Aun. You just don't want to lose. Again."

Aun and Fang both looked dumbfounded.

"Zia, do you know what the definition of a one night stand *is*? It still counts even if you killed the guy afterwards."

Zifeara cocked an ear, starting to get annoyed at what he was implying. "Wait wait wait, are you trying to tell me luring a guy somewhere alone, letting him *think* he's going to get some, and biting a *hole in his throat* is your definition of a one night stand? Fang, what have you been doing while I've been gone?"

They both continued to stare at Zifeara in utter confusion, but Fang was the first to drop it.

"You know what, whatever. Your turn Aun."

Aun shook his head slowly but continued, "Sure. Fine. Uuuuuuum, never have I ever made my siblings cry."

Fang looked dubious that this was true, but he put a finger up. He remembered accidentally opening a door and hitting Melody right in the face with it. Zifeara didn't have to put a finger up for that either– she and Mortis never saw each other enough to really be upset with one another. Aun was happy he had at least moved Fang closer to losing than he had been, but now it was Zifeara's turn.

"Never have I ever... been *caught* staring at someone's ass." Zifeara was smug as Aun and Fang both hung their heads. Aun had lost, but she knew how to get them both in the end.

"Well, now we have to find something else to do. Aun has officially lost three out of five," Fang said.

"I would say we could play I Spy, but everything besides us and the occasional herds of grazers is either brown grass or green grass. So what else?" Zifeara ventured.

All three thought for a while before Aun spoke up. "You know, I did have a few things I wanted to ask you since you are all knowing, after all." That last bit he clearly said with heavy sarcasm, but he continued, "As long as you don't mind hearing yourself talk, Zifeara."

In their current line up to play their game, they had the horses walking with Thrush in front, Heme in the middle, and Treble at the back so Zifeara could easily ride sidesaddle and see them both. Now the two boys looked expectantly at her, as though she were about to tell them a story before bedtime.

"Yeah, shoot Aun, we've got the time."

Aun made himself more comfortable and asked, "So, I know I'm not really supposed to ask about your job or whatever, but if you and Fang really are from the future, how did you get here?"

Zifeara reached into her bag to pull her time crystal out and show him. "This was given to me in order to help me do my job. This crystal can make a bridge between two points in time; the one the world is currently experiencing and right now, where you are. It sounds hard to believe, but I've been in this exact time once before. The *first* time right now happened." Seeing the complete and utter lack of comprehension still gracing his features, Zifeara tried something else.

"Here, this is the way I had it explained to me; picture a wagon wheel. Time is sort of like that wheel. The wheel creates itself and gets longer as it turns. There are many spokes that hold the wheel up and help it to roll, but the spokes are each connected to only two points on the wheel. This crystal opens up a pathway along one of the spokes– the one closest to where I exist in the future. Since each spoke only goes between two points, I can't jump to any time I want, only the time directly opposite me. Your time, *right now,* is the exact opposite from the point where new time is being created and added onto our wheel. Does that make any sense?"

Aun stared, but it was obvious by the way his eyes were moving that he was thinking really hard about what he'd just been told. "So, where you're from... in the future... there's nothing before you? Just everything else after you?"

Zifeara nodded quickly, glad that this was easier to explain than she thought. "Yes, exactly! The only really confusing part is the part where I live through each time twice. The reason I have to be back here in the first place is because our time wheel is moving along, having a nice ride, but then it hits a pothole. A cosmic pothole that alters events from the way they were the first time. Time changes most often when someone has figured out how to bend the rules of the universe. I, very specifically, am here to keep people from breaking the rule saying they have to die. A surprising number of people this time around have found some way to make themselves immortal, a power very few are allowed in this world. It gets insanely annoying after a while, to tell you the truth. There are only four true immortals in the world and it has to stay that way. I get to those who have broken the rule and find whatever loophole it is keeping them alive, and I put an end to it. Only true immortality can keep you from permanently dying no matter what happens to you, so most often man-made immortality just keeps you from aging. A quick bite to the throat or stab through the vital organs usually gets the job done, most of the time."

Aun was still for a while before he seemed to be done absorbing what Zifeara had just told him. "Wow, I didn't think it would be that easy to trick you into telling me what your job is."

Zifeara narrowed her eyes and her ears pointed back. She had gotten too caught up in trying to explain how things worked and had forgotten she didn't want to let Aun in on her secret just yet. Well, one of her secrets. Fang was extremely quiet, trying not to take sides but also trying not to laugh; he knew very well how carried away Zifeara could get explaining just about anything. She used to do it all the time when he was a kid.

"So, if you're immortal, that's only one. Who else is there?" Aun pressed.

Once Zifeara had pouted for what she felt was long enough, she let out a sigh. "My brother. Mortis is what mortals tend to refer to as the 'Grim Reaper'. He's responsible for collecting the souls of all beings once they've died. The only souls he can't get to are the ones I have to take care of. That's why they call it cheating death; you're robbing Mortis of the ability to do his job. It never seems to bother him though- not a lot gets to him. He just waits for me to take care of it and comes back later. If I'm lucky, I get to see him come for the soul I just freed up. It's actually one of the only times I get to see my brother... He's far busier than I am."

Zifeara didn't exactly look sad, but she did show a momentary twinge of regret. She sometimes wished their lives crossed over more, but that simply wasn't the way things worked. Instead, she treasured the brief glimpses she got of Mortis; he at least always had a smile for her and appreciated what she did for him. Now, if only she could make her visits to her mother's that infrequent, maybe she'd finally stop hearing about how damn cute Fang was.

"Well, that's pretty cool, I guess." Aun paused for further thought. "That's two?" he prompted, bringing Zifeara back to the present conversation.

"Oh right, sorry." Zifeara continued, "The other immortal I'm not thrilled about. It does require you to answer sort of an odd question, though. How religious are you, Aun?"

He gave Zifeara a wary look. "Uh, not very I guess. Most of my clan believes in Farrah, the deity of the forest, so I know a lot about the elementals. That's really the only religion I've heard a lot of. Why?"

Zifeara looked back to Fang who was once again trying not to laugh. He had a hand over his mouth, knowing exactly where this was going. He had met Lucifer on many an occasion and was wondering if Zifeara would omit the part about the Queen of Hell being a bit of a gossipy, over-excited mom.

"Well," Zifeara hesitated, "I don't want to tell you that everything you've thought your whole life is wrong... buuuuuut you're wrong. Being that I was there for most of the world's history, I can safely tell you that only *one* of the religions is correct. Those who believe in Dios and Lucifer have been right this entire time. They are the only two gods there are."

Aun's mouth hung open as he scanned her face for any indication that she was messing with him again. When he found none, a slight waver crept into his voice. "Whoa, what? How could you possibly know that? Just because you've been around a while, how does that mean you know which religion is right?"

Zifeara smiled, very ready to blow the poor kid's mind. "Because the true gods gave me my immortality. According to Diists, those who believe Dios is their only salvation, Dios and his sister Lucifer created all life in this world; Dios making the good creatures and Lucifer the bad. Which would you say I am, Aun?"

Aun knew a trap when he saw one. He tried to be very vague about his answer. "Well, if what you're telling me is true, you're helping keep the natural order of the world. But you really don't seem like an angel..."

She threw him a bone since he was clearly trying not to offend her. "You're right, I'm not. I come from the other side. If I have a brother, I must have a mother, yeah?"

Zifeara and Fang could clearly see the wheels in Aun's head trying to turn before finally slipping and spinning like mad. "No fucking way. There's no way you're...?"

"Essentially the Princess of Hell. In the flesh."

Aun just stared with his mouth slightly open. Granted, this was a lot to process, but Zifeara was starting to think she had broken him.

"So if you're... then who is..." Aun trailed off, staring worriedly at Zifeara, assuming she would understand what he was asking.

"My cousin," she replied. "Dios created himself a son- 'perfect' like him. His name is Gideon, and he's a whingy little asshole. He shows up at pretty much every inconvenient time I can think of to try to get me to behave myself and convert to an angel, like him. He really doesn't understand how the world works. Or how not related to him I wish I were."

"Okay, so Mortis, you, and your angel cousin are running around, duking it out for moral control or whatever. Cool. That's two for Lucifer, so the fourth must be an angel or something too, right?"

Aun looked to Zifeara, seeming almost hopeful that there was some sense of justice in the universe. This time Fang couldn't help it, he straight up burst out laughing, tears forming at the corners of his eyes. Yeah right. Him, an angel.

Aun looked irritated as always. "What, was that really such a dumb assumption? Balance of the forces that be and whatever? *What*?"

Now Zifeara was laughing too. Knowing what she did about Fang's soul, she couldn't help but giggle at how close to right the tiger was. Soul of a saint, sold to the devil. "Hold up, Aun," she said between fits, "The 'or something' fits a bit better. A very long time ago I met someone special. Someone who wanted to be my friend even though I am what I am. Someone I stole from the most powerful being in the universe for."

¤ ¤ ¤

This was going to work. This *had* to work. Zifeara and Lucifer had gone over their plan almost nonstop for about twenty-six hours now. They had to execute this perfectly. There would be no second chances.

The locked door in Lucifer's room that she kept hidden in her closet was now ajar, and inside was open space. Not empty air; stars and planets that stretched on and on, asteroids endlessly drifted past and complete silence hung over everything like a wet blanket. Mother and daughter stood in the doorway, watching the cosmos go about its business without a care in the world. Lucifer snapped her fingers and slowly the asteroids nearest to them stopped and came together, forming a jagged set of stairs in front of the door. The two proceeded to climb.

After five minutes of silent scaling, the asteroids stopped in front of... Absolutely nothing. Lucifer was not a patient demon. Not at all. Which was why Father Time always made her wait. Finally a large, shining door formed itself out of passing stardust and swung inward, allowing the demons into the realm of the true gods.

Father Time was standing in a large room, made of what looked like white marble with towering columns holding up a ceiling of the same material. He was huge, standing at around three times Zifeara's height. She never understood how anyone could like white this much; something about it was unsettling to her and she only used the color sparingly in her own house.

Time held his arms out, and Lucifer ran to jump into them, growing in size to match her father's proportions. "Father! I haven't seen you in so long! Where's Mother?"

Time beamed at his only girl. "She's this way, in the sitting room. Your brother is already waiting for you as well. Zifeara, come here, dear. How are you?"

He knelt down to see her and Zifeara gave her most convincing smile, obligingly hugging her grandfather. "I've been well, thank you. Work has been a little slow as of late, but I'm enjoying spending some time entertaining myself."

"Good, good," Time said approvingly, ushering the two of them through a large archway that led to a hallway of many doors. "Now Zifeara, Gideon has been excited to see you. I expect you two to run along and play nicely; I'd like to catch up with your mother and uncle for a while first. Then, I have a surprise for you and your cousin."

Zifeara made a face before she could stop herself. "Grandfather, I would enjoy spending time with Gideon more if he weren't so... preachy."

Time chuckled softly. "Fret not my dear, I've told him to behave himself as well. Go on now."

Time held his hand out to a door on his left and Zifeara opened it, letting herself in. The room looked rather like a large library, complete with oversized armchairs and roaring fireplace. This was the knowledge of the universe, as cataloged by Time himself. He did so very like to be thorough and organized.

"Zifeara!"

In one of those armchairs sat a thin, fragile looking boy who jumped to his feet when he saw her. He bore long, curly blonde hair and two large, white wings on his back that were so bright they almost glowed. Gideon looked sweet, but Zifeara found him annoying more often than anything. She didn't hate him, per se, but he wasn't her favorite person to spend time with. That person was the entire reason she was about to do what she had spent so long planning. She was trained for this; it would be fine.

"Hey, Gid. How's life for you?"

Gideon gave a happy little hop and ran to embrace his cousin, stopping just short of actually touching her. He at least remembered this time that Zifeara hated it when he hugged her. Instead he cleared his throat and held out his hand for her to shake.

"Life is good, Zee. And how are you?"

Zifeara genuinely smiled. Gideon really was trying not to piss her off. For once. She took his hand and gently pulled him closer to very briefly hug him. She could feel him tense with elation over her uncharacteristic actions and trying so hard to contain himself.

"I'm fine. I've been feeling kind of strange lately to be fair. Almost... what most people consider normal, I suppose."

Gideon looked confused and giddy all at the same time. "What do you mean? Like you're getting more emotions again?"

Zifeara nodded. "Yeah, I think so. It's kind of weird, I... I think I'm... Oh never mind, it's silly of me."

Gideon's eyes widened and he urged her to go on. "No, it isn't! You're what, Zee?"

This was it. Gideon was taking the bait. Zifeara knew it would be easy to get him hooked; he was always far too trusting.

She did her best to look embarrassed, lowering her eyes to the floor and tilting her ears back. Attempting to embody the word 'demure'. "Don't laugh. I... I think I'm in love, Gid."

He almost shot up to the ceiling. He had flapped his wings firmly a few times to let out his excitement and was trying very hard not to squeal with joy. Gideon had never thought his cousin, someone made so evil, would finally learn the most important emotion of all.

"Gideon, shhh!"

Landing again, he took both of Zifeara's hands. "I'm sorry, I can't help it! Who is he? What is he like? Is he... wait. Zifeara, I... oh. I'm... really sorry. I'm happy for you but..."

Zifeara looked back down. Gideon realized she wouldn't be able to spend forever with whoever she had supposedly come to love. Perfect.

"Gideon, I know I have no right to ask this of you, but I need your help. He and I have been together for quite a while now, but if I don't do something soon, he'll be too old to really enjoy his life anymore. Mother had an idea, but I need you to help me make this work. I need one of grandfather's vials."

Gideon became paler than she had ever seen him. His hands began to shake and he spoke in a whisper. "Zifeara... I don't think I could possibly do something like that. Father would be furious, and stealing is wrong."

Zifeara made her eyes tear up a little as she had done many times before. "Gideon, don't you always lecture me about second chances and forgiveness? I just want this one chance to have something good in my life. He could turn me around. He already has. Without him, I feel like I could snap. Just thinking about it makes me upset enough to consider taking it out on an entire village."

Gideon knew this was a backhanded threat, but his cousin had always been weird like that. He considered his options for a moment. This may be his chance to finally get her to see things his way; love was a powerful force, and he'd seen it do wonders. "What exactly do you want me to do?"

Zifeara smiled softly. "Your part is very easy. I just need you to toss me the vial. The state of my soul prevents me from crossing the threshold of the room grandfather keeps them in, a precaution to keep Mother from walking in and taking them all, but you can. I'll make sure the coast is clear and get it back safe and sound. *Please* Gideon, you're my only hope."

The poor angel couldn't say no to the pleading of his only other family member. "A-alright, Zifeara. Do you know which room it is?"

Zifeara let go of Gideon's hands and motioned for him to follow her. They swiftly made their way down the long hallway, passing door after door. Gideon had no idea what was in most of these rooms and he wasn't sure how Zifeara knew either. Finally, she stopped at a door with a tiny gold star above it. Opening the door, she made a shooing motion, and Gideon looked inside. The room was entirely blank, no patterns on anything, just a bright empty space with six white marble pillars standing just a few yards away from the door. They were fat, and three of them were bare. The other three had small vials sitting perfectly in the middle of them, each containing what looked like the vast reach of space they had traversed to get to their grandparents home.

Before he could make a sound, Zifeara pushed him in the door and quietly hissed, "Hide!"

Gideon nervously whined but quickly lifted slightly off the ground and swooped behind one of the large pillars, tucking his wings as close to himself as he could.

He could hear his grandfather's stern voice from the doorway, "Zifeara. What are you doing by that room, child?"

Zifeara sounded calm as ever. Gideon knew she must be freaking out like he was, but she lied for him. "Gideon and I were spending time together, just like you said. We're playing hide and seek and I'm trying to find him. I forgot which room this was... He wouldn't be hiding in here though, that would be cheating and he would *never*."

Zifeara closed the door to the room, but Gideon didn't relax. He didn't dare loosen up until he heard his cousin's voice from the doorway again. "He bought it. C'mon, Gid, quick!"

Gideon unfurled his wings and shot out from behind the pillar, snatching the vial off it and clearing the room in the blink of an eye. "Here, get this out of here, I don't want to do this anymore- that really scared me."

Zifeara already had her time crystal in hand and the second she had a firm grip on the vial, she dropped it and jumped through.

Lucifer had excused herself from the conversation with her parents just in time. She appeared to Fang and presented him with his deal.

"Of course, Lucifer. I'll give you my soul in exchange for immortality, just like Zifeara's."

Lucifer didn't think she had time for this, but the curiosity was killing her. "Dear child, why do you want this so badly? Surely Zifeara has tried to talk you out of it?"

Fang nodded but replied seriously, "She has but... she shouldn't have to do this alone. I want to be there for her like she was for me."

The Queen of Hell would have been touched if she did sentimental crap like that. "Alright, dear. Shake my hand and it's a deal."

Fang took the devil's hand and it felt like touching a hot stove. As he recoiled from the sting, an old piece of parchment with writing appeared in front of him along with an ancient looking quill. The scroll had written on it what he had just agreed to, but more words were appearing.

"Fang, dear, I want you to take care of Zifeara. If she needs you for something, truly needs you, I mean, you must assist her. If you don't, you will start to suffer physical repercussions until you become more cooperative. It will become excruciatingly painful at its worst, and it will eventually drive you insane should you ignore her. Do you find that a fair addition? You must sign this contract in your own blood."

Fang looked to the Mother of all demons, a determined fire in his eyes. He was as frightened as anyone face to face with the devil should be, but this wasn't for him. This was for the woman that had given his life meaning. All of this would pale in comparison to the smile Zifeara would surely have for him once she returned. He was hers now. He wanted to be. Fang used the metal tip of the quill to cut into the meat of his palm before dipping the instrument in the blood and signing his full, real name on the scroll. Looking back to Lucifer, she smiled at him in a mischievous way.

As she began to fade and leave Fang alone in his own room once more, she quietly murmured, "Welcome home, Mortichai."

With that, she appeared in back in Hell just after her daughter had. Zifeara quickly handed her mother the vial and Lucifer walked to her desk, putting it in a drawer for later.

"Well? Are we good?" Zifeara's concern showed in her wavering voice.

Lucifer turned and rested a hand on her daughter's head, right in between her ears. "Flawless performance as always, love. The deal is done."

Zifeara let out a massive sigh and they made the walk back to the God Realm. Just in time as well. They arrived in the foyer to see Time stomp furiously out of the sitting room.

"Where is it?!" he thundered loudly enough to shake the room, "What have you done?"

Zifeara dove behind her mother, looking and feeling for all the world like a scared child for probably the first time in her life. Dios appeared from the doorway as well with Gideon trailing behind him, clearly trying not to cry. Because, of course, the second he'd done something he shouldn't have, he'd gone running to tell his daddy like that sap he was. Mother Nature was the last to make her way in, cloak of ever-changing foliage trailing behind her, looking quite composed as usual.

Lucifer had been prepared for this too, of course. "Father, don't we do whatever we can to make our children happy?"

Father Time's face was red with fury and he continued to bellow, making Gideon cringe and hide behind his clearly upset father. "And what does Zifeara need with *two* vials of immortality? Who only knows what monstrosity she'll use it on! Not only did you have the *nerve* to steal from me, but your girl *lied* to poor Gideon as an end to your horrid means. We all know Zifeara has never felt love, but of course Gideon would be the easiest to convince otherwise. Give it here. *Now*, Lucifer."

The devil kept her calm smile throughout. She knew she had won. "I can't father. It's no longer mine to give." Before Time could ask what she meant, Lucifer continued, "I can't void a contract once it's made. You know that."

Mother Nature glanced from her partner, who couldn't seem to settle on fury or amazement, to her grandson who was still on the verge of a mental breakdown, to her granddaughter who seemed ready to run and hide. "I'm sure Zifeara had a good reason to do this."

Everyone turned to look at the Goddess. "Your grandfather is upset about the way you chose to go about this, love. Why didn't you simply ask for the vial?"

Zifeara answered, but didn't emerge from behind her mother, "Grandfather wouldn't have given it to me. He knows I'm evil, knows I have to be. He would never have believed me even I told him what it was really for. He doesn't listen, he only commands."

Time was speechless. He didn't really think himself that insensitive to his own family's wishes.

Nature simply smiled, softly clapping her hands together. "I think this family visit is over. I expect the next time I see you all here, you'll have the latest recipient of the elixir with you so that we may determine if they may keep their immortality or not." And with that, she turned to wander back through the archway, traversing the hallway of doors.

While everyone was distracted, Zifeara had gotten Gideon's attention. He still looked to be on the verge of tears but honestly, Zifeara felt kind of bad for him. For once. He was about to get into massive amounts of trouble, but had done her a huge favor. She smiled at him and gently mouthed the words 'thank you, Gid'. He stared at her in surprise for a moment but then wiped his eyes on his sleeve and returned the sentiment. She may not have really been in love, but she clearly wanted the vial for someone else. This really wasn't for her. And she'd never thanked him for anything before.

After everyone had gone home, Zifeara went to go get Fang ready to sleep before taking his vial. It was only a day before his birthday, after all.

CHAPTER 13

The Thrill of the Hunt

S o who did you steal from? What did you take?" Aun was still looking at her, ready to hear a tale of grand adventure.

Zifeara refocused after remembering one of the most stressful days of her career. She turned back to him and winked. "Well, since you tricked me into telling you what I do for work, you'll get to wonder about that a little longer. If you don't drop it, you don't get any more answers at all."

Aun gaped at her for a minute before looking to the other member of their party. "Do you know who it is?"

Fang had just recovered from his laughing spell and was slightly gasping for the air he didn't really need. "Ahhh, of course I do. If Zifeara is going to make you wait, I won't spoil it. You'll find out eventually."

Now fully pouting, Aun was done asking questions for the day and moved Thrush back behind Treble so he could turn around and not have to look at either of them anymore. Orro Heme once again led, moving swiftly over the flat ground. Zifeara began teaching Fang the types of weaponry common in this time period; katanas, staffs, chain scythes, even tiny rockets in places where gunpowder had just been discovered. He had to know what he was up against. The Arneirs plodded on into the night, Aun well asleep but both immortals still awake, looking at the stars and enjoying the quiet of the night.

Zifeara sat up, listening intently around them. "Orro Heme, woah. Hold up."

Her steed stopped, as did the girls behind him, and Fang too stirred to see what the problem was. He turned the dial on his headphones, allowing him to hear closer to his true perception of volume, which was actually a tad better than Zifeara's.

"Zia, over there. It sounds big." He pointed to a spot over a slight hill far to the left and in front of them. "What do you think it is?"

She listened more intently, not quite hearing exactly what her friend had. "I'll go check it out. Heme, keep moving but veer to the right. Give it a wide berth 'til I know what we're dealing with. I'm thinking it's one of two things and really hoping it isn't the second."

Zifeara shifted to a raven just as Aun woke. He was starting to pick up on whatever Fang had and was quickly alert. "Huh? Fang what is that? Where's Zifeara?"

Fang pointed to her just as Zifeara crested the hill, beginning to circle the source of the noise. She made a few passes before tucking her wings and falling, pulling back up just in time to rocket herself back to the worried group. Landing on Heme's back, Zifeara shifted before her sharp talons hurt the poor horse.

"It's okay. Luckily that's just a herd of Farrowers. They don't pose any threat," Zifeara said as Aun shrugged and settled back in to sleep.

She began to explain the creature in question to Fang, remembering they'd be extinct in a few hundred years. "They're these massive herd animals who live for so long that they each have a colony of birds that live in their tree-like horns. The birds drill holes into them and nest there for generations. Farrowers are several storys tall, anywhere from two at birth, to six as an adult bull. Their shaggy hair often obscures their eyes, so they just wander wherever the day takes them. Unfortunately, Farrowers will die out around five hundred years from now; with mankind's expansion and plains fires, they don't make it. I'm sure we'll see more of them on the way through this area, though."

The next morning, Zifeara halted the horses. She had been carrying several jugs of water in her bag in case they couldn't find any for their mounts, which she produced and set out so they could drink.

"Alright Fang, day one of training is today. Think you're ready?"

Fang sounded far too excited for his own good. "Hell yeah I am! What are we starting with?"

Zifeara smiled gently, knowing Fang was not going to do well at first. "Unfortunately, you've never been good at tracking a moving target, so let's start with that. Aun, get over here! I'm in need of your services."

The tiger grumbled and made his way over. "Zifeara, we haven't even eaten yet today, why are we doing this so early?"

She gave him a smug grin. "Because you're going to earn your breakfast today. You don't help, I don't feed you."

Aun scowled but gave up. "Fine. So what are we doing?"

"Teaching Fang how to hit a moving target. Large tiger form, please," she said making a shooing motion with her hand. Aun carried his sour expression into his shift, morphing to a different tiger than usual. This one was about a tiger and a half and had large upper canine teeth, each one at least five inches long. It had the same cumbersome bat ears they were used to seeing, though they looked less massive on such a big cat.

She tilted one of her ears back in amusement. He must have been getting more comfortable with them to look like that. "Aun, I don't think I've ever seen you as your true inner tiger. I had almost forgotten your kind are saber-toothed. Alright, would you please run back and forth through the grass about... fifty feet away? Fang is going to try to accurately hit your vital organs."

Catching the look Aun was giving her, she shook her head. "Oh, don't worry so much. I'll make sure he actually switches to the paint bullets."

Aun sulked off to go take up his spot while Fang put in the bright white paint clips. Not only did the white paint stand out more on just about everything, it also glowed in the dark, which aided in the night drills Zifeara would surely want to run eventually.

Fang signaled he was ready, so Aun began to run to and fro, staying somewhat in the same area he started in. Fang took five shots, each of which missed anything that would prove fatal. He fired three more before Zifeara figured out what he was doing wrong and intervened.

"You're shooting like this is a video game. Sure, you shoot where your target is going to be, but in the real world you also have to watch your target's body language. You can see Aun bend his wrists just as he puts on the initial burst of momentum beginning his stride. He brings his back legs forward and for a moment, only his front paws touch the ground. You have to shoot just as your target holds still for that brief second, aiming just barely in front of where you're trying to hit them."

Zifeara shifted herself taller and stood right behind him, putting her arms around him to lay her hands over his and move his gun with him. He knew she couldn't possibly understand that this wasn't helping him concentrate in the least, but he forced himself to pay attention. He watched as she aimed to the side of where he just had been and slightly higher, moving with Aun as he turned to run back again. Just as the tiger moved his hind paws to meet his front ones, Zifeara put pressure on Fang's trigger finger and made him fire. The shot hit its mark, right below the tiger's ear, making him roar and come to a screeching halt to shake his head. Fang could feel Zifeara giggle next to his ear as she let go of his hands and shrank behind him. Well, he was well awake for the morning.

"That definitely would have killed him. Sorry, Aun," she shouted to him. "Once more please. Then we can eat!"

Aun roared in protest. It was amazing how disgruntled he could sound as another species.

"C'mon Aun, you're going to get hit with a lot of paint over the coming days, so am I. I'll clean it off you when we're done."

That seemed to shut him up and he began to run again. This time, without Zifeara's guidance, Fang took more careful aim. It took him a little longer, but this time when he fired, he at least hit Aun closer to anything important. Being shot in the shoulder may not have been fatal, but it was a start.

"Atta boy! That's at least an improvement. The good news is you've always been a fast learner, Fang," Zifeara said as she waved Aun back.

As Aun changed back, the white paint became even more visible and he looked extremely unhappy about having to be the target. "Hey, next time you let him shoot you with this crap. How exactly do you plan to get this gunk off? It doesn't feel like-"

Zifeara cut Aun off by putting a hand on his head, right over the paint, and very quickly burning it off. "My fire can be very specific," she said as she ran her hand over the paint on his shoulder, singeing that one off as well.

"Well, that's not what I was expecting," Aun half-mumbled. "Can we eat now?"

Scarfing down the remainder of the meat Zifeara had saved in her bag, she made Aun aware of the situation. "Hey, that was the last of our food. I did say I would train you too, right?"

Aun looked interested. "Yeah, what did you have in mind?"

"I was thinking I could start with pack hunting." Zifeara indicated somewhere over the horizon by dipping her head. "There were buffalo tracks here when we settled down this morning. They can't have gone too far away. Feel like running?"

Aun grinned. "Yeah, I'm definitely up for that. You're thinking wolf right? Big cat would be too slow for this kind of area, I think."

Zifeara nodded. "That's right. The trick to taking down a big herd animal is easier than you think. C'mon, I'll get Fang and the horses on their way, then we'll go."

Zifeara gave instructions to Heme so he could tend to the other two horses, then told Fang he'd be on his own for a little bit. He didn't look happy.

"Zia, what if something happens while you're both gone? I'm not saying I'm convinced something will, but still. You know I'm not good enough to..."

Zifeara reached up to ruffle his hair. "Fang, I wouldn't be leaving you to take care of the horses if I thought you couldn't. You may not have much training yet, but you aren't an idiot. If something happens, I trust you to deal with it. Besides, we aren't going too far away, and we can quickly fly back here. I'm just teaching Aun how to hunt a little better. You both have a lot to learn."

Hearing Zifeara say she trusted him made Fang feel a bit better, so he told her to be careful and watched as she turned and began to run, changing into the large black wolf that was still so unfamiliar to him.

She really does belong out here in the wild... Fang thought as she ran up to Aun, who had already shifted and was waiting for her. The two sniffed the ground for signs of what they'd be tracking and seemed to converse for a moment before dashing off, leaving Fang to get the horses moving. He mounted his horse, calling out to Heme to get going.

As he reclined on the filly's back, he pulled his MP3 player out of his pocket. Fang didn't feel like playing music, but he had brought some gadgets and a solar charger with him so he could still listen. His headphones worked just like normal headphones, connecting wirelessly to his device. Putting a song on[11] and telling the player to put everything on shuffle, he sighed heavily.

"Alright Treb, just us now. It must be boring for her to be stuck here with me all the time since I can't do any of what Aun can..."

Forgetting the Arneirs all understood the common language, Fang was surprised when Treble craned her neck back to gently nuzzle his hair, offering a comforting whinny. Heme had also turned to look behind him, tossing his head and snorting. Even Thrush had come to stand next to Treble, her eyes looking as though she were smiling and bumping her muzzle into his knee. Fang was pretty sure they were trying to cheer him up, something he hadn't expected, especially from horses, extra smart or not.

"Thanks, guys. I may not be able to understand you like Zia can, but I get it. Let's go."

Aun was excited to get some one-on-one time with Zifeara so he could show her what he could do. Having no friends as a kid, he had spent all of his time practicing his shifts and moving around as various animals through his forest. He had never gotten to hunt with another wolf before, so he was beyond stoked for the experience. They tracked the buffalo to their herd of about fifty animals, creeping up through the brush so they wouldn't be seen.

Zifeara quietly told Aun what to do and the hunt was on. They moved to either side of the herd, being careful to avoid being spotted until just the right moment. She was impressed Aun was doing so well. Giving the signal in the form of a curt bark, Aun rushed from his spot and began barking furiously at the buffalo, causing them to begin running. Zifeara started to run as well, issuing her own snarls to the herd, helping to corral them and determine which among them was the slowest. Sure enough, one adolescent started to fall behind and they closed in on it.

Barking more instructions to Aun, Zifeara started running faster than the animal while Aun dropped behind, preventing it from slowing down. Zifeara quickly rammed the side of the buffalo, just enough to throw it off balance but not enough to get her trampled. The young bull slipped, tumbling to the ground, where Aun had kept up just enough to quickly grab its neck and kill it.

Sporting a wolfy grin as she trotted up to the rusty wolf, furiously wagging his tail and panting by the kill, Zifeara nudged Aun with her muzzle. "Good job for your first go. Did you have fun?"

"Hell yeah! That was fuckin' awesome! I can't believe I never thought to ram it and make it trip," he said. "One question, though? How do we get this back?"

Zifeara looked at the carcass. "The same way we move anything around. Drain the blood and cut it up. I have a ton of jars in this bag of mine and I was planning on

---

[11] "I'm Gonna Be (500 Miles)" – The Proclaimers

bringing some blood back for Fang since he couldn't come. He's gonna want to taste this, I know he is."

Aun cast a sideways glance at her. "You and Fang are pretty close, huh?"

Zifeara shifted back to herself and scoffed. "Of course I am, he's my best friend. He's probably the only person I've ever completely trusted."

Aun shifted back as well. "Fair enough, but you haven't considered him as anything... else?"

Zifeara glared at him like he'd just called her hideous. "Oh gods, you sound like my mom. No, I haven't. Is it really so hard to believe I can be friends with a guy? I have tons of guy friends. I can think of at least five others off the top of my head, excluding Fang!"

Aun held his hands up to show he didn't mean anything by it, but snuck in a another comment on the subject, "So you don't have a boyfriend then. Good to know."

Zifeara turned her ears back and grabbed Aun's face, pushing him out of her way so she could start draining the body. He stifled a laugh and waited for his share of blood. Once he was full, they cut up the buffalo to fit in Zifeara's bag. After stowing the meat, the two shifted to birds to fly back to find the horses.

¤ ¤ ¤

The trip through the plains was fairly uneventful and Zifeara was thankful for it. Most of the time the group passed either a herd of grazers, a small predator who couldn't hurt them if it wanted to, a pack of wild dogs, or a large cat. A few of the cats eyed the horses, but one roar from her or Aun sent them running. They also passed by some small groups of nomads who moved with the herd migrations, but only stopped long enough to trade them for more water when they couldn't find any.

Every morning, Zifeara would train Fang to shoot better, often being the target herself now that he had the basic concept down. He found that she was far harder to hit than Aun, however. Fang could only hit her every seventh shot or so and he was starting to get discouraged.

"Zifeara, I don't feel like I'm getting any better. I've honestly been trying not to use my visor for anything more than improving my vision, but I might have to start using the tracking reticle. You're really hard to hit."

Zifeara sighed. "Just give it some time, hun. You're good, but it takes practice. Why don't you try Aun again until you can hit him consistently, then I'll go for you."

Aun swiveled an ear at the mention of his name. He was not excited to be it again. "Aw, man, I was just getting used to not getting hit with paint."

Zifeara shook her head at him. "Aun, you've only been shot twice. I've been doing this for a week now. Come on, it's well past your turn."

Aun rolled his eyes but got up and shifted his form obligingly. After a few rounds, Fang hit him with every other shot, and some were even fatal. Zifeara couldn't figure out what she was doing differently that Aun wasn't. Hell, he was even harder to see since tigers were meant to blend into this sort of terrain. She was seriously stumped by the time Aun had called it quits.

"Alright, I'm *well* enough covered in this shit for today. I'm done. Zifeara, you're going to have to start bribing me to do this shit with him," Aun complained.

"Bribing you with what, Stripes? Rearranging your face?" Fang jeered.

Aun stuck his tongue out like a child, but Zifeara just glared. "Aun, I'm kindly letting you come on this trip with us, feeding you half the time, and helping you get back the gem Torvak stole from your clan. Is it really too much to ask to have you run some drills with Fang? I'm considering that payment for the training I'm giving *you*. Have I not been teaching you different ways to hunt and answering most of your questions?"

The tiger looked sheepishly at the ground. "Well, no, you've done all that..."

"Alright, so you don't get to complain. Just because he hasn't hit me as often doesn't mean you're allowed to whine. Now, shut up while I get breakfast going," Zifeara said as she began pulling raw buffalo out of her bag.

She and Aun had caught it the day before as charras, a sort of cheetah-dog hybrid. Aun had never seen one before until he'd spotted them hunting, and Zifeara had showed him what one looked like up close so she could teach him how they worked and hunted. Shifting back, he sat down and tried not to look at Fang's smug face after he got scolded. Zifeara doled out food, cleaned Aun off, and later ran a few more drills with Fang before they got moving.

The next time she saw a band of nomads, she asked if they had seen anyone like Torvak, just as she did with all the others they had passed. This time, the good plains people affirmed they had and were nice enough to tell her when and which direction he was heading. They were on the right track still. Torvak sounded to only be about a week ahead of them, if that. The other good news was that they would reach the edge of the plains before the storms came in. Summer meant monsoon rains out here.

The forest they were heading towards was classed as montane, meaning the plains would be rapidly sloping upwards, creating cooler temperatures and supporting groves of pine and birch. The way up was grassy and gorgeous, forming gentle hills until the other side of the forest where it turned more mountainous. Aun had never seen pine trees before, so he, at least, was excited.

That night they had to stop to let the horses sleep, and for the first time in quite a while, Fang dreamt of Zifeara. It wasn't anywhere near as good as the last dream he'd had about her though. Instead, it was a nightmare about walking through a dense forest, heart racing and eyes darting to and fro. He had lost both her and Aun, but there was *something* here with him. Something creeping up on him. It weaved through the bushes and ferns, never in the place he swore he saw it last, and every time he pointed a pistol at it, it vanished. Finally he heard it run up behind him but as he turned to shoot, he was frozen. The black panther moved almost like a snake through the grass, huge fangs and claws exposed as it leapt right for him, deep indigo eyes full of primal hunger.

Waking with a start, he accidentally hit Zifeara, who he had been holding on to, and she almost bit him. Realizing he was scared for some reason and hadn't been aware that he'd smacked her, Zifeara calmed down again. "Fang, hey, what's the matter? What happened?"

He was still freaking out, but at the same time he didn't have the heart to tell Zifeara he just had a dream about her being nothing more than a mindless animal. "Sorry, I just... had a really bad dream. Zia, I don't suppose I could... just take a break from this time? Not go home for good, just a day or two?"

She had a feeling this might happen. Zifeara knew it would be hard for him to adjust to this time since it was so drastically different from what he was used to. If she were honest, she was majorly proud of him for not complaining about much of anything while they had been moving.

"Of course you can, Fang," she started. "All we have to do is send you back through the portal and you'll pop up in my house just like I do when I come back. You just have to think about how long you'd like to be gone and pick an exact time for me to come back and get you. As you're well aware, we can't text from two different times. The service here sucks."

That got him to crack a smile and he thought a moment. "Can I get three days starting tomorrow?"

"That's all?"

"Mhm. I don't want to miss out on too much excitement. We might see a tree or even a rock any day now!"

Now he was back to normal. She giggled quietly before looking back up to meet his gaze again. "I'll be sure to tell you all about our first rock. We'll send you off in the morning instead of doing drills. Think you can go back to sleep on your own?"

Fang gave it some thought, but the bloodthirsty eyes of the panther in his dream flashed through his mind and he felt guilty. Having Zifeara sing to him would probably stop his brain from imagining her as a monster. "I... could use a little help."

Zifeara smiled gently and laid him back down with her, wrapping an arm around his broad shoulders and stroking his hair. As she began to sing,[12] Fang assured himself that there was no way Zifeara would ever do anything bad to him. She loved him, even if not in the way he loved him, and she could never hurt him. In the middle of the song he drifted off, not having any more dreams at all that night.

---

[12] "Six Weeks" – Of Monsters and Men

CHAPTER 14

Best Friends Are The Worst

I t felt good to sleep in his own bed again. It felt even better to take a real shower and sleep in his own bed, *clean.* Fang loved running around with Zifeara, but spending all day in the woods on a horse really made him miss running water. He had taken his first day completely off, spending way too long in the shower, taking a nap, and playing video games. His second day he spent in much the same way, but now it was late afternoon and he was starting to get hungry. Fang decided to text a friend of his to see if he was up for dinner.

Most of his friends worked in the entertainment industry as well, and Todd was no exception. He worked in a nightclub further downtown than the Cave called The Down Under. His club was themed after the Island of Turak which sat 'down under' Queylinth and had some pretty weird wildlife running around in its scrubland.

Todd Tulayne was a short, charming jackalope; he looked so young that he was usually mistaken for a teenager. He was twenty-two, but he didn't really do much to make himself look more like an adult. Shaggy brown hair surrounded his lengthy rabbit ears and short horns, and framed his heavily freckled face. Even though his horns were only about 6" each, Todd sometimes forgot they were there and bumped them on things. At 5'7" Todd was as tall as he'd ever be, but what he lacked in height, he made up for in personality.

If Fang had to describe him in a sentence, he would say that Todd was a loud, likeable little bastard, but that would probably earn him a punch to the arm. Todd was the only one Fang ever really felt comfortable talking to about his problem with Zifeara- at least when he was sober. Out of all his friends, Todd was the only one who had a relationship with his girlfriend similar to how he and Zifeara already were. He was happy his friend found such a great girl, but Fang never quite understood how it happened.

Lolliva Van Pelt was an albino rabbit, about on the same side of gorgeous as Zifeara. She always insisted on being called Lolli and was rather sweet so long as you were on her good side. Lolli wasn't a genius per se, but she was very good at using her looks to get what she wanted. She was well aware she could make a living out of it, so she did. She modeled lingerie for the most wide-spread retailer of expensive and fancy undergarments on the continent. And somehow Todd got her to date him. She claimed it was his sense of humor, but Fang wasn't entirely sure he believed her, nor did he want to know the real reason.

Fang's phone buzzed, offering a return text asking when and where Todd could meet him. He quickly typed back their favorite restaurant, a ramen place about halfway between their clubs, and in an hour. Fang got himself dressed and ready to go, getting in his car and cranking the radio. Hopefully they could take a break and go have fun for the night.

Despite taking his time getting to the restaurant, he was still ten minutes early. Fang sat at a bar table by the window, watching the gathering clouds outside. Summer was coming and New Tinning usually got at least a little drizzle every other day around this time of year. He was starting to wonder if it was raining where Zia was right now. He silently hoped Aun was ugly when wet like most cats, especially with those giant ears of his.

"Why are you always so damn early?" A familiar voice next to him signaled Todd's arrival.

Fang turned and smiled, happy to see his friend. "I was just sitting in my house doing nothing, I may as well have come here. That and I guess I'm used to it because Zifeara's..."

Todd gave an impish grin, his sage green eyes reflecting friendly ridicule. "Never on time? Yeah, I know. Speaking of, I thought you were on vacation dude, what are you doing *here*?"

As they ordered, he caught Todd up to speed on all the current nonsense since he left and his new major issue.

"Hm..." Todd thought about where to start. "What does she think of the tiger?"

Fang laid his head in his hand and leaned on the table, stirring his noodles. "I don't know. It's weird enough Zifeara let him go with her, but she doesn't really treat him the same way she does any of us. She is teaching him things though, so she doesn't *dislike* him. I just wish more than anything I could at least say Aun was unattractive- news flash- he's kinda hot. It sucks because he's technically my age but he's a cocky little shit and it seems to make Zifeara laugh. I can't tell if she's laughing because he's charming or because he's an idiot."

Todd nodded in understanding. "Yeah, that is tricky. Well, I guess all you can do is wait and see. I don't suppose this is giving you any more motivation to see if Zifeara would go out with you, huh? Seems like it's getting down to the wire now that you have some competition."

"Yeah, no. We've spent time together, but we're never actually alone, unless she sends Aun out hunting. Since we're almost constantly moving, it isn't easy to just... go have fun. This isn't the vacation I had in mind."

Todd didn't want to laugh at his friend's plight, but he did anyway. "Well, yeah, this wasn't going to be a *honeymoon!*" Seeing his best friend's face start to color at the word only spurred him on. "What did you expect? Snuggling by the fire? Long romantic walks through the demon infested forest? Kissing under wild mistletoe? Taking a steamy midnight dip in-"

"*Todd!* **Shut. Up.**" Fang knew he was blushing hard and Todd was always an ass about this sort of thing, despite his good advice.

It may have taken the better part of five minutes, but the jackalope quelled his laughter. "Alright, alright. You know I can't help it, you've only been doing this for almost four years now. So, what's your winning plan for working around the cat?"

Fang shoved more food in his mouth while his face cooled down. He was tempted to push Todd out of his seat, but he was also kind of used to this; he was always a dick before he imparted his best ideas, like a really fluffy troll under a bridge of sarcastic comments. They acted like brothers more than anything, and usually, if they hung out with Sara, she'd have whacked Todd over the head and told him to lay off when he went too far. Most of the major DJs in New Tinning knew each other, but they all acted like family.

"Depends," Fang started. "If he becomes more of a problem we'll see, but for now I'm just going to try and get more of Zifeara's attention. We can't spend an awful lot of time not making progress towards where we need to be, but most of those extra moments she's using to train me. She's teaching me all sorts of useful skills to help me survive there, but she still has to do her job, too. I don't know, I feel bad for taking up her time, but... I dunno..." He hated when he didn't have the words to explain something.

Todd was done teasing now and he lightly smacked Fang on the back. "Dude, c'mon. You've been in love with Zifeara for forever now, you gotta start doing something about it. Now that there's someone she may not say no to, if you don't get a move on you'll just kill yourself over it. Start small, bring her a daisy or something. You've had at least one girlfriend, right? You should know how to girl by now."

Fang rolled his eyes. "Yes Todd, three. Zifeara doesn't do normal girl-dating-stuff. None of the other girls were the same for obvious reasons and none of them ever made me feel like she does. My brain forgets everything I know with her and I become a babbling idiot. When I look at her and she looks back a certain way, like... I just get stupid? It's hard to explain."

Todd chuckled to himself. "You're so weird, Fang. Sara's off tonight, too, why don't we go out? It'll help clear your head and we could hit up Dewy's club. Hell, maybe Dewy can give you some insight on your problem- he's kind of like Aun isn't he?"

"Goddamn Todd, you know I don't want to deal with fucking Dewford. *Ever.* He's becoming more and more of an asshole and I really don't have the patience for him, especially tonight."

Dewford Jisst was the DJ at the Congo, the jungle themed place by the bay. He was a jaguar and he took his DJ name, DewClaw, as a pun on his first name. He had been hitting on Zifeara for the past five years, and it was what helped Fang realize that he liked her more than he used to. One night he became a little too protective during one of Dewy's attempts to get Zia on a date and was left to think about why he'd reacted so harshly.

Problem with all that was, it meant Fang didn't like Dewford in the slightest. He was always so pushy with Zifeara and now that Fang was getting closer to telling her how he felt, Dewy was getting more and more aggressive with his efforts. Not physically, but he was pestering her more every time they came into contact and it was really starting to piss Fang off.

Todd shrugged, obviously trying to hide his troublemaker smirk. "Well, in that case we could always go somewhere else. I don't care one way or the other for Dewy."

Fang text Sara to see where she wanted to go, telling her the Congo was out. In the response a few minutes later, Sara picked the club with the loudest, hardest music she could. Sometimes Fang wondered if she were secretly psychic and knew he didn't want to do much talking. He informed Todd they would be heading to the Scrapyard per Sara's request, and they agreed he'd go get her and meet the jackalope at his house to pick him up second.

Once they parted ways, Fang took a walk until it was time to go get Sara. He was always the designated driver, but only by technicality; his car drove itself, allowing everyone to drink if they wanted to. Driving to a high-class condo overlooking the bay, Fang told Digit to go park and got out, ringing the buzzer at the tall gate into the lobby. The Seashell Shore condo was one of the most pleasant in New Tinning. It was a ten story place and had a community terrace with one of the city's most unobstructed views of the harbor, making it a highly coveted location for wealthy aquatic demons. Sara's uncle owned the place, so of course she lived on the very highest floor.

Once the buzzer sounded, a female voice came through the speaker, asking Fang his name and intended visitee.

"Hey, Carol, it's Fang," he said into the box.

There was a pause and then the gate swung open, allowing him into the spacious lobby.

"Hello, Fang! I assume Sara knows you're coming. I haven't seen you at the SoundCave lately, is everything okay?" Carol was the nice, human lady who worked the night shift, and Fang had given her an invitation for the SoundCave once he learned she had a wild side. She liked to go out on her nights off and he had seen her in his club many times.

"Yeah, I'm fine, Carol, I'm just on a bit of a vacation. Is DJ BloodMoon getting the hang of things yet?"

Fang had looked around for his temporary replacement pretty hard before he left, and Lyric Jasper seemed to fit into his staff of misfits perfectly.

He was a cat demon of the regular domestic variety, and was just barely twenty years old. He was probably a good five inches shorter than Fang, with triangular ears and a long tail that made him look unassuming and innocent. The young man had just been kicked out by his parents for dropping out of college when he'd met Fang. Lyric, as an aspiring DJ, recognized Fang and proceeded to lose his mind. They got to talking and made arrangements for the kid to work at the Cave, something which brought him close to fainting before thanking Fang a million times. Lyric chose his DJ name because he was born under a blood moon and Fang liked that it fit the theme of his club as well.

"I think he's pretty good. Obviously no one could ever replace you, but he keeps everything going well. And he's pretty cute. Good job," she said with a wink. Fang chuckled with her and bid her goodnight, making his way to the elevator. He was happy to hear his home was being looked after.

Going down the hallway of the 10th floor, he stopped just in front of his friend's place to knock, but the door swung open. All 110 pounds of tiny shark jumped on him, a pretty standard greeting between the two, and Sara looked up to her friend. "Heya, Fang! I knew you'd be coming soon, so I'm ready to go. So, if you're here, where's Zifeara?"

Fang put her down, sighed, and began explaining how things were going while they got to his car and made their way to go meet Todd. As soon as he put Sara and Todd together, they both started brainstorming ways for Fang to get on the other side of the friendship fence. He had to spend the entire car ride telling them to shut up and drop it.

"Guys, for the last time, I just want to go have fun tonight. I will turn this car around if you don't knock it off."

Sara gave Fang a sly grin he had come to know as her being up to no good. "But Fang, unless we've given you a good idea already, you need help. It's been almost four years next month and you have competition she might be considering by the sound of it. I can't *wait* to meet this guy. She's bringing him here, right?"

Fang opened his mouth to tell her that was ridiculous, but he stopped short. It might be fun to watch Aun flail helplessly around in this time. Then Fang could laugh at him for not knowing anything for a change.

"I dunno, Sara, it depends on if I can talk Zia into it or not. I guilted her into taking me with her, but..."

Todd laughed and shoved Fang's shoulder from the backseat. "Dude, shut up! Zifeara never says no to you for long. You may not be able to ask her out, but you're the only one who can work puppy dog eyes on her."

Fang flushed slightly. "Th-that's not true! She says no to me all the time..."

Sara was giggling now as well and chimed in. "Fang, you're the most spoiled child ever. She bought you a house, a club, and massive amounts of tech because you wanted it, you're *immortal*, she takes you to the SpinOff every year, and now you get to run around in a different time period. She *never* says no to you. When was the last time she said no and actually *meant* it?"

Fang continued to blush but made intense eye contact with the floor mats as he thought about it for way too long. His friends were both looking at him expectantly. He couldn't think of a single time.

Todd broke the silence first. "See, falling in love with your sugar mama is hard, isn't it?"

Sara quickly moved to the other side of the back seat since she knew these boys well enough to know what was coming. Fang reached back and grabbed one of Todd's horns, bending him towards the floor uncomfortably. The only fight the jackalope could muster was slapping uselessly at Fang's arm and saying 'ow' in rapid succession.

Fang glared at him, all while getting even redder in the face. "Take it back, Todd. You can't say that about Zifeara!"

They scuffled all the way to the Scrapyard, Todd quickly jumping out as soon as D1g1t parked the car.

As Fang got out himself, he shook his head and mumbled, "Yeah, you better run, bunny boy."

[13]This club had a steampunk theme and boasted the loudest music in New Tinning. It was easy to lose yourself completely in the hard bass, and the drinks could knock an ogre on its ass. It may have looked like an old warehouse on the outside, but the interior was covered in machinery that moved for the sake of moving and looking awesome. They had a few DJs, but no one in the group knew them too well since the Scrapyard wasn't really a place you went to socialize. The bouncer on the door was one of Vhans' friends, so he ushered Fang and the others right through, getting a fist bump from each of them on the way in. Fang dialed his headphones almost all the way up just to be able exist without blowing his eardrums, but he still felt the floor shaking in time with the music.

As per usual, Fang and Todd both stuck to Sara like glue, not only because of her size but because she tended to get distracted while dancing. The last time Fang couldn't find her it was because she had accidentally migrated to the complete

---

[13] "Sabotage" - Kura

opposite end of the club. If other guys wanted to come dance with Sara, they'd move off a touch, but she had to make them. Call it some sort of brotherly instinct, but he hated leaving her even remotely by herself at times like this.

The set was good[14], and at some point Fang and Sara returned to the bar for round two. Todd resisted, being a bit of a lightweight, and Lolli would kill him if Fang had to carry the poor idiot into the house again. Sara may have been small, but she could drink almost as much as Fang could, and he always said it was because the alcohol was scared of her too and that it knew better.

The trio stayed until just shy of dawn before they finally decided to call it quits and take Todd home first. Sara had stated she was starving so Fang took her for breakfast on the way back to her place. He was reasonably knackered and food helped reinvigorate him. They chatted while eating, before finally circling back around to everyone's favorite drama.

"Ya know, Fang, I get that it's gonna be hard to find the right time to tell her, but what is it you're so damn worried about? Maybe knowing that'll help you figure out what to do."

Fang thought about it as best he could given the circumstances. "Well... I dunno how far along she is, emotionally. I dunno if she even knows what love feels like or if she's ever even had a crush before. She doesn't just *talk* about this kinda thing an' any time I've asked her, she gets grouchy about it an' won't talk to me. That, or she seems... sad or something. I know she has a type she finds attractive, hell if I could tell ya *what* it is, but that's about it, really. Fuck, I can't say if she's even, like, *thought* about sex or just knows who's pretty to her? If I just blurt out whatever I'm thinking, it might be too abrupt for her an' freak her out, but subtlety when it comes to flirting is *not* Zifeara's forte. 'M havin' a hard time finding the middle ground."

Sara nodded thoughtfully while Fang laid his torso on the table forlornly. "'M'kay, so what it sounds like you should do is change how you treat her in tiny increments- sorta ease her into it. If she asks what you're doin', just ask what she means. If she's catching on, then it's probably working and you might have a chance. Ya just gotta gauge her reaction to things and see if you're on the right track."

Fang looked up from his spot on the laminate table, shoving more pancake into his mouth. Sara had a point. He had to start doing something the second he got back, but he had to be very careful about it.

"Yeah, you're probably right. Thanks, Sara. At least I can talk to *you* about this without wanting to hit you today."

They both laughed and he asked about Sara's love life. She was at the 'just getting a cat' stage. Once they finished their food and argued about who was paying, he drove her home.

---

[14] "La Da Dee" - Cody Simpson

Now that the sun was up, retreating into his basement home made Fang feel even more like the stereotypical vampire most people thought he was. He didn't even bother locating his pajamas- he just took all his clothes off and threw them about the floor, deciding to deal with them tomorrow, when he tripped on them. Flopping down onto his bed, he was asleep in minutes.

CHAPTER 15

Destructive Dreaming

Zifeara had described having memory dreams, something he hadn't yet encountered, but she said he probably would. She had explained that the older you become as an immortal, the more your brain likes to exercise its muscles and relive memories so you don't get rusty at recalling old things. This was why she looked as though she were reading sometimes when she had to remember specific information; her brain was just flipping through pages of the countless books in the library that was her mind. That night he had his first memory dream and it was... kind of weird.

Fang was in his room, but he could have sworn the sheets weren't the ones he currently had on the bed. He was tangled in blankets and it looked as though he was just waking up. His phone began to ring and he could tell from the song[15] that played it was Zifeara.

He let it ring for a little bit just to hear more of the tune before he picked up. "Hey, Zia, what's up?"

"Well hopefully, you are. Were you coming to get me or was I heading over there?"

Fang felt like he was watching some kind of weird movie; he wasn't seeing this from his own eyes; he was almost... standing in his room while it happened to the other him. He could hear Zifeara's voice as if she were right next to him, but he always had his phone volume impossibly low since it was right next to his ear after all.

"Oh, shit, right. Um... funny story. I'm not even dressed. If you come get me, I'll be ready by the time you get here," he had said, embarrassed.

He could almost hear her roll her eyes over the phone. "Alright, but you better hurry up. I want to spend all day there and I don't want to wait for you to make yourself beautiful. Go get dressed, you nut."

---

15 "True To Me" – Metro Station

As she hung up, he jumped out of bed and ran around trying to quickly decide what he was going to wear. Fang suddenly knew when this was. This was when he took Zifeara to the carnival a few years ago. They hadn't gone together since he was a kid, and she secretly loved them. This was only about a year after he started his crush. It was one of his early attempts at confessing his feelings, and probably his worst to date.

He picked his favorite red and black striped shirt and a nice pair of black jeans, tripping over and cursing at clothes from the night before which he'd had forgotten to pick up, then rushed to the bathroom to get ready. He got dressed and wet his hair down, combing it before vigorously ruffling it all, the only way he had ever dealt with his mess of hair. He grabbed his phone and put his headphones on, double checking his room for anything he had forgotten. Grabbing his jacket, his phone meowed at him, alerting him to Zifeara's text that she'd be there in five minutes. He always forgot how fast her damn car was.

Things started getting kind of blurry as a few scenes faded in and out, as if there was something interfering with his brain's signal. He and Zifeara were riding a roller coaster, then sitting on oddly colored horses on the carousel, and then he won her another fish for her collection. Zifeara had a pond built behind her house specifically to harbor all the goldfish Fang had won her over the years at various festivals. The first fish ever, Snow, had grown to be a little over two feet long now and always came to the surface to see Zifeara when she went to feed them. The scene faded further and came back to them on the Ferris wheel. They always waited for nighttime to do this one so they could see the carnival with all the lights on.

This was the moment. That awful moment where the universe decided to hate him. Zifeara had just pointed to something on the ground when they hit the top of the wheel, the conductor stopping it so people could enjoy the view. And because Fang had asked him to earlier.

"Hey, Zia? Can I ask you something?"

She looked so happy right then it hurt. "Well, of course, hun, anything. What's up?"

Fang swallowed hard and tried so hard not to look her in the eye. "Well, uh, we've been together for a really long time, right? I... I was just wondering-"

With a loud boom, something bright flashed in one of the stands on the ground near the bottom of the wheel. Flames quickly enveloped one of the tents covering a food stand and people were running around frantically trying to put distance in between them and the growing inferno. You had to be kidding. The wheel started moving again, and quickly, as the conductor was trying to get everyone off and away from the danger. By the looks of it, one of the propane tanks in the hotdog stand had exploded, sending a column of fire dangerously close to the Ferris wheel. Luckily, no one was hurt aside from the poor hotdog guy, but that incident ended the whole trip.

Once they got off the wheel and were making their way towards the gate, Zifeara turned back to him. "Well that was unexpected. There's something kind of funny about the teeny tiny scorched hotdogs though. Fang, what were you trying to tell me?"

His brain had frozen and panicked, as it far too often did around her. He hadn't steeled himself for this again. "Oh, um, I was just going to tell you how much I... I'm really happy right now. Just in general."

He could feel his face on fire and Zifeara laughed and took his arm. "Yeah, me too. I'm glad you're my best friend."

All he could remember thinking was not only how much of an utter loser he was for having so much trouble doing something he'd been working up to for a week now, but also how much the words 'best friend' hurt at that particular moment in time. He had shriveled pieces of hotdog charcoal of all things to blame for it.

The scene blurred and turned into something else. This was a little less than a year ago. He was in Zifeara's house, climbing her stairs. Graham was trying to tell him she wasn't ready, as per usual, but he wasn't having it. He was going to go yell at her for being late. Oh gods, *no*. He had tried so hard for so long to forget about this. This was why he *never* went anywhere near upstairs before she was done anymore.

As he crested the stairs, he heard Zifeara singing and was planning to sneak up and slam his hand on her door to scare the crap out of her. It was the cutest thing in the world when she had her tail fluffed up and was mad at him. Instead of getting to do that, however, it looked like Graham accidentally hadn't shut the door all the way earlier when he told her to hurry up and that small crack was apparently an idiot trap. Fang's first compulsion was to look through it before his brain actually thought. He really wished he hadn't.

Instead of being in the bathroom still like he thought she'd be, Zifeara was next to her bed about to grab the outfit she had laid out for tonight. And she was completely naked. Now that Fang was immortal, his brain took a permanent polaroid and he could never unsee it. At least he only saw the side of her and nothing more detailed since she had just brought her shirt to her chest, but it was *enough*. Every once in awhile, something would bring the image of side-boob and an awful lot of fantastically perfect ass up and he would have to suppress it very quickly. He, of course, could *never* tell her he'd seen this, but it haunted him, always. That night he purposefully drank way too much so he would have to go home early since he couldn't bear to look at her at all for the next week.

Fang woke up that morning absolutely on fire and completely bothered. He decided a cold shower would be the best way to attempt to rescrub that picture out of his mind. If he didn't, that perfect, well-formed figure of hers, minus the clothes would be all he would see for the next several days. Zifeara was coming back for him tomorrow morning. He would have to do something wholesome today to get rid of this image.

Once he got out of the shower, which hadn't helped at all, he called his sister. She invited him over for tea and he hastily accepted. Seeing her would definitely clear his head. So would seeing his nephew. He drove across town to her suburban house, a two story white Victorian with the cliché white picket fence and flowers in the front yard.

The second he parked and stepped out, he was set upon by a small child. "*Uncle Fang!*" The young boy jumped and attached himself to Fang's leg, holding on for dear life as Fang began to lurch towards the house.

"Hahaha, hello, Morris. Someday you're going to get too big for this, you know."

The muffled reply came, "Nuh-uh, I'm only four and you're reeaaally tall!"

Fang giggled and Frankenstein-walked into the house, through the open front door his over-excited nephew hadn't closed, and into the kitchen.

Melody had just put tea on a tray and glanced over to him with a broad smile. "I see Morris found you. I don't know how he always does that, I didn't tell him you were coming."

They all sat in the living room where Morris detached himself in favor of sitting almost on top of his uncle on the couch. Fang asked him questions until his lacking attention span couldn't take it anymore and he zoomed off to do something else.

Fang laughed. "Gods, how do you keep up with him? He has the energy of all three of us put together."

Melody sighed contentedly. "I know he does. You gotta do what you gotta do when you're a mom, including move a hundred miles an hour. Now that he can really talk, he's never quiet either. He's the best. We're getting him a puppy for Einrit this year."

Fang gazed at his sister fondly. Several years ago she had gotten married to a demon who was so sweet to her at first but turned into a huge asshole a month into their marriage. She had been walked home that night from orchestra practice by the shy violinist she used to think was interested in her, but he seemed bothered, as if he wanted to say something to her.

As soon as he left and Melody got into the house, her husband went into a rage, accusing her of cheating on him with the violinist. He hit her. When you play the cello, you get used to *moving* a cello, even though it's heavy. Melody broke her cello on her soon-to-be-ex husband's head for hitting her and called the cops. The divorce papers were started that night but the violinist, Theo, had come running back. He wanted so badly to tell her that he couldn't stop thinking about her and that he loved her, but she was married. Imagine his surprise when he got back to her house.

He offered to let Melody stay at his house so she wouldn't be alone, and the rest was history. She found out she was pregnant two months after they got married. Theo was a raven demon, but their son turned out looking more like Fang did when he was young. He had black curly hair and massive ears, which he'd hopefully grow into. His eyes were a deep orange, almost red, and he was drowning in freckles all over his pale skin. Morris was born Einrit morning and Fang spoiled the ever living hell out of that kid. He was way too excited to be an uncle.

"A dog would be cool. Help him get rid of some of that chaotic energy. How's work?"

"Work is good, as usual. I'm probably buying a new cello soon, mine is starting to show its age. Theo just restrung his violin and we're thinking of starting Morris on piano lessons once he hits school age. He's always obsessed with the piano in the theater," Melody said.

Standing and smoothing out her skirt, his sister offered him her hand. "Alright, time for uncle duty: you're coming to the park with us. We almost always go on Saturdays, and the weather is too nice to make an exception just because you're here."

Fang was more than willing and even bribed Morris to put his jacket and shoes on by telling him the sooner he got ready, the sooner he could have the present in the backseat of his car. The young boy was out the door, fully dressed in an instant. Melody buckled him in and they were off, Morris unwrapping the new set of dinosaurs he had gotten to replace his old, faded ones. Morris loved extinct animals almost as much as he liked bugs.

Once at their destination, Fang and Melody walked around in pleasant conversation as Morris made the dinosaurs fly all over the park. He must have given an involuntary sigh, because Melody's demeanor instantly changed from carefree to concerned.

"You okay, Mortichai? You seem off."

His sister was the only one who ever reliably called him by his actual name despite being the *whole reason* everyone called him 'Fang' now. "Yeah, Mel, I'm fine. I just have something on my mind I wish I didn't."

Melody nudged him with her elbow. "Zifeara?"

Fang looked down at her and shook his head. "I see where Morris gets it. How did you know?"

Her eyebrows shot up at him as if to imply that he was crazy. "Fang, I'm married and have a kid. If I couldn't tell you were insanely in love with Zifeara just by the way you *look* at her, I could tell by how you act around her. It's been what, three, four years since you started sighing a lot in her presence? You get lost in your own little world when you're together- it's honestly really cute. Plus, you're my brother, how could I *not* know?"

Fang slouched his shoulders and kicked at a rock. "I had a dream about her last night I'd give my left eye to not think about ever again. It wasn't bad but... It's problematic," he grumbled.

Melody grinned and poked his side. "Ah, you had one of *those* dreams. They are hard to forget."

"Kind of. Sort of. Let's just say it'll make it hard for me to see her tomorrow."

He knew she was sympathetic to his plight, but that didn't stop her from laughing at him. "I can imagine. I assume you'd like me to stop talking about it and start distracting you?"

"See, this is why you're my favorite sister."

They got ice cream while Morris was on the swings and spent a few hours there before it was time to return. Fang drove them home and said a fond goodbye, his nephew back to clinging to his leg. Once he pried his biggest fan off and left, Fang made one more stop on the way home.

The huge, wrought iron fence stretched for what seemed like miles around the grassy field, an oak or two scattered around the general landscape. Amongst the stone benches and towering angels, Fang made his way to his mother's headstone. It was right under the only willow tree in the entirety of Dawnfall Cemetery. He sat on the ground just in front of it and inhaled deeply, taking in the lovely smell of grass and trees.

"Hey, Mom. Sorry I haven't been by in a while, I've got a lot going on right now. I know that isn't an excuse but... Anyway, I was just at Melody's and saw Morris. I'm so surprised at how... *us* that kid is. He's a Nightstalker for sure, haha. I'm finally running around in the past with Zifeara and it's awesome but... I'm kinda lost. It's definitely hard to get used to, and there's this new guy we're traveling with who's got his eye on her too. Who wouldn't, she's amazing, but still. I don't want to rush Zifeara into something she isn't ready for and my friends have already given me good advice, but I still feel nervous as hell. There are so many things that could go wrong. She... she can't hate me right? Like, even if she says no, we'll still be friends? Right? Ugh, I'm so pathetic."

Fang leaned forward and pressed his head against the stone. "I wish you were still here, Mom. You could give sagely mom advice or something. Everything sounds reasonable coming from my friends, but it would be different from you."

The wind blew quickly and forcefully, sending a dried flower right across Fang's lap. He stared at it for a moment, before leaning back up with a sorrowful smile on his face.

"Yeah, you're right. I have to try. Thanks, Mom, you're the best. I'll see you later."

He got up to go home, readying himself to resume his escapades in the past.

CHAPTER 16

Bonding, I Guess?

Zifeara had dropped Fang off in their own time but didn't stick around. She didn't have any time to waste since they were rather close to the edge of the plains. Once they made it to the forest on the other side, she had a pretty good idea of where they needed to go to catch Torvak. If he had taken the Lightning gem, he must be after other intensely elemental stones.

Oranda was the largest city for quite a distance from the plains and was home to a massive population of well-to-do humans and demons of all types. In fact, Oranda was predominantly human, but many people came from all over to trade at the expansive marketplace. The eldest son of the founding family of this market was also a trader of exotic items. Ryu Harizuka was the richest human in the world at the moment, mostly because of his inherited wealth, but also his sharp business sense. He would trade almost anything he owned for the right price, and Zifeara had a small stockpile of 'obtained' items to sell to him. She was hoping that, with some persuasion, he would let her take one of his rare gems for safekeeping since she was almost 100 percent certain Torvak would be paying him a visit.

Ryu had found one of the largest and most difficult to display gems discovered to date. The world's largest ruby had to be contained in thick glass at all times due to its constant radiation of heat. The Inferno Ruby, as it came to be known, would slowly char and combust any flammable material too close to it, so its thick glass case sat upon a stone pedestal, deep under the Harizuka castle. It would still take a few days to get to Oranda, but Zifeara was optimistic about their chances of arriving there swiftly.

"Alright, loser, let's get going."

Aun looked at her just as she came back through the portal, thinking the trip would have taken her longer. "Well that was fast. And also not nice. Are you going to be pissy with me the entire time Fang is gone?"

Zifeara rolled her eyes and laughed. "No, it's just an expression. Speaking of being sans Fang, you and I have three days to get to the forest."

Aun looked down sharply, showing his annoyance. "Um, why exactly? What's the matter with how fast we're going now?"

"Are you kidding me?" Zifeara asked. "Did you forget we're actively chasing a madman? If Torvak took your gem, I think I know what he's up to and we have to hustle." Hurrying to make sure the horses were set and ready to leave, she somewhat mumbled the thought roiling around in her head, "That, and there's somewhere I have to be very soon."

Aun went to ask her where that might be, but she cut him off, "Plus if we make the horses run, we can run alongside them, further improving your stamina and getting you trained up. This won't be an easy fight when we do catch up to that asshole."

Aun thought about it and she was right-he had never spent a lot of time as anything but a predator. His forest was great for deer, but even then it was difficult to run without catching an antler on something in most places. "Alright, fine. We rest at night and run during the day?"

Zifeara nodded and turned to her horse, explaining to Heme and the other two what the new plan was. She shifted herself into a large pure black mare and looked to Aun. He changed as well, looking more like a mustang with his orange and black patterning, and they were off. The first day they spent chatting on the way, laughing as they enjoyed running free. They made a massive amount of progress and if they continued at this rate, they'd be camping in the forest by the next night.

For this evening, however, Zifeara was starting to teach Aun hand to hand combat in case he was ever caught between shifts. Considering most tigers were never taught such techniques, he was not doing well.

"Aun, come on, I'm not even trying. I know this is a new concept for you, but just block one hit. I haven't even tried to kick you yet."

Aun glared. "Zifeara, you're way fucking faster than me, how am I supposed to actually do anything?"

She sighed. "Considering I've been going slow for you, maybe do what I tell you? I've showed you what to do a dozen times at least, but you keep trying to shift." Hmmmm... Perhaps the way to motivate him was to piss him off. She knew that worked for her. "You know, maybe I should wait for Fang to come back. He's more your speed since he can't keep up with me either."

Aun looked even less happy at being equated to Fang in terms of combat prowess. "Hey, at least I'm good at shifting. I don't really see how teaching me to fight with just my hands is going to help me at all."

Zifeara raised an eyebrow, quickly moving behind Aun and wrapping her claws around his throat. "Go ahead, shift. Push your neck further into the thing threatening to kill you, or get small enough for me to crush you. *Or*, how about you do something to get out that won't kill you?"

He wasn't expecting her to be this close and she was obnoxiously right. If he couldn't shift... there was another way for him to save his own skin and he thought maybe she had forgotten where he was from. He wasn't above proving a point right now- she'd compared him to *Fang*. Trying not to overdo it, Aun took a deep breath, feeling the familiar tingle across his skin of building static, and electrocuted the shit out of her. Much to his surprise, that didn't make Zifeara let go. All that did was seemingly piss her off. Since she had hold of Aun's throat anyway, she knocked his legs out from under him and slammed him to the ground.

"That was not what I meant and you know it. You better start getting good. Fang has a head start on this, you know. I started teaching him a while ago."

Aun grit his teeth. Laying there, pinned to the ground, was not really how he expected training to go, and he felt Zifeara was having a little too much fun. That, and he really didn't want to believe Fang could be any better than him in any regard. Thinking about how Zifeara was positioned, Aun tried to figure out exactly what it was she wanted him to do to get her off him. She had him around the neck, sure, but the rest of her body was right over him, save for her legs. Oh, that was obvious.

Aun swung his legs sideways, wrapping them around Zifeara's and quickly rolled, switching their positions. Coming out of the roll, Aun used one of his arms to move Zifeara's hand off his throat and held it above her head.

"Can we do real training now?"

She just shook her head and looked up at him smugly. "You're not going to be so cocky when Fang kicks your ass. He can at least almost hit me."

Aun just rolled his eyes and got up, still holding on to one of Zifeara's arms to pull her upright. "Whatever. I still feel like your time would be best spent on teaching me to shift better. I've *never* been too slow on that."

Zifeara sighed and gave up. "Alright, sure. It's still not going to be what you had in mind, though. I'm trying to help you work on the things you suck at and have very little practice with- that's the *point* of training, Aun."

He lowered his ears, looking irritated at being told what to do, but he gave a resigned huff. "Alright, fine, have it your way. If it'll get you to teach me something more useful, sooner, so be it."

Okay, since pissing him off didn't work, but maybe tough love would. Zifeara whistled for Orro Heme. The horses had been resting a while, and he was well enough energized to move again. As Heme trotted over, Aun's ears swiveled backwards. "Zifeara, what are you doing? I thought we were spending the night here..."

Zifeara jumped up onto her horse's back and looked down. "Aun, I am a several thousand year old being. I'm doing what I have to do and have always done. Fang convinced me to take him along and I have because he's important to me and wants to help me get my job done. *You*, on the other hand, I have no use for. I let you come with me because you seem alright for a mortal and you're going to the same place. If you don't want to hear what I have to teach you, I don't have to teach you. Nor do I even have to let you follow me. Since the wisdom of a nineteen year old sheltered tiger boy seems to outweigh a ten thousand year old demigod, I'll be taking my leave. You *clearly* don't need me."

As soon as Orro Heme took two steps forward, Aun became distressed and stepped in front of the horse to stop him. "Wait, you can't be serious. I- I'm sorry. Please don't go, I'm sorry."

She sounded skeptical. "You'll actually try to learn the things I'm attempting to teach you?"

Aun's expression settled into something that made him look twelve; helpless, innocent and super cute. It almost made Zifeara feel bad for trying this to slap the smug out of him. Damn it, this was like dealing with Fang all over again.

Aun still had his ears lowered. "Yeah. I'll pay attention. Honest. I... I guess I was being kind of a brat. You're right."

Zifeara stared at him a moment before letting herself back down. She walked up to the still ashamed looking tiger and put a single finger in the middle of his chest. "You're goddamn right I'm right. And don't you forget it, you stripey whelp."

Her smug grin returned, prompting Aun to perk back up. "Now, come tomorrow morning, you and I are going to practice your hand to hand. Once you get a little better at that, I'm going to teach you the value of non-predatory animals."

Aun nodded. "Okay. Do we need to go hunting again?"

"We'll hunt right before we hit the forest, but after that, no. The nice part is, once we get to the forest, there's a river we can cross and I can teach you different things in that terrain, and even how to fish if you haven't done that much."

The rest of the night, Zifeara told stories of the first time she lived through this particular time period, including tracing the route she took on the map and a few animals she'd seen that weren't here anymore. They finally fell asleep, Aun once again dreaming of the unknown man he was becoming familiar with, and Zifeara dreaming of memories not so very long ago.

¤ ¤ ¤

"Zifeara, where are we going?" Fang asked.

Graham was driving her car into downtown New Tinning for a shopping trip. In the seat next to her, Fang was very small and this must have been just a week after she took him home since he was still wearing fairly ragged clothes. Zifeara sometimes forgot how tiny Fang used to be since he towered over her now.

"We're going to go get you some new clothes. You can't wear that for forever." She glanced down at him and he seemed nervous. He wouldn't look at her, constantly shifting about in his seat and digging at the skin around his nails.

"Are... are you sure? I used to only get new clothes once in awhile. Is it really okay?"

She laughed and ruffled his hair lightly, trying to get him used to being touched with no negative outcome. "Of course it is, honey, I wouldn't be taking you if it weren't. Besides, one day, when I teach you the value of money, I'll also teach you why it doesn't mean anything to me. You'll understand someday."

Zifeara not only sold priceless artifacts in 'pristine' condition, she also wrote a series of very popular novels, owned several archeological dig sites that she knew the exact locations of by way of time travel cheating, and owned many pieces of land that she rented out. Her time traveling had a funny way of making her secretly the wealthiest person to have ever existed. She could more than afford to spoil the absolute hell out of one small child.

Fang still looked uncertain about all of this, but he was even more fidgety once they got to the store. Graham dropped them off to go do some errands, so they had all afternoon to get what they'd come for. This particular store had all sorts of clothes but most of them looked handsomely designed.

Once greeted by the cashier, who she knew fairly well, Zifeara knelt down to Fang's level.

"Alright Fang, I know you're worried about picking things out for yourself, but I don't want you to look at how much anything costs. Trust me, I can more than afford anything you get here. Now, go find seven shirts, seven pairs of pants, two sets of pajamas, matching socks, and two new pairs of shoes. Pick out whatever you like. I'll be right here, go on."

She shooed him off and turned to the cashier, a young human girl with cheery green eyes. She was looking at Zifeara with a 'what have you been up to lately' sort of expression.

"Zifeara, who is your adorable little charge? I didn't think you had any nieces or nephews... and he can't be-?"

Zifeara chuckled and shook her head quickly. "No, no, no, he isn't mine. Well, not exactly anyway. I'm sort of adopting him."

While she was conversing, Fang had gone around looking at clothes like he was told. It took him almost forty minutes to gather everything, but he kept making trips between clothes racks and the counter, glancing worriedly at Zifeara every time he brought something new to his pile. She just smiled and encouraged him to finish getting what she had asked, so he did. Once he had everything and Zifeara counted, she asked if Fang was sure he liked everything he chose, to which he instantly replied yes. She just shrugged and paid for the pile, most of which Fang insisted he carry himself once they were in bags.

"Zifeara, are you *really* sure I can have all of this? I mean, super positive?"

She had answered yes to that same question for absolutely everything she got him that day, including school supplies, some new toys, and even a few things for his room in her house. Once Graham picked them up and they made their way home, she set all the bags on his bed, told him to unpack and that she'd get him for dinner in an hour. What Zifeara had come back into his room to later was not at all what she expected.

Fang was sitting in the pile of bags, all still completely full, and he was crying, knees pulled up to his chest.

"Fang, what's the matter, love? Why didn't you put any of this away?"

She moved a few things so she could sit behind him on the bed. He shuddered slightly when she softly set her hands on his shoulders, but that was to be expected from any orphan with trust issues.

"Zifeara..." Fang started between sobs, "I don't feel like I deserve any of this. I- I'm not your family and... and it feels wrong to accept a-all of this stuff. Why are you being so nice to me? I can't- can't do anything for you."

Zifeara seriously couldn't believe this was the problem he was having. She had thought he'd be ecstatic over finally having nice things. "Fang, I took you in because I wanted to. I can't expect you to go around with one pair of clothes forever. You may not be family, but we can be friends, right?"

Fang nodded and she continued, "Well I take good care of my friends and when they need something, I help them. You need a place to live and clothes to wear and you need to go to school next year. You didn't think you were staying here for free did you? I expect you to get good grades and do really well, that way you can make all this up to me. Does that sound fair?"

Fang though a moment, slowly calming down. "Kinda. Still seems like you're doing more, though."

She smiled reassuringly. "Tell you what, you be a good kid and it won't be work at all, okay?"

He nodded slowly and looked down, clearly thinking about something. When he met her gaze again, his big red eyes bore the most serious, absolute resolve she'd ever seen from someone so young. "Mortichai."

Zifeara perked her ears. "What now?"

"My name is really Mortichai. Fang is just a nickname my family called me."

Zifeara almost couldn't contain herself; she had just brought the most adorable child into her house. "Alright, which would you prefer I called you, then?"

He thought again. "I like Fang. I was never Mortichai unless mom was really happy or I was in trouble."

She giggled. "Well, I'm glad you told me."

He continued to stare at her, his determination no less diminished. "Do you think if I had a nickname for you that no one else ever, ever called you, we'd be like, *best friends?*"

Zifeara considered it. No one besides her idiot cousin ever called her anything else anyway. "I don't see why not. What did you have in mind?"

"...Can I call you Zia?"

That had taken her by surprise. She hadn't expected anything a four year old came up with to be reasonable, much the less kind of... nice.

"I think I can get used to that. Now, help me put all your things away, Graham has dinner ready."

As the memory faded, it was quickly replaced by another. Zifeara was sitting in bed, reading a book and generally waiting for the same thing she did almost every night back when Fang was young. Hearing her door creak open, she glanced up as he peeked his head in. He looked older now, probably only eight or so, but he still had the same issue most nights. From about the second week he had lived with her to not long after his twelfth birthday, Fang couldn't sleep by himself.

"Zia?"

She put her book down and moved her covers around. "Yeah, come on. Does it have to be a story tonight?"

He shuffled in and climbed up onto Zifeara's intricate, four-poster king-sized bed. Snuggling up to her, he looked very tired. It was unusually late for Fang to come in here, so he must have tried to sleep on his own.

"I'd like a story... Zia, in your stories there's never a prince or anything. All the girls at school always go on about princes and castles and stuff. I want that."

Zifeara looked down at his hopeful face and grimaced. She knew exactly what he was expecting and was aware she couldn't deliver. "Fang, those are fairy tales. A lot of those things don't happen in real life. I don't really have a story like that for you."

Fang looked a bit disappointed for a moment before his face brightened again. "Do you have a story about knights and dragons? Both of those things are real, right?"

Sighing, she gave up. Zifeara couldn't say no to him twice.

"Once upon a random time, there was a girl. The girl went on many great adventures and saw many wondrous things." Fang had mouthed this first part with her since she always started her stories this way.

She spoke slowly, in a low and mysterious tone. "The girl had a dark and terrible secret that she never told to anyone; every time the full moon rose into the sky, she would turn into a horrible, massive dragon. The dragon knew no right or wrong, only destruction and chaos.

One night while the dragon ran amok, a brave knight came forth to challenge it, intending to slay the beast once and for all. The knight had wings of white and was armed with a silver trident that gleamed in the moonlight. The knight fought bravely, severely wounding the dragon, but no matter how many times it went down, the monster came back stronger and angrier than the last time.

Eventually the knight's strength waned, causing him to lose the battle. With his wings stained red with his own blood, he was certain this was the end for him, bowing his head and praying the thing finished him off quickly. Just before the dragon struck the final blow, the brilliant morning sun crested over the hill, spilling the first rays of daylight over the beast, making it roar in pain and rage. The dragon began changing- shrinking and becoming more human, eventually turning back into the girl. Though the knight was tired and injured, he still carried her to safety and cared for her until she regained her strength. When the girl came to, the knight was asleep and she couldn't bear to face him knowing what she had done. She left that night to continue on, off to other adventures in other times."

The instant it was clear that she was done, the noise started. "Zia, can the girl get rid of the dragon? Why can't she stay with the knight? Did she ever see him again? If he kills the dragon, will she die too?"

Fang was asking a lot of questions that she didn't have the energy to answer at the moment; the full moon had only been a night ago and she was tired. Besides, Zifeara wanted to wait until he was older to tell him all these stories she kept telling him about 'the girl' were not only true... but about her. She didn't want to scare him.

"Fang, hush. You have your story, now settle in. You'll have to wait 'til next time to know any more."

She reached over to turn off the light, rolling back to see him opening his mouth to argue. Zifeara pushed Fang's head under the covers, fondly messing up his hair. "Go to bed, munchkin."

He giggled and popped back up. "Okay, fine. Will you at least sing to me?"

She smiled and hugged him to her. She was so glad she had taken him in... he had become impossibly important to her in the last few years. "Sure. Tomorrow is Saturday, wanna go to the zoo?"

Fang nodded enthusiastically and closed his eyes as she began to hum their special song.

CHAPTER 17

Multiple Cats Make a Clowder

Aun hit the ground, once again failing to block Zifeara's kick.

"Jeez, Zifeara. You're being kind of vicious today, don't you think?" Picking himself back up and rubbing his shoulder, he was covered in dust already and they hadn't been at it for very long.

Zifeara had woken up in a mood. Not only did she feel pissy, but she was noticing that for some reason... she was dreaming about Fang a lot. She wasn't sure why, but it made her anxious- like it was trying to tell her something. She didn't think it was because she was seeing more of him. This hadn't happened when she saw Fang every day for almost two months straight. She hadn't had a dream about him more than once then, but now she'd had several in just half as long.

"Well, considering how easy I was on you the first time, I thought you might do better if I legitimized the threat. C'mon, again."

Aun had concern written all over his face. "Zifeara, are you okay? You're not still mad at me from yesterday, are you?"

"No, it's not you, I just... sort of woke up in a bad mood. Sorry, I'll go a little easier," she replied.

Aun brushed himself off. "No, I think you're right, actually. I feel like I move quicker when you do hit me harder. It at least gives me a reason to get better faster."

She felt a little bad about being bitchy with him and tried to lighten up. By the time they had to get moving, Aun could reasonably block a few kicks and swipes.

This day they had decided to fly over their horses, working on different aerial maneuvers and enjoying the breeze sweeping the plains. It was cloudy again, but by night they had made it to the forest's edge ahead of schedule. Tomorrow she could spend part of the day training Aun in the forest, but once she retrieved Fang the day after, she would have to leave the boys alone for a short while. The full moon was only three days away. She had to put as much room between her and her friends as possible before the It came out for its night of terror.

The next morning, the air was filled with the sound of jousting bucks, separating on occasion to kick at and jab at each other. The larger buck shifted to a ram during his charge, knocking into the deer and pushing the wind out of its chest. In response, the buck began coiling its rapidly changing body around the poor goat, tongue flicking in and out as the python began constricting. The large snake's scales slipped loose as the goat massively shrank and a small sparrow flew swiftly away, landing on a tree branch far away from the reptile. The giant snake reared up, rapidly flicking its tail. It coiled tightly and propelled itself as a spring, shifting scales to fur and landing gracefully above the bird, slender cat tail wrapping around the small feathered creature. Furious chirping became violent hissing as it became a cat-on-cat fight across the branches of nearby trees. The black cat lost its footing, falling backwards off the branch, vindictively extending all of its claws to drag the orange feline with it. Landing in a pile on the ground, both cats looked at each other in surprise before slowly changing into their normal forms, laughter manifesting with their familiar features.

"Hahahaha, alright, you win, Zifeara. The python was pretty good."

"Are you kidding, the ram was perfect. You did really well this time, Aun."

They laughed a moment more before they both realized Aun was still essentially on top of her. Rapidly coloring, he cleared his throat and quickly got up, holding his hand out to help Zifeara, looking away. Not looking at him either, Zifeara took his hand and got up, very careful to let go the second she was standing.

"Hey, so, um, wanna get moving? I know you want to make a ton of progress while it'll be fast."

Zifeara responded rather quickly, "Uh, yeah, that's fine. Going through the forest won't be as fast as the plains, so if we wanted to take today a little easier, we could just walk with the horses."

They agreed on that and tried not to talk awkwardly about nothing in particular for a while, just so the silence wouldn't set in.

Around noon, however, they heard another group of travelers approaching. Aun and Zifeara turned back, guiding their steeds so they didn't look like wild horses. A group of men came into view, all humans carrying a variety of weapons and laughing loudly at the conversation they were having. Great. Bandits. The pair exchanged a glance and made sure they looked super serious. Humans could be pretty easy to intimidate when you were a demon in this time, but they were also outnumbered. The bandits could try something stupid.

Spotting the demons and their horses, the bandits looked unsure of what to do at first. The tallest of them pushed to the front, clearly intending to make a stand. They'd gone the stupid route. Sighing, Aun stepped forward first, motioning to Zifeara he'd deal with them. She almost laughed at him right in front of the humans- him thinking he would protect her like some simple woman. Then she thought better of it; she should let him practice what she'd been teaching him.

The large bandit had an equally large sword, but he was not expecting Aun to be a shifter. Aun became his true tiger form, massive fangs prominently displayed, taking a protective stance in front of his party. The cat roared, electricity crackling over his fur, making the bandit falter and wisely step back. The others shot worried looks to each other before at the big guy, who quickly jerked his head to indicate they should run like hell. Moving rather hastily around the still growling tiger, Zifeara, and the horses, the cowardly men beat a quick retreat.

Aun followed them with his eyes and made a face as a tiger that very clearly expressed disdain. Once they were far enough gone, he turned back. "Well shit, I was hoping for a good brawl. Fuckin' humans, right?"

"Cut them some slack, if I didn't have any natural way to defend myself, I'd be afraid of a really big kitty with lightning powers and teeth the size of my entire dick too."

Aun snickered before laughing so hard he had to lie down, massive paws kicking at the dirt once in a while as he settled. The worst they encountered the rest of the way were small goblins who were so easily disposed of, even Treble trampled one to death.

Camping in a rocky overhang that night, Zifeara asked Aun more about his childhood.

"Haha, yeah, you don't really want to know," he said, looking a little melancholy. Zifeara's inquisitive expression caused him to sigh. "I'll spare you the sob story of the only tiger for miles around who wasn't all tiger. You don't want to hear about all the times he was bullied, by adults and children, or how his best friend was his own sister. It's really kind of a mood killer."

Aun focused on the fire they had made and one of his ears flopped over slightly, as though he was irritated at himself for having a rough time as a child.

"Well, if it's any consolation," Zifeara said softly, "in the future the world is ruled by hybrids, so your clan is wrong for thinking poorly of you for being different."

Aun looked at her, smiling stiffly. "Thanks. Unfortunately I don't live in your time, though. Currently, I'm a freak."

Reaching over, she gently grabbed the closest of Aun's ears, tilting his head towards her and making him faintly blush. There were very few times girls played with his ears and those times had ended somewhere he absolutely did not think Zifeara was going.

"Freaks are the best people, Aun," she murmured as she softly rubbed the velvety fur of his ear, causing him to inadvertently purr quietly. "I don't think I've ever liked anyone normal. Besides, your clan doesn't know what they're missing; the bigger your ears, the better it feels to have them pet. I should know, mine are massive. At least your ears are cute on you."

Aun didn't even know he purred. Had tigers always purred? No girl had ever made him purr before. And did Zifeara just call him *cute*?!

"Zi-Zifeara... Knock it off..."

She giggled and let go. "Didn't know how good it feels to have your ears scratched, did you? Don't worry, we're going all over the world on this trip; you'll find either somewhere you like and want to stay, or somewhere where someone likes you just as you are. You'll find a place to be happy."

Aun was surprised how hard it was to flirt with Zifeara. His brain was telling him to say something smooth, like 'but I'm happy right here', but his mouth didn't work. He was just focusing on not purring like an idiot because he knew she could hear it. Not only that but... he wasn't used to people being nice to him like this for longer than it took to sleep with him, and it was throwing him off his game.

As if Zifeara could read his mind she laughed again. "Yes, all big cats do purr. I do too since I'm part leopard, but no one is ever close enough to me to get me to do it."

Aun's brain blurted out the first thing that came to it, "Not even Fang?"

Zifeara's eyes widened a little as she was clearly not expecting that. "Come to think of it, no. Fang doesn't pet me. That'd be kind of weird considering we're just friends."

Now he was back on track. He raised an eyebrow at her, grinning. "And yet you were just petting *me* because...?"

Scowling slightly, Zifeara tilted her ears in annoyance. "Oh, shut up. You were being all depressed and pitiful. Go to sleep."

That night Aun dreamt of the man again. He was running through the pines, looking around their trunks. He didn't feel worried as if he were running *from* something, he felt as though he were... looking *for* something. He heard giggling. The laugh sounded familiar and movement to his right made him turn quickly. He just barely caught something long and slender darting behind one of the trees. It looked a lot like a tail; a very familiar tail. He heard the giggling again and put the two things together. Quickly ducking around the questionable tree, he almost ran his face into Zifeara. In fact, he had come inches away from kissing her. She blushed and pushed him away, backing up and continuing to laugh. He could feel the heat rise in his face, but he reached out and grabbed hold of Zifeara's arm, gently pulling her back. She stared at him before bumping her head into his chest and resting it there a moment. It wasn't a hug, but she was definitely pressed against him in what would be considered an affectionate way. Alright, it was official; Aun was confused and there was something going on here. This guy obviously knew Zifeara, but the big question remained. Who the actual fuck was he?

That morning, Zifeara was making use of the mountainous terrain to do some agility drills with Aun. There was a nice rocky outcropping nearby with jagged rocks jutting out at weird angles, so Zifeara ran him through several shifts to jump over the formation. She even ran him through as himself, which was probably the least graceful run he had. She always went through with him as the same animal so he could see where he went wrong. All in all, it was fun, but they had to keep going.

While moving further through the forest, Aun began his line of questioning again. "So, in the future, what do you do? If you keep coming here, then is there not a lot for you to do there?"

She looked towards him and smiled. "Yeah, in the future, magic and such isn't used quite as often, so work is easy there. I basically get to go on vacation to the future when I don't have to be here."

Aun thought this over for a moment before asking, "What do you even do there? Like, more for fun and stuff, I mean? It must be really different."

Zifeara related the last day she and Fang had just gone out before going to Todd's club. They had gone shopping for some new clothes before playing some video games to waste time until all the clubs opened for the night. She described her friends and the Down Under, eventually getting to her own house. Aun almost couldn't believe Zifeara had a house as large and as... different as she had described. Most of her house was decorated in her three favorite colors; black, purple, and red, and she favored dark stone and marble.

"Do I ever get to come see any of this? Fang goes back and forth, so there's clearly no rule against being in a time that isn't your own."

"Hmm, maybe. I suppose that could be your reward for doing well with training. Sure, why not. If you do really well with your training in the next few months, you can come see our time," Zifeara said.

Accepting that as fair enough, Aun didn't press the 'few months' part. He'd convince her to take him sooner, it just wasn't an argument to have today.

Zifeara and Aun had decided deer would be the traveling animal of the day, so the horse caravan was led by a buck and doe, buck at the head of the party. While traversing a birch grove, Aun stopped short, causing the others to stop behind him. He had a bad feeling about this area and he returned to his normal form to make use of his large ears. What he heard sounded large and unhappy. As it got closer, Zifeara shifted as well, recognizing the sounds.

"Well, at least we found lunch. That sounds like a bear."

Aun sounded surprised. "You can eat bear? I always heard they were sort of gross."

Before Zifeara could answer, a very sour looking bear came into view, eyeing the group hungrily. Deciding he could take them, the beast reared up, roaring and slamming his paws on the ground.

"Alright, I'll distract it. You go for the throat. All you have to be is faster than it."

Zifeara turned to her panther form and ran around the bear several times as its massive paws swiped at her, badly missing. Aun turned tiger and waited for his moment to take out the creature. Zifeara jumped on its back, causing the bear to stand in an attempt to shake her, and Aun went for it. Moving in a zigzag, he launched himself at its exposed neck, but the beast swung a formidable paw, raking his claws across Aun's face and sending him flying. Zifeara quickly moved herself so she could sink her teeth into the back of the bear's neck, further distracting him from the tiger's second attempt. This time Aun got him, shoving his lengthy fangs through the its thick fur and muscle, finally getting into the vital area to damage arteries and windpipe. The bear only struggled a little before collapsing, Zifeara nimbly landing and changing back.

Aun had blood running down his face, but he was lucky; the strike had come a few inches from hitting his eye. He shifted back as well, using the back of his hand to press to his scratches and stem the bleeding.

"Aun, let me see, you're going to get it infected if you touch it too much." Zifeara hurried over to where he was grumbling about the bear getting him so easily and moved his hand, allowing fresh blood to dribble down the tiger's face.

"I'm fine, I've had worse. Way worse. Tiger claws are far sharper." Aun shooed her and went to put his hand back on his face.

She grabbed his hand, giving him a very stern admonishment. "Aun, you do realize I have extensive medical knowledge, right? I can get that to stop in seconds if you'd just listen to me."

"Zifeara, I've taken care of myself for the last thirteen years, I'm pretty sure I can take care of myself now! This is really not something I need you for. It's a scratch."

Aun was becoming more agitated the more she tried to help. He was not used to someone caring this much, if at all, that he got hurt. His brother and father began teaching him how to fight at a pretty young age, but they'd always told him to suck it up and keep going as soon as anything happened to him. He'd just figured that's how it was; you fight, you get hurt, who cares- fight more. He sulked off to sit down and deal with the blood while he waited for Zifeara to cook.

She looked after him, confused at why he was suddenly so angry, but whatever. If he wanted to be touchy, fine; she'd just dress the bear and eat it herself. She skinned and cooked up their fallen foe after whistling to their horses that it was safe to return. They had backed off to get well away from the fight, but poked their heads back into view past a tight grove of trees. After making a fire, Zifeara took a leg and began to eat.

Twenty minutes passed before Aun reemerged and sat down, quietly carving off some food for himself. They ate in silence, but Zifeara could feel him glance at her every once in awhile. She paid him no mind and finished her food, getting up to dismember and pack the bear away in her bag. He was so big that he'd feed them for quite some time. Once she had finished, Zifeara called to her horse so they all could carry on.

Before she could get on, Aun grabbed her hand. "Hey..."

As Zifeara turned to look at the tiger, he actually hugged her. Speechless, she froze. It didn't last long and Aun immediately beckoned Thrush over upon letting go, but it was enough to leave Zifeara feeling confused as hell.

"Most of my life no one ever really batted an eye if something happened to me," Aun said, more to Thrush than to her, "I haven't really known you very long but you're the only one who seems concerned that anything happens to me. You don't have to like me. You don't even need me. But you're probably the closest thing I have to a friend. What... what I'm trying to say is; I'm sorry I'm kind of a jerk. I'm not used to having friends."

Zifeara sighed, then smiled. "I know how you feel." Aun looked back at her, confused, and she elaborated, "I've been alive a very long time, Aun. I didn't start out the way I am now. I started with no emotions whatsoever. I was created to destroy things and kill people, so I didn't need feelings. I've had to learn every single one the hard way. As you can imagine, being an emotionless husk doesn't really endear people to you, so I spent a majority of my time completely alone. I used to be okay with it, but several hundred years ago, I learned an emotion I didn't really want... loneliness. Sure, I've made friends here and there, hell, I even have some religious worshipers, but you and Fang are the first two to ever come with me and just... hang out. It's been really nice having you both, truthfully. I've enjoyed having company."

Aun considered hugging her again, but Zifeara seemed to be over it. She vaulted Heme, who snorted at the other two horses and Thrush looked at her rider expectantly. Aun shook his head and got onto his mare, leaving well enough alone; this was the sort of thing that was best left when the conversation ended.

By the time night rolled around, they had gotten well into the mountains. It was early enough in summer to still be rather chilly before the sun had even set, so when camp was made the horses stood as close together as possible for warmth. Zifeara pulled out both sleeping bags and this time Aun accepted one; he was no stranger to the cold, but he didn't spend the night outside in it very often. They passed the night in silence, Zifeara opting to read while Aun turned in early.

Zifeara didn't really feel like sleeping, so she finished her book and ate more, eventually digging around in her bag for Fang's MP3 player. She was pretty sure he hadn't taken it and she was right. She listened to music until dawn and hearing Fang's favorite songs made her hope tomorrow would go well. If she flew all day she could probably cover enough ground to get to the decently sized town of Rishiro to the north. She liked that town well enough, but if destroying it would keep her dragon away from Oranda, and more importantly her friends, then so be it. The It would take the lowest hanging fruit and would waste a lot of time trying to get to Oranda all in one night if she flew far enough away.

CHAPTER 18

Why Did You Leave Them Alone Together

I t was finally time to get Fang. Zifeara opened up her portal and went through before Aun had even stirred. Her house was quiet when she stepped in since even Graham wasn't up yet to start morning chores. She text Fang to see if he was already awake and heard a cat meow. Zifeara didn't own a cat. It sounded like it came from upstairs so she began heading up to see if Lola had snuck a cat in here. Zifeara wouldn't have been mad, she just would have liked to know about it considering it was *her* house, even if she wasn't there a lot of the time. As soon as she made it up the first few stairs, something moved on the upper floor and it sounded way too big to be a cat. Bracing herself for the sport of ejecting idiot burglars from her home, Zifeara sat very still and listened. There was only one of them, and she was pretty sure they were in her room. They didn't sound like they were rummaging around, but instead coming towards her. When Fang came around the corner of her hallway yawning, she had almost shifted and jumped on him.

"Fang? What the hell are you doing here? You scared the crap out of me and I almost kicked your ass just now!"

"Oh, sorry, Zia. I would have told you I was here, but I can't exactly text you in the past and I didn't know when you were coming. I figured it would be easier if I were right here when you got back. That, and Lola baked me a mountain of desserts last night."

Zifeara shook her head and made for the game room, Fang following close behind.

"Alright, look," she said as she sat down. "I would have much rather left the two of you and the horses here, but I don't think Aun can handle the time difference yet. I feel like being here would really freak him out. So... I'm going to have to leave the two of you to keep moving while I get as far away from where you're heading as I can."

Fang knew this would happen eventually, but he didn't know what the plan would be. Since Zifeara lost herself to the dragon once every month, he also knew she was used to diverting it. That didn't really make it any less worrying. He must have been giving her a very concerned look because Zifeara tried to smile.

"It'll be okay. If I fly hard and far enough, there's no way it will come back for you guys with another town so close by. I just need you to keep moving. I don't care how tired the horses are, get off and walk yourselves if you have to. You. Are. *Not*. Stopping. Understand?" Fang nodded solemnly and Zifeara brightened again. "And no fighting with Aun. I know you two don't like each other, but behave yourself."

Fang pretended to revert back to a child and put some serious whine in his voice to try to make her less somber again. "Awww, Ziaaa. I don't wanna babysit the kitty. He's dumb and ugly and mean to me!"

Zifeara giggled. "Look on the bright side, I did you a favor; I started him on hand to hand."

Fang gave a disinterested pout like he didn't understand why this was helpful to him, so she made it obvious. "I expect you won't skimp on training just because I'm gone, you know. An hour or two won't make much of a difference on your head start with as fast as I fly. I've taught you more than I have him, and he's been a cocky little shit about having to learn this. Kick his ass, Fang."

A maniacal glint passed through Fang's eyes and he smiled widely. "Yeah? You mean it?" Zifeara nodded and Fang got up quickly, holding his hand out to her. "Well, shit, let's go. I can't wait for this."

She laughed again as he helped her up. "Don't be so excited. I'm expecting you to be the responsible one- you are technically older, after all. And I'm giving you homework. Here," she pulled a book out her bag. It was worn and the pages were quite yellowed. It had a picture of flowers on the front that looked rather pretty, but the title was 'Wild Plants to Know and Fear.'

Fang raised an eyebrow, but Zifeara made him take it. "Trust me, there's going to be a time when you need to know not to put something horribly poisonous in your mouth and I won't be there to stop you. It won't kill you of course, but the aftermath of poisoning yourself isn't pleasant either. Since you have a photographic memory now, you may as well put it to practical use." She also took her bag and handed it to him since she wouldn't need it for a while. "Here, all you have to do is reach in and think about what you're looking for. It'll be there. Let's go."

"Hey, Zia?"

Zifeara stopped short. She was really hoping he wasn't about to ask what she thought he would.

Fang managed to look worried and sympathetic all at the same time. "Do I... um, do I ever get to know what happens? I know you don't like to talk about the It, but... you've only ever told me about the mark. I'd still like to know how it works."

Zifeara subconsciously reached her hand around to touch her shoulder. Three days before she turned, a bruise-like mark resembling a pair of wings to mirror her dragon's began appearing across her skin. It took up all of her upper back and darkened as it got closer to the time, foreshadowing her inner monster rising to the surface. On the night of the full moon, it looked like a tattoo, completely black and causing the skin around it to gain a raised texture.

"Fang, I honestly don't think you do want to know. The It isn't to be taken lightly; it spends all night destroying as much as it possibly can, killing as many people, animals, and anything breathing as it's able to. At least the second the first rays of sunlight hit It, it has to get back inside. The only upside is, so long as it's stuck inside me, it can't do whatever it wants. It only gets one night."

His expression didn't really change. "Zifeara, you're- you're the one person in the world I tell everything to. I'm going to be around just as long as you are, you should have someone you can talk about this with. It might make you feel at least a little better to tell someone what it's like. I'm here for you. I always have been."

He took both of her hands in his, brushing his thumbs across her knuckles. The sincerity in both his voice and eyes gave her a feeling she really didn't want to think about right now; a confusing mix of regret, shame, and... something else she didn't have a word for.

"Mortichai..."

Zifeara knew she didn't have *time* to be emotional. If she was going to give the boys time for training and getting enough flying distance between her and them, they had to go soon.

"Maybe one of these times I'll tell you. For now, we have to scram. C'mon then."

Before she could receive any more protest, she produced her crystal and dropped it, grabbing Fang's shoulder and practically throwing him through.

On the other side, he stared at the unfamiliar terrain. Wow... they really had made a lot of progress without him. It didn't look like they were anywhere near the plains anymore.

"Alright, Fang," Zifeara said quietly so as not to wake Aun, "I better get started. I have a long way to go."

Before she could turn, he grabbed her hand one more time and pulled her quickly towards him, hugging her tightly. "Don't worry about us, Zia. I'll make sure we're still okay by the time you come back."

Zifeara smiled and returned his embrace, briefly burying her face in his chest. "I know you will. I don't know that I can make it back any sooner than tomorrow night. Depending on how... bad it is, I may be later. You should make it to Oranda tonight if you keep going like I said and don't spend too long training this morning. Stay somewhere nice when you get there, there's plenty of gold in my bag. Don't be too hard on Aun."

She moved away, slowly letting go of Fang's hand and giving her best reassuring smile, turning her gaze to the sky. Becoming a small falcon, she circled once and screeched before shooting off northward.

Fang watched her go, trying to imagine what was in store for Zifeara tonight. She had never told him anything about what happened to her when that thing came out, besides the wings manifesting on her back, so he could only fear the worst. Once she was out of sight, Fang turned to see Aun, still sound asleep in one of Zifeara's sleeping bags, not a care in the world. He moved towards their friend, but it made the horses stir. Once Treble saw Fang, she snorted and pawed at the ground in excitement, which in turn, woke Aun.

A tiger exploded out of the sleeping bag, snarling in Fang's direction, still bleary with sleep. Fang was having serious Deja vu. This tiger was... less attractive somehow. Fang was surprised it occurred to him that he could tell the difference between Zifeara's tiger and Aun. The big ass teeth Aun bore were a dead giveaway, but he still looked different.

"Hey, furball. Good to see you're still here."

Aun realized what was going on and gave a half-hearted snarl. He was about to lay back down, but Fang had other plans for him.

"Hey no, up and at 'em. Zifeara already left and she told me where you are in your training. I'm supposed to test you this morning."

Aun paused. He had forgotten that Zifeara said he was expected to spar with Fang while she was gone. His scowl turned to a smug grin, exposing the full length of his canines. "Right. I'm supposed to kick your ass today," he growled deeply.

Fang stood, one hand on his hips, one eyebrow raised. "Is that what Zifeara told you? Because she said that exact same thing to *me* this morning. C'mon then, let's have you."

Aun sneered and shifted to his regular self. "Yeah right, Zifeara told me I was doing pretty well. You think you're ready for this, but you aren't, Twiggy."

Fang just smiled confidently and took a defensive posture, motioning for him to start. Glaring, Aun took an aggressive stance, fully intending on playing Zifeara's part this morning; hitting hard and fast. That was his first mistake. Fang was trained to keep her at bay, so he was well prepared for the first hit Aun tried to make. He deflected Aun's first two swipes and flat out smacked him upside the head, pushing the tiger back with a shove to the chest afterwards. Aun didn't falter much, but it was enough. Fang used that small misstep to kick Aun's feet out from under him.

The obnoxious part about cats was how good of a job their tails did at keeping them balanced. Instead of hitting the floor, Aun used this as a chance to drop and spin, kicking his leg out to try to bring Fang down to his level. The wonderful part about cats is that they all think they're clever until you prove them to be otherwise. Fang jumped as if he were playing jump rope, easily avoiding Aun's sweep and backflipping far enough away to be out of reach.

Landing back in a perfect stance, Fang couldn't help but laugh a little. He wasn't going to be the bigger man when it came to this. "What were you saying about kicking my ass? Because I'm pretty sure it isn't going well for you."

Irritated, Aun made a valiant second attempt. Launching into a volley of jabs and kicks, he was determined not to lose. Fang either blocked or countered every hit, eventually starting to get cocky about it. He was now throwing flair into avoiding being hit by his younger counterpart, flipping over Aun and spinning around him when he could get away with it. Finally, rage proved to be the determining factor when Aun lost it and yelled, moving too fast for Fang to keep up. Aun caught him right in the jaw, putting an end to happy fun times. Recoiling from the hit, Fang tasted blood. Having such sharp teeth could be a pain in the ass sometimes.

Straightening up, he looked to Aun, who was panting slightly, but seemed proud of himself.

"Congratulations, you finally managed to hit me. Once. Zifeara would be laughing right now."

Losing his smile, Aun retorted, "Oh yeah? What makes you think that?"

Moving quickly, Fang faked a swing and maneuvered behind Aun, hitting the back of his knees and pushing him forward, making sure to grab his arms. Landing on top of the tiger and knocking the wind out of him, Fang tried not to sound too smug.

"Because if she were being as hard on you as she is on me, I wouldn't have won this in one move. I've still never hit her. If you have, she's dumbed down your training for you."

Struggling to get up and finding himself unable to, Aun decided he'd had enough. He shifted back into his tiger form and threw Fang off of him, spinning around to pin his opponent and gain the upper hand. While Fang was on the ground, Aun turned to meet a sight he didn't expect. He had placed his head in exactly the right spot to meet the barrel of one of Fang's pistols. Aun was pretty certain the gun was *not* loaded with paint, and remembering what that thing had done to the deer the group had eaten so long ago, he froze.

"Wanna see who's faster?" Fang's expression was deathly serious and he had absolutely no humor in his tone or eyes. "No one likes a sore loser, Aun. Now get your stripey hide up and get ready for breakfast. We're on our own today."

All the fur along Aun's spine bristled. He had never heard Fang say anything even remotely serious, but now that it was just the two of them, he was very different. Aun slowly backed up and sat, glaring but obviously outmatched.

Fang didn't lower his gun. "I'm not a fan of you either, but think of it this way; if I shoot you and claim self-defense when Zifeara gets back, you can't say otherwise, and she trusts me with her life. There's literally no way she wouldn't believe me. So cool it."

Aun wasn't liking this new Fang. He had a spine. "And who made you the boss? I'm pretty sure I'm not required to listen to you," he growled.

Fang took the gun off the tiger, returning it to the holsters he had carefully hidden in his silk shirt. "For your information, Zifeara most definitely *did* say I was the responsible one before she took off. And since I'm betting you want to stay on her good side as much as anyone with half a brain, I suggest you behave yourself, kitty."

Aun shifted back to normal and started to say something else, but Fang had already begun digging for breakfast in Zifeara's bag. He pulled out a raw hunk of bear from the other night and held it out towards Aun. "Do you know how to cook? I assume you do, but still."

Aun snatched the meat and said roughly, "Yeah, yeah, make me a fire. I'll try to find a good pair of spit sticks."

Fang gave his best sarcastic smile and started gathering sticks. At least Zifeara had taught him how a flint and steel worked, and she always kept a set in her bag, probably for this exact reason, now that he thought about it.

Once they finished breakfast, Fang made sure they wasted no more time and headed out. He told the horses the only stops they were allowed until they hit Oranda would be for water, and they seemed okay with that. On one such stop, Aun seemed to be staring an awful lot.

"Alright, *what* Aun? There has to be some reason you've been glaring at me for this long," Fang sighed.

Aun narrowed his eyes. "What is your deal? I don't understand why Zifeara has you. If you haven't been here with her before, then what are you for?"

Fang was speechless for a moment. Regaining his ability to process what Aun had just said to him, he was indignant. "What am I *for*? I'm her best friend. I'm for all the time Zifeara has when she isn't doing her job. Zifeara always comes to me to de-stress and have fun- to have someone who knows her better than anyone else that she can talk to. To have someone who doesn't judge her for what she is. That's what I'm *for*. I see the side of her no one else gets the privilege to; the best side she has."

Aun became even more agitated, his tail flicking behind him. "And exactly how long have you been in love with her?"

Now it was Fang's turn to be annoyed. "I don't recall saying I was. Besides, we've always been friends. It's never been anything else."

Aun was looking at him like he had just told the biggest lie ever, so Fang continued, "Do you have any idea how hard it is to watch your closest friend get hit on by guy after guy twenty-four seven? I'm naturally protective because I *have* to be so that she doesn't have to deal with that all the time."

Fang turned to make the horses hurry up and drink faster so he could bail on the conversation, but Aun wasn't letting up.

"But what if she wanted it?"

He stopped in his tracks. "Excuse me?"

Turning back around, he saw Aun was smiling, happy to have found that one thing he could do to get to him. "What if she wanted to be with a guy and you're stopping her from doing it?"

Aun leaned against a tree while Fang thought about it quickly. Zifeara would have told him to lay off then, right? She never had any problem saying exactly what was on her mind, so if he were intruding, she'd make him stop... unless she was worried about hurting his feelings. No, she'd still tell him. Right?

Aun was enjoying getting back at Fang for this morning. "Didn't think about that, did you? It might happen soon enough. She and I got on great without you–"

Fang cleared the space between them in only a couple of strides, slamming Aun against his tree. "So help me, you do *anything* to her and she comes to me upset, I will straight up murder you in the slowest way I can think of. Forget about what *she'd* do to you if you pissed her off, she wouldn't have enough left of you to end."

Even though Fang had him pinned to the tree, it was only by the collar of his shirt. Aun could have easily shoved him out of the way, but something wasn't right. Aun was scared shitless. He had never found Fang particularly threatening before, but something was very different now. He could feel the hair on the back of his neck stand and his tail was bristling, telling him he was in a lot of trouble. But why? Logically he *knew* Fang didn't scare him, so why was he more scared now than when Fang had a pistol pointed at him?

Fang held his death glare for a moment more before dropping Aun's shirt and turning away, trying not to go with the self-defense story for shooting the tiger right there and then.

Aun calmed down almost immediately after Fang had stopped looking at him, but instead of asking the pertinent question, another fell out of his mouth. "It's been *that* long, huh?"

Fang almost turned back to ask what he meant, but realized soon enough. "Shut up, Aun. You barely even *know* her; to you she's just a pretty piece of ass."

"And funny, and too smart for her own good, and incredibly fun to be with."

Now Fang did turn back around, unable to disagree but still able to glare at the smug, dreamy look Aun had on his face.

The tiger was lost in his own head for a few seconds. "And bossy."

Fang couldn't be quite as angry as he'd started out. Aun was right, all of those were things he loved about Zifeara, even the bossy part. Zifeara was almost more attractive then.

He sighed. "Just go get your horse. We have to get to Oranda by tonight and I don't know how far we still have to go."

They both got ready to leave, but Aun had the last word. "You know I don't care, right? It doesn't matter to me how long you've known her, I'm going to even the odds. By the time we get all this sorted, she'll be just as tempted to stay with me as she will be to go with you."

There was only so much that counting to one hundred could do, but Fang started counting anyway. *One, two, three, four, won't think about killing this shithead anymore. Five, six, seven, eight, I'd have to get my story straight. Nine -*

Counting stopped working by around fifty, so Fang started reading the book Zifeara had given him to try to keep from thinking too hard about his conversation with Aun, and how his violent outbursts were beginning to worry him. He only got halfway through before he became distracted. He started thinking about all the things Todd had said when they were talking last. Zifeara didn't even like daisies. He'd have to do something though; if Aun really was about to get serious, so would he. Once Zifeara got back from her problem time, he'd have to give it a shot at least.

Looking around at where they were, Fang figured this was probably a great area for growing vegetables that thrived in cold weather. If he could have something cooked by the time she got back, he could show her how resourceful he was becoming, especially if he picked everything himself instead of buying it. Well, at least picking most of it. He would definitely find what he could, including the meat. Fang hadn't hunted without Zifeara yet but he was pretty sure he could handle it. Zifeara loved elk stew. This was definitely where he had the upper hand; he knew exactly what she did and didn't like whereas Aun had to figure that out.

Feeling a little better, Fang spaced out for a while until he noticed it getting rather dark. The surrounding trees were thinning out gradually as they were coming down into a valley, passing one or two human travelers on the road. It was most likely an hour until the sun fully set, and a large city was spreading itself out before them. They'd made it to Oranda. Now they had to find somewhere to stay, safe from the utter horror the unsuspecting city a day's trip north was about to succumb to.

¤ ¤ ¤

Zifeara had been right; she could see Rishiro already and she still had about two hours 'til the sun set. She flew past the town, just to give herself some extra safety distance and found herself a cave to sit in when she only had around a half hour left. She always liked watching the sunset, especially when it would be the last nice thing she'd experience for the next several hours.

One of the many things she didn't talk about with Fang to avoid worrying him was anything to do with this process. This was the proof that she really was a monster.

This dragon of hers had been documented in various ways throughout history and was known to mortals only as the It. As a twisted hobby, Zifeara enjoyed collecting the most interesting pieces of art depicting the It- and on rare occasions, her. She thought it was funny in a morbid way, like collecting her own autograph or something.

As the sun dipped below the horizon and the last rays of light vanished, Zifeara took a deep breath in. She felt her heart slow to a stop before rapidly beating harder and faster than even the toughest fight could have managed. Her heart began swelling, the first piece of her inner horror to take shape. Zifeara grit her teeth as all of her bones followed, elongating where they could, snapping and reforming where they had to. Her skin began stretching and dulling in color, adopting a bluish hue. She had been sitting a minute ago, but now she doubled over, her quickly growing claws raking the rock mouth of the cave. The dark wings on her back began to separate from her body and expand; long, straight black horns burst from her forehead and curled backwards.

Unable to contain it anymore, Zifeara let out a guttural scream, which distorted into a half roar, half anguished cry. The transformation always hurt like hell. The new talons on the dragon's hands continued to grow until they became scythe-like. Its tail stretched to about half the length of its body and by the time it had stopped growing, the thing was barely able to fit in the cave. The It was about the same size as stacking six bull elephants in a two by three pile. Eyes closed, the monster sat still a moment, deeply inhaling and scenting the air. When its eyes finally snapped open, it grinned a terrifyingly wide smile, massive razor-sharp fangs glinting in the moonlight. The It could smell humans nearby. It was dinner time and its favorite food was on the menu.

CHAPTER 19

Bloody Sunday

Crickets chirping and moon rising, a small figure moved through the quiet streets of Rishiro towards the forest. The young girl had gotten into the habit of sneaking out to the woods at night when she couldn't sleep. Everyone in her family went to bed stupidly early and it drove her crazy. Wandering in amongst the trees, she hummed quietly to herself. She froze when she heard something moving in the trees to her left. The full moon was casting plenty of silver-blue light, but she couldn't see anything out of the ordinary. She quickly stepped back, intending to return home; something out here was making her nervous. Once she was halfway to the town, that nervousness turned to dread, her blood freezing in her veins. She couldn't hear the crickets anymore. She may have only been seven, but she knew that was a bad sign. Turning slowly, she saw something moving behind her.

It was a color almost indistinguishable from the moonlight around it, save for the large black horns on its head. As soon as she realized what danger she was in, the dragon opened its eyes. It had bent down to be perfectly eye level with the small child, mostly for maximum horrific effect. Its eyes were strange; instead of having whites the base was black, and in place of irises and pupils it had a single shape, similar to half a yin-yang symbol. This was silver in color and unwavering in its stare. The girl stood still a moment, processing the unholy monstrosity behind her, before finally breaking into a run, screaming as she tried to get back to her home.

The dragon toyed with her, staying just far enough behind the girl as to not catch her until she reached the edge of town. A few people came out of their houses to see what was going on. Just as the girl came into view of the townsfolk, the dragon lunged, scooping her up in its jaws and crunching down, tearing her in half. As her torso fell to the ground and spilled her remaining organs and blood, the quiet, peaceful night turned into a cacophony of frantic screams and calls to arms. The It waited patiently for more villagers to emerge from their doomed dwellings with weapons until the small mob started actively trying to hurt it.

Claws, fangs, tail, and fire all descended upon these people, methodically eliminating them in the most gruesome or painful ways possible, sparing neither man nor beast. Homes were crushed, families devoured, land decimated, and souls returned to their caretakers. Once the majority of people were disposed of, the It's favorite game began; stalking the fleeing mothers, stragglers, and abandoned children. Their fear and the crushing of their determination to get away was truly what the night was all about.

The It enjoyed itself all throughout the night and by dawn, very few residents of Rishiro were even still alive. Seeing the sun approaching, the dragon raised its head and snarled, crushing the human still in its jaws. It turned tail and ran further into the forest and away from its handiwork, returning to the cave it had emerged from. Arriving just in time, the first ray of sunlight struck the dragon as it ducked into the crevasse.

The monster reacted as though it were submerged in acid- hitting the ground and flailing wildly, roaring in rage and pain. As the It thrashed, it slowly began shrinking and reverting back to its mortal-shaped prison. Moving less and less, the form taking shape began breathing heavily in ragged gasps and laid still on the cold stone of the cave.

Zifeara was back. As she consciously slowed her breathing, she cursed to herself. She was exhausted and ached all over. She was in no condition to fly to Oranda any time soon. Not only that, but she had forgotten to kill herself something for when she came back because she was so preoccupied with pointless thoughts. Now was one of the times she was thankful for the type of fire demon she was. Slowly shifting herself slightly, Zifeara gathered a few small rocks near her and swallowed them down her now snake-like throat. She could turn literally anything into energy if she gave her body long enough to melt it down. After ingesting probably twenty pounds of stone, she lay still, letting sleep speed her recovery so she could get back to her friends.

¤ ¤ ¤

Shooting the elk was easy enough. Dressing it turned out to be the hard part. While Fang had gotten himself a very nice knife during his wander around Oranda specifically for this, that didn't mean he was a pro at skinning and carving a kill. Zifeara had shown him how, but she also had centuries of experience. While not glamorous, field dressing an animal did have its perks if you had a thing for the taste of blood. It was just like regular cooking where you got to sample your food first.

Full of blood and a desire to impress, Fang did his best to get all of the elk into Zifeara's bag, and he really needed a bath afterwards. On his walk back to town, he collected some wild carrots and tubers he had seen, as well as wild spices he was familiar with. He was hoping Zifeara would be back soon, though she did warn him it could be as late as tonight that she'd make it to Oranda. If he started cooking this afternoon, he could have late lunch or early dinner to serve, so he had time to kill before he started the stew.

The hotel he had chosen was very nice, just like Zifeara had told him it should be. In fact, it was the largest bathhouse in Oranda as well as a hotel, so when he returned to their room, Fang grabbed one of the robes provided by the staff. He had been in a few of the smaller bathhouses Zifeara had made them stop at on the way, but never one that had been built out of the surrounding rock over a natural spring, or one that was large enough to have public pools. This was a huge draw for folks all over the region, so it was already busy when Fang got there.

He had forgotten that in this time it wasn't awkward to be undressed in front of complete strangers, but he really needed to wash the blood off. Zifeara would not be happy if she came back to a bloody bed. Despite how shy he could be sometimes, he was quite comfortable with his own body; he just wasn't used to being undressed in such a public setting. He rinsed most of the gore off in an area that was akin to a natural shower where the spring water was diverted over a cluster of rocks that created a waterfall before settling into the main bath. This pool had benches carved from the same stone as everything else all along the edges, so you could sit and soak without having to float. The rock pool was expansive and many different groups of humans, demons, and other assorted races were relaxing in the pleasantly steaming water as well.

Fang was surprised so many of the demons he had seen were a very distinct species of animal and not hybrids as they were in his time. While there were, of course, regular animals like Lola and Sara, he encountered far more mixes like Todd. Jackalopes were all varying degrees of deer and rabbit, even in the wild, but most of what he had seen here were one or the other.

It was loud too, at least to his sensitive ears, but the water felt amazing enough to let him relax anyway. Just as he was about to close his eyes and fully melt, Fang heard a dejected sigh from behind him.

"Great, you're here too." Aun was standing there, one ear tilted in annoyance. "Move over, everywhere else has too many people."

For once, Fang was in no mood to argue, so he scooted over as Aun got in. He couldn't really decide if it were a point of pride or not that he was... *bigger* than Aun without being a shifter, but he thought better of bringing it up. It was really just an unimportant guy thing, and yet it made him feel a little better.

"What are you grinning at, Scarecrow?" Aun was still on the warm side of irritated, but being in the water had made him chill out a little, clear by the lack of true venom in his tone. He sounded less like he actually wanted a fight and more tired.

"Nothing, it's just so... different here. We don't have places like this where I'm from."

Aun raised an eyebrow. "Then how do you get clean?"

Fang shook his head. "No, we have rooms in our houses with running water that we can turn on and off. Like controlling a waterfall. You can fill a tub with water in this room too, but it's way smaller than this. Really only big enough for one person. Or two if you get a big bath. Zifeara's can fit, like, four people."

Now the annoyed lilt came back into Aun's voice. "How do you know how many people fit in her bathing pool?"

"Dude, first of all, it's called a bathtub, and secondly, I've been to her house. I've *lived* in her house. I know parts of that house no one else has ever seen. It's what happens when you have the curiosity of a toddler."

He rolled his eyes, but realized Aun looked confused. "Fang, how old are you?"

Fang almost told the truth before realizing Aun hadn't figured it out yet. "Nineteen. I've had long enough to explore that place though; I've lived with Zifeara since I was five."

"There's no way she's related to you. She can't be or you wouldn't be so attracted to her. Unless you're *that* kind of freak," Aun said fairly matter-of-factly.

Ignoring that second part, he leaned his head back onto the warm stone and sank further into the water. "As much as it pains me to say it, you aren't wrong. I'm adopted. Zifeara raised me, that's all."

Aun sounded almost sympathetic for a second. "That explains a lot. Mom, Dad, or both?"

Fang didn't really mind talking about his family anymore, so long as no one brought up his brother. "Dad is in prison for killing Mom. I took my sister and ran. Zifeara happened to find me after my sister got taken into a really nice family, and for some reason she kept me. You asked like there's something wrong with yours, too."

The tiger gazed across the bath. He adopted what sounded like a well-practiced lack of emotion. "Never met my mom. She ditched me with Dad when I was only a few hours old. Around here, a tiger that isn't all tiger is worthless, but Dad chose not to kill me. He and my brother would kick the crap out of me in training so the rest of the village wouldn't, but my brother has always been a dick. My sister was the only one ever nice to me, so it was kind of like having a mom. It's why I was so fast to leave, really."

Fang sort of felt bad for being harsh; Aun must be so cocky because inside everything hurt. He was the exact opposite when he was young, but in his time he was treated like any other demon.

Aun saw the look Fang was giving him and cleared his throat. "It's fine, I left. They'd probably rather I not come back, so maybe I won't."

The two sat in mutual silence for a time, trying not to think about finding something they connected on. After a while they simultaneously got up to leave. Fang burst out laughing when he realized Aun had looked down to compare for himself and was sorely disappointed. This was like being an insecure teenager again.

"Shut up, it doesn't matter when you're a shifter," Aun grumbled.

"Sure, sure," he still chuckled. Oh yeah, personal point of pride.

Once they got back to the room, Fang went to put his headphones back on, but noticed Aun staring again.

"They're for cancelling out noise. My ears are really sensitive and without these, everything is way too loud. They play music, too," he said.

"Music?" Aun tilted his head a little.

Fang sighed. "Here, it's easier to show you. Your music comes from instruments, just like ours, but in our time we can store the sound for later. Hold still."

He put one of his headphones near Aun's ear and fished out his MP3 player, [16]selecting something easy to get the tiger used to very new age music. At first Aun cringed as if the earpiece had shocked him, but he quickly relaxed, astounded and mesmerized by what he was hearing. Fang handed him the other half and Aun listened intently.

Once the song had finished, Aun remained motionless a moment before loudly exclaiming, "What the *actual fuck* was that?!"

Fang spent the better part of the night explaining how it worked and answering various other questions before the two of them passed out, forgetting about the stew. He had expected to be woken up by Zifeara coming in and laying down next to him, but no such luck.

The next morning, Fang just laid around, thinking on if there was anything he could add to his stew that he had forgotten yesterday. Nothing came to mind, so he simply went out to stroll through the market yet again to see if that helped him realize what was missing. After snagging a few spices that didn't grow in this climate, Fang was confident this was going to be the best stew ever.

While he had received basic cooking lessons from Graham as a teenager, he had taught himself to make many dishes during his time as a bachelor. He was convinced he was simply adequate at cooking and baking, but all of his friends told him he was very good. Zifeara demanded he make pancakes absolutely every time she stayed at his place after a night out. In fact, sometimes she'd forego going home to her own house just so he would have to make her breakfast. Fang was more than willing to oblige.

He was just about to head back to the room when a stall caught his eye. It didn't look special, just another jewelry stand, but what he did see was someone turn over a necklace that appeared to have a dragon on it. Fang stepped up to the stall just as the customer returned the necklace to its spot on the table. He picked the necklace up and

---

[16] "Lisztomania" - Phoenix

stared at the figure carved into the ivory that made up the base of the pendant. The ivory was dyed in places to give it the colors that made up the creature on it. Something in his head was screaming that he had seen this somewhere before. The dragon was blue with long black horns and very sharp-looking claws that seemed too long for its hands. Its eyes were black pits and it had large, bat-like wings. Overall, it could be described by some as disturbing, but Fang could only think of where in the world he had seen such an unsettling creature. He didn't even hear the merchant come up to him.

"Interesting isn't it?"

Fang jumped a little at the man's words, and the vendor laughed apologetically. "I beg your pardon, I have always had a bad habit of sneaking up on people. I got that in a far away land from a man who carved it himself. He said he had seen this thing once and it was a force to be reckoned with. I thought he was mad, but I'm a trader by trade, so I bought it, ha ha!"

Even though it still felt odd using Zifeara's money, Fang had to have the necklace. He had to show her so she could bloody tell him what this was and why he recognized it. He paid the man and tucked the necklace away, eager to begin cooking. Zifeara could be back at any moment and he had to get started.

The staff at the bath house said he was more than welcome to use the kitchen so long as he stayed out of the way of dinner preparations, so he wasted no more time in getting the stew going and letting it simmer, tasting it after a bit. It was still missing something. Something sharp but not too strong. Something like... like... Smacking himself in the forehead, Fang cursed himself for being so stupid. It was the taste of onion he was thinking of, but onion itself was too harsh. He needed celery. And he had seen some out in the woods too, he just hadn't thought to grab it.

Evening was coming, but with the few hours of light he had left, Fang made his way back out, heading to the small, swampy pond he had seen the celery near. After snapping a few stems off, he left to return home, proud of himself for identifying what his glorious stew lacked. When he was almost within sight of town again, he removed some of leaves so he could sample a piece. He didn't hate celery by itself, but it also occurred to him that he'd ruin the stew if ancient wild celery tasted like utter bullshit compared to modern farmed celery. After taking a bite and finding it different but not displeasing, Fang carried on before hearing a loud screeching above him. The small hawk circled twice before dropping, landing solidly on the ground. Zifeara was finally here and his stew wasn't even done.

"Zifeara! I'm glad you're back, how did it go? Er, never mind. I, um, I have something to make you feel better! I'm making dinner!"

Fang was already bombarding her with small talk and she had just barely made it here. Zifeara adored Fang, really she did, but sometimes all she wanted was silence. After waking up, having recovered some energy from the rocks she'd eaten, Zifeara hauled ass getting back, picking off some squirrels and other easy prey where she could to keep her strength up without landing. All she wanted to do was pass out until morning.

"That's nice Fang. What are you-" She stopped short. Zifeara stared at the plants in his hands, really hoping she was just tired from the flight. "Fang... what are you holding?"

His smile was broad and proud, for all the world beaming like a child on graduation day from elementary school. "I'm making you one of your favorites; elk stew! I gathered almost everything in it myself, even the elk! I was missing a flavor though, so I went out to get celery. Why, do you not like celery? I can leave it out if you don't, that's fine... What?"

Zifeara could feel herself getting steadily more angry as he talked.

"You didn't read the damn book, did you?"

Fang's face fell. "W-well... not entirely. I started to, but I might have gotten a little distracted. Aun and I..."

He stopped talking, looking crestfallen. Zifeara practically stomped over to him, digging her hand into her bag which he had at his side. She brought out the book, lightly smacked him on the head with it, and flipped to a little more than halfway through.

Holding it open for Fang to see, she glared expectantly while he read aloud, "'Killer Cooking; Poisonous Plants that Resemble... Benign Food'..." He looked back up, meeting her cold gaze.

"The first thing you do after *not* reading the whole book on poisonous plants was to go out and **pick plants** you plan to *eat*?!"

Fang looked down at his celery, wondering what exactly he was holding to make her so mad. She almost never raised her voice at him. "Zifeara, I... what is this?"

She sighed. "You're holding hemlock, Fang." Before he could protest that he wasn't stupid and he knew what *hemlock* looked like, she cut him off, "Water dropwort hemlock grows in marshy areas and looks nearly *identical* to celery. At least you didn't eat it yet and poison yourself."

When his countenance denoted that he was even further upset, Zifeara gaped at him. "No... you didn't? I... How long ago?"

"Um... just before you landed?"

Zifeara rubbed the bridge of her nose, closing her eyes and visibly straining to not outright yell. "Fang, you're about to be violently ill. Poison doesn't kill you anymore, but you don't pass it easily either. Throw the rest of that crap somewhere and pick a bush."

Before he could ask for clarification, Fang felt his stomach turn as if he'd just done a loop on a rollercoaster. Then it burned. Dropping the stalks of hemlock where he stood, he suddenly found a favorite bush and vehemently emptied the offending plant and bile into it. Instead of a color one might expect, the fluid came out black and with the consistency of oil. He retched several times, even after there was nothing left. It was the only time vomiting had been that awful for him. He felt dizzy afterwards, but the pain subsided quickly.

Zifeara stood, expectantly waiting for him to be done. The perfect picture of health once again though moderately sheepish, Fang stepped up to her side to lead the way back to the hotel.

"Fang," Zifeara sounded very serious, "that would have killed Aun, you know."

At first he couldn't tell if she was simply pointing the fact out or chastising him for potentially murdering her friend. She paused as if she were waiting for a response but turned to head into town before getting one. She moved at a pace that was hard for him to keep up with despite his longer stride and assumed they were staying in the bath house. Zifeara looked to Fang once they were in the lobby and he knew what she wanted.

"226," was all he said.

She moved quickly up the stairs to get to the room while he simply slunk off to the kitchen to finish his celery-less stew. Now he couldn't care less how it turned out.

It was around midnight when Fang hauled the borrowed cauldron up to their room. For a demon, it wasn't all that heavy, but a human would have had trouble getting the massive amount of stew up the stairs. When he opened the door, Aun had smelled him coming and was sitting straight up on his bed, staring expectantly. Zifeara, however, was laying face down on their bed, hair still damp from the bath, completely out. Fang simply sighed, dug bowls out of her bag, and handed one to Aun so he could eat.

"Wow. This... is actually really good," Aun said through a mouthful of stew.

Fang debated heavily with himself before deciding to wake Zifeara, ultimately reasoning she needed food more than sleep right now. After gently shaking her awake, he managed to coax her out of bed to inhale stew - about four bowls worth. Yeah, she was starving. Once it seemed she was no longer angry, Fang finally tasted the product of all his hard work. It needed celery.

"Your cooking is good, as always. I'm impressed you got most of this yourself, though. Maybe I can make a hunter out of you yet," Zifeara said with a grin.

It did make him feel a little better to hear Zifeara say she appreciated the food, but Fang was convinced she'd be mad about the hemlock thing for a very long time. In fact once everyone had settled in for the night after eating the entirety of the stew in one go, Fang read the book. Twice.

It was around dawn that he realized he hadn't slept, but it didn't really matter; Zifeara could have quizzed him on just about any plant that would kill Aun and he'd have all the answers. He promised himself that he'd ask her for more books when they headed out on the road next. Fang was going to take all of this very seriously from now on; it wasn't a vacation anymore.

CHAPTER 20

Only a Slight Abuse of Power

Once Zifeara woke up that morning, she led Aun and Fang through the town, past the market, and up a winding road towards the massive castle on the hill above Oranda. This castle was a red and green behemoth; easily five stories tall and the size of a standard football field on each floor. It's sloping pagoda roofs cast imposing shadows here and there with the angle of the sun, decorative creatures made of gold adorning each corner. All of its columns stood firm and straight, silently bearing the burden of the house's weight.

"Zifeara, what is this place," Fang asked, agape at the building's lavish appearance.

"This is why we're in Oranda," was all she offered in return.

Zifeara hated this castle. She always found it far too garish, but she never pointed this out to its owner. Ryu's great-great-grandfather had built this place and Ryu didn't want it to be altered in any way. He actually went to great lengths to preserve the palace and everything in it. Regardless, she thought it was ugly as sin.

The two guards at the massive double doors saw Zifeara coming and hastily pushed them open, bowing deeply as she and her companions passed into the mansion. The man in the hall standing next to the towering central staircase looked up from whatever it was he was writing on a piece of parchment, looked back down, and did a quick double take.

"Zi-Zifeara," he stammered, "A pleasure to see you again. Master Harizuka is currently in business dealings upstairs, but I'll let him know you're here. I must beg a moment of your time."

As he hurried off, Aun shot Fang a look. "Is it just me, or did the way that guy seemed to piss himself at the sight of Zifeara kind of make you think she's been less than nice to him before?"

Zifeara turned one of her ears down at the accusation, but Fang simply replied in a far too innocent tone of voice, "What, Zia? *Never!* She's always an absolute peach."

She glared at the both of them. "I'll have you know that weasely little man was a complete ass to me. Exactly *once*."

Further ignoring her companions, Zifeara started to climb the large hardwood staircase. She knew the foreman had intended for her to stay downstairs, but she couldn't have cared less what he wanted; she was the most invaluable trade partner Ryu had and would ever have, and they were both well aware.

Fang and Aun quickly moved to follow, but Zifeara held a finger up and pointed to a room off to the left. "Oh no you don't, you two wait down here. It's bad business to bring strangers to the table. This will only take me a few minutes if Ryu knows what's good for him."

Stopping on the fourth floor, Zifeara saw the foreman come out of a room, clearly surprised to see her. "Miss! What are you doing up here? I was coming down to inform you that Mr. Harizuka-"

"Is ready to see you."

The voice from the room the foreman had just left was deep and commanding, yet still gentle. The man it came from emerged behind his servant, his dark brown hair highlighting his warm smile. Ryu's hazel eyes had a way of putting you at ease, which was probably one of the reasons he always excelled at making sales.

"You know we don't make Zifeara wait, Ko. Please come in, my dear. I'm sure you have something good for me since it's been so long since your last visit," Ryu said.

Moving into the spacious room Ryu used as his office, he held his hand over one of the two luxurious armchairs stationed in front of a massive marble desk.

Zifeara perched herself in one and waited for him to take his seat before beginning. "Ryu, I've come to you about something very important. I'm hoping all the time we've spent in good relations will garner enough trust to make this easy. I think you're about to be in danger."

He looked surprised, but allowed her to continue without interruption. "I'm currently looking for a man who is collecting very specific stones for his own purposes and I believe you're his next stop. He wants the Inferno Ruby. It is *imperative* he not be allowed to take it from you. I'd like to ask you for it now so that I can be a step ahead of him."

Zifeara opened her bag above the table, a large quantity of gemstones of varying natures and sizes pouring out. There was a *lot* of money on this desk.

"I'm willing to give you these in exchange for it and as soon as I've taken care of this man, I'll return the ruby to you as well."

Ryu looked at Zifeara very seriously, folding his hands in front of him. "And you think if I don't have it, he'll just move along?"

She sighed. "Well, no. I was also going to urge you to move yourself and most of your wealth discreetly out of the castle until I can be sure you'll be safe. *Please*, Ryu.

You may be a good business partner, but I also consider you a friend. I can't make you leave, but I highly suggest you take my advice."

He looked down to his desk solemnly, clearly weighing his options. After several minutes of silence, Ryu stood. "Very well. This is only because you've never proven yourself untrustworthy and have definitely had a hand in my current and continued fortune. Follow me."

He led the way back down all of the stairs and into the castle's subterranean vault. Coming to a large metal door, he produced a key from a chain around his neck and unlocked it. There, in the center of a small stone room, an obsidian pillar stood holding a red gem about the size of an orange but with an irregular, jagged shape. The stone gave off a faint light from beneath a thick box of glass. Ryu moved aside to allow Zifeara in, since he was well aware she could touch the stone. She was the one who helped him get it in here, after all.

After placing the rock in her bag, Zifeara held her hand out to him. "Thank you. It may take me quite some time to return this to you, but I need to make sure that until this man is dead, he can't possibly get his hands on it."

Ryu shook her hand and nodded his understanding. Once they were back upstairs, he began instructing his servants on moving valuables out in carts of produce and to be as stealthy as possible. Fang and Aun heard the commotion and peeked out from the sitting room, seeing Zifeara motioning for them to leave.

"I'm assuming that went well?" Fang asked on the way back through town.

Zifeara smiled contentedly. "Yes, actually. I didn't even have to touch him to get what I wanted this time."

Fang's face- and heart- dropped. "*This* time?"

"In his early trading days, Ryu didn't want to listen to a word I said. He didn't think a *woman* could benefit him in any way. Therefore I had to... soften him up a little, I suppose," Zifeara said with a smirk. "He's never had the nerve to disrespect me since. We've disagreed on things, but he always makes time for me."

Aun became curious. "Exactly how much did you have to do to make him cooperate?"

"Not as much as I thought I'd have to honestly. He was as easy as a saunter around his desk and a huskier tone of voice. He was *gone* once I sat in his lap. And has stayed gone ever since."

Now the tiger looked dubious, and maybe a tad disappointed. "That's *it*? That's really all you had to do?"

Zifeara clicked her tongue, mildly irked. "Aun, I was made for this. If you've ever met a kitsune and she tried to reel you in, imagine that times ten and that's me. You do *not* want to mess with me when I want something or you'll come to drooling on the floor and feeling *very* unfulfilled."

Aun still didn't seem to give her words much credence, but Fang chose to be silent. He would rather not have thought about how far she'd had to go to get what she wanted. Zifeara had, of course, never done any such thing to him since he'd have to be insane to say no to her, but he imagined that all it would take would be for her to smile at him. He might be able to hold out until she asked him sweetly. Fang really never wanted to find out, especially with his current... situation. Instead he decided to change the subject.

"So, now that you have whatever it was we came to get, where are we going?"

"We aren't going anywhere yet," Zifeara answered, "because if I'm right, Torvak will be making his appearance quite soon. And I would very much like to beat his face through his skull. I mean, meet him."

Aun turned to give a look of surprise at her vehemence, but Fang just scowled.

Catching his look, Zifeara responded, "What? Do you know how much trouble this guy will cause me if I don't kill him now? Plus, if he's all the necromancer said he was, this dude is going to be difficult to stop once he gets going. One doesn't obtain minions by chance; you either work hard for them or scare enough people into doing what you want. Last I checked, Terravak was run by some rich fat guy named Suta, not a creepy fuck named Torvak."

CHAPTER 21

The Enemy of the Day

The three made their way back to the inn after checking on their horses in the stables. They had dinner and returned to their room to rest, settling in for a good night's rest. Except for Zifeara. She sat stock still on the windowsill as a small cat, staring unblinking into the night.

Once Fang realized she wasn't coming to bed, he joined her. "What are you looking at, Zia?"

"The castle," she said without moving an inch. "I've had a bad feeling ever since we got back. I hate to say it, but I almost wish I wasn't right. I don't know if Ryu has had enough time to get out."

Fang followed her gaze to the imposing silhouette on the hill, still in the bright moonlight. They both stood there for quite some time, neither speaking. Just as he looked to his feline friend to break the silence, he watched as her fur bristled and ears perked.

"Fang..." The warning her voice carried made his own hair stand on end.

He quickly looked back to the building to see what looked like a lit lamp glowing in one of the windows of the ground floor. The gentle lamp light soon revealed itself to be much more ominous as it wavered erratically and grew, becoming a blaze very rapidly. Harizuka castle was on fire.

"Fang, open the window," Zifeara commanded urgently.

He complied, allowing her to leap deftly into the night, changing from cat to raven seamlessly.

As she sped towards the growing inferno, Fang rushed to shake Aun into consciousness. "C'mon, he's here. Zifeara's already going, we have to move, now!"

To his credit, Aun roused himself in record time and made for the window. Seeing his cohort wasn't following, he gave an exasperated sigh. "Fang, we're only on the second floor- the fall isn't far and you'll waste time going down the stairs. Just jump."

Aun was right... this was no time to be scared of such a short fall. Aun lept from the window, landing and quickly changing to his tiger form, looking back up to urge him out. Fang jumped and though his landing wasn't a perfect ten, it wasn't as bad as he'd thought it would be.

Aun growled once Fang had regained his footing. "Don't make a habit out of this, but get on. You run too slow."

Fang lept to do as Aun had asked, and the tiger starting to sprint before he had even gotten on securely. Holding onto nothing but fur was harder than keeping hold of a horse, but no one had even a second to spare; they had to go help Zifeara and they both felt the urgency of the situation. Not one of them knew who they were truly up against.

Zifeara entered the castle through a window on the fourth floor. This was where Ryu's bedroom was and was also the only window large enough to break through without hitting anything besides glass at her current size. The blaze had grown irrationally fast, meaning there was no way Torvak had just set a normal fire; he had to be a fire demon in order to keep this going. A strong one.

Once she had smashed through the glass, Zifeara rolled and shifted along the floor, crouching and scanning the room. Seeing no one, she descended the quickly failing stairs. The fire was too loud to hear anything unsubstantial over, so she would need to physically seek her target. If she was lucky, it would be seek and *destroy*, but she'd see about that when she got to him. Even if this fire wasn't natural, it still couldn't hurt her. She moved room to room, ducking in just enough to be certain Torvak wasn't there before moving on to the next. It wasn't until she got to Ryu's library that she found what she was after.

A man of around six feet tall was furiously tearing down decorative stone plinths that once housed jewels but now lay empty. His leathery black wings obscured much of his back, but Zifeara could tell he was sharply dressed; the tail of his crimson cloak forming a small puddle of fabric on the floor. As she stepped closer, the man must have sensed her and turned. His skin was grey, his eyes a piercing yellow, but where there should have been white, there was only blackness. His hair was a dark red, similar to a deep cherry wood and much of it was trapped in a bun on his head; secured by two extravagant looking skewers. His long pointed ears were pierced in several places and he had a faint scar over his left eye. He also had two red marks on either side of his face. While they looked like claw marks, they were too uniform in shape and size.

Zifeara would have guessed he was anywhere from thirty to eighty, mostly because with many demon species it was hard to judge lifespan, but before she could make a move for him, he smiled. His mouth was deceptively wide. It had looked of normal proportions, but as he grinned it pulled just wide enough to be disturbing.

His sharp teeth all came to fine points like a steel trap but his voice was smooth as silk. "You must be the one I've heard so much about. Zifeara, is it? You're much lovelier in person than I was led to believe. I don't suppose you'd be willing to tell me where Master Harizuka has gone to since you've come to attempt to kill me, would you?"

Zifeara glared. She didn't like that he sounded as though he knew exactly who she was. It never made things easier if the target had done his homework. "I assume you're here for the Inferno Ruby, then? I'm afraid it isn't here; Ryu has left for a business trip and taken it with him. Didn't say where he was going. You are, however, correct about why I'm here, Torvak. Though if you give up the ghost now, I won't have to do this. Immortality isn't what you think it is."

Zifeara knew she couldn't reason with crazy, but she also believed it didn't hurt to try. If talking this guy out of doing the immortality thing would save her five months of travel, she'd do it.

He laughed, a deep, sickening sound, and his teeth caused him to hiss involuntarily from inhaling quickly. "I'm afraid not my dear. I've worked too hard to get where I am, though you are most welcome to join me. From what I've heard of you, you'd make an excellent queen for a worldwide empire. Don't be put off by these teeth, I'd make it worth your while," he leered.

That was it- this guy was getting more than killed. He was getting to know what spitting out his own testicles through sheer force propelling them through his body felt like.

Hearing something crash downstairs, Torvak's expression changed from creepy smugness to annoyance. He reached into the satchel tied at his side for some object, but Zifeara didn't let him get to it. She charged him, going full panther, but this jerk was fast, giving his large wings a quick flap to dodge. Torvak drew a long sabre from a golden sheath tied at his waist.

"Come now, we both know this won't end favorably. I've heard of all your little tricks and have arrived prepared. Animals don't do well against weaponry."

While he was right on one count, Zifeara bet that Torvak didn't know as much as he thought. Ryu kept weapons in his study for decoration, but some of them were fully functional. The wall nearest Zifeara held a few fancy katanas, all mostly for show, but one. Ryu's father had used it to defend this land and he kept it polished and sharpened to perfection. As she shifted to her normal form and took hold of this sword, raising it in a position to signal she was ready for a duel, Torvak's eyes widened.

"Asshole, you don't know a damn *thing* about me. If you did, you'd know you really aren't my type."

She lunged forward again, this time putting her extensive weapons experience to use. Unfortunately, Torvak was very good with his sword as well. Block after block and graze after close miss, they seemed evenly matched. All the while, splintering wood, roaring, and several muted shots sounded from downstairs. Took the boys long enough to get here. Zifeara wondered what they could possibly be dealing with.

Distracted by the thought, Zifeara hissed as Torvak finally got a good jab in. She had managed to move back, but he still pierced her abdomen. Thank the gods she didn't have a normal human anatomy or it might have been bad. He came at her again, swinging in quick succession, giving her no time to do much else besides defend herself and look for a chance to try and shift her tail long enough to catch his legs. This guy may have been fast, but she had the experience to win. The searing pain that rocketed through her entire right side as she stumbled back from blocking the heavy swing that followed suggested otherwise. Even though he clearly saw her falter, Torvak backed off.

"I knew normal toxins would burn up in your bloodstream, therefore my blade is coated in one specifically designed to kill fire demons. Now, I do believe I must be going, this castle is starting to come down and I have stones to collect. It was wonderful meeting you," Torvak said calmly as he sheathed his sword and spread his wings.

He spun and with a flourish of his cape, he waltzed upstairs like nothing was amiss. While the thought of pursuing him definitely crossed her mind, the poison in her veins felt like something that wasn't to be taken lightly; it could be any concoction of substances, and she didn't know how hard it would be to recover from. It did hurt to move, but it was certainly only going to get worse the longer she took to get herself downstairs. The burning was starting to move slowly into her torso. She needed help.

As she limped through the fire on what was left of the stairs, she finally made it to the ground floor to see it littered with dead imps. They were all red and most of them either had their throats missing or limbs violently removed. She did notice that a few of had suspiciously round holes in them though. Torvak had brought friends to assist him in searching the castle but they had run into her own friends. She couldn't help but feel a little proud despite the situation; it was clear that Fang was getting better based on the locations of those bullet holes.

Just as Zifeara was about to call out for the boys, a tiger came crashing through a mostly disintegrated wall with a few imps clinging to it. As it roared and fought the small pests off, Fang emerged from a different room entirely, a little bit of blood dripping from one of his sleeves. He took aim near Aun, shooting an imp the tiger had thrown but not killed. He took three shots to finally end it as his hand was shaking too much to be accurate. It didn't escape her notice that he wasn't using his dominant shooting arm.

Fang turned once the imp was dead and caught sight of Zifeara as she was halfway down the stairs. He went to ask if she'd taken care of Torvak, but stopped when he noticed she was gripping her side. Before he could move to her aid, a large part of the ceiling collapsed just in front of him, making her hurry down the remaining stairs and towards the front doors.

"Come on, we need to get you two out of here, now!"

Fang wasted no time, moving the second Zifeara had, and Aun ran swiftly to the door as well, the last dead imp still in his mouth.

Finally outside and certain her friends were both present, Zifeara dropped to her knees. The pain was now everywhere except for her head and the very ends of her left extremities. She was hoping that was as far as it could get since maybe she hadn't gotten a full dosage.

Fang was on her in an instant. "Zifeara, what happened? Where are you hurt? What can I do?"

The awful thing about poisons intended for fire demons was that it prevented her body from healing as quickly as it should, and it also took longer to expel the toxin. It was definitely trying to clear itself as Zifeara felt her stomach turning, but she knew the last time this happened it had taken her a few hours to recover fully.

"It's not as bad as it looks, promise. He got me with a sword covered in an unpleasant toxin that hurts like a bitch and just generally sucks. Let's get back to the inn and we'll deal with it there. Are you two okay?"

Aun had been licking a scratch on his shoulder just behind them and he nodded that he was, but Fang sort of hid his left arm behind his torso.

"We're fine, Zia. Let me pick you up and we'll get you into bed."

She looked at him sympathetically. "Thank you, love, but I think Aun would be faster since your arm is hurt and he's bigger."

The tiger trotted over and chuffed, offering his shoulder so Zifeara could get on his back. Aun grinned so that Fang could see it and began hurrying their injured girl back to the inn. Fang managed to keep up, but just barely. Zifeara had been right, as per usual, but that didn't bring him any comfort.

Once in the room, Aun laid on the floor and licked the few battle wounds he had sustained. He was the least injured of the three. Fang attempted to get Zifeara to let him see what he could do for her wound, but she grabbed his bloody sleeve and pulled him onto the bed with her. She slid it up to reveal the rather large, ugly bite on his arm.

"Fine, huh?"

He looked at her sheepishly, mostly embarrassed that she instantly knew he'd tried to be a tough guy for her. Truth was, that bite burned like hell- enough to have made that side virtually useless earlier.

Zifeara dug around in her bag, producing some jars of gross-looking paste in two colors, one yellow and one white, along with some gauze. She smeared the yellow gunk on Fang's bite and quickly wrapped it, making him wonder what the white one was for.

"Fire imp bites don't naturally heal well but this should clear it up in a couple of days and make it hurt less in the meantime. Aun, will you leave for a few minutes? I have to deal with this hole in my side," she asked, wincing slightly from being upright to fix Fang's arm.

"What? Why just me? Why does he get to stay," Aun complained, his voice still deep and gravely from his shifted form.

"Because I need his help. Now, shoo," she said curtly.

Aun grumbled his way out of the room and Zifeara handed Fang the roll of gauze.

"This poison will take a while to pass through my system so I need you to help me wrap this to keep the salve on. It draws the stuff out so I don't have to try to throw it up." Before Fang could even agree to anything, Zifeara removed her shirt and used it to stem the fresh blood oozing from her wound at the sudden movement.

"I hate this shit. It's the one time being hurt is just inconvenient as opposed to being something I can be dead a while for." Grabbing the white stuff jar, she quickly plugged the wound with a large glob and turned around so that Fang could move the gauze around her without too much trouble.

While Fang had seen her in a bikini top before, he wasn't prepared for this. He found out that Zifeara didn't care to be historically accurate when it came to bras, and the one she was wearing was super cute too; entirely black with little red bats on it. Thankfully he managed to not stare too hard and focus on being useful since she was hurt. With Zifeara's instruction he did a pretty good job of dressing her wound, but he had tried not to touch even a centimeter of her bare skin. It was bad enough that she had just whipped her shirt off right in front of him, but he really didn't need that extra temptation. Looking anywhere else was hard enough that he almost missed her telling him he should wash the blood out of his shirt downstairs so he could hang it up tonight and have it dry by tomorrow.

"Zifeara, why don't you just burn the blood out of these?"

She opened her mouth to offer an explanation, but stopped short, "Actually, I could do for yours. Give it here."

He removed his shirt and handed it to her, watching as it began to blaze without burning. Fang had to assume he must be delicious due to the smell it produced. It smelled sort of like cooked deer, if he had to place it. He had never thought he was so gamey.

Instead of handing him his shirt back, however, Zifeara handed him hers. "Will you go wash mine, though? My blood doesn't burn for obvious reasons so I'd still have to get it clean eventually."

Taking her shirt, Fang got up and held his other hand out. "Sure. Can I have mine back, though? I do have to go all the way down to the kitchen for a sink and washboard."

That familiar, trouble-making grin spread across her face and Zifeara moved his shirt behind her back. "No. I'm keeping yours as collateral, just to make sure you do a good job."

Reddening slightly, he protested this assumption that he couldn't manage a shirt. "Zifeara, after all this time do you really think I can't handle *laundry*? Of all things?"

She giggled, coughing a little. "No, I just like making your life a little harder. You wanna fight me for it? Even hurt, I could more than take you~!"

It was times like these Fang wished he could think of a good way to easily tell Zifeara what it was she was doing to him. She was always at her most irresistible to him during her gentle teasing and now she was doing it *half in her underwear*.

"You know I'm not going to fight you, you brat," he mumbled, shaking his head and turning away to do as she had asked. The faster he did, the less time Aun would have to ogle her once he was allowed back in.

Making his way down the stairs, Fang received a few giggles, and several of the hotel's maids looked him over as they went about cleaning the empty rooms and floors for the night. He was going to have to get Zifeara back for this *somehow*; he could feel his entire body growing hot from how completely embarrassing this was. Finally getting to the kitchen, he found Aun raiding the pantry for late night snacks since he had been banished from their room.

"Uh, Fang? Where's your shirt, man?" the tiger asked, looking him up and down.

"Well, Zifeara took it to burn my blood out and now she won't give it back 'til I clean hers. Because her blood doesn't burn. All she had to do was ask, but nooo- she had to make me walk past damn near *every* woman employed here since they're all out cleaning right now!" He waved his arms emphatically as if to illustrate exactly how bothered he was, but the younger man merely blinked a few times before shrugging.

"You say that like it's a problem. Well, you have fun washing clothes. I'm taking snacks back up. Zifeara's probably as hungry as I am by now," Aun said as he piled fruits and biscuits into a small sack.

"You know," Fang began, "you're about to go past an awful lot of staff who will see you taking all of that."

Aun grinned, "Who said I was using the stairs? I'm going outside and back in through our window! This isn't my first raid. Later, shirtless loser."

With that and a tiny salute, Aun did indeed back his way out the door to the alley just outside. Fang rolled his eyes and went to the sinks, looking in all the cupboards until he finally found where they kept their towels and cleaning things. Flammable or not, Zifeara's blood was just as susceptible to soap and water as anything else.

Watching all the red swirl around in the basin, Fang wondered for the first time what hers actually tasted like. He had never had blood that wasn't from an animal, despite there being bars in New Tinning designed specifically for those who drank it. Loads of different humans and demons alike showed up at these places to either satisfy their thirst for warm, exotic blood or to earn some money providing for those who drank in a place they were guaranteed to be safe. Fang had never been to one, mostly because he thought it'd be kind of awkward. Sure he craved blood like a frog craved water, but he'd never once been able to bring himself to try and get it from the source. There was something about it that just made him feel wrong even though it was socially acceptable and even something his race was born for.

This had never happened to him before; smelling the blood coming out of Zifeara's shirt gave him that sort of hazy feeling the boar had the first time. Just the scent was making his mouth water. He'd never smelled anything like it. *Zifeara would never know he'd done it.*

As soon as he had the thought, Fang felt ashamed of himself and it snapped him back to reality. He'd know and it would be *really* creepy. Putting it out of his mind, he quickly finished what he was doing and gave the shirt a good wringing to get most of the water out. Zifeara could dry her own damn laundry.

Moving as fast as he could past the still staring staff, he returned to their room, finding Zifeara with an apple shoved in her mouth digging for something in her bag and Aun talking with his mouth full about some type of fruit he was gorging on.

Looking up at his return, Zifeara removed the food from her face. "There you are. Do you remember what the hell that book was called, about that island where people started dropping like flies and their land was blighted and they had to fix it and whatever? I can't quite remember for some reason or another so I can't find it."

Aun swallowed, turning his ears back. "How in the world do you expect him to know what you're on about based on-"

"Catahullowa's Curse?" Fang asked, "The one with that super buff dude and the weird bird things?"

Zifeara's eyes brightened. "Yes! That's the one!" She rummaged just a bit more before producing a thick book and handing it to Aun.

"How in the world did you even..." he said, mouth slightly ajar.

"When you've known someone well enough for a long time, you don't have to make any sense for them to know what you mean," Zifeara replied, finally taking an actual bite out of her apple.

"True," Fang said plopping himself on their bed. "Now, where did you stash my shirt, woman?"

Zifeara just continued to eat, eyes crinkling with amusement over her fruit and her tail wagging slightly in enjoyment of her continued torment of her friend.

After maintaining unwavering eye contact with her for a solid ten seconds, Fang narrowed his eyes. "It's under the bed, isn't it?"

Grin turning to a mock pout, Zifeara gave up. "You're no fun."

Fang threw the freshly clean shirt he was holding at her, dipping under their bed and retrieving his. Hearing her giggle through another mouthful, he couldn't help but laugh too. He'd get her back for this... once he stopped being so goddamn in love.

CHAPTER 22

I Lie Because You Need Me To. Probably.

Fang had about five seconds to make this shot. He'd already missed twice and was in a lot of trouble now. He aimed well, but his target was faster, watching him move and correcting to avoid being hit. *Three seconds.* Now it was down to the wire and the shot would be point blank. He had to make this. Pulling the trigger again, he barely even grazed its shoulder. Fuck. *One second.* That was it. Fang closed his eyes as he was hit full force and slammed to the ground, the massive jaws inches from his throat. The heavy weight on his chest would have robbed him of precious air, had he needed it. He could feel the pinpricks of pain as the sharp fangs closed in around his neck, promising at least to cut off blood flow, at most to cut off his head. Slowly the pressure lessened as he kept his eyes shut, dreading what awaited him.

"You're dead," a whisper brushed by his ear, soft enough that he almost couldn't hear it. He finally looked up. Zifeara was laying on him, no longer the slick panther he had been trying to shoot, just hanging out on his chest, looking unimpressed.

"*Dios*, Fang, I don't get it. You did fine when Aun ran at you earlier- more than fine even, why can you not hit me *literally* to save your life?"

Stammering due to her close proximity and suggestive posture, Fang didn't really have an answer. "I-I don't know Zia... You're just so... fast. Aun runs slower and, well, you don't. Besides, I only technically killed Aun maybe, like, twice out of five times. I think? Um..."

Zifeara rolled off him and stood, holding her hand out to pull him up. "I thought since you proved yourself well enough against the imps at Ryu's, you were ready for things coming *at* you, but this doesn't feel like you're doing as well as you could be. I don't think there's *that* much of a difference between Aun and I. Is there? Tell me what I'm doing wrong, I *want* you to get this so badly."

Fang scratched the back of his head, trying to think of a better excuse besides her just being really quick and not wanting to shoot her, even with what he knew was paint. He was fully aware this couldn't possibly hurt her, but... he just couldn't do it.

She looked to their younger friend, still using a wet rag to wipe paint out of his hair while he awaited proper clean up. "I don't know Zifeara, you have more experience with guns than I do, so maybe that's it? You inherently know how to move and I don't?"

They had been drilling Fang harder since leaving Oranda almost a week ago, attempting to get him to aim well under the pressure of being actively attacked as opposed to being the supporting fire for everyone else. He wasn't doing spectacularly well. Sure, he'd hit Aun well enough to seriously injure him and eventually kill him, but none of his *initial* shots had been fatal. And forget about hitting Zifeara. Fang couldn't even *mortally wound* her yet.

Sighing, she threw in the towel. "That's enough for today, we have to get going. C'mere Aun, let me get that off you."

"Maybe it's just my reaction time under pressure," Fang said aloud, causing Zifeara to look back towards him. "Since I can usually at least hit Aun, maybe my brain reasons that since he's hurt I have time to take another shot before I'm in danger. You're just so quick that I can't hit you at all, so I panic and do worse." To him, that sounded like as good a reason as any.

Zifeara considered this for a moment. "That could be, yeah. I'll have to think about what to do with you, then. We'll figure it out tomorrow, let's go."

Getting back on the trail, the group was heading to where Zifeara thought Torvak might go next. The mountainous forest they were in stretched on for quite a while, but the massive lake in the middle of it supported a large group of people who had dredged up a very special stone centuries ago. The massive quartz was the color of mud even after being washed numerous times and seemed to be able to predict earthquakes. Anytime a quake was near, the stone began to ring, similar to a tuning fork, and would continue for up to three days before it hit. The stronger the shake, the longer it rang.

The villagers considered it sacred since it had such a connection to the soil and had saved them from disaster many times. Which made it ripe for the stealing if you wanted elemental stones to grant immortality. Moving through the mountains wasn't the fastest either, the rockier terrain frequently robbing them of clear paths. This was still a forest, so they weren't in the Hasagawa range quite yet. Zifeara had them skirt it for the sake of speed.

This stretch was, however, perfect for reading, which Fang was doing a lot of. Zifeara was surprised when he asked for books the first day out of Oranda but had refused the sci-fi novels he usually loved in favor of medical texts and field guides. She actually kind of felt a little guilty for giving him such shit over the hemlock, but if this was the result then so be it. He took everything she had to offer eagerly and she hadn't felt this proud of him since he graduated second in his class in high school. He had never been to college, since it would be a waste of time, but she didn't think he was trying to make up for it now. It seemed to her he genuinely wanted to know more about the world around him. She must have been staring at Fang while she was thinking because he looked up, feeling as though he were being watched.

"What?" he asked, somewhat absentmindedly.

"Oh nothing, it's just cool that you've taken such a serious interest in learning important things lately, that's all. Hell, some of the stuff you've asked me for doesn't even really apply to you, but you've read it anyway. It's nice to see you reading."

He shrugged and went back to his book, reclining on Treble's back and moving his tome in such a way that she couldn't see his widening giddy smile. Reading *was* nice. It made him smarter than Aun. Zifeara liked smarter.

The path they were on was large enough so that all three horses could walk side by side, but that never lasted very long. Tonight, they would have to rest, so they chose a rocky outcropping that very nearly formed a large cave.

Settling in, Aun was now favoring a sleeping bag since there were few suitable trees for him to sleep in. He had to admit, it was pretty comfortable. He had borrowed some books too, though he had chosen ones written very close to his own time he hadn't read before. Zifeara had books from all periods and it was proving to be fun to read. Aun's village only had so many books and he didn't often get a chance to trade with neighboring clans, so he was taking advantage of this trove of an unlimited library while it lasted.

Zifeara looked from one reading boy to the other and chuckled. "My gods, it's almost boring having you two so absorbed. If it wasn't so damn fulfilling to watch you both enjoying reading for once, I'd tell you to knock it off!"

They both looked up and at each other, almost unaware they had both lapsed into book comas for the past several days.

"Zifeara, what do you read in your time off? It must be strange since you remember everything every time," Aun asked.

"I still reread every single book I have periodically," she replied, settling in to sleep. "Just because I remember what happens doesn't mean I don't still enjoy it. Plus, I write my own books, so I can always make up new stories as I go."

"What do you write?" Aun pressed.

Zifeara took a book out of her bag and tossed it over to him. The cover had a young lady on it, walking down a school hallway, people staring in shock as she had ears and a tail while no one else did. She looked mostly like a cat demon surrounded by humans. "It's about an alien princess who flees an arranged marriage on her home world to go live amongst her favorite creatures to study: humans. Her planet is made up entirely of a race of technologically advanced shapeshifters and the human planet is called

Earth. She tries to fit in and has misadventures. You can read it if you like, but I'm working on book three right now, so you might want to wait."

"Wait," he ventured, "you named your all human planet after *dirt*? Like, the earth beneath our feet, Earth?"

Zifeara shrugged. "Sure, it seemed funny to me."

Fang chimed in over his own tome, "It's pretty good. I think you'll like it, honestly. Even if you don't understand some of the technology, it's easy enough to explain."

Aun shrugged. "Yeah, I'm game. I'll start this one after I finish the one I'm on."

He threw her book back for safekeeping and continued reading his story about a man trapped at sea. Once everyone settled in for sleep, stories gave way to dreams for all.

While Aun dreamed a muddled mix of things of his home and his mystery man's life, Fang was dreaming of something else that had happened a long time ago. He was facing a mirror in his old room at Zifeara's house and was dressed rather sharply. This had to have been for his senior prom since that was the only time in his life he'd ever worn a tuxedo. At Zifeara's insistence, of course. He turned and left, going downstairs and waiting to receive the keys to the new car Zifeara had bought him for his birthday, along with the SoundCave.

"Mortichai, what's the one rule?" Zifeara was holding the keys just behind her enough that he couldn't take them, but not so much that he couldn't see them.

"Conduct myself with grace and intelligence no matter what I do?"

Her stern look melted into a bittersweet smile as she sighed. "You're your own man now at eighteen and I can't tell you how to live your life, but I can try to keep you from making an ass of yourself. At least you listen. Go on then, have fun, and for Dios' sake, don't forget that you have a center console in that car. Use it wisely."

She tossed him the keys, which he very nearly didn't catch, but he didn't have time to ask what she meant about the console before she went back up the stairs to her room; he had to go pick up his date. This new car drove to its destination automatically since Fang was too blind to manually drive himself, so he decided to investigate what Zifeara could possibly have meant. As it turned out, Zifeara meant to embarrass the ever-living shit out of him.

She legitimately, and not in any form of jest, had placed a few condoms in amongst his other things. Taking the entire ride to his date's house to recover any composure he had left, he made sure to hide them under other things just in case for any conceivable reason he needed to open it in front of her.

Bridget and Fang had been friends for years; at least since middle school. She had transferred to their class from the region just south of Queylinth, the small island nation of Carrig. She was a magpie, her long iridescent black wings tipped in white and far too large for her slender frame. She always looked as though one strong gust of wind would carry her off. Her pale skin contrasted immensely with her straight black hair, similar in appearance to her wings, and her dark eyes always made her look a bit sad. Bridget had a pretty rough time making the switch, as most of the children at school had known each other for years, so there were very specific cliques already standing.

Fang had seen her and simply thought she looked a lot like he had when he started school, so had said hello. She had proven to be very intelligent but also very shy, tending to stick to her drawing pad like glue. Bridget was the only one who had managed to get better grades than he did in the entire school come graduation day. They had done everything together for so long, it only seemed natural for him to develop a bit of a crush.

Once he arrived at Bridget's house, he noticed she was waiting outside, wearing a floor length dress as black as her wings. As nice as the evening had been, this was before Fang had become immortal, so only bits and pieces of the memory were swirling around. By the end of it, however, it turned out Zifeara was completely right; that was in fact, the night he lost his virginity, and had figured out that his car had collapsible seats. He and Bridget had dated for about two years before they both agreed to just go back to being friends. They had a good run, but she wanted to move back to Carrig for school and there was no way in Hell or elsewhere Fang was leaving New Tinning. Changing over to some other time, Fang continued to realize with memories of his second ex that he definitely had a type.

Meanwhile, Zifeara found herself sitting in a clearing covered in snow, somewhere mountainous and rocky. She would have guessed they were in the alpine section of Marien, but it was hard to be sure. Large, defined flakes were falling and the surrounding area was dead silent; devoid of any signs of life. She knew this meant her mother had something else for her to do, but she wasn't expecting Lucifer to make a tame entrance compared to her usual antics.

The Queen of Hell simply strode through the few trees there were, scorching bark and melting snow as she moved. "Hello, sweetheart. How's the adventure coming? Your boys look like they're getting along better."

Zifeara rose to meet her mother. "Yeah, I think they are, oddly enough. It's weird, they're both currently reading a lot and not talking to each other. It's preferable to fighting, so I'll take it. So, what do I have to do now?"

"Well, I have a small errand for you, but it will take you awhile to get to where you need to be," she said matter of factly. "In the bustling city of Usakara there is currently a kitsune stealing and ingesting souls. Since she works in a brothel- an excellent business choice- this means she's been taking souls that are mine in particular. I need her taken care of as soon as you get there."

"Yeah, we should be able to make it there in about two weeks I think," Zifeara said, "though we'll see how quickly we can actually get there." They were probably going to have to pass through that damn place anyway, now it just meant they'd be spending longer than she'd like there. She hated that town.

Lucifer nodded and changed the subject to less formal matters. "You know, it's been so much fun watching you all lately, but I can't help but notice how much trouble Fang has been having aiming correctly when it comes to hitting you. Have you thought of why that would be?"

Zifeara shook her head and ran a hand through her hair. "I don't know what I'm doing wrong! He can shoot Aun alright, not perfectly but he's getting much better, so I don't know what I'm doing differently. He thinks it's just because I'm faster, but I can't help but think it's something else. I can't put my finger on it, but... something is up with him. He says he's fine every time I ask... The stress of being in another time might be getting to him. I *knew* this would happen."

Lucifer smiled a knowing but unsettling smile. She could read the negative emotions surging through beings at any given time and could watch what was happening during said emotion, so she very familiar with what Fang's issue was. She enjoyed watching him suffer through it, however, so there was no way she was spoiling this surprise. She could, completely and without a shred of regret, stir the pot of shit that was brewing.

"Maybe you're working harder instead of smarter, dear." Zifeara gave her mother a questioning look so Lucifer continued her thought. "What if you could trick him into doing better? Doesn't he usually do best providing covering fire?"

She waited, watching her daughter think and try to imagine the exact scenario she had in mind. One more gentle push should connect the dots. "You and Aun are both shapeshifters, right?"

Lucifer could almost see the light bulb burst over Zifeara's head. "Do... do you really think that would work? *Why* would that work...? I'd have to send him out hunting so I could make sure Aun is close enough to... That's insane, but it might do the trick."

Lucifer simply waved and turned to go back the way she came, leaving her daughter to wake.

¤ ¤ ¤

"Alright, Aun, we have to get this right the first time- I have no idea how long he'll be gone."

She had sent Fang off for their morning hunt even though he could have sworn they still had some food left. He did know for certain that questioning Zifeara was ill advised, so out he went. She helped Aun shift into as perfect a copy of herself as she could possibly manage and made him practice turning into and speaking as her on command, over and over again, until they could hear Fang coming back around forty minutes after he had left.

Once he had deposited his catch somewhere it would be easy for Zifeara to cook it, Fang looked to the stretch of forest his friends were standing in. The land was flat but had several rocks jutting here and there off to one side, and it looked as though they were talking about some sort of maneuver Zifeara wanted the already-shifted tiger to do. They appeared ready to do morning training before breakfast. As he switched his clips out and began to walk towards them, Zia caught sight of him and motioned that she'd like him to wait where he was.

She turned away from him to say something to Aun before yelling over her shoulder. "Alright, Fang, we're doing something a little different today. Try to hit Aun."

Fang didn't see how this was different from any other day, but there was something about Zifeara that seemed... wrong. He couldn't tell if it was just the way she sounded or the way she was standing, but she was just plain off. Before he could ask, he noticed that Aun had wandered off to the side and stretched out slightly, preparing to do his part, but he wasn't aimed right for their normal pacing run. The tiger crouched and hadn't waited for Zifeara to return and watch how he was holding his gun or aiming. She had turned towards him, but Zifeara stood her ground, arms crossed and relaxed. Aun bolted forward, kicking up dust and instead of moving straight across as he usually did for target practice, or even running towards *him*, he made a beeline for Zifeara. She wasn't even looking at the tiger.

Something was completely wrong about this. Aun wasn't slowing down, he was eyeing his target to figure out where he was going to make contact, and he was moving in a way that made it hard to predict his actions. *Aun was going to hurt Zifeara.* Fang reflexively aimed and fired, mostly forgetting he was armed with paint now. He fired twice, both shots finding their mark right between the eyes, one higher than the other.

Aun roared and skidded to a halt, inches from touching Zifeara's back. Fang shakily exhaled the breath he hadn't realized he'd been holding as the tiger peeked around her and went to speak. It was *not* Aun's voice that came out of that cat.

"Holy shit, I can't believe that actually worked! You hit me. Fatally. *Twice!*" Zifeara was beside herself and suddenly it clicked in Fang's head. If *that* was Zifeara...

Aun's voice coming from Zifeara's mouth was unsettling, to put it lightly. "Well, I'll be damned. Who knew. I guess it was because you're you; he aimed just fine as long as he thought you were me. Thanks, Fang, good to know I can *trust you*... asshole."

As both of his friends returned to their normal selves, all Fang could do was stare. He had really managed to hit Zifeara dead on. He just had to think he was saving her. *Dios*, he sucked. Speaking of whom, Zifeara had run over to congratulate him on the impossible, but had chosen to do so by tackle hugging him.

She threw her arms around his neck, bumping their foreheads together. "See, I *knew* you could do it! It was all in your head and we just had to *make* you do it. Now let's do it again, but without the lying."

The next several times Zifeara ran at him, even as faster predators, he had managed to land good shots, at least half of which were fatal. He was getting better. Immediately. She had done it- she had fixed him entirely and now it was just practice. Lucifer sat on her throne, deep down in Hell, laughing her ass off.

Fang felt like an idiot; literally all it took to turn him into an absolute sharpshooter was to think Zifeara was in trouble. She was, without a doubt, going to give him shit about this- he could feel it already. Meanwhile she and Aun were raving about what a good performance he'd given since he wasn't used to having to copy someone's appearance or voice to a T.

"That was definitely impressive, Aun. I didn't think you'd be able to get it down so well so fast. This means tomorrow morning we can start alternating between training Fang and working on your shifting. Your unshifted combat still needs work too..."

Aun shrugged. "Yeah, it does, but I think I've gotten better since we started."

Zifeara nodded. "You have, but you still haven't hit me solidly yet. Actually *neither* of you have. We'll work on that next, but for now, we still have to get to Tsuruya."

CHAPTER 23

Missed Opportunities

Once night fell, the horses seemed nervous and Zifeara asked Orro Heme what was wrong.

"He says something doesn't feel right, that there's something in these woods that wants to hurt us. He isn't exactly wrong, there are a few unsavory creatures in this part of the world, but I haven't heard much of anything major lately, have you guys?"

Fang turned his headphones off and listened. Aun perked his ears up as well, but neither boy heard anything aside from regular animal life and a few of the mischievous tiny goblins and faeries that inhabited any forest. Zifeara shifted to get an aerial view of their surroundings, but she couldn't see much out of the ordinary either. She did, however, take Aun off with her to dispatch a group of venomfang wolves they would have to go through to continue on the path. Once they were dead, she moved the horses along, staying on foot just in case whatever was scaring them showed itself.

As soon as daybreak hit, Zifeara took them on a little detour to get water from a small stream. The water flowed swiftly at all times of the year, but it was almost warm now that summer was well underway. The stream also lead to a small pond before continuing on through the hills, providing the perfect place to relax for a moment. Seeing the water was relatively clear, Aun decided now would be a great time for shapeshifting shenanigans. Zifeara was sitting on a decently sized boulder having already filled the jugs. She had her feet in the pool and was describing the city they were heading to for Fang.

Aun quietly turned to his tiger form, all 400 pounds artfully sneaking. Fang also had his feet in the water, but he was lying down on a smaller, flatter rock on the other side of Zifeara, so he couldn't see the large cat. Once close enough, Aun leapt up onto Zifeara's rock just behind her, using his girth to press against her back and shoved her off into the pond. Fang shot upright at the splashing noise to see Zifeara treading water, hair everywhere and glaring hard at the tiger perched upon her rock in hysterics. Seeing Zifeara looking like a wet housecat made Fang crack up as well. Huffing, she disappeared below the surface and was under just long enough for the laughter to die down and cause both boys to look at each other with concern.

"Do you think she's-" Aun didn't get to finish his sentence.

A crocodile burst through the still surface of the water and grabbed on to Fang's legs, managing to fit both of them perfectly between all the teeth as not to be painful. Dragging him back into the pond, Zifeara let herself sink to the bottom and settle on the soft silt, hopefully giving Aun enough time to worry about being next. Fang knew he wasn't going to drown, so once the initial panic had passed, he stilled, legs held fast, arms crossed and giving his toothy captor a disapproving glare. She made a deep rumbling sound that was intermittent and must have been the large reptile equivalent of mocking him. Zifeara opened her mouth slightly to release him, changing in size and becoming smaller while much furrier. The otter swam a few circles around him, checking him over to confirm she hadn't really hurt him and chittering happily to assure him it was all in good fun before shooting up and out of the water.

Fang hadn't made it the entire twelve or so feet to the surface when something splashed back down into the pond just near his head. Now there were two otters, squabbling and pawing at each other as they raced and spiraled around the entirety of the body of water. Fang just sat patiently, not wanting to swim further in case the water weasels decided to run into him. He did not need to be in the middle of that scratching and squeaking. He was content to watch anyway; he had always liked otters and how gracefully they moved through the water. Even while play fighting, Zifeara and Aun were turning and gliding as though they had been born as otters and just forgot about it sometimes.

Aun had to go back up for air but Zifeara simply turned to glance his way. Otters always look like happy creatures, but she seemed especially jubilant, like she was having so much fun. It wasn't every day she got to do this with someone; shifters were a rare thing, even in their time. Fang realized with a twinge of sadness that she was starting to treat Aun similarly to how she treated him. It was great that she had a new friend but didn't bode well for his chances with her. He hauled himself out, content to watch the other two play from land where he was out of the way. After a bit more frolicking and general tomfoolery, the otters decided they were done as well.

"Aun, when have *you* seen an otter? They aren't endemic to your waters and aren't very common to any region near yours," Zifeara asked. "As good as you're getting at this, I don't think you had nearly enough time to copy me while I was latched onto your face."

Fang was sort of sad he'd missed that particular sequence of events.

Aun laughed somewhat wistfully, still wringing water out of the bottom of his shirt. "Believe it or not, once in a while we get traveling traders and whatever who have pretty good relations with all the tiger clans. They travel coast to coast up through our forest, passing goods between us all since most of the elements don't like each other. One trader we knew pretty well had a pet otter that he picked up from the southern coast at one of the port towns. He used to let me play with it when I was a cub and I loved that little guy."

That night Zifeara had them stop for the horses to sleep but chose to read after dinner instead of rest. While Fang wasn't particularly tired, he had managed to fall asleep sitting next to her as she absentmindedly hummed from time to time while she read. He awoke to something lightly tapping on his head. He sat up quickly to see Zifeara standing behind him, starting to back up towards the woods around the clearing they were camping in and motioning for him to follow. She held a finger over her lips and pointed to Aun, and Fang guessed he was meant to let the sleeping cat lie. He got up as silently as he could, following his friend into the dark forest.

Once they were a bit away from camp, Zifeara whispered, "I wanted to show you something cool around here, but I don't think Aun would care. Besides, it's been kinda hectic lately and I haven't really taken you guys anywhere interesting that I know about. This is one of my favorite spots so we can't miss it!"

Fang smiled and followed eagerly, his heart beating fast at the prospect of having Zifeara to himself for a while. He might be able to do this. Hell, he had just managed to finally shoot her, he might have it in him. Pushing through a stand of dense shrubs, they came out to what looked like a short, narrow opening in a tall rock face.

"C'mon, in here. It widens out once you get inside," she said, already crawling into the deep void that was this cave.

Fang swallowed hard and ducked inside. It was so dark that the moonlight outside didn't make it more than a few inches into the cave.

"Zifeara," Fang called softly, "Zia, where did you go?" He didn't receive an answer nor did he see any light from where she might be. He sighed, turning his headphones off. She was testing him even now that they were supposed to be having fun.

He pressed his tongue against the roof of his mouth and brought it down hard, making a high-pitched clicking sound- like hitting two stones together. While his race had gained the ability to echolocate centuries ago, most of them never really needed to do it anymore considering all the technology available to them. The sound bouncing off solid objects formed something like a snapshot of the surrounding area which Fang could visualize and interpret with speed. Granted, he may have been a little rusty with the skill, which was probably why Zifeara was making him do this. That and she just *liked* messing with him.

The cave was large enough for him to stand in now but was mostly a jagged corridor for about 100 feet in front of him, at the end of which he had just seen the tip of Zifeara's tail vanish to the right. Fang walked forward, clicking as he went to avoid sharp stones on the floor, and turned to his right. A faint blue glow was coming from up ahead and the closer he got, the more he could see the floor slope downwards and around another corner.

Finally coming into an open area, Fang found the source of the light. Mushrooms of all sizes from a marble to a football littered the floor and climbed about two feet up the walls in places, all around what looked to be a cavern full of water. On the ceiling, thousands of tiny mushrooms hung like stars in the night sky and created a galaxy that reflected in the pool below. Fang's mouth hung open for a solid minute as he looked around, eventually spotting Zifeara sitting on an open patch of ground just shy of the water, looking at him expectantly.

"It's amazing, isn't it? This cave has been here for a little over 2,000 years and every time I come in, it looks even more impressive."

He sat down next to her, shoulder to shoulder, the blue glow softly illuminating them both. The more of the room he took in, the more he realized there was so much he would have missed out on learning had he not been so insistent that he come on this trip. This was something that just didn't exist in the time he lived in and even people in this time likely weren't aware of its existence, given how hidden the cave was. It was stirring an awful lot of emotion in him for fungus.

"Zia, those aren't really mushrooms on the ceiling, are they? They look like they're... moving."

Her smile broadened and her eyes were wide, reflecting the glow of the cave just as accurately as the pool at her feet. "No, not exactly. What you're seeing are small, grub-like insects moving across hammocks of sticky silk. They've formed a symbiotic relationship with the mushrooms in this cave; the grubs actually grow small mushrooms on their backs to attract flying insects passing through to the other side and they get stuck in the silk. The grub pulls the insect into its mouth full of garbage disposal teeth and digests it, later secreting a sort of nectar which it then dabs at the base of its mushrooms. Sometimes the flying insects get confused and fly to the lights reflected in the water, where they're then eaten by blind cave fish who sense the vibrations. It's ridiculously amazing, the fish-"

Watching Zifeara explain all of this with such animated detail and a look of absolute wonder in her eyes made Fang's heart swell. He loved it when she got really into something and lost herself talking about it. It was stupidly cute and she didn't do it often. Even with all her time seeing all there was to see, she could still be fascinated with something she watched take shape and had returned to again and again over the centuries. Zifeara made immortality seem not so bad.

Turning to see if Fang was as enthralled as she was, Zifeara instead found him staring at her.

"Whaaat?" she asked, feeling self-conscious.

She knew she did have a tendency to ramble, which is why she thought Aun would be bored. That, and a bunch of bugs probably weren't interesting to someone who had lived in a forest all their lives.

"N-nothing," Fang replied hurriedly. "It's just really cool that you know all of this, that's... that's all."

He had looked away, but Zifeara thought he was acting strangely. They had been talking very softly since Fang wasn't wearing his headphones and they didn't want to scare the cave dwellers, but this silence seemed abnormally heavy for the two of them. Zifeara could usually sit next to Fang without saying anything for hours, but she couldn't place why this was so different. Had she said something weird? More often than not when she had gone on a knowledge tangent, he just let her and asked questions along the way, but it felt like he was trying to humor her this time. Like he wanted to say something but politely wasn't.

As if things weren't weird enough, he started displaying what she knew to be one of his nervous ticks. Since she had leaned back, she was close enough to feel when he gently rested a few of his long fingers across hers. He always touched her in some minute way if he was stressed enough- said it calmed him down to know she was right there. He didn't look at her again, instead watching the blobs of light he now knew to be grubs crawl slowly across their sticky threads. She didn't move in the slightest. Whatever storm was moving through his head right now, he'd tell her as soon as he figured out how. They told each other just about everything, so he was well aware she was beyond receptive to hearing out his insecurities.

After watching the insects move around for several minutes, Fang finally broke the awkward silence. "Hey Zifeara?"

"Y-yeah?" she asked with concern.

Great, he had made her uncomfortable because he was nervous. Somehow he'd thought touching her would make this easier and it *really* hadn't.

"You..." *Come on, just fucking get it over with- tell her you love her you incompetent fool.* There was nothing *but* perfect romantic atmosphere in this cave, besides the fact that there were hideous bugs above them. If he knew Zifeara half as well as he should, that wasn't exactly a negative.

"You know that... you're the most important person in the world to me, right?" That was *not* how he wanted it to come out; he sounded way too overbearing. This was not a good start.

"I- I mean sure, Fang. We've been through a lot together and I can't think of many people I've liked as much as I like you," Zifeara said looking a little flustered. Her ears were tilting away from him, not all the way down yet and she was doing that thing with her tail; just the very tip of it always started to twitch when she was nervous.

As far as Fang could tell, she appeared to be the kind of embarrassed people only get when they aren't sure of what to do in a situation they've never been in before, which was definitely uncommon for Zifeara. He couldn't remember the last time he had seen her that way and he honestly didn't know if that was a good thing or not.

She continued talking, clearly not intending to let the silence take over again, "Well, obviously if I went through all the trouble of turning you immortal, I *must* like you in particular. I'd probably never get to do that again for anyone else..."

Fang had lost track of where he had been going with this for just long enough to let the stupid fall out of his mouth. "Would you want to do it for anyone else?"

Shit, that wasn't even *close* to what he had needed to say. Zifeara turned to look at him immediately, her expression halfway between confused and indignant. Before Fang could try to correct himself, her face lit up as though she had an epiphany.

"Is *that* what this is about?"

He tensed, face quickly heating up and held his breath. Of course she knew what was going on. She must have noticed his erratic behavior recently, especially upon meeting Aun, and pieced it all together. He was doomed. She was going to tell him off and that would be the end of everything.

Zifeara relaxed and laughed, removing her hand from under his to use it to gently shove him. "You're *jealous,* aren't you?"

"Wha- of-? What do I have to be jealous *of*!?"

Now she was sitting up straighter, sitting up on her knees in that way-too-excited-puppy way she did every so often when she was about to give him hell. "Fang, no one could *ever* replace you as my best friend, we're too good together. Aun is fun, yeah, but he could never be you! You silly jealous bat- you feel like you're getting replaced!"

Fang still didn't exhale. He was dumbfounded. She really hadn't figured it out, she just thought he didn't want to share her attention. That wasn't untrue, but Zifeara truly *was* oblivious to all the blatantly obvious signs that he was smitten and how he'd been trying to flirt with her in the softest way possible for the past couple of days. He couldn't believe she hadn't noticed by now- like- he'd just done the gentle hand touching, what more did he even *have* at this point? He refused to be obnoxious about it like the tiger. That was not how you treated a lady, especially not one important to you.

For just about the millionth time, Fang chickened out as Zifeara continued to tease him about thinking he was becoming less important to her, backhandedly assuring him that could never happen. While he appreciated the sentiment, it wasn't helping to ease the red out of his practically glowing cheeks, nor was the fact that she was leaning on him for a better angle to poke at all the places in his ribs she knew made him laugh. By the time they were both giggling messes and he shoved her off, he pretended to look back down at the water, trying to collect his thoughts and settle back down. That wasn't completely the worst attempt at this to date, but it was always his mouth that ruined it. He couldn't just *kiss her* either. That gave her no options and would likely end with him on fire.

Eventually they got up to leave, making their way back out of the cave, and Zifeara grabbed his hand once they were in the open.

"Hey." She looked up at him and smiled, pulling him into a hug. "I meant it; there's not one living soul I would trade you for. Nobody else could possibly be *my* DJ."

Fang held her close, taking comfort in at least being the most important person in her world too, even if it wasn't in the way he wanted to be. He loved Zifeara more than anything and love was patient, if more often than not a bumbling idiot that couldn't think straight. It had to be patient or it ran the risk of ruining everything you had and quite possibly blowing up in your face in a very literal sense.

CHAPTER 24

Stick Smacking

As morning came, Aun was the first one awake. He hadn't dreamt of that guy, but he had been dreaming of his own family. He had gone back after years of exploring the world and they were all just gone; simply vanished without any sign of what had happened to them. He thought he really shouldn't have cared since they were never all that special to him, but he felt very unsettled. He figured he was just a little homesick from being somewhere new and went for a walk to shake it off. He began to shift into his tiger form, but thought about the training Zifeara was making him do to acclimate him to unusual shifts and decided to be something out of his comfort zone today.

It turned out being a squirrel was kind of fun. He jumped from branch to branch through the trees, watching a few other animals below him and enjoying the feel of the rough bark beneath his paws. He was beginning to understand why Zifeara had insisted he try new animals. There was no way he'd tell her as much though- she'd be far too smug about it.

While out and about, he came across a small meadow, tucked neatly in a grove of trees. Since spring had just passed, the grassy area was full of flowers of all types, taking advantage of the bountiful sunlight and absence of snow. Skittering down his current tree, Aun shifted back into his tiger form once he was in the open in case a hawk or some other predator decided he looked tasty. He didn't really want to deal with that right now.

As he strode into the flower grove, he inhaled deeply. Some of these flowers grew in his forest too, but they mixed with the smells of unfamiliar flora and it was a little disorienting. It smelled so much like home but so different all at once. He looked around and made sure no one had followed him out here before indulging in one of his favorite childish activities; he flopped himself down and rolled in the fresh grass, infusing his fur with the smell of the plants and the warmth of the morning sun they held. It was a silly looking thing for a giant, fearsome cat to do, but it always served to calm him down when he was feeling stressed. It was hard to worry when you could smell nature and wiggle around like a cub. He lay on his back soaking up the strengthening rays and breathing in the soothing scent of freshly crushed grass for quite some time before he decided he best head back. The other two would surely be up soon, no doubt deciding they needed to use him for something fighting related.

Aun got up to go but paused, examining the spread of flowers and myriad of colors before him. He shifted briefly and wandered back through, gathering a few different types of blooms in red and white before turning cat again and holding the flowers as gently as his saber fangs would allow. Heading back to camp, he couldn't remember if he had asked Zifeara what her favorite color was or not, but he figured red was a pretty safe choice and white went with everything.

By the time he made into their clearing, Fang and Zifeara were deep in discussion about where he could be since they needed to either train or get going.

Zifeara caught sight of him first. "I don't know, Fang. I'm gonna fly up and - oh, there you are, Aun. I was just about to come find you. What have you got there?"

Since his mouth was full, Aun simply walked up to her and sat down, extending his neck to indicate he'd like Zifeara to take the flowers from him.

"What are these for?"

Once he had released the bundle, Aun chose to remain shifted, his voice deep and grumbly. "Well, I thought you'd like them. Do you not like red?"

Zifeara stared from the tiger to the flowers, entirely unsure of what to make of them. "N-no, I like red. I just... I don't know why you'd bother..."

He nonchalantly licked one of his paws to clean behind an ear. "Well, I haven't exactly been the easiest person to deal with this entire time, so I figured I should probably do something to start making up for it."

Zifeara recalled the last time someone had given her flowers just for the sake of doing it, but that had happened a very long time ago, and the man responsible for it was well gone, unfortunately. She had truthfully liked him quite a bit. He definitely hadn't been a giant tiger, though. "Thank you, Aun. I'll find something to do with these. Uh, until then we should get started for today... It's your turn."

"Cool, what are we doing this time?"

Zifeara was starting to be slightly suspicious of Aun being so agreeable today. He hadn't been this way the entire time they'd been going. "Well I figured we'd try you at polearms today. I've seen some bamboo and other sturdy sticks around and you've never done that before."

Expecting resistance, she was surprised to be met with eager acceptance.

"So you mean I get to hit Fang with a *stick*? Awesome."

Fang was looking at Aun as if he were crazy. It's like the tiger could sense today was a bad day to turn into someone reasonable and likeable- at least likable to Zifeara.

"That's... kind of the spirit I suppose? Fang, you *are* going to be in on this as well. I would imagine it's been a long time since you've practiced," Zifeara said, attempting to get Heme to hold still enough to lay her new flowers on his back.

She wasn't wrong. Fang hadn't really been given any reason to practice, but he was willing to bet once they got going he'd remember everything. Zifeara located enough bamboo for the three of them and heated it just enough to dry the canes out. She began walking Aun through how to hold and wield it while Fang focused on stretching and going through the motions of swinging and blocking imaginary foes.

Half an hour later, Zifeara thought Aun was as ready as he was going to get. "Alright, let's do this. Fang, you show him first, and please be gentle. I'll get to you once I think Aun's done well enough."

Aun took the stance Zifeara had shown him and Fang began, trying to remember he was supposed to be teaching. He really wanted to absolutely whip Aun and win, especially with it being clear the tiger was going to start seriously trying to get Zifeara to like him. Fang wanted to look good at the only thing he was confident he did well. At least Aun was even worse at this than he was hand-to-hand. His progress was slow enough that Zifeara declared him done for the day after another half hour so that she could get to Fang.

"Alright, you ready?" she asked.

Fang was absolutely ready. He knew he wasn't going to win, but if he could do well enough to keep her from hitting him at all, there would be high praise and admiration from Zifeara in it for him. Plus, it was fun. He had this. Holding his staff in proper position, he smiled confidently.

"Let's go. I actually think I'm okay at this one, so I'm ready for you, Zia."

She reflected his expression. "Alright, but don't think I'll be easy on you. You have more practice than Aun does so I expect you to be damn near at my level by now."

Fang nodded and prepared to roll since her first move was always to make sure he was light on his toes. As he expected, Zifeara wasted no time warming him up. She darted right for him, swinging her pole upwards to try to catch him under his staff should he choose to block. It was exactly why he always rolled. While doing so, he half-heartedly tried to knock Zifeara off balance, swinging for her legs just in case she wasn't paying attention. She was, of course, and jumped, bringing her pole down towards his head while he was on his back. This time Fang did block, quickly turning over and wrenching her staff to the side while backing up, ready for Zifeara's inevitable charge forward. Charge she did, jabbing at exactly where his vital organs were, making sure he needed to block or it would hurt like hell. Fang was almost surprised he was doing so well considering that Zifeara was going a little harder than she usually did. Muscle memory was an amazing thing for keeping him from getting hit as well as reminding him of her usual habits.

Zifeara was going through as many standard motions for polearms as she could think of just to make sure Fang still knew how to do this so that she didn't hurt him too badly. Seeing how well he was doing thus far, she decided it was time to mix it up. She backed off a little, inviting an attack and hoping her friend would take it. Luckily he did. Fang tried to move around her, attempting to get far enough to her sides that she couldn't reach around to counter his hits. When this failed, he began trying to hit her with either side of his staff in as quick a succession as he could manage. Zifeara was of course blocking every hit, but she was impressed; Fang was doing far better than she had expected him to. It was almost a challenge.

While blocking one of Fang's hits, she gave him a good shove as well, putting herself back on the offensive. They clashed canes, moving all over the clearing they had slept in. Zifeara was ready to end this since she and Fang had been sparring for almost an hour. She was pretty sure their staves were about done and there was no way he was going to hit her at this rate. Besides, they had to get going for the day.

Fang had lost track of how long they'd been sparring, but he had to admit this was one training session he was enjoying; he was good at it and he didn't have to touch Zifeara at all so he could keep focused. That being said, Zifeara was starting to get serious by the feel of the impacts on his cane; she was swinging her pole harder and he had to start backing up to maintain his ability to block without getting grazed. They were getting close to the tree line so he was planning to use the tree immediately to the left behind him to evade her strike and hopefully get close to hitting her.

Unfortunately, it seemed Zifeara had other plans. She began striking alternately between his legs and his head, effectively shepherding him lest he be hit. Hard. Just as Fang felt as though he were very close to the tree he had planned to use to escape, Zifeara increased the frequency of her strikes, making it impossible for him to do anything but keep her at bay.

With a solid shove, Zifeara forced him to take one more step back, effectively cornering him against a tall tree. She immediately pressed her staff against his, making a wall of herself so he wasn't going anywhere. He was glaring at her rather defiantly as though he were determined to free himself and it made her laugh.

"Fang, don't give me that look, we have to stop so we can get moving. I had to put an end to this eventually."

He blinked several times as though he suddenly remembered they were only training and he wasn't in a real fight. "Huh? How long have we been going? It can't have been that long, can it?" He was still straining against her, trying to keep himself from being completely immobilized, "I was just about to perform some amazing maneuvers and finally win!"

Zifeara laughed harder, still not letting up. Fang had never hit her, much less won a match against her and she was going to keep it that way. "Were you now? Based on how you're sweating and I'm fine, I think you're still a little ways off from beating me. I am impressed though, you did insanely well, Fang. I had forgotten that this was the thing you excelled in."

Even after she had declared them done and there was no way for him to break the block she had him in, Fang was still looking for a way out and he hadn't lessened his resistance. Zifeara couldn't tell if he expected her to try to get a finishing hit in, but he was usually not this *forceful* about their sparring. It was nice he was taking his combat training so seriously, but she'd never seen him try this hard. He had nearly hit her a few times during the session, but she also hadn't managed to hit him either. She almost wanted to let him have this one, just so that maybe he'd get better from the confidence it would give him. Almost.

"Fang, we're done, ease up. I don't want to back up only to have to hit you."

He looked down at her suspiciously. "You aren't going to hit me if I drop it first?"

"Why would I do that? You've won as far as I'm concerned, this is the best you've ever done against me. I haven't hit you yet, have I?" she asked indignantly.

Zifeara was right. She hadn't hit him at all, which was highly unusual for their fights. Pretty much every time they sparred, Fang at least got one good smack just to make him want to block more thoroughly. It never hurt really, she only did it to motivate him into doing better. Now that he was coming down off his adrenaline fueled confidence, he realized this was exactly what he had wanted. He had his praise so he could probably drop it now. Plus as an added bonus the only thing keeping her from pressing him against a tree with her entire body were two sticks. Oh, that was not a good thought to have right now.

"Okay, you're right, of course. Back up, I won't move. Promise," he said quickly.

Zifeara raised an eyebrow but did slowly lessen the pressure she was holding him with, Fang standing stock still and letting her move off. He tossed his staff off to the side once she was far enough away and she did the same.

"Alright then. Let's get on with it!"

Zifeara motioned for Orro Heme to come to her and he did so, careful not to displace the flowers still on his back. Which had given her an idea. As they moved forward along their trail and the boys read and bickered over random things, Zifeara talked to her horse, weaving her flowers into his mane.

He wasn't super sure he enjoyed it since it looked so girly for a male horse, but Zifeara had made a pattern of skulls and velvety red swirls since those were the colors she had so he accepted it. He really wasn't in much of a position to argue since she was temporarily his person, but much to his surprise, Zifeara had been pretty reasonable with her expectations. She treated all of them well and Orro Heme hadn't foreseen that when he agreed to go with her. That, and he definitely hadn't expected them to get names. At the ranch all the horses were simply called according to their color and gender if necessary, so Treble had been the black and white, Thrush was the tan mare, but he had always been 'the bad one'. They hadn't cared that he could understand. He was just a horse.

¤ ¤ ¤

It takes a certain level of skill to manage a large group of people. It takes an even higher level of skill to manage an entire city of witless lowlifes who couldn't plan a surprise birthday party successfully, much the less anything of importance. It was very hard work having to spend an entire day writing out page after page of detailed instructions in between long days of flight in order to keep his glorious empire going. Some days Torvak wondered how some of his minions had even managed to survive for as long as they had without his direction. This routine was costing him precious time, but he had requested a few of his choice forces to come to his aid and hopefully help him slow that witch of a shifter down. He was certain she was onto his plan and would try to stop him. Luckily he had gotten started before she realized what he was doing, but it was most inconvenient that he had attracted her attention now.

Torvak had known he would have to deal with Zifeara at some point - all beings seeking immortality did - but he was so hoping it would wait until he had gathered his stones. Still, from what he had read, she was defeatable; all he had to do was kill her and steal her head. The few pieces of literature he could find about her claimed this was the most thorough way to keep her down. Granted it was unproven since the scripture had mentioned that no one had ever managed this feat, but Torvak was a pioneer. He had gone places and done things that no one before him ever had. He could definitely kill one pretentious bitch bent on keeping him from what he wanted. He most certainly had before, and he surely would again before this task was over. Then he could have all the women he wanted as he slowly took over the better part of the world, ushering in a new era of human enslavement to demon kind.

CHAPTER 25

Inappropriate Times for Emotions

H ey Zifeara?" Aun had gotten bored of reading, bored of running near the horses, and just bored in general.

She looked up at him from a strange glowing device with letters on it, which she was tapping at in order to make words.

"Can I ask you more stuff? I'm out of things to do and hearing Fang's voice is making me want to shift my ears off."

While the other man in question glared at the book he was reading, she sighed and turned the thing off, putting it in her bag.

"Okay, first of all, don't be a dick. Secondly, what's on your mind?"

"Well," he started, "I uh, was kinda curious about something the Tall Wonder said the other day, actually."

Fang snapped his attention up from his tome about demons from this time period. "What? Why would you ask her and not me if it was something I said?" he asked, worried what the tiger could possibly related to anything they'd been talking about.

Aun gave a dismissive wave of his hand. "Because it pertains more to her than you. I wanted to know why you decided to *keep* him. He said he was only a little kid at the time and you don't strike me as the type of woman who's into raising a family, frankly."

As much as Fang was angry that the tiger would dare ask such a personal question... he kind of wanted to know what she'd say. She would never give him a straight answer when he asked so he had since given up.

Zifeara stared at both of their curious faces, annoyed that they had decided to gang up on her. Fang was definitely giving her an extra pleading look she was having a hard time saying no to.

"Ugh, fine, stop looking at me like that. There was a point in my life where I realized I was beginning to feel sorry for other sentient beings. It started small and only with animals; things like tossing scraps of food to wild animals that looked lean, rescuing kittens from fires that weren't out of my way, bringing orphaned puppies to families that would keep them, stuff that wasn't a big deal.

All of that changed when I saved a child for the first time - a *human* child. He was only two and his family had been killed by raiders. They were planning on keeping him, using him as a slave for the rest of his life. I was flying overhead, on my way elsewhere, and I heard their conversation. I meant to keep moving as children were of no concern of mine, but he cried and cried, screaming louder than I'd ever heard a human scream. I have no idea what came over me but I was pissed. I killed every single one of those raiders and took him, leaving him with a family in the next town I stopped in. It was a strange feeling. I was happy I'd done it."

"Fast forward a long while and, well," Zifeara slid her eyes to Fang, "there you were. You weren't the only other kid I'd helped, but you were the tiniest, scrawniest, most helpless urchin any demon had *ever* produced. Dios, you were so small."

Fang smiled that wonderfully caddywhompus smile of his, always up to the left, as he could tell Zifeara was just giving him shit as she often did.

"At first I... well honestly I had planned to take you to one of the orphanages in New Tinning and make sure you were taken care of. But..."

She sort of trailed off, half hoping they wouldn't bother making her continue.

"But what, Zia? What was it?" Fang gave her a weird look Zifeara was having a hard time placing. It wasn't admiration, but it wasn't curiosity either.

"Zifeara?" While she was staring at Fang, Aun had gotten testy. He was such an impatient boy.

"Something was different about you," she continued, still looking at her friend of almost thirty two years, "you felt different. Like it wasn't just help you needed. Like no one else could do what I could for you. Like it *had* to be me. So I kept the little whelp."

Her grin had returned. Fang had always loved her grin and he often wondered if she ever noticed how perfectly it mirrored his. Her mouth always pulled to the right.

"And lo and behold he grew into the geekiest, lankiest, most perfectly imperfect model of a man I've ever seen. What *have* I done."

"Aw, Zifeara- I think that's just about the nicest thing you've ever said to my face." Fang was half sarcastically sweet and half puppy love giddy. That really was the nicest thing she had ever said about him as far as he was concerned. He was also pleasantly surprised at her reaction.

Her face became a little flushed and Fang would recognize that tail flick anywhere. "Oh shut up - you know what I meant. Can't you two ask anything less obnoxious?"

Aun was very ready to move the conversation onward. It was not somewhere he wanted to linger, nor the answer he'd been after. "Yeah, I guess I can. Explain to me this whole 'Dios-Lucifer' thing. I don't know anything about the religion or how it actually works, to be honest."

¤ ¤ ¤

"So what you're telling me is, in the future, it's really *not* frowned upon to sleep with more than one girl at a time?!" Aun had moved on from pestering Zifeara to pestering Fang.

The two had moved their horses together to hold their rather unusual conversation.

"Well no," Fang was explaining, "In the future we focus less on traditional views and old ideas in order to try to enjoy ourselves more. It's been centuries since anyone in my part of the world said you had to commit yourself to any one partner or that you couldn't *be* gay or have a different idea of how your own sexuality works. If you're born a girl but you want to be a boy but you still like girls, it's whatever, no one is going to tell you you're wrong. We've decided that kind of thing isn't important."

Zifeara had her head buried in her work. She was writing her third novel and this was a conversation she had no desire to be included in, so she had made Heme outpace them. She didn't think she needed to be part of 'guy chat' and had been tuning out every single word between them for the better part of half an hour.

Aun was flabbergasted. The future sounded awesome and he was stuck here. He wanted in on this. "So, uh, when do we go into the future? I think I could be quite comfortable there."

Fang remembered what Sara had said about wanting to meet Aun. "Well, that's all up to Zifeara. If she wants to take you with her, then whenever that is. I have no control over that."

Both of them looked to Zifeara, still very much absorbed and not paying a lick of attention to them.

"So speaking of..." Aun said lowering his voice and gaining that glint in his eye that Fang was starting to hate, "is she it? The only one you've ever...?"

It took a moment of uncertainty for Fang to figure out what he was asking. "The only? Oh. *Oh.* No, of course not. Not that it's any of your business, but no."

The younger man was being oddly friendly as of late considering the two of them were sworn to despise each other until Zifeara had either chosen one of them or told them both to piss off. Now this felt more like a sleepover.

"Oh come on, surely you keep track- you're still a guy! I'll tell you if you tell me," Aun said mischievously.

Fang rolled his eyes but gave in. It would become a big loud deal if he didn't, he could just *feel it*. He did not need Zifeara to start paying attention to their discussion right now. "Fine. Three. My first was the day after my eighteenth birthday, actually. Happy now?"

Aun clapped a hand over his mouth but it didn't quite suppress his snickering. "You live in an age of heightened sexual freedom and it took you 'til you were *eighteen* to get laid?"

He was sorry he'd ever thought this would make Aun shut up. "You act like that's a bad thing. I'm glad I waited; I did it with my best friend in the back of my brand new car on a cliff overlooking the entire city we lived in under a nearly full moon! And it was fantastic!"

Aun looked dubious, eyeing him even though the tiger was well aware of exactly what it was he was packing downstairs. "Fantastic for you. How long did you last, a whole five minutes?"

This time Fang settled in. Clearly this conversation was not going to end nor was there any point in attempting to keep any information to himself. Aun would surely take reluctance to share as some form of shortcoming in this petty competition.

"Well, I would assume it was a good deal longer than that considering by the time we were done, I had not only turned my headphones up because she was shouting my name a little too loudly but I had also needed to let her take a break for a moment. I'd say I did quite well enough."

Aun didn't want to believe Fang could be telling the truth, but there was nothing in his voice or demeanor to suggest he was embellishing to improve his standing. Which was fine, he had the Skeleton beat. "Even if that *is* the truth, I've still done better. In the same amount of time, no less, since we're damn near the same age. I have been with thirteen women and started at the age of sixteen. Four tigers, three rabbits, two does, a falcon, a reptilian which I deeply regret, a cat, and my crowning glory; a kitsune."

Fang raised his eyebrows. He was impressed, but felt no shame. He'd had an uncounted number of women very nearly beg for the chance to bed him, mostly because of his fame and wealth, but he chose to refuse them simply because he wasn't interested. Living in an age after the sexual revolution meant things worked in both directions; not having an absolute ton of sex with everyone who offered wasn't looked down upon either.

"More doesn't really mean *better*, at least not to me. I've gone with women I liked, not just anyone who'd have me."

"Well it's so much easier in your time," Aun said defensively. "Here with me being," he pointed to his ears, "*me*, I've worked for every one of those. It was a challenge with a high payoff. I'm surprised so many of them were tigers, truthfully. I thought they'd be the hardest to win over, but I'm pretty sure it was the danger of being caught with someone so taboo that did it for them. I'm not complaining, it's the only thing my damn ears have ever done for me."

Fang just shook his head, but Aun was feeling confident since he had, in his mind, won this battle. "I'll prove it to you."

Before Fang could stop him, he leaned slightly over Thrush's head. "Hey Zifeara! Zifeara, listen for a second!"

Hearing her own name more than once, she finally looked up, just as Fang strove to hide himself behind Treble's neck as much as he could physically manage. Since he had Zifeara's attention, Aun wasted no time in getting to the point. He wanted to see what would happen.

"Quick question, who's ears do you think are sexier, mine or Fang's?" He grabbed one of his own ears for emphasis while jerking the thumb of his other hand to his hiding cohort.

Zifeara blinked a few times, her mouth slightly open and brow furrowed, trying to fathom if she had heard the tiger correctly. "I- I beg your pardon?"

Aun crossed his arms over his horse's head and was leaning on them, awaiting an answer. Thrush snorted and he was fairly certain it was in amusement. "You heard me, be honest. Mine or his?"

Comprehending what she had been asked to do, Zifeara reddened sharply, ears falling completely flat. "Wh- A-Aun, what have you two been on about!? I am absolutely *not* going to dignify that with an answer!" She quickly put her face behind her tablet, attempting to hide her embarrassment.

"Oh come on, Zifeara! Surely you have an opinion! You definitely spend enough time with both of us to have given it some thought."

"Shove off, shithead!" was all he vehemently got in response.

Aun laughed and returned to reclining sideways along Thrush's back to wag his eyebrows at Fang, remarking loudly enough for Zifeara to hear him, "Bet it's mine- that's why she doesn't want to say anything. She'd hurt your feelings and-"

Before Fang could unbury his burning face from his hands to glare furiously at the tiger, a singular apple glanced off Aun's head, making a rather loud thunking sound.

"OW! What the-?"

There was no way that could have come from anywhere other than Zifeara's bag since this was definitely not apple country. Or season. Looking forward, both Fang and Aun could see she wasn't even remotely acknowledging them anymore, but her tail was hanging down off to Heme's side and was flicking rapidly in annoyance.

Aun turned to him and they both just stared at each other, unsure of where this left them.

Fang could only keep so much hope out of his tone. "Does... does that mean it's mine?"

A second apple was forthcoming.

¤ ¤ ¤

Punch, punch, block. Roll, kick, spring, punch, block.

Zifeara had been training both boys in hand-to-hand every morning since the polearms lesson. She didn't think it was terribly important that Aun wasn't very good at such things; unarmed combat was a far more pertinent skill for him to master. The tiger was already done for the day, having shown minimal improvement, and now it was Fang's turn.

Zifeara couldn't believe it; Fang was doing better by the day, and was even becoming quite a handful for her to keep up with. He wasn't just improving in combat, either; by day they fought and by night they talked, discussing the things he had learned by reading and elaborating on his new knowledge.

Today Fang was giving her a damn good fight. After only forty minutes, she was already putting in full effort to dodge each blow. She had gotten in a few solid hits herself, but so far that had only served to redouble his efforts. As with all their training sessions, Aun observed from the sidelines, learning what he could to apply to their next match.

Zifeara kicked Fang to the ground and moved to win, hoping to pin him down, rendering his arms unusable, but things did not go as planned. For once, he was ready. Just as she moved towards him, he regained himself. He rolled just enough to use his legs to vault Zifeara over him, tossing her far enough away that he had time to get up. She, of course, landed on her feet before springing back at him, but this was no longer an easy win. When had he gotten so good?

She was on him again in an instant, but she'd lost her advantage. Fang managed to knock her legs, putting her on unsteady footing. She lashed out to make him as unstable as she was, but he was on point for the turnaround. He jumped before she could make contact, spinning his body as he went, getting one last kick in before he hit the floor. Zifeara had most definitely taught him how to perform a roundhouse kick, but he very rarely got the chance to use it against her. She hadn't made it past trying to hit him. He connected with the side of her head, halting her forward progress and turning her sideways. She stood dead still.

Once Fang had landed and realized what he'd done, any color he had in his pale complexion vanished faster than a rowboat in a hurricane. "Oh... *shit*."

He approached her, arms extended and hands palm up, but ready to defend against the much expected retaliation.

She shuddered once before she finally made a sound. "Ha... hahahahahaha! I'll be damned. You finally did it." She looked up to reveal that she was laughing, tears at the corners of her eyes and no hint of anger whatsoever. "After all this time, you actually *hit* me."

Fang was speechless. He *had* finally hit her. He had done the impossible.

Zifeara jumped on him, hanging on his shoulders and ruffling his hair. "Look at you: managing to hit me in hand to hand *and* in a split second with your guns. You're. Doing. So. *Well!*"

All his color came flooding back in, plus a little extra thanks to her exuberant praise. "Zifeara, are... are you okay? I didn't hurt you?"

He grabbed her waist and lifted, just to keep her from putting all her weight on his shoulders, but he immediately regretted doing so. It now put her extremely close to his face and this made it very hard to look directly at her. Fang was well aware that this of all things shouldn't be making him anywhere near this bothered, but the adrenaline the fight had pumping through him was not helping in the slightest.

"Are you kidding me? Hurt *me*? Fang, I've been hurt worse- by far less intimidating things than you- you barely fazed me in the grand scheme of things. But you did it!" She hugged him tightly, burying her face into his shoulder from a moment. She was so proud of him.

Fang took this moment to look at Aun, who was quietly fuming off to the side. Fang gave him a sort of shrug and a shit-eating grin since this was surely one step away from the ultimate reward possible; so very close to obtaining the much coveted kiss from their princess.

"Hey Fang?"

Zifeara was looking directly at him, and he made the mistake of turning towards her, as he usually did when responding to his own name. With her face inches from his, Fang damn near dropped her out of surprise. "You, uh, you can put me down, you know."

He did so quickly. "Y-yeah, I guess I can. Um, what kind of books do we have for today?"

"Whatever you want, really," she said digging through her bag, "You know the basics of pretty much everything here with as much reading as you've been doing, so just pick a subject."

Fang thought about it while she was looking over a few titles. "You know, now that I think about it, what can *you* teach me on the way there? I'm sure you know a lot that I'm not going to find in a book, Zia."

She looked back to her friend, excited to share her vast wealth of knowledge with someone who could benefit from it just as much as she had. "Well... Pick a subject I guess!"

They spent the day discussing the practical applications of poisons in various forms, how to tell the difference between a kitsune and a regular fox demon, and some of the strangest demons Zifeara had ever seen. By night, they all opted to sleep amongst the horses, but for once, no one dreamt of anything meaningful.

CHAPTER 26

The Bone Zone

According to Zifeara, Tsuruya was only one more full day's journey away. Anxious to reach their destination, they skipped training in favor of travel. The bad news was, the summer monsoons had crossed the plains up into the mountains the party was currently moving through. It had been raining heavily since dawn, causing everyone to be flat out grumpy, and the mud it was producing was slowing the horses down. Zifeara created a massive shield of fire to put over their heads and keep them all from getting wet, but this also meant she was eating all day to keep her energy up. By early evening, one of them was going to have to go hunting in order to keep her fed.

Zifeara could feel the protest about to come from Aun at having to go hunting in the worst sort of weather for catching anything in, but Fang didn't give him the chance. "I'll go, Zia. You should stay here and keep the horses dry while they move."

"Fang, that's very sweet of you, but that isn't going to happen. You have no idea how to track in any sort weather plus your sense of smell is barely better than a human's at distance. What we're going to do is keep going until we find a cave or something to safely shelter in and then we send you home so you can get something there. It's about time we treat ourselves anyway, you've both been working pretty hard."

Aun watched Fang's face light up. "You mean it? I can bring back anything I want?"

Zifeara chuckled. "Sure, just make sure to leave something in my pantry so Lola and Graham don't starve!"

Soon enough, they found a cave, concealed by tons of moss and shrubs. They coaxed the horses inside once they made a path through the overgrowth, but upon entering it, Aun spoke up.

"Zifeara, I don't like it in here... It feels weird."

She stood, studying the place and scenting the air. It was dark for sure, but once she lit her hand on fire and walked further in, it looked just like an average cave and she smelled nothing alive. She didn't know what Aun was sensing, but she knew from experience that gut feelings were often true.

"Okay, we'll only be here for a few minutes, then. In you go, Fang. Be quick, yeah?" Zifeara produced her time crystal and promptly dropped it, handing him her bag and ushering him through.

Appearing in Zifeara's foyer, Fang scared the absolute hell out of Lola. She screamed, dropping the stack of dishes she was carrying and causing them to shatter on the floor.

"*DIOS!* Fang, h-h-how did you *do* that? Y-you just-!"

Graham came rushing into the room from the kitchen and grimaced at the new mess. He knew very well that Zifeara could quite literally show up at any moment, out of thin air no less. "Lola, calm yourself. It is only Master Fang after all. I'm assuming since Zifeara is not with us, you require something, young master?"

"Yeah, I came to grab some food to take back with me, but I gotta be quick. I'm just going to raid the pantry real fast, okay?"

"Of course, Master Fang, take whatever you like. We just did the shopping yesterday so you should have plenty to choose from." Graham nodded.

Fang turned sheepishly to the much smaller girl. "Sorry, Lola, I didn't mean to scare you. Sorry about the plates, too..."

She looked embarrassed that she had just dropped them all. "No, it's alright, Fang. It wasn't really your fault, I just didn't expect someone to pop up right next to me!"

Fang smiled and ruffled her hair, hastening to get into the pantry. Once he was out of sight, Lola exhaled loudly. She was usually so happy to see Fang. Graham cleared his throat next to her.

He extended his arm towards her with a broom, but he didn't look cross for once. "Best get to cleaning this up. We'll need to order replacement dishes in the morning."

"You aren't mad at me, Graham?" she ventured.

The old goat shook his head and chuckled. "Not this time. I was young and new to this place once too, you know. The first time Zifeara did that to me, I dropped the *good* tea set. She scared the ever-loving hell out of me twice more before I got used to it. Zifeara, and apparently now Master Fang, is full of surprises."

Meanwhile, Aun sat, tiger form and all, staring into the darkness of the cave. He was creeped out, but he couldn't find any logical explanation for the feeling. "I don't get it, Zifeara. Something feels bad about this place but I can't for the life of me figure out *why*. It doesn't smell weird, I can't hear anything... It's just a cave, right?"

She considered it a moment before walking towards the looming darkness, hand outstretched and again ablaze. She had already started a small fire near the mouth even though they wouldn't be there long, but now she was curious.

"Woah, woah, what the hell do you think you're doing? Get back here!" Aun grabbed the back of her shirt in his mouth, holding her back.

"Oh, stop being a scaredy cat, Aun. You stay here with the horses and yell for me if I'm not back in twenty minutes. I want to see what's freaking you out because I don't feel it. I can't die, remember? I'll be fine, now let go."

He actually growled at her, low and deep, but one stiff glare and a slightly forceful thump on the nose and he begrudgingly released her shirt.

Zifeara wandered in, her fire lighting up her silhouette until she was out of range of Aun's watchful gaze. The cave was lengthier than she'd expected and had several twists and turns, but eventually let out into a large cavern. She found exactly what had been giving the tiger a case of the heebie jeebies.

There were bones scattered everywhere; hundreds of *human* bones. Zifeara quickly counted at least four dozen skulls of various sizes. There were also primitive tools near some of them, some with small, mysterious trinkets. What really made her blood run cold were the scorch marks across most of the floor and some of the walls... All of these people had burned to death.

Looking to the opposite wall, Zifeara spotted a large opening which she had to guess lead outside. Based on what appeared to be old claw marks around the other entrance, it looked like something big got in here and torched the place and Zifeara was really hoping it wasn't what she thought it was. More often than not, however, some things in life just won't stay buried.

On the wall closest to her, Zifeara saw colors and that caught her eye. It looked like whoever had tried to hide in here had been painting to keep themselves busy. The scene on the wall showed animals of several types fleeing and tents with people coming out of them, all armed with either spears or bows, attempting to fight off a large, blue dragon.

Zifeara recognized that hideous thing anywhere, even crudely finger painted. That was definitely her. There was also a round white orb just over the dragon's head which she assumed to be the moon, so there wasn't really any room for doubt. Her dragon must have gone after this little tribe of people and cornered them in here. They were trying to warn anyone else who came into this cave that something was out there.

Zifeara didn't want to stay there anymore. Fang should be ready to return and Aun was probably still jittery and nervous. The instant she was back in sight, the tiger looked immensely relieved.

"Oh good, you're okay. I was thinking of coming to find you. What was in there?"

Zifeara very seriously considered lying and telling Aun he was just being paranoid. The only problem with doing that was making him doubt his own instinct, which for someone in this time, was very important. "Well, I can see why you were creeped out. There's a boneyard back there. Bunch of humans."

Aun's ears flattened. "Oh Hell. Any idea what killed them?"

This time she did lie. She didn't want him to know about this yet. "No, it could have been any number of things. But that's all it was; a lot of skeletons that you're afraid of."

He didn't make any clever retorts as he usually did when she teased him about something; instead Aun just glanced behind her into the cave.

"If you say so..." Aun couldn't shake the feeling he had, but if Zifeara said it was skeletons then there must have been skeletons. What reason did she have to lie about a bunch of dead people?

Zifeara opened her portal once more and Fang came back, distributing odd-looking bags and boxes of what Aun assumed to be food.

"Guys, why is this covered in weird clear paper? Is this meant to annoy me?"

Both of his futuristic friends snorted, but Zifeara did answer him. "It's called plastic, Aun. It keeps food from going bad as fast, but yes, it is also meant to irritate you. Just cut it open!"

Aun had to watch how Fang opened his bag of something known as 'chips' without spilling them on the floor before attempting it himself, but once he was in, Aun adored future food. Every single thing he put in his mouth was delicious, but he discovered that he really liked cookies. And these tiny little things that tasted like chocolate but were spongy and covered in sweet clay. Zifeara informed him they were called cakes. Aun loved cake.

Once back on the horses and moving again, still shoving food in their mouths, Zifeara was trying to form a plan for taking the quartz.

"I literally have no idea how we're going to get this thing," she said in between bites, "As far as I know, this rock is guarded at all times by temple monks. I think they're mostly human, but still. I don't want to have to murder people for something I just intend to borrow."

Fang swallowed his chips. "Well, maybe we can pull some secret agent stuff! Do they have a hole in their roof? Can we tunnel under the stone? Is it in a locked room?"

Zifeara just laughed. She appreciated his enthusiasm, though. "Fang, I really don't know- I haven't made a point of seeing the thing any of the times I've been there. I've seen the temple but I've never been inside."

She didn't seem worried, so Fang was confident she'd think of something. "That reminds me, you have another job too, don't you Zia?"

"W-what? How did you...?"

She hadn't told him about the job yet and he assumed it was because she wanted to focus on the Terra Quartz first.

"You woke up the other night. You never cling to me like that unless your Mom has been by."

"I have done no such thing!" Zifeara was starting to faintly blush again. "I do not cling to anything."

"Uh-huh, sure you don't." Fang didn't usually get to be on the antagonistic end of giving shit in their relationship, but when he did, he took full advantage of it. "Other things you also don't do in your sleep are snore or mumble or curl your tail around my-"

Since the horses were all right next to each other to stay under the fire umbrella, Zifeara managed to lean over and shove the rest of the cake she was about to eat into Fang's mouth to shut him up.

He just sniggered and took a bite, continuing to talk with his mouth now full. "So what *is* the new job?"

Zifeara crossed her arms and held her head high, just the way she usually did when she refused to admit she ever did anything embarrassing.

"Yeah Zifeara," Aun chimed in. "Who's next? Bandit leader? Terribly powerful sorcerer? Another maniac?"

Still not looking at anything but the trail they were on, Zifeara relented. "Kitsune."

Aun just about choked on the food he'd put in his mouth. "Wait, what?! *Why?*"

She relaxed again and stroked Orro Heme's neck. "Kitsunes can grow to be very powerful beings; sometimes the older ones get a little carried away and start to get power hungry. Think they can simply take over with their charm and they move past just stealing life forces. They start eating souls and outliving their natural lifespan."

Fang and Aun just stared at each other.

"Hey Aun, didn't you just tell me the other day you'd been with a kitsune before?"

"*What?*" Zifeara whipped around, tone laden with worry. "Aun, do you have *any* idea what that could do to you? How many tails did it have?"

He didn't really understand what the big deal was. As ruthless as kitsunes could be, they were really just fox demons with a wild side and terrifying abilities. "Oh, Zifeara, calm down. She just had one tail and she wanted to fool around. Kitsunes need practice too. Besides, even if she did take a little life, it was well worth every minute. She was amazing."

Zifeara and Fang were just exchanging looks, hers far more filled with disdain. "Fang, do me a favor."

"Yeah, Zia."

She went from disdain to dead serious. "Don't *ever* mess around with a kitsune. It's stupid and reckless and a good way to get yourself into some real shit. Kitsunes are very dangerous."

She was glaring at Aun, but he just shrugged and continued to eat his chips. "Regardless, that's who I've got next. She's in a town a few days away from the Terra Quartz, but we'll deal with that when we have to."

They continued to eat as the horses pressed on, finally arriving in the massive city of Tsuruya in the early hours of the morning. Getting into their room for the duration of their stay, everyone decided to take a quick nap; they had a long day of infiltration ahead of them and needed the energy. Aun was happy to be tucked into a bed again, but it didn't keep him from dreaming that night.

He was somewhere in that pine forest he knew the wolf guy lived in. He was a wolf himself, running after the fleeing tail of a deer. There was another wolf running with him, black just like he was, speeding up past the prey. The other wolf barked once and ran itself into the deer, knocking it down so that he could deliver the finishing bite. He knew this tactic and that other wolf looked very familiar. Once they had eaten their fill, they spent a while just walking, doing nothing in particular.

He had been the one to break the silence. "Hey Zifeara?" This voice always sounded so foreign to him but he could very clearly pick out the nervous undertone to it. She looked his way and he continued, "How, um, how long were you planning to stay? Have you decided yet?"

Zifeara held eye contact for a moment before speaking, looking to the ground as she did. "Well really it depends on when I get another job... I'd like to stay as long as I can but I have to go as soon as something comes up."

He gazed at her and said cautiously, "Have... you ever considered taking someone with you?"

She stopped walking and said his name, even though Aun still couldn't tell what it was. "I don't know that I... could. I get myself into a lot of situations that would be dangerous for mortals, so I think it would be unwise. For both of us."

"But Zifeara," he protested, reaching out to take her hands in his, "I... I don't really have anything to do with my life. It's boring here and all I can really do is look for a mate and settle down. I don't want to do that. Besides... you're..." He hadn't finished his sentence and looked down. He knew he was embarrassed with where he'd been going with that.

After a tense silence, Zifeara huffed. "Look, I'll think about it, okay? I don't make promises I can't keep."

He had looked back up, but he still felt so sad; he had spent the last couple of weeks falling head over heels for Zifeara and he couldn't bear to let her go off and leave him behind. *He was so in love with her.* He must have been making a face because Zifeara smiled mischievously and playfully jumped on him, shifting back to her wolf form and crushing him a little.

"Don't pout at me, I've been having a fun time here and I'd like to continue to do so. Perk up!"

He smiled and shifted as well, flipping her off him and the two wrestled around, laughing and pretending to growl at each other. At one point, he had pinned her and while she was struggling their noses touched. Were they human, their lips could have brushed and the thought sent electricity down his spine. They both tensed for a split second before he quickly got up and suggested they head home. Gods, he wanted to kiss her.

CHAPTER 27

I Think Lying To Holy Men Is a Sin

Auun... C'mon, get up."

Aun opened his eyes and grumbled. Zifeara was standing over him and petting his head to rouse him. This was definitely among the nicest ways to wake up he could think of, though it could easily be improved.

"Fang is out grabbing breakfast from the morning market already. He's going to meet us at the steps to the temple."

Aun was groggy from dreaming and was laying on his stomach, his face pressed into the bed. He had one emerald eye open, lazily looking her over. "Mmm, what are the odds of you getting into this bed with me and giving it five more minutes before you make me move?"

Zifeara tilted one of her ears back and crossed her arms. "Far worse than your odds of me kicking your ass for asking that. Get up."

He grinned sleepily. "Aww, but I bet you'd do it for Fang. What does he have that I don't, huh?"

"Enough common sense to know that I am not a patient woman. Now shut up before I get mad and decide to *make you* shut up." Her demeanor shifted to truly irritated, suggesting he not press his luck any further.

Aun sighed and stretched. "Oh fine. One of these days I'm going to do something so cool, you'll *have* to sleep with me for a change."

Zifeara grabbed one of his ears, making him tilt his head awkwardly. "Aun, as it currently stands, my mother will *build a water park in Hell* before I'd sleep with you. She hates water. Now stop fucking with me and get your striped hide in gear before I knock those stripes right *off*."

¤ ¤ ¤

189

Torvak had instructed his minions to install fire charges all throughout the forest surrounding Tsuruya before his arrival so all he had to do was get there, and he was close now. Assuming a certain shapeshifter hadn't already made it to the city herself, Torvak could simply detonate the charges and the temple monks would have to scramble to put out the fire. They doubled as the town's fire service, after all. With only a handful left guarding the Terra Quartz, he could simply swoop in, kill anyone remaining, and take it.

He was making decent progress on obtaining the stones for his ritual, though he was beginning to wonder exactly how much of a pain Zifeara would continue to be. He was fairly certain that she either had the Inferno Ruby herself or knew where it was, so at some point he would need her; but at the same time, competing with her for the stones was going to get old fast. He was just hoping she didn't know exactly which ones he was after or how many he needed.

¤ ¤ ¤

Fang had already eaten his breakfast and was waiting for Zifeara to get Aun out of bed. The tiger had managed to sleep through both of them leaving this morning somehow. He must have been in a pretty good food coma from yesterday.

The temple he sat in front of was somewhat small, a modest home for their most valued treasure. It was made entirely of marble and most of it stood open to the air; just a roof supported by pillars carved into statues of a very muscular man. The only enclosed part of the structure had one double door where a few men were standing guard. All of them were in matching tan robes with no facial hair and shaved heads.

As far as he could gather, there were three men guarding the stone at all times, but they changed shifts on a set schedule. In their down time, it looked like the other monks moved to and from the larger temple on the other side of the market to give prayers to their elemental deity and do whatever else monks did. He was sure Zifeara could think of something with this, especially once she found more information.

Fang had definitely heard the expression 'speak of the devil', but he hadn't thought it applied to the devil's daughter as well. Then again, it was hard to be surprised by the appearance of the person you're thinking about the all the time. Zifeara had Aun in tow as she rounded a corner into the market surrounding their temple target. The wretch looked like he hadn't gotten any sleep. Poor him.

Fang waved them over before handing them their breakfast and telling Zifeara what he had learned while she ate. "So what are you thinking? How are we going to get this thing?"

Zifeara chewed quietly for a moment, eyes scanning the ground in front of her as she ran through scenarios in her head. He thought she had spaced out, but just as he was about to say something else, she piped up, "I don't suppose figuring out which monks are on guard duty next is going to be easy, do you?"

Fang also considered this. "Hmm. Well, how do you figure they determine that? I don't think they'd have a big old chart on the wall or anything like that. I take it we should go down to the other temple and nose around?"

"Listen, do you two think you can do this on your own? Now that I'm up and I've moved, I kinda..." Aun had barely touched his food for once, and he had his head in his hands, "feel like absolute Farrower shit today."

Fang and Zifeara both looked at him like he was speaking another language but he didn't care; he was starting to feel awful.

"Aun, why didn't you tell me you didn't feel well earlier instead of being a smart ass? I would have let you sleep." Zifeara had moved to be right in front of him.

"When you first woke me, I thought I was just tired since I'd been dreaming all night. Now I'm not hungry, I'm dizzy, and my head hurts."

Zifeara knelt down and took his chin to lift his head up, making him look at her. She turned his head this way and that, studying his eyes as they followed hers. "Does it being so bright out hurt your eyes?"

"Not really. It just kinda sucks to be upright."

She sighed.

"Fang, new plan. There could be any number of things Aun has, we have to take him back to the room so I can figure this out. Once we're back we'll talk about how you and I are getting that rock. Can you still shift, Aun? I'll carry you home if you get smaller," Zifeara offered. Aun grumbled and shrank, his usually playful tabby cat looking a little more like roadkill. She picked him up, holding him less like a cat and more like a baby. "Alright, we'll figure out what's wrong with you, get you on the way to being better, and *then* go do work. I swear you mortals get sick every five minutes."

Aun regained consciousness as Zifeara laid him on his bed under the blankets, gently shaking him to get him to turn back into himself. He did, though he did so very slowly. She looked worried, but he was in no condition to appreciate her fussing over him for once. She was saying something but he couldn't really tell what; he faded out of awareness pretty quickly. While Aun was trying to communicate to her he couldn't stay awake, he also couldn't tell if he was forming real words or not. He felt like he was on fire and for all he cared, he could be. He just wanted to go back to sleep.

"Fang, this isn't good." Zifeara had laid Aun on his bed, but he was only awake for a moment before he passed out. She had her hand on his head and the tiger was certainly running a fever now. From the symptoms Aun had told her earlier, this level of escalation was something serious.

"What do you think it is? Can you..." Zifeara knew Fang wasn't exactly Aun's best friend, but he sounded concerned enough.

"I'm... I'm not sure. Not yet. I can think of a few things he may have contracted, none of them favorable, but until he manifests one more symptom, I don't know for sure which he could have. All I can really do right now is give him something for his fever and come back later. Let's hurry up and get this stupid rock taken care of so I can watch Aun. If he starts shaking or coughing a lot, he'll be fine. If he starts losing his color... we have a real, honest to Dios problem."

"What do you mean? Like he moves closer to my skin tone as opposed to yours?" As much as Fang didn't like Aun, he didn't truly want the tiger to just drop dead. That would upset Zifeara and he'd grown a bit fond of the asshole. In a 'laugh when he falls over but check if he's okay' kind of way.

"No Fang," she shook her head, "I mean starts to literally lose his color. Think of sliding the grayscale bar on a picture on your computer; he'll have the color start fading out of his entire body. If that happens... I can't fix him."

Zifeara produced a dried plant from her bag and began plucking the leaves off. She had half a handful before she crushed it into a ball. Once it was about the size of a marble, she gently opened Aun's mouth and pushed it to the back of his throat, quickly closing it again. He tried to cough but she held his jaw firmly shut, making him swallow instead.

"C'mon, we have to go. I can only hope these monks make it easy for us."

The monastery the monks lived in was a moderately sized wooden building; two stories with many windows and modest green paint. There was nothing to make it stand out at all. On the inside, however, it was all well-polished floors and gemstones inlaid into murals on the wall depicting the illustrious history of Tsuruya. There were several statues of Ruuta, the god of the mountains, littered around the place in various shrines, but all in all this was like any other temple. Zifeara knew this because she had spent a little while crawling around on the ceiling scoping the place out. At least most monks valued all forms of life too much to bother the lizard on the roof and just went about their business.

Sometimes she was pretty sure fate was just laughing at her, though. There really was a big fuckin' chart on the wall detailing who was on guard duty at all times for the next week. She would have slapped Fang upside the head out of spite if getting this sorted ASAP wasn't currently life or death. Now she just had to find-

"Irah! Going out to tend the garden before your turn with the crystal?"

Two monks met in the hallway she was in.

"Actually, I was going to take a walk today, would you mind doing the garden? See you later, Muto."

As the monks bowed to each other, the one called Irah moved perfectly for Zifeara to let go and land in the sash he had slung over his shoulder. The monk took her out of the temple, through the garden they grew their own vegetables in, and out on a small mountain trail. Zifeara waited until they were out of sight of the village before shifting into a large python, quickly wrapping her coils around Irah's face so he couldn't cry out, depriving him of just enough oxygen to keep him unconscious for a moment. It was all she needed. To ensure he was out for long enough, she slipped him a little dose of a nasty cocktail of plants she had made ahead of time for just such occasions, and moved him into a bush well off the trail.

She assumed the monk's appearance, practicing the voice she had heard him use quickly. She was a master of lies, so it didn't take her long to get it down well enough to fool his friends. Zifeara had been doing this for centuries. She began walking towards the temple where the Quartz was kept, going slowly so as not to arrive too early. Now Fang just had to do his part.

"Ah, you must be one of the temple monks," Fang had said as he felt Zifeara run into him 'accidentally' in her new body, "I was just here on a pilgrimage to see the Terra Quartz and I was wondering if you would let me in to see it? Only for a moment..."

Fang knew he had to make their conversation believable and also loud enough that anyone around them could hear if they felt like it so no one suspected a thing. Apparently it was common for pilgrims to come from across the continent to touch the stone some deemed 'The Heart of Ruuta'. It was a convenient route to the stone.

Zifeara had pulled another set of clothes out of her bag for him to change into so he looked the part. She even had a hood to complete the outfit so that hopefully the guards couldn't get a good look at Fang. Now they just had to stay cool.

Coming up to the monks who hadn't quite switched out yet, Zifeara explained they had a pilgrim and that she didn't mind letting him in to see the stone even though it was a bit early to start her shift. The other monks viewed it as dedication to their duty and let them in without any problems, closing the doors behind them.

"Okay, Fang," Zifeara whispered in the unfamiliar voice of another, "I saw them do this earlier; they'll let you out, check on the stone, then let me out. I'll nab it the second they stop looking at me, so when you get out, thank them a lot. Keep them busy, got it?"

He nodded, the excitement of helping her do her job for once making it hard to keep level-headed. Fang gave it another minute, then knocked on the door. The monks did indeed let him out, looking in to see Zifeara bowing as he left, her bag hidden and open behind her back. Sure enough, they stopped looking at her and wished him well.

He spoke slowly and insisted on touching their hands as much as possible, making a pest of himself in a way the holy men couldn't refute. "Thank you so much for this chance to see the Quartz. It is truly an honor. It must be so gratifying to serve Ruuta in such a noble way. I bid you all the fondest of farewells."

Zifeara came out and they closed the doors. She stated that before her shift really began, she would have to relieve herself and made her way behind the temple, towards the woods. Once she was out of sight, there was no more monk; Zifeara simply sauntered herself back out of the forest and the real monks were none the wiser.

She and Fang didn't speak until they made it past the market where none of the monks could see him. Just before he said anything, she held her hand up and he high-fived her.

"Zifeara, are all of your jobs this easy?"

She laughed, but it was short-lived. "Oh, I *wish*. There is almost *never* not a problem. Speaking of problem, though..."

She turned to go back to their inn, still very worried about their friend.

CHAPTER 28

In Which Aun Dies

While Fang changed out of the borrowed clothes, Zifeara felt Aun's head again to see if what she had given him had at least helped. They'd only been gone two-ish hours, but it should have worked by now if it were going to do anything. Unfortunately, the tiger was still abnormally warm. Zifeara huffed, digging around in her bag and producing several books which she placed on the floor. She grabbed the first book on the stack, laid herself next to Aun, and began to read at an incredible speed. From time to time she would stare at him for a moment, only to resume reading.

Fang wasn't sure what to do with this situation. He had never seen her so invested in another person before him to this extent. She was really... *She really cared about Aun.*

"Zifeara?"

She grunted an acknowledgement. He was quiet. He had lost her to this.

He was silent long enough that she had very nearly forgotten he had said anything. "What, Fang? I'm obviously kinda busy at this particular moment."

"I... I was going to ask if there was anything I could do while you're reading... To help."

She made eye contact over her book. "Oh. Thank you, hun, but since I don't know for sure what Aun has, I don't know what I need. I have a ton of Soursop left so I can try to manage his fever, but other than that, I can't really send you out for anything. If a monk sees and somehow recognizes you, we might be screwed. Just... hang out, alright?" She tossed her bag over to him before continuing, "Entertain yourself, please."

He sighed. Fang hadn't been sick in so long, he had forgotten what it was like. Now all he could do was hope the tiger didn't have whatever his best friend was so worried about. Zifeara sat there for a full hour, reading all seven books she'd produced. Three of them were actually modern medical texts, so while he absentmindedly played with his guitar, he wondered how bad this could really be. Would she go as far as taking Aun back to their time to get him taken care of?

Zifeara vindictively dumped all of her books onto the floor. She had them piled up next to her as she finished each one, but now she didn't even want to look at them anymore. If Aun really did have chromeoplasmosis as she feared, there was absolutely nothing she could do. Symptoms could hide themselves for years, only revealing the affliction by the time it was too late to receive treatment.

It was a pretty rare disease, only contracted by shifters, usually through contact with another who already had it. Far more abnormally, it was brought on by a run in with a contaminated prysmawolf; wolves whose coats slowly cycled through more colors than were perceptible by the human eye. They were rare beasts, but chromeoplasmosis was basically rabies for them. She highly doubted Aun had ever seen a prysmawolf.

"Fang, what else did Aun tell you related to that kitsune? Had he... had he mentioned a shifter?"

Fang stopped strumming. "Uhm... No. No he didn't. He gave me a running count of girls he had been with, but he listed them all as one kind of animal. Why?"

She looked down to Aun's sleeping face, drawing her knees up to her chest, ignoring the growing ache it harbored. "If he starts to drain color like I said he might... there's only one place he could have contracted the disease which causes that. He would have gotten it from another shifter. So if he hadn't been with a shifter before, I could at least rule that out..."

Fang stared, completely unable to comprehend the irony befalling the tiger. "Are you trying to tell me that the guy giving me all kinds of shit for not sleeping around more has a *fatal STD!*?"

"*Mortichai Fang Nightstalker!*" Zifeara was glaring at him intensely, and she *never* called him by his full name.

Zifeara was furious but didn't want to wake their friend by being too loud again. "No, what I'm saying is, we better hope that is exactly what Aun *doesn't* have because if he does, he *is* going to die. We can't treat it this late in its progression, even in our time, which I would gladly take him to if it would help. Dios, Fang, I know you two don't get along, but that's a *horrible* thing to joke about. He's not even twenty years old..."

"I... I'm sorry, Zia. It's not that I don't care, I'm just... trying not to think it could be the worst case scenario. That's all."

She gave Fang one more harsh look for good measure before resigning herself to silence. All she could do was wait to see which illness showed itself. Zifeara hadn't even known Aun that long, so being this upset felt irrational, but... though he was obnoxiously forward and kind of bratty sometimes, she felt Aun was important to her. When you can count your true friends on both hands and have room to spare, anyone you have even an unexplained connection to becomes important. Zifeara could only think of three people in her lifetime that had won her over that fast and one of them was sitting on the other bed, passing time and sulking, just like she was.

She sat in the same place until early evening, checking Aun's fever, making him drink water, and administering more medicine as time allowed. It wasn't helping, but she could still try. Eventually, she heard a commotion and looked outside; it seemed the changing of the guard had revealed their earlier heist. She watched monks scramble around like ants, but currently it brought her no comfort.

By late evening, Aun wasn't able to swallow voluntarily anymore. Grabbing one of his hands to check his pulse, Zifeara put her own hand over her mouth. The tips of Aun's fingers were pale, as though he had been too cold for a while. Fang noticed her frantically digging through the blankets, but she provided no response to his questions about what she was doing. Once she found Aun's tail, she held it up for Fang to see for himself. About an inch of it was white where it had been orange this morning. Zifeara's eyes started to water. She had *maybe* hours to say goodbye to one of her friends and he couldn't even hear her.

"It's happening... He's... he's got it."

The explosions couldn't have been timed any better. People outside started yelling about a fire and before you could say 'ain't that about a bitch,' all the monks were hurrying to make a bucket chain to start dousing the sudden blaze that had erupted in the town's forest. Opening the window and quickly looking around, Zifeara saw a majority of the trees surrounding the town completely engulfed in flames. They couldn't stay here.

"Fang we have to-"

The soft rush of wings cut her off, preceding the figure flying right past them, toward the fire. Her mind immediately jumped to Torvak and she nearly spit flames of her own at his brazenness, but then she realized the sound didn't match up with the demon. Such a delicate swoosh came from feathers. Torvak definitely didn't have feathers. But Zifeara knew someone who did and that person tended to be drawn to natural disasters.

"Zifeara, what is it, what did you see?" Fang now, too, was hanging out their window. "Was it Torvak?"

Zifeara all but hissed, "Gideon."

Fang looked at her in disbelief. "Wait, what?"

She was about to say something else, but as she looked to Fang, her eyes widened as realization dawned on her. "*GIDEON!* Fang, if the fire is threatening to burn the inn down, grab Aun, get to the horses and start heading east out of town as fast as you can manage, I'll catch up. Unless this building is going to come down, *stay here*. Got me?"

"Yeah, I got you, Zia. What-"

Zifeara jumped out their window, not even bothering to shift and hitting the ground running to catch up to the figure now hovering about the forest fire as he shouted orders to the monks below.

The thin, blond boy flapped his massive, white wings, keeping himself aloft so he could see the extent of the situation. He pushed his long, curly hair out of his sky blue eyes as the wind generated from his wings always put it in his way. A majority of the Tsuruya forest was consumed with fire, but only on the side where the temple resided. Someone must have been after the Terra Quartz again. He darted into the temple, pushing the doors open, hovering just above the ground. The stone was gone. He sighed. Keeping the fire away from the village was priority number one then.

He returned to the air, calling out to all the monks, "Ho there! Please keep calm, I'm here to help! I need you all to get everyone as far away from this as you can! If you don't, I'm afraid there will be casualties. Please, hurry, go!"

The holy men all scrambled to do as he said, more so out of panic as opposed to any sort of recognition. They didn't believe in angels. But that was fine, Gideon helped anyone who needed him, regardless of what they believed. That was the true spirit of mercy. He heard someone running up behind him, but before he could turn to tell them to get back, a very familiar voice washed over him.

"Gideon!" Zifeara called out to her cousin, watching him turn rapidly in surprise.

"Zifeara? What are you-"

"Gideon, listen to me. I didn't start this fire, but I know who did. I'm going to help you put this thing out."

The angel was beyond confused and for good reason. Zifeara had killed him a few times in all the years they'd spent running around on their planet, so an offer of assistance was unprecedented.

"Zee, why would you-?"

She looked at him very sternly. "Because I need a favor. Much more kosher than the last one, I *promise*. No lies, no anything. Just straight up trading one service for another. What do you need?" She stared her cousin down, daring him to say no.

"I... I... Okay, Zee. One favor for another. Can you start digging me a trench?"

She nodded and shifted into a house-sized ox, tilting her head to ram one of her horns into the ground. She began furiously ploughing the soil, making a deep trench the fire couldn't spread over and flinging dirt on the inferno here and there.

Gideon flew to the opposite end of the fire from where Zifeara had started. He held himself steady over the blaze and began beating his wings as fast as he could, slowly but surely extinguishing it. This wasn't his first fire, no thanks to *someone*. By the time he and his cousin had met in the middle, only one structure had caught fire because neither of them had quite gotten to it yet.

The angel moved to put the building out while Zifeara kept digging to give them extra assurance that it was contained, but something she saw out of the corner of her eye caught her attention. Another figure was flying very quickly out of Tsuruya, and this one had large, bat-like wings. The flash of crimson gave him away. Zifeara took a deep breath in... and then she let Torvak go and kept digging. She had to keep her word or Gideon would just assume she had left and would probably do the same. Once the fire was dealt with, Gideon landed and moved to hug his cousin as he always did.

"Gid, we don't have time for this. Come with me."

He backed up. "Oh, right, what was so important? What is it that you need?"

On the way back to the inn he kept talking, happy his cousin was being strangely amiable for once. "Wow, Zifeara, you did a really great job with that fire. I'm not surprised at that, but uh, I am surprised you're being so helpful right now. Oh! If you didn't start the fire, who did? And where did the Terra Quartz go? Do you know? Please tell me you do."

Zifeara took another steadying breath so she didn't yell at him to shut the hell up and began explaining about Torvak and the stones and how she had the Quartz right now, but only for safekeeping. She couldn't have cared less about a ringing rock. They had made it to Zifeara's room by the time she had finished.

"So what do you-"

"*Gideon*, please stop talking. I'll tell you if you give me a damn second to breathe. I may not have to, but it is nice."

He put his hands behind his back as a sign he was going to be patient and listen now.

Zifeara opened the door to the room they were in front of and the first thing Gideon saw was what appeared to be a tiger hybrid asleep in the bed across the room. As Zifeara led him closer, however, it became apparent that this young man was very ill. He was sweating and his breathing was distressingly shallow. It was obvious that his hair wasn't supposed to be that color; it was *turning* white, only the roots of it still orange. Gideon watched his cousin freeze and then rush over to place one of her large ears on the young man's chest and listen carefully for a moment.

"Gideon, this is what I needed you for. This is my friend, Aun, and he has an illness I can't cure. He's going to die very soon if you don't help him. *Please* Gideon, I know you can."

Hearing the excessive stress in his usually stoic cousin's voice and struck with his own strong desire to aid the sick, the angel wasted no time. He placed a hand over Aun's mouth and stilled in concentration. The tiger slowly stopped breathing.

Fang moved out from the corner of the room he'd been waiting in, no longer able to stand idly by as his best friend had a meltdown. She was nervously flicking her tail while shifting her weight from one foot to another and was chewing her bottom lip. He set a hand firmly on Zifeara's shoulder, rubbing his thumb along the edge of her collar bone. From all the stories she'd told him, if there was one thing he knew her cousin excelled at besides talking her fucking ears off, it was this.

Aun's chest heaved. Gideon removed his hand as the tiger rolled himself quickly over the edge of the bed and spewed what looked like tar from his mouth, retching several times afterwards. Zifeara raced forward and caught him before he fell all the way to the floor. Aun wasn't even conscious long enough for her to ask if he felt better, passing out from the strain of expelling the illness from his body. She tucked him into bed and listened to his heart again. It was weak and slightly erratic, but it already sounded stronger than it had. He was going to make it.

Gideon moved backwards a bit, giving his cousin room to express her relief by worrying over her friend. He ran into something he could swear hadn't been there a moment ago. Yelping, he spun around only to find another man behind him.

As scary as this guy looked, he simply held a hand out in a way that would suggest he meant no harm and said, "Easy, it's alright. Is Aun going to be okay?"

Gideon was eyeing him up and down, since this man had to be at least half a foot taller than him and his appearance made the angel nervous. That and knowing his cousin, the kind of company she kept was not likely favorable. "Y-y-yes. He'll be fine. Um, where did-? How-? Who-?"

He shot a glance at Zifeara who was smiling weakly, still kneeling by the bed. "Oh right. After all of the history you have together, you two have never met."

Turning back to face the stranger yet again, Gideon was surprised to see a shy smile looking down at him.

"Zifeara, what do you mean? I don't... wait." It suddenly clicked. "You're? *No. Way.* Ohmygosh it's so nice to finally meet you! You... really aren't what I expected and yet..." Gideon looked from the other immortal back to his cousin. "You two look really cute together."

With as much color as Zifeara didn't have in her face from dealing with Aun, Fang now had enough for the both of them. "I- *no*- that isn't- w-we aren't..."

Zifeara smacked herself in the face, dragging her hand slowly downwards. "Gideon, how many times do I have to tell you that *I. Lied. To. You.* Fang is my best friend. I've *never* been in love, Gideon. He's who I stole the vial for yes, but not for that reason. Now as nice as this has been, and I really appreciate what you've done, will you please *fuck off*? I absolutely don't have the energy for you anymore. You can give me the same shit you always do about repenting or whatever next time. I'll even ignore that insultingly stupid thing you just said about Fang, okay? Please, don't today. Let me like you for *just. One. Day.*"

Clamping his mouth shut, Gideon skirted around Zifeara, making his way over to the open window. Her eyes followed him the entire way, a grimace plastered to her usually lovely face. As he sat down and swung his legs out, careful to duck his wings far enough under the top of the frame, he turned back for just a moment.

Before Zifeara could cut him off and tell him to go, all he said was, "You're welcome." And just like that, he pushed himself out.

Zifeara moved to the window and slammed it shut as fast as she was able.

She turned and slid down the wall. "*Fetka* Anhael. I have had just about enough fun for one day, how about you?"

Fang flopped down onto their bed, talking mostly to the ceiling now, "Yeah, I think I'm good. So Aun is going to live now?"

"Yeah. Yeah, he is. It's the one thing Gideon is good for."

Zifeara got back up, moving over to triple-check that their friend seemed stable. The white hadn't spread and he was breathing well now. It would take a day or two for him to fully recover with as close to meeting her brother as he had come. Mortis may not have personally collected every soul there was to be had, but they saw him all the same. She wondered what he would have looked like to Aun.

¤ ¤ ¤

Everything was darker than night was supposed to be. He was warm and somewhere very comfortable. He was moving, barely, but he was. Aun slowly opened his eyes, his lids heavy and uncooperative. He felt as though he were made of rocks. Scanning the room, he could see the edge of the other bed and part of the lump in it. Zifeara and Fang must have come back from stealing the rock and gone to bed already. Why was he so tired? If he had slept all day, he should have kicked whatever the hell he had earlier, like he always did after a nap, and felt ready to take on the world. The longer he kept his eyes open, the more alert he was getting. Aun remembered he wasn't as still as he should be for laying down. He tried to move of his own accord, but he barely stirred. The gentle rocking stopped.

"Aun?"

Zifeara's voice sounded a lot closer than the other bed. Actually, it sounded right next to his ear. A hand on his shoulder sat him up further and it was only then he realized he'd been so comfortable because he had been asleep on Zifeara's arm.

"Huh? Whr, wha?" He couldn't seem to form words. His mouth may as well have been full of leaves.

"Easy, you're still kind of out of it. Do you remember how you didn't feel well?" She brushed the hair that always hung over his eye further out of his face. *What... what was going on?*

He sort of nodded his head.

"Well, that was yesterday morning, Aun. Last night we had some pretty crazy adventures." Zifeara explained to him what had happened and exactly how close to death he had been. By the time she was done, he was much more alert. Weak, but sitting upright on his own and making sentences.

"I... I don't know which one was a shifter. Really I don't. I, um. Thank you, Zifeara. I wouldn't have made it if you hadn't..."

She just smiled. "Honestly, you're super lucky my dumb cousin was here; I couldn't do a thing for you. And, bonus points, you didn't even have to talk to him."

Aun laughed, which then turned into a cough, which then became a desire to lay back down.

"You know," Zifeara said, a teasing tone creeping into her voice, "damn near dying was a pretty stupid way to get me to sleep with you. I thought you said you were going to do something *cool*. Dying isn't cool. Trust me, I know."

Aun laughed again, much softer this time, raising a fist slightly in the air. "Worth it. When is Lady Lucifer selling tickets for her glorious water park?"

"Shut up. Go back to bed." She grumbled at him, but he could swear her usual aggravated edge was missing.

He leaned back onto her shoulder, not as comfortable as he was earlier. "Zifeara?"

She tilted her head away from his so she could look down at him. "Yeah?"

He turned a little pink, the first bit of color to return to him besides his hair. He may as well risk it; he'd essentially come back from the dead today. "Will... will you sing to me, too?"

She reddened as well, a good deal more than he had. "I... You know what, sure. Settle in."

Neither of them knew their conversation had woken Fang up or that he was becoming at least a little upset at losing his special privileges, but once he heard what Zifeara chose to sing[17] to the tiger, he let it go. Aun was essentially a scared child, just as he once was.

Zifeara put an arm around Aun's shoulders, pulling him backwards further so he was lying just next to her head. He was thoroughly comfortable again, looking up at her as she stared straight onward. Once she got to the chorus of her song however, the tears that had begun to sting his eyes finally fell. No one had ever said anything this nice about him, much the less sung it to him in a lullaby. About halfway through she really poured on her talent, causing him to become less sad and more drowsy. By the end of the song, he was finally out. He had never slept so well in his entire life.

---

[17] "Wanderer's Lullaby" – Adriana Figueroa

CHAPTER 29

Big Toothy Puppies

Being stuck inside was murder no matter how terrible he still felt. He'd been ordered to stay in bed until it was certain he was fit as he would get. With the level of activity he'd been getting used to, Aun was desperate to move around by day three. Begging to at least take a walk, lest he start getting fat, he thankfully obtained the desired result.

"Sure, Aun, but are you positive you're up to moving around? You were still pretty out of it yesterday." Zifeara had been extra worried about him while he was recovering from the after effects of nearly getting in line for reincarnation.

"Yeah, I feel loads better and if I sit still another minute, I'm going to scream. C'mon, at least let me run outside? We don't even have to go hunting, I just *need* to move."

He and Zifeara went to walk around the town while Fang was busy cooking. He was trying very hard to make as much food as possible before they had to leave again, so Zifeara left him her bag full of supplies from the morning market. It would hopefully keep him preoccupied and out of trouble.

Zifeara only let Aun get to the outskirts of town, staying close in case anything happened. She wasn't sure how much better he actually was and how much he was just trying to tough it out. Once she hesitantly allowed him past town limits and out into the forest, Aun did try to shift. The problem with chromeoplasmosis was that it confused a shifter's cells, not only draining them of their coloring but rendering them stuck in whatever form they'd taken when the disease took hold. Since it was incurable, she was unsure if her friend would ever shift again regardless of how well he had been recovering. After some very obvious difficulty and ignored cautions about pushing himself too far, Aun looked like he always did as a wolf; rusty fur sleek and eyes bright. She let out a sigh of relief and shifted her form to match.

They walked in silence for a while, enjoying the summer warmth.

"Zifeara, can I ask you something kinda heavy- with no hint of sarcasm or jest- and have you think about it?"

She tilted her head. "Yeah, of course. I am concerned as to why you sound so somber out of nowhere, but go on."

Aun bared his toothy grin. "You know, I could very easily ask you to just bring the Thunder Gem back once you've taken care of Torvak. I know where it is and there isn't much I can do about it. Realistically, all I *can* do is wait for you to kill him anyway. I survived something I shouldn't have. I should take Thrush and go home and see my family."

Zifeara stopped walking and stared at Aun in shock. He had every right to go home whenever he wanted, but she hadn't considered this would make him give up on the journey.

She lowered her ears and tail in resignation, but before she could speak, Aun continued, "I *should*, but all this has done has made me want the exact opposite. Zifeara, I know you told me Lucifer does contracts, but do you?"

Her mouth pressed into a firm line before opening to reply. "Well, no. I don't collect souls, I free them up for my brother. Aun, where are you going with this...?"

He wagged his tail, still smiling like an idiot. "Well, I realized I've never felt so alive running around doing all this fighting with you. I don't think I ever want to go home at this rate. I was wondering... if I could make a living out of doing this; with you. Bodyguard isn't the right word since you could kick my ass in ninety-nine out of a hundred fights, and I don't like the sound of assistant, but I figured..."

"Would you take the title of 'friend'?" Zifeara was staring off into the forest, looking about as awkward as a wolf could.

Aun couldn't believe what she had just said, or how she had managed to say it so seriously, since it was pretty lame.

She refused to look at him. "Aun, this is my job and mine alone; I was created *solely* for this purpose. You can follow me around if you want, but it isn't business. It's personal. Frankly, you're lucky to get that. I've never been in the habit of letting anyone come with me before, so don't sweat it. You can just come along as a friend, for as long as you want."

Zifeara being so sentimental over the past couple of days had really thrown Aun off his game. He wasn't used to the lack of sass or any form of snark she usually offered. "Are you sure? I'm known for being trouble," he said in a joking tone. He wished he was kidding, but tigers will be tigers in this day and age.

Zifeara looked back at him and sounded like her old self for a moment. "And I'm known for centuries of murder. Aun, I like you. That's an accomplishment in itself, but not many people want to stick around, so you can do what you want. If you wanna go, fine, but you can always stay. Or come back. I'll be around. I'm always around."

Aun's tail stopped wagging. She had just offered something his own family had never even given him. "Zifeara, I don't want to go anywhere but wherever you're going. Fuck my family. They don't even like me."

She continued to smile, "Well okay, then. Let's get you back into shape so we can keep going. Think you can run yet?"

"Oh, I think I can manage somehow." Darting off into the woods to hear her call after him about being careful was so rewarding.

¤ ¤ ¤

Today the road was long and winding but the three of them were happy, healthy, and getting along perfectly for once.

Aun couldn't help noticing how being so close to death makes you really just enjoy life a little more. With Zifeara's training, the ever-changing scenery, and generally nothing to worry about, things were looking up for him. He felt almost at 100 percent and had successfully convinced Zifeara that he'd be okay to keep going. Now on the path to Usakara, the three of them were eating leftovers from all the food Fang had made. Aun hated to admit it, but every single bit of it was delicious.

"Fang, how much did you even manage to make? You were cooking all day but we've been eating for two now," Zifeara asked in awe of the sheer amount of food that he just kept pulling out of her bag for them.

He merely smiled. "I honestly don't think you know how easy it is to make about seven different dishes at once when you have a whole kitchen at your disposal, much less when you have an entire kitchen *all day* and nothing better to do. I probably have two more days worth in here still. Haha, you act like I don't cook for you all the time."

She shoved another one of the rolls in her mouth and talked through it. "Well yeah, but hell, this is a *lot* of food. And it's all really good."

Fang was always happy when she liked his cooking, but he had only wasted the entire day in the kitchen so that he didn't have to be around while Zifeara spent her day in bed with Aun. That first day he had still been pretty bad, so she had to help him drink and kept a very close watch over him. At least now that they were back on the road everything was fairly normal again - except that Zifeara and Aun were problematically close. Granted, since Aun was feeling better, he had his sleeping-with-Zifeara privileges retracted, but that didn't mean everything was the same. She had lost some of her reserved nature when dealing with the tiger, Fang could tell. They were both on almost the same footing now; the only thing separating them was the history he and Zifeara had. Well, that and the fact that he was smarter.

"Fang!" Zifeara's voice snapped him back to attention. "Did you hear a single thing I said just now?"

"Uh... no, I didn't. Sorry, I got lost for a second. What?"

She rolled her eyes and sighed. "I said when we get to the next city, you and Aun are going to have to be far more cautious. Usakara is a horrible cesspool of bullshit. Thieves, prostitutes, a thriving black market for just about anything revolting, you name it. The crime rings in this city are out of control, it's just not my problem. The kitsune we're after does work in a brothel, but I don't have to destroy the whole thing to stop her."

Aun piped up at this point. "I would imagine brothels are actually pretty good for team Lucifer, right?"

Zifeara's tone oozed sarcasm. "Oh good, you *do* pay attention sometimes!" Despite his mock glare, Aun said nothing and Zifeara continued, "The point is, you two are going to have to either stick to me like glue or just stay holed up in the hotel. Also..."

She paused, clearly debating on the best way to word whatever was on her mind. "Catching a kitsune can be pretty easy if they've gotten too cocky, but I'm not sure either of you are quite prepared for this. You've never gotten to see me take a mark nor have you seen the process I usually have to go through for it."

Aun looked at Zifeara as though she had essentially called him a baby. "Zifeara, please. What could you possibly do to surprise us? I'm well acquainted with both brutal shapeshifter murder and many forms of sexual deviance. If anything, all that could surprise me is what you're planning to wear for this. I doubt you, of all people, wear men's clothing to a fancy brothel."

Now she definitely wasn't going to tell them how she was planning to get to the kitsune. This particular tactic seemed best left a surprise. "You say that, but I can imagine you are severely underestimating what I'm about to have to do. You think this is going to be a snap of my fingers. Are you forgetting that there are times this line of work gets me killed?"

"Speaking of, Zia," Fang interjected, "you were going to tell us about the first time you actually died, but we got distracted by imps and you never did..."

As much as Fang would never ever revel in any harm coming to Zifeara, he was abundantly curious as to what death was like. He knew he'd find out someday, but he'd like to have an idea of what to expect.

¤ ¤ ¤

Zifeara was starting to get impatient. Her target was moving constantly and had been doing so for the week she had been tailing him. This man was powerful and had business dealings all over the continent, but he didn't even stop to sleep. He always slept while en route to his next deal, surrounded by his caravan of bodyguards. The demons he had chosen to protect him would be an insurmountable measure of trouble for her to fight, and honestly Zifeara didn't want to deal with them if she didn't have to.

She had tried to drop into the carriage as something small and catch the man by surprise first, but he seemed to have a sixth sense of when he was in danger. Ever since he almost caught her, he kept guards in his carriage as well. She would have just set his carriage on fire, but luck tended to be a bit of a dick to her; her target was immune. She had so hoped not to have to go dragon for this, but it looked somewhat unavoidable. She was still not terribly experienced at maintaining her largest shifts for extended periods so she was uncertain if it would even be an option, though at the rate things were going, she might have to try.

Zifeara waited until the cover of night to steal herself away and rest on the top of the carriage. She had become a moth, and her new plan seemed as good as any. Even immortals could be crushed to death. Ensuring she had positioned herself over the appropriate side of the vehicle, she shifted quickly, the hulking form of her newly reptilian body effortlessly flattening the wood and people below her. The remaining guards reacted rapidly, leaping into action to try to spear and lance and fire arrows at the dragon which had just taken out their master's carriage.

Zifeara unleashed fire all around her, killing many of the bodyguards, though just as many either avoided it or were unaffected. They fought her, and they fought hard. It was ultimately too much; Zifeara's strength waned. She couldn't keep this form any longer; while she tried to shift into a much smaller raven, one of the lancers had managed to intercept her. His long weapon pierced her chest mid-form, dropping her to the ground. At first she still tried to move. Zifeara had been wounded many times before and was usually in enough of a stable state to get to safety. She thought differently once her body refused to obey her commands.

She was a mangled mess somewhere between bird and dragon, unable to become one or the other. Her feathered dragon hand/wing clutched at the hole in her chest, but she could produce no fire. In fact, she felt something wet make contact with her talons before she should have been able to feel blood. Something sloshed itself out of her chest and onto her hand.

Zifeara looked down and very much hoped what she thought she saw was just a byproduct of the woozieness brought on by rapid blood loss. The thing she was now holding had what looked suspiciously like the left ventricle of a standard heart exposed to the air and was ragged where the lance had torn through it. The worst part was how it was still slightly quivering; trying desperately to continue its function, further asserting itself as a misplaced vital organ. Zifeara lurched forward. She was definitely conscious and now in searing pain, but her body was not only refusing to shift, but now also unable to do much of anything.

She was on her knees and falling ever closer to the ground before it dawned on her. She didn't need oxygen to survive. It was the lack of circulation that was keeping her down. She was simply losing too much blood. That and since the blood wasn't moving within her, there was no friction in her veins to draw even the slightest bit of energy from so she wasn't healing fast enough. Zifeara knew her internal workings were complicated, but she had never bothered to ask her mother more about it before. But now she knew it was possible. She was dying.

Her vision began clouding, not drastically at first, just enough so that nothing was as clear as it should be. The remaining guards were all talking about what to do now that their employer was deceased. Zifeara could still hear just fine, though things were sounding a little more like she was underwater the longer this went on. It was as her sight finally departed that she felt something... different. It felt like drifting off to sleep, the pain of the hole in her chest being replaced with a cold feeling. Her last thoughts were that this must be the heat leaving her body and wondering what would happen upon her return.

It was the middle of the night when Zifeara sat straight up, gasping for the air she didn't need but had sorely missed. She panted heavily for a moment before taking in her surroundings. Someone had moved her off the road she had collapsed on. She was alive again, gripping at the spot in her breast which had sported a large gap last she had seen. Zifeara was back to the way she should be; a perfect picture of health. She rose slowly from the ground, not trusting her legs to hold her immediately. Once convinced she'd be okay, Zifeara took off; a lone bat in the darkness of the evening.

¤ ¤ ¤

"Wait, you were *awake* the whole time? That... that really sucks, Zifeara," Aun offered sympathetically.

Zifeara simply shrugged in response. "It sounds weird to say, but honestly, you kind of get used to it and it becomes nothing more than an inconvenience. I think the last time I died, my last thought was literally 'Ah shit, not again' before I was out. It isn't a big deal."

"Zia, what-" Fang abruptly stopped talking and Zifeara recognized the look of concentration on his face. He was listening. Sure enough, her friend turned his headphones down and swiveled his head around.

Aun's ears perked as well, fidgeting and turning this way and that to pinpoint the sound. The horses stopped walking, feeling their rider's nervous energy.

"Aun, what is that?" Fang whispered, knowing Zifeara either couldn't hear it at all or that the sound was still too far off for her to pick it up. The initial noise was swift, alerting Fang to its presence, but if he hadn't lowered the volume on his precious ear guards, he wouldn't be hearing it now. It was a low keening sound; similar to wolf song, but it was definitely not wolves. Whatever this was sounded far more vicious. And bigger. And it was getting closer.

Zifeara soon heard the noise as well. "Oh hell. Hyenadons. We need to be ready for them; these things never give up on something they think they can eat. Aun, with me.

Fang, you keep them away from the horses. They'll surely go for them. Don't shoot at their heads, their skulls are too thick. Go for the heart or neck to hit the windpipe."

They quickly moved the horses up against a rocky hill, so that there was only one direction the beasts could come from.

Zifeara and Aun shifted, equally matched in size for once.

The tiger shot her a glance and the panther's deep voice reflected just how large of a cat she was now, "Hyenadons are no lightweights. A full grown female can tip the scales at just over 600 pounds, so being the smaller one does me no good here. Don't hesitate to use your electricity, Aun. These things are vicious and won't just run away when outmatched; any advantage you have over them, *use*. Got me?"

The tiger dipped his head. "Got you."

Zifeara turned to glance at their unshifted companion, who met her gaze, pistols out and ready. "Fang?"

"Got you." He didn't sound nervous, but his eyes betrayed him. These were about to be the most dangerous things he'd ever faced and he was *entrusted* with three lives. Zifeara thought he could do this. He *would* do this.

The panther smirked her approval and turned to face forward, the strange, high-pitched barking and whining noises drawing nearer. She had known they couldn't out-run these things, so she had chosen to prepare for them instead. Now all they had to worry about were the trap-like jaws and they'd be fine.

The first hyenadon burst from the underbrush and made a beeline for the nearest prey animal, Fang. It didn't give Zifeara time to try to talk to them, instead making her jump to intercept it before he could even take aim.

Extending her claws to cut a windpipe or jut through a heart was easy enough, but the rest of the pack had caught up.

Four more large females came crashing into view, snarling and sizing up what they wanted most. Three dove towards Aun while Fang had taken the fourth, delivering a crack shot to its chest.

Zifeara tried to aid the tiger, but the Queen of the pack finally showed herself, surrounded by her small handful of males. Seven hyenadons was a *lot*, and she could only hope that Aun would be able to handle himself.

The tiger stood stock still as the females descended upon him, only to roar as he unleashed what had to be a few *thousand* volts of electricity. Not all elementals could throw their talents like Zifeara could; he'd needed them to get close to hit them all at once.

The Queen gave a curt bark and her males started moving, all six of them rushing for the horses. This was why it was beyond helpful for Fang to have more than one gun. He was quick to take shots at two of them, though the second one he only wounded enough to make it slow down.

Zifeara blocked two more males, latching onto one while shifting her tail to spear through the second. The other two almost made it to the horses when the tiger freed himself of the heavy corpses on top of him and sprang, knocking into one and sending them all tumbling to the side. While this gave Fang time to get another few shots off, he couldn't hit anything vital from where they had landed; not without hitting their friend.

Nipping at her wherever they could, the hyenadons Zifeara fought did minimal damage before she took them out. The huge, spotted mass of teeth and claws that slammed into her afterwards was *not* happy.

The Queen was frothing at the mouth as she endeavored to fit as much of the large cat that had killed her favorite boys in her jaws as she could. Her clawed paws raked down Zifeara's sides, digging deep into her flesh and that was about the time she followed the tiger's example.

Zifeara set her pelt on fire, causing the larger female to yelp and abandon her vindictive biting. Just as the Queen scrambled to get up, two more shots rang out, the bullets imbedding themselves in her thick shoulders. Fang may not have been able to kill her that way, but he could distract her from her biggest problem.

Growling, Zifeara turned and launched herself at the Queen, trying to at least get at her throat. The mass of fur that collided with the already unstable beast from the other side toppled them, dropping all 600 plus pounds onto Zifeara and immobilizing her. The hyenadon rolled, devolving into a strange mix of barking, yipping, and cackling. As the black cleared from her vision, Zifeara could see Aun perched on the Queen's back.

The tiger had sunk his teeth and claws in and was holding on for all he was worth. Small arcs of electricity crackled across his fur, making it all stand slightly before he discharged, stun locking the hyenadon. Her muscles tensed from the sheer voltage flooding her mammoth frame, twitching violently as Aun disentangled himself, heavily panting and limping back from the body.

"Fang, make sure she's dead. I don't believe it 'til there's no way she could get up." Zifeara stood on shaky legs, still in the process of getting feeling back into them.

Her friend nodded, coming around the front of the beast and firing a few times into where her heart had to be. The spasms died down quickly and Zifeara finally looked at the tiger more closely. He was covered in scratches, some far larger than others, and had a good size chunk taken out of his shoulder. His fur was still sparking here and there, but Aun was very clearly ready to drop. She hustled to his side and he leaned all his weight on her, trying to catch his breath.

"Aun, are you okay? Why in the world would you try to get the big one? I could have done that..."

He smirked before wincing. "Almost got you. Coulda grabbed your neck..."

Before she could protest, Fang came around to stand beside them. "He's right Zifeara, she pointed her head down far enough that she could have gotten your neck in her jaws... He kinda just saved you..."

Aun was slowly shifting back to normal and would have hit dirt if Zifeara hadn't been faster. He grumbled at her as she picked him up, carrying him toward the horses. "Eh, 'm fine. Been hurt worse, 'm just tired."

"Tired or not, you're pretty beat up and I'm going to have to do something about this huge bite. Especially if you stopped me from dying when you probably should have just let her get me. Even if it had killed me, I would have come back. You would not."

Aun tried to protest further, but that stopped when she set him down to lean on the rock cliff and promptly whipped his shirt over his head. The only sound he could manage was a subdued yelp and the faint blush overtaking his face wasn't something she had expected from the boy who treated flirting like a well-loved pastime.

Pulling out what she needed from her bag, Zifeara turned Aun's face to look at her. "This is going to hurt a little bit, nothing I can do about that, but let me know if I'm pushing too hard when I wrap your shoulder up, okay?"

Though his eyes were a little bleary, he was paying attention, mouth forming a thin line as he nodded. This was a far cry from how he had reacted the last time she had tried to help him with his injuries, meaning he was either too tired from expending that much electricity at once or he was actually starting to trust her. The latter would be nice considering she had a hand in saving his life once now, but in this day and age, trust was hard to come by for most.

Hovering over the bite on his shoulder with the bottle of rubbing alcohol she'd produced, she offered one more sympathetic glance before tipping it. Aun hissed through his clenched teeth but didn't move, steeling himself against the sting. After she'd mopped up the mess, he handled being wrapped well. Zifeara got lost in methodically moving her roll of gauze up and over, over and under, until Fang's voice behind her snapped her out of the repetitive trance.

"Is he going to be alright?"

Fang was used to seeing her and Aun race about and play-fight for hours on end without stopping, so this had to be and odd sight for him. As far as he knew, the tiger had the energy of an unsupervised toddler and that battle should not have worn him out so thoroughly.

"Oh yeah, he'll be fine." Zifeara tied the gauze off, shoving unused supplies back into her bag. "He's just worn out."

"Why?"

Aun's sarcastic tone popped into the conversation as he wasn't content to be talked about right in front of his face. "Because unlike some people," he nodded his head at her, "I don't have an endless source of energy. There's only so much electricity I can produce before I drop dead from exhaustion. They say it gets easier with age but, uh... not being all tiger doesn't really help me keep up with the curve. I only meant to discharge once- when I let the first three pile on top of me, but..."

"Like I said, next time don't be the hero." Zifeara playfully ruffled his hair as she stood back up. "If it comes to that, just let her eat me. I'd rather be out of commission for a day than have you get hurt."

She turned to meet Fang's ruby gaze and her ears tilted back slightly. *"Either of you."*

As much as it looked like there was about to be a debate about this, she didn't let it happen, instead shuffling Aun to his feet.

"Come on, let's get going. I'd prefer we not be spotted by some of the things that are going to turn up for these bodies. We're almost where we need to be."

CHAPTER 30

Everyone Is a Little Bit Gay

O f all the things Zifeara said Usakara would be, the most jarring to Aun was how *big* it was. His village had somewhere in the realm of 150 people in it and his was one of the biggest clans of tigers, as well as the oldest. His home was not small nor was the wall that encased it.

As soon as they had come through the mountain pass and had gotten their first look at the place, he couldn't seem to close his mouth. This city had to house *thousands* of people, either permanently or as transients and that was... a little scary honestly. The wall around the city towered over them as they passed through the gates, dwarfing the one he was used to by at least a story.

Once they got into the city, however, the next thing to render him speechless was the mixed grab bag of species passing before his eyes. The tiger couldn't even place what most of these people were, much the less the ones that clearly weren't just a straight animal hybrid. He gaped as he saw people that had legs which bent at odd angles and yet had no problems walking, with too many or not enough eyes, with spines in places that *should not* have spines, and with more skin colors than he'd ever seen or thought possible. He even saw people he seriously could not tell the gender of to save his striped hide.

He was only aware Zifeara was talking to him because Orro Heme waited for Thrush to walk up to his side and there were fingers being snapped next to his head.

"Pay attention, country boy. I know culture shock is consuming but I only want to say this to both of you once more. Usakara is dangerous in a way neither of you are familiar with. This place is infamous for being an unsavory shithole. It has an abundant black market, is a stop on a sentient trafficking circuit, and life has no value here. We stick together or you stay in our room while we have to be here, understand?"

Aun nodded and turned back to inspect the people they were passing. Even though he supposed they looked normal for a town this size, what did he know? He'd never left home before. He hadn't been alive for so much as two decades. He'd been wrong about looks before. While he was taking everything in, Zifeara and Fang talked about something or another he wasn't paying attention to 'til they made it to what could only be described as 'the fancy part of town.'

Seeing the looks the boys were giving her, Zifeara shrugged. "I know someone. I always do, but in this town, if you don't stay on the good side, you might die in your sleep. Life is easier when you have connections."

She had the horses trot on to the only palace that seemed to be open to the public. The massive white structure had accents of blue and gold, an expansive courtyard within an even larger garden, and what looked to be a smaller palace for their steeds.

Every stable they'd been to had an attendant to take care of their horses, but the man who took the reins of their precious mounts looked immaculate. While he had the lower half of a horse himself, he stood with his back rod straight and not a hair in his sweeping ponytail was out of place. He didn't even have a speck of dirt on his clothes.

"Zifeara, where *are* we?" Fang had the appropriate amount of awe in his tone, but she merely smiled and turned to lead the way inside.

"Just because I have work to do doesn't mean I can't see a friend once in a while. I think you'll like Ming-Da. She's... entertaining."

The double redwood doors barring the entrance to the main building were pulled inward by two more staff and the glaring brightness of the main lobby was instantaneous. From the polished marble floors to the white upholstery on the birchwood chairs, to the lightly colored tapestries hung on the white walls - everything in this building was so...

"Dios, I haven't seen *hospitals* this clean." Once they were inside, Fang was less impressed and had a sour taste in his mouth.

"Well, everything should be clean when you're the most affluent spa on this side of Urterra."

Fang tilted his head slightly. "Ur...? Oh jeez, the continent hasn't even split yet? I knew we were in the past but I didn't think we were that far."

Currently, Marien only had one landmass and several islands to its name. A series of violent earthquakes over the next thousand years would trigger the separation of the supercontinent into smaller portions, scattering its inhabitants and forming the world the future was familiar with. That was a far less fun time if Zifeara remembered correctly. It was much harder to find the people she needed to when even the world itself didn't stay in one place for long.

She shrugged and made her way to the front desk, leaning on the counter to address the rather furry creature manning it. "Good day. Would Lady Chei be in her office today?"

The seemingly sentient mass of hair raised what could pass as arms from its paperwork, bringing them up to part the fur on its face to reveal disproportionately large golden eyes. "Hmm? I believe she is, who may I say is seeking her?"

"Zifeara Nightshade. She knows exactly who I am, though this time I have two guests as well."

The thing nodded, picking up a small bell and shook it, causing a pleasant chime to echo off the stone. Zifeara was about to smack Aun upside the head for staring gormlessly at the poor girl, but the arrival of another staff member snapped him out of it. The young man who'd come to receive instructions for informing their mistress of the arrival of important guests was by far stranger than his coworker.

His stalked eyes darted between who he was speaking to and his surroundings every few moments. The human-looking upper half of his body bordered the uncanny valley, slightly bulkier in places humans shouldn't be. His ruddy skin, if you could call it that, had an odd sheen to it, especially in places where it connected in small plates. It mirrored the chitinous armor of his four legs, which worked in perfect tandem to propel him back up the staircase he'd emerged from at nightmarish speed.

While she could see the benefit to such a design, Zifeara would never be able to watch a crab scuttle without inwardly shuddering slightly. Based on the look on Fang's face, witnessing a crab climb stairs ever again might make him cry, and Aun wasn't faring much better. They had to stop this.

"Listen, while we're here, you two need to stop staring at people like that. I know this is a lot to take in, but it's rude and I have a reputation to keep. Plus it might get you stabbed or something if you look at the wrong person that way."

Aun pressed closer to her, dropping his volume to barely a whisper. "Okay, but what *is* the... person... at the desk?"

"That's Ari and she's a Mirrow. She looks like an upright cat under all that fur, two to five tails depending on species, usually only two eyes but sometimes three."

Now it was Fang's turn to be surprised. "*She's* a Mirrow?"

Zifeara rolled her eyes. "Yes. She just has long hair and doesn't like to cut it. Now will you-"

"Zifeara?"

The rather feminine voice behind them cut her off and she immediately whipped around to run towards her friend. The last time Zifeara had been through here, Ming had been busy and couldn't see her. They both crashed into each other and she lifted the shorter woman off the floor.

At a glance, Ming-Da Chei was a well put together noblewoman. Her plentiful black hair was gathered in a tight bun atop her head, her sharp features spoke of an authority few dared to question, and her tan skin glowed like rays of the setting sun over ocean sand. She appeared remarkably human though she was a hybrid, the only things giving her away being that she had four arms and a stubby tail protruding from the end of her spine.

Her onyx eyes sparkled as she released her friend from the tight embrace. "Gods, I'm so sorry I missed you last time! I have so much to tell you about and you better-"

She stopped mid-sentence and directed her attention towards the two men she didn't recognize.

"Zifeara? Who are your..." she eyed them both up and down before continuing, "guests?"

Zifeara settled into an easy smile and motioned her boys forward, setting a hand on each man's shoulder as she introduced them. "This is Fang Nightstalker, my best friend, and Aun Thunderfang, another good friend of mine. This is Ming-Da Chei, matron of the bathhouse."

After greetings had been exchanged, Ming eagerly led the group out of the lobby and into the main area of the spa. Sunlight filtered in through the glass ceiling, bathing everything in warm rays. Bamboo walls separated out several small chambers, each with either a flat table or a plush chair in it. Past all of these were chambers a little more spaced out and a bit larger, with even fancier chairs and a small army of people standing around them. As soon as they caught sight of their mistress, the staff sorted into two groups according to their gender, and stood patiently by one of four stalls.

Ming turned and placed herself between Zifeara and her boys, holding her hand out towards the group of girls. "You two will be on this side, thank you."

Fang and Aun both looked at each other, neither missing the grin Zifeara cast them over her shoulder as she proceeded into one of the sections.

It was the tiger that spoke up first. "For what, exactly?"

Ming's smile was as welcoming as it was mischievous. "Well you're in a spa, it would be remiss of me not to indulge my guests in all I have to offer."

As she disappeared into the stall next to Zifeara's and small curtains were pulled shut over both, the women huddled around the boys, ushering each into their own section. They were told to change into the bathrobes sitting on the chair before the curtains were pulled shut and they were left to do just that.

Fang was exceptionally unhappy to discover that his didn't fit very well since he was taller than a standard human by far, but he wasn't sure how to bring this issue up to the staff. They barely gave him enough time to change before hustling him further down the row of stalls. The next chamber had chairs built with backs at odd angles, and basins on wooden pedestals resting behind them. He had never been to a spa himself, but at least he knew what they were for. He had to persuade the industrious people ready to dote on him to let him remove his headphones and then to speak softly while they worked, but they were ready to serve and he got his way.

When Fang looked over to see how Aun was taking it all since the chairs were not separated, he was almost surprised to find that the tiger was practically melting into his seat already. One of the women- decidedly some type of dog- was busy running warm water through his hair, careful not to get it in his ears while another had started filing his nails. The tiger's tail was wagging slowly back and forth.

He couldn't say he was particularly thrilled about having complete strangers touch him so much at first, but Fang could see the appeal as soon as the faun washing his hair started to rub at his scalp. It didn't hurt that he could not only hear Zifeara as his ears were unobstructed, but see her as well. She was just as relaxed as Aun currently was, giggling with her girlfriend about what shenanigans had taken place in the city since her last visit. It sounded mostly like high society gossip from what he could tell, but seeing her comfortable made him relax. Zifeara was only off high alert in this time when she was convinced they were safe.

He was fine with his hair and his nails, but he became expressly nervous again when they asked him to move down to the next stall and lay on one of the tables. Then they asked him to take his robe off.

Aun seemed to care much less, undressing before anyone had shielded their new chamber from view and shamelessly winked at the female staff when they began to whisper amongst themselves. It wasn't until the area mirroring theirs gained its occupants that Fang realized what they were trying to do for him. Ming and Zifeara were already out of their robes and instead had *very* short towels covering themselves. They both hopped up on a table, stomach down, and carried on whatever conversation they were having while two of the larger men in their group hovered nearby.

As soon as she looked up to check on her boys, the gleeful gleam in Zifeara's eyes clouded over with worry. "Fang? What's the matter, hun?"

Scratching the back of his head, he didn't really have a good answer for her. Not to mention that he was a little... distracted now. "Uh... I don't uhm, don't think I want to..."

"You don't have to do anything you don't want to. I'll warn you though, the massage is the best part of this entire thing and if you try it, you'll like it."

Wait, the *what*? That could only mean- The men from before cracked their knuckles and moved to the women's tables, grabbing a couple of towels and delicately draping them over both girls rears so they could shift their first towels around. The alarms went off in Fang's head. That big, thoroughly muscled blonde stud was about to have his hands all over the one thing in this world or any other Fang would kill for, and she was going to let him.

"I'm serious, Fang; if it makes you so uncomfortable, you can go sit in a chair again and they can-" Zifeara gave a soft gasp as something cold dribbled onto her back, "do something way less invasive. I know I certainly didn't sign up for this part the first few times either. Though, based on the state Aun is in, you may want to reconsider, hahaha."

Turning to see what she meant, he discovered that the tiger was laying on his face, ears back, tail flicking, completely blissed out. The girl running her hands over his back was smiling and humming softly. It almost covered the other sound coming from his side. It took Fang a little too long to realize that Aun was *purring*.

He gave up. Avoiding looking back across the way since he'd surely snap if he did, Fang laid on his table. He only took the robe off once the peppy little mouse waiting to provide his massage handed him his towel, mandating *some* level of personal dignity be retained. He situated himself to his satisfaction and tried to keep his eyes closed so that he could just ignore the looks he was getting. Nothing stopped him from hearing the staff giggle about how cute it was that he was so shy, but he could do his best to listen to what Zifeara was discussing with her friend instead and bury is burning face in his arms.

He wasn't sure how such a small woman could muster the strength to turn every single one of his bones to jelly, but he was happy he'd decided to submit himself to this. Zifeara was right, this was the best part. Soon the chatter around him melted into the same drone as the girl worked him over, rubbing the ache out of spots he didn't even know could be sore. Fang swore he was almost falling asleep until something made his ears perk.

"Miss Zifeara? I'm finished, are you certain there's nothing *else* I can do for you?"

Cracking an eye open and combating the haze settling over his mind, Fang glared towards the table Zifeara was still lazing on.

"Hmm? Oh, no Ruda. You know I'm not into that."

The man looked a bit put out, but Ming chimed in and it made Fang tense hard enough that he heard his mouse pout.

"It doesn't have to be him, you know. You have your pick of literally anyone in my employ. Just point and they're yours."

Were they... talking about what he thought they were? They couldn't be, right? This was a high class place and he was just overreacting.

Zifeara sat up, holding her towel to her chest and reaching for her robe. "No thanks, but I think I will take some extra time on my feet instead. That felt great and I'm definitely about it."

Fang almost settled back down until both the girl massaging Aun and himself stopped, coming around to the front of the tables with their robes in hand. Aun was slow to grumble himself into a sitting position and redress, but Fang was faster. He was pretty sure they were talking about him again, but he couldn't quite hear them past the hot blood storming through his ears.

Both masseurs left and were replaced by a new girl that stopped in front of Aun. She seemed to be some sort of rabbit if her tail and legs were any indication. "Sir?"

Her voice was soft as silk and as soon as Aun looked at her, she started to faintly blush. "Is there something else I can do for you? The back rooms are spacious and comfortable..."

The tiger blinked slowly a few times, ears rising until they were fully erect as he processed what was being offered to him. "I... Really?"

Fang's jaw was practically on the floor. While both boys looked to Ming-Da, she merely nodded and rose from her own table. Zifeara smiled and rolled her eyes as she asked her friend a question about dinner and left her boys to do what they would. Oh no, okay, this was...

The girl that came around the corner from the other section stopped in front of Fang, barely a few inches from his knees where they were hanging off the table. Her long dark hair fell to her waist, small furry ears tilted in embarrassment, lithe black tail twitching behind her, lagoon blue eyes looking up at him shyly. *Dios,* she could almost be related to Zifeara. He hadn't seen a girl he found this pretty in a long time. She was for him.

She took one of his hands and pulled as Aun and his new 'friend' started heading back to wherever they were supposed to be further *serviced.* Fang could swear through the burning heat climbing his neck that he could taste bile on his tongue. This wasn't okay. She didn't want to be doing this- doing *him.* This was prostitution and he probably couldn't go through with it without throwing up.

The cat tugged again and Fang shook his head, swallowing thickly. "N-no, I... Thank you, but I'm- I'm good."

Her ears perked and she tilted her head, seemingly confused at why he would refuse such a thing. Fang was starting to think she was mute and it just made him feel worse. He stood from his table, hands raised to his chest and backed down the corridor towards where Zifeara had been going. By then, Aun had turned his head to shoot an incredulous look over his shoulder.

As soon as Fang took a faltering step back, the tiger had turned all the way around and placed himself next to the other cat. "Dude, what is *wrong* with you?"

He draped his arm over the girl's shoulder and sneered at Fang before heading the way the rabbit had been leading him. He put an arm over her shoulder, too. "Don't feel bad, he has no idea what he's missing. I'll be more than happy to make it up to you."

The second they stopped looking at him, Fang nearly tripped over his own feet to go the opposite direction. He wanted nothing to do with that; not only was it morally objectionable, but... no one really *did it* for him anymore- not since he figured out he might be more than a little invested in his best friend. He hadn't particularly been in the habit of sampling the selection laid out before him pretty much every night at work, but there were times he'd considered it. The only thing stopping him was his own guilt. Any time he thought he might want to try again, he couldn't imagine being situated intimately with the woman actually in front of him. Picturing Zifeara while he was with someone else was definitely rude, but it was also *dangerous.* It was just a matter of time until he slipped up if he did unspeakable things to her in his head too often.

As soon as Fang half-fell into the stall Zifeara and Ming has repositioned themselves in, their conversation came to a halt.

Zifeara raised an eyebrow at him, clearly not expecting him to still be here, but it was Ming that spoke. She frowned and the tone of her voice was of one who'd been told something was amiss. "What's the matter? I thought you would have liked Oona, was there a reason you didn't? I can get all the girls together if you-"

"No!" Fang hadn't meant to cut her off so forcefully, so he dialed the panic down a little. "N-no, she was fine- nice! She was a nice girl I'm sure, but I don't- I didn't want to- why are they...?"

Shooing the man at her feet out of her way, Zifeara stood up, taking both of Fang's hands and trying to dissuade him from blowing a gasket. "Hey, shhhh. It's alright, I told you it was perfectly fine to opt out of something you didn't want here. Ming's spa is also the high-end brothel; the only one in town that pays its girls a decent wage and gives them the choice to refuse clients that don't treat them well. They do it because they're okay with it and it makes them extra money- not because they're forced to. Do you want to come sit down with me?"

Gods, yes. At this point Fang didn't even care what the context of their conversation had been, he wanted Zifeara close. She was painfully aware he didn't handle things like this well; she'd been with him to plenty of events where his fans had been a little too pushy and knew it gave him anxiety.

He nodded his head in a jerky motion and she was quick to pull and spin him around to sit in the chair she had been in. She nudged her foot between his ankles, prompting him to spread his legs so she could sit in between them on what was left of the chair. Fang leaned all the way back, allowing her to be as comfortable as she could get with her back to his chest. She picked the conversation back up with Ming and, aside from one last worried glance, the other woman entirely dropped the issue he was having.

Fang snaked his arms around Zifeara's stomach, ignoring the pointed looks he was getting from the male staff returning to their task of tending to the girls. He needed to calm back down and couldn't have cared less what they thought. Zifeara was his more than she was theirs, no matter what they were doing for her. This was the way they always sat when he was starting to get overwhelmed around other people; she made a protective wall of herself in front of him and it had never failed to comfort him before.

He wasn't keeping track of time, but at some point the staff were done and they were ushered to their room for the night. They had an hour before dinner was served, and that gave them plenty of time to settle in. Following a staff member to the third floor, the room they were given was spacious and had its own bathroom attached- something they hadn't seen yet in this time. While Fang laid on their bed to read,

Zifeara locked herself in for a bath to wash all the oil from her massage off. She could have burned it, but she seemed intent on soaking in the huge tub.

She wasn't out yet when the door to the room opened again. If Aun had looked boneless earlier, then he had no muscle left now. He dragged himself across the room, collapsing face first onto the bed Fang didn't occupy with a heavy sigh.

Fang eyed him before returning to his book. "Ambition can be one's downfall, you know."

It was muffled by sheets, but the tiger's tone definitely had a gleefully exhausted waver to it. "What*ever* dude, I haven't been this happy in years. Can we stay? Like, forever?"

The other boy rolled his eyes and shook his head. "Maybe *you* can, but I bet you'd have to find a way to make yourself useful. Besides, don't you have something you're supposed to be doing right now? Like for your people?"

Aun raised an arm off the bed to make a swatting motion at him, which Fang couldn't help but chuckle at. The tiger turned his head slightly to better be heard.

"You really don't know what you missed out on."

Closing his tome, Fang couldn't help but sound unimpressed. "How so?"

"They were fighting over you, you know– over which one got to take you back. Gods if I understand *why*."

Flattering as that was, he didn't regret passing the offer up. He didn't take kindly to Aun's last comment, however. "I don't see why that's so unbelievable. What about six foot four, pale as hell, and insanely unruly dark hair *isn't* sexy in your time?"

His companion cracked an eye open to glare. "It makes you look like a vampire!"

Fang threw his hands up. "I *am* a vampire!"

The door to the bathroom opened in a small cloud of steam and Zifeara stepped out, wringing her hair and burning it dry as she went. "Boys, boys, you're both very pretty. Head downstairs for dinner, I'll catch up with you in a second."

Aun griped about just barely laying down, but got up anyway, ignoring Zifeara's comment about it being his own fault he was so worn out.

As Fang passed her on his way out, he couldn't hide his curiosity. "What's your hangup? You're rarely the last one to dinner."

He would never get tired of the troublemaking glint in her eye, but the timing of it was concerning. "I still have business to take care of, hun; we came here for a job, after all. I'm going to leave for work right after we eat, so I'm going to slip into something more appropriate for the task."

He hummed, exiting their room and closing the door to leave her to it. He was about halfway down the stairwell when the noise from the dining room hit him. Fang smacked himself in the forehead. He could hear the din from downstairs already because he'd forgotten to put his headphones back on. Sighing at having to climb the stairs again but unable to go without them, he hustled to get back to their room. He hoped Zifeara was done so that he didn't have to wait too long.

Turning out of the stairwell, he came inches from smacking right into someone else. He was only spared the embarrassment because they seemed to have faster reflexes than him, stopping on a dime before they hit his chest. Fang was apologizing to the man before he even saw him. The guy was at most four inches shorter than him and was clearly some sort of mutty hybrid. His ears were a good size, possibly feline with the way they nestled into his inky hair, alert thanks to the near mishap. His tail wagged slightly, full and dark as his hair. Fang would almost bet money on it being from a wolf or at least a dog. He was pretty solidly built for his size, likely close to Fang's weight too if not a bit thinner.

"Sorry man, I wasn't looking where-"

When Fang got to his eyes, he forgot how to form words. He missed the smirk spreading across the man's face; he was too stunned by the consuming shade of purple haunting the other's irises. He could recognize that color anywhere at any time. He'd been staring at it reverently for thirty two years. The molten blood slowly climbing his neck nearly made Fang choke.

"Z... Zifeara...?"

Those eyes, paired with the shit-eating grin he was sporting, couldn't have been any more solid proof than if Zifeara had picked it up and hit him with it.

The man smiled and placed a single finger in the middle of Fang's chest, dragging it down as he walked around to get to the stairs.

"Zephyr," he practically purred.

Fang could only watch him descend as he glanced over his shoulder and winked before disappearing. He was glued to the spot. The heat had worked its way not only into his face, but also into his very core. This was stupid. Fang had never felt like this while looking at another man before- hell, he'd only ever felt this way a few times *at all*. He wasn't gay. *He wasn't gay. He'd **never been gay.***

He felt a little gay.

CHAPTER 31

Gender Means Literally Nothing

S tepping into the old building, the hardwood floors creaked under his feet. The place wasn't in disrepair, it'd just been standing for a long time. Dark columns climbed the cream walls, dutifully bearing the complaining ceiling. The older woman at the desk looked him up and down as he shut the sliding door behind him. His sensitive ears picked up the sounds of sheer bliss from several of the surrounding rooms, making him inwardly cringe at what he was here for.

"Is Yahei in tonight?"

The woman nodded but pointed to one of a few chairs lining the left wall. "She is, but she's with someone right now. No guarantee she'll take you either; she's choosy about her clientele. Wait 'til she gets a look at you."

He dipped his head in acknowledgement and took a seat. *Yeah, of course she's picky. You can afford to be when you look like a well fed kitsune does.*

Looking around and trying to ignore the noise from other rooms while he waited, he took note of the few windows he could see. Listened to the way the roof creaked to try to determine if it had a gap somewhere. Turned off his sense of smell to avoid the overbearing scent of sex. Observed how little attention the woman at the desk afforded her surroundings in favor of her book. Assessed the mouse holes in the walls.

He stood tall and straight when the kitsune leaned around the corner of the hallway, eyeing him curiously.

"He here for me, Kim?"

"Yeah. In or out?"

She spent an awfully long time staring at his crotch before nodding. "In. Come with me, sugar." She crooked a finger his way before starting back down towards her room.

He followed, noting that she had her flaxen tails all tied together. She had five. He was going to have to play this up big time for her to drop her guard and it made him grimace. She slid open a screen and he didn't hesitate to duck inside, immediately making himself comfortable on the bed like he wasn't going to need another bath later.

"So what do you want, baby? There isn't anything I don't do, at least not for a cutie like you." Her tone dripped silk down his ears, disarming in a maddening way to those with less resistance.

He made a show of grazing her body with his gaze, stopping on the shoulder she had exposed from her robe. That'd do. He held his hands out. "On my lap. Face me."

She giggled, moving to do as he asked, all while batting her ochre eyes in what she thought was a seductive way. "Ooh, direct. I like it. Tell me what to do, I'll give you everything you want, baby."

Gods he wanted to gag. *Yeah, like a slow death. Bet the feisty ones taste better.*

The very second her legs were straddled over his thighs, her tongue was in his mouth and he sighed, resigned to doing this properly. It wasn't as if he'd never kissed someone before, far from it, but he did love when he got to skip that part. He let her do her damnedest to impress him, thoughts drifting to recall the last time he'd had to go through such a charade to accomplish the task. Had to have been that rich noble a year or so back. Desire of all the ladies, but very, very gay.

Once he felt he'd had quite enough of that, he remembered he was supposed to be having a reaction to all this effort she was putting forth. Forcing extra blood slowly into his cock, he pulled the woman from his mouth and rolled his hips, achieving the desired result. She gasped through her teeth, smiling down at him.

"Mmmm, I thought you might have been big, but *Ruuta!*"

He wasn't sure if she was saying that to butter him up or because she actually meant it, but he didn't care. She was sufficiently convinced he was no threat. Humming in response, he grabbed her jaw and turned her head, working his mouth down the column of her neck. Laving his tongue over her pulse point confirmed that he had the right spot. She giggled as he scraped his teeth over the flesh, grinding her hips down onto what she had been *hoping* to spear herself on tonight.

Shifting at speed was an art and as his fangs sliced through muscle and artery, he had her wrists in hand before she could stop him, tentacles climbing her arms to ensure there would be no escape. It was usually very simple to use the initial shock of a surprise attack to turn a situation entirely in his favor and at least this was one of those times. Sort of made up for all the crap he'd had to do to get here. The choking sounds she was making and the scrabbling of clawed feet on the floor was drowned out by all the other noise in this place.

It didn't take too long to drain enough blood that it would prove fatal, meaning he could release her and finally get out of here. Disentangling himself, he let her slide to the floor. He had no desire to wait for his brother tonight. Not here. Standing, burning the blood off himself only took but a few moments. After that, it was as easy as turning to a small black mouse and scampering through a hole by the door. This building was old and all old buildings have mice. Some a bit more murderous than others.

¤ ¤ ¤

"*Alright*, so let me get this straight."

Aun had been a mess ever since he had shown up to dinner this way, but now as he laid arms behind his head, Zephyr couldn't help but smirk. He followed the tiger with his eyes, the younger man pacing endlessly. He couldn't believe it had never occurred to Aun that as a shifter, he could morph his own gender.

"You out of nowhere decided to be a guy one day and just... *did it*? No thought, no planning- just standing there normally one minute and had a dick the next!?"

It was too hard to keep a straight face with Aun making this much of a fuss. Zephyr laughed as he stood, moving to set a hand on the tiger's shoulder. Aun hadn't failed to complain about being shorter, either.

"Look dude, it took me a while to figure out how I looked as a man. When you first shift your gender, you turn into how you *think* you should look, not how you actually do. I'm an anatomy whiz; I know the inner working of a male in any species down to an exact science. Since you seem like you might really be as much of a ladies man as you claim, you should know what a girl looks like by now."

The sarcasm dripping from his mouth didn't seem to faze Aun too much in the grand scheme of things, though one of his ears did tilt a bit. He was likely choosing to just take that insult and move on. Zephyr put his hands on the boys hips and moved him further from the bed.

"Come on, let's have it. Give me your best impression of a female you."

Aun looked at him like he was crazy, but the wheels were clearly turning in his brain. It didn't escape Zephyr's attention that Fang had been intensely quiet the entire time he'd been gender bent, but it was understandable. He had never seen Zifeara as anything other than a woman before. Hell, even when she was an animal, she was usually still female.

Aun took a deep breath in before slowly changing size. He shrank a few inches, shoulders becoming more narrow, facial features and eyes softening. His hair grew longer, now completely covering the left side of his face and sweeping back over his shoulders. Zephyr could feel her hips widen, but not by enough. She wasn't super proportional, but it wasn't bad for a first try.

"Hmm." Moving a circle around her, he could see Aun's tail flicking. This always felt weird at first. "Your hips are too narrow; you'll never survive birthing a baby with those. Still too masculine. Your chest is too big for your height. You either need to gain a few inches back or take a size off. Just because you *like* feeling a big rack doesn't mean you need it. It's a pain in the ass anyway. Speaking of ass, you don't have one. Take what's coming off your chest and put it back there."

Huffing, Aun implemented the suggestions and shuffled her weight around. She was fidgeting, playing with her fingers and shifting from foot to foot. She was clearly acclimating to a different set of genitalia and Zephyr had a decent idea that she'd done that wrong on the inside too. Not that it mattered at the moment.

Looking the new changes over, he slowly nodded his head. "Very good, Aun. Looks more realistic." Taking her jaw in his hand and turning her face side to side, he grinned. "Very cute."

The light blush spreading across her cheeks was also cute. Zephyr let go and dug around in his bag to produce a mirror so Aun could see what she'd accomplished. Sitting himself down next to Fang, he watched the tiger take it all in.

"You..."

Sliding his eyes to the side, it was easy to see the hesitation painted on his best friend's face. Fang didn't know what to do with this. Zephyr raised an eyebrow but it didn't prompt Fang to finish his thought.

"What? I know you aren't used to be me being male, but you've been awfully quiet this whole time. I'm not a completely new person, you know."

Fang narrowed his eyes and it took a minute before he decided on how to phrase his issue. "You... feel different. Like you're acting differently."

"Do I? Might have something to do with how freeing it is to be a dude." Zephyr laid back down, just as he had been before. "You'd be surprised how little flack I take in this time just from switching genders."

"I don't know, you're kind of-"

Fang couldn't think of the word he wanted. Or even set of words. He was thinking something along the lines of 'being a cocky bastard' or 'seem like you might be a douchebag', but at the same time, Zephyr still had all of Zifeara's snark, all of her dedicated teasing, all of her nothing-can-touch-me attitude. It just seemed somewhat repackaged and wrapped up in a ribbon of testosterone. Maybe it was just throwing him off to hear Zifeara's voice two octaves lower slipping through a squared jaw and tumbling down what looked to be a body rivaling his own. The eyes were the same, but everything else was so... foreign.

Aun had been testing her voice out, trying to get it to stick, but now she crossed the room and kicked one of Zephyr's feet. When he looked up, she had her hands on her hips. "Okay. I think this is passable, yeah?"

Zephyr's smile was unsettlingly mischievous. "One way to find out, babe."

Fang almost choked on his own tongue. *Babe!? If anyone was, **he** should be babe.*

Zephyr draped an arm across Aun's shoulders and started moving them towards the door. "You know how to flirt with girls, but if you can adapt that to men, you are so set. That and you need to find a more feminine name you like. I doubt anyone will question it, but you'd be surprised how referring to yourself differently helps you get into character."

"Where are you two going?" Now Fang was up and couldn't have been any more concerned about what leaving these two together would produce.

Casting him a devious look over his shoulder, Zephyr winked. "I think it's time I taught our young friend the one skill I excel in with no effort; the art of the hustle."

¤ ¤ ¤

"What a pretty name... Where are you from, honey? I've never seen stripes like yours before."

On her third try, she was doing much better. Zephyr was keeping a close eye on her from a table at the back, but his ears could pick up the sound of the man's voice with no problems. Bringing Aun into one of the taverns on the shittier side of town was proving to be a wise move. Men saw such a clean, pretty girl here and jumped at the chance to deviate from their usual single-silver whores. Didn't hurt that she was starting to become decent at female body language either.

The man currently chatting Aun- Aurora- up had probably the worst way of storing money he intended to keep. He had it stuffed in a flimsy pouch attached to the sash around his waist, and she was determined to relieve him of it. Zephyr had already done a quick round of pickpocket practice and told her exactly how to abort if she was caught in her attempt.

"Can I buy you a drink? This place has great rum- all the way from the coast!"

Zephyr chuckled to himself. There was no way this guy was actually going to get Aurora *that* kind of liquor, but he was trying to win her over fast. He seemed a little shocked at how well she slammed her shot, but it didn't deter him and Zephyr almost lost his lunch. He couldn't *wait* until later in the night so that he could see all of Aun's very unladylike habits surface despite his current form. Teaching a new hustler was hilarious, especially since he could still hear Fang's disapproval ringing in his ears.

This dude had already been tipsy when they got here, but two more shots in and it was impossibly easy for Aurora to skim a hand along his waist, whispering something into his ear and cutting the drawstring of his pouch with her claws. She had successfully filched his money and had done it efficiently. He was strangely proud of her. The second the man tried to reciprocate and get handsy with her, Zephyr stood up. He knew when things were about to go too far. Coming up behind them, he made sure to pull her back from the guy when he grabbed her waist.

"There you are, baby! I've been looking for you. Who's your..." Zephyr made certain to smile at the guy, "*friend*?"

"Oh, no one, Zephyr. We were just having a nice conversation! Time to go home already?"

"'Fraid so, buttercup. Come on."

She made sure to be extra sweet and innocent while bidding farewell to the man who couldn't be glaring any harder if he tried. The second they were out of the bar and ducked into the connecting alley, Zephyr finally let out the laugh he'd been holding in.

"Hahahaha, good gods girl, you're learning fast! Did that hurt? You sounded so sweet I swear you have to have a cavity by now!"

Aurora snorted, holding up the stolen pouch. "Y'know, I thought it'd be harder than this? You really just do this whenever y'want to, huh?"

He shrugged. "Well, not so much anymore. When I first started needing money for things, sure, but now I have so much that there's no reason for me to. Meaning," he pushed the purse closer to her chest, "that's all yours. You earned it, you keep it."

Her ears tilted like he had told her Einrit wasn't coming this year. "I... it's... mine?"

"Well yeah, what am I going to do with *more* money? I didn't scam a guy well enough to get it, you did. You think learning was its own reward or something?"

Eyes slowly lowering the small bag, Aurora's voice was meek and nearly revenant. "I've... never had my own money before..."

Placing a hand on her shoulder, Zephyr smiled warmly. "First time for everything. Wanna get more?"

The almost sad aura faded quickly, replaced by a gleam of excitement. "Do I!? I wanna make enough to get new clothes!"

Laughing maybe a little too loudly, he clapped her across the back and started moving towards the next seedy watering hole. "Well let's go then, pussy cat. Gotta get to the money before it's spent!"

Aurora was learning how to work sex appeal alarmingly fast.[18] It probably didn't help that all the drinks she was getting were going to her head, but as soon as she figured out showing a little skin made her marks pay even *less* attention, she was working it. There was something almost *primal* about being coveted so much that you could do anything you wanted. Considering she was used to being reprimanded for every single thing she did, this kind of freedom made her feel untouchable. Leveraging sex appeal was so much easier as a woman, mismatched ears or not.

It had gotten to the point that Zifeara reverted back to help her. One pretty girl was bad enough, but the two of them together were very quickly liberating coins from their rightful owners hands. While taking a break and searching for their next target, the girls fell into a topic of conversation Zifeara hadn't expected to land on.

---

[18] "Primitive" – Richard Vission

"Nope, no way, not even for money. He's just too ugly, I can't do it." Aurora giggled and downed the rest of her water before pointing to someone else. "What about him?"

Zifeara looked the man up and down. "And you think he's attractive enough? Straight as you are?"

"Look." The tiger laid a hand over one of the immortal's. "Just 'cause I'm straight doesn't mean I'm not able to say when another man is attractive. Bein' a girl has made me consider my standards more thoroughly, but I know when a guy's good looking."

Zifeara hummed to herself, trying to pinpoint what sort of man Aurora had gone for most of the night, but the fingers over hers stroked softly and it gave her pause. Meeting those beautiful emerald eyes, the sliver of gold in them seemed to shine more brightly than ever.

"I'd say I was surprised to find that you make such a handsome man, but I really wasn't. Makes sense, lookin' at the status quo again."

And of course Aun was still in there somewhere. Zifeara rolled her eyes and removed her hand from the table, but it didn't stop the grin from forming on her face. Sometimes Aun was a pain in the ass when he tried to flirt with her, but other times it was just funny. He was aware she had millenia of experience with men and yet he was so confident that he could make it work. There was something endearing about his tenacity, and yet he still wasn't quite tempting. It was more... *cute* to watch him try. With how well their night had gone, she was almost in the mood to indulge his silly nonsense.

"You know, I'm curious. What is it you think you'd even do if that worked for once?"

Aurora's eyes widened and for just a fraction of a second, she slipped. Her features hardened, almost becoming masculine again. "Wh-what?"

"If I said alright- right here, right now, let's *go*. What would you even do with yourself?"

Now that she was processing what it was that was being said to her, she was sitting up straighter, mouth slightly agape.

Zifeara just shook her head. "That's what I thought. Come on, we should actually go back to our room; it's almost closing time."

She stood and ignored all the noise around her, the drunken jocularity and men trying to get one last shot in with her before giving up. She heard Aurora get up and follow her outside, but what she wasn't prepared for was the toned arms pinning her to the side of the tavern once outside. While it made her flinch very minutely, she wasn't exactly worried when she met Aun's lidded, verdant gaze. He had dropped all pretense of being female and was completely himself again.

"What makes you think I haven't thought about it?"

229

"Everyone has thought about it. Comes with looking like I do." Zifeara's tone was even, but something about the way his own rumbled dangerously in his chest had a warm lizard writhing in her stomach. "The difference is, you know me. Know what I could *do to you* if you tried anything I wasn't happy about. I asked more because I have a funny feeling that you're all talk, no rock."

While he was unfamiliar with the expression, he seemed to understand its meaning. The thoroughly drunken smirk across his face held no menace, but his whispered words certainly did. "Wanna find out?"

Alright. This had gone far enough for her liking. Zifeara's look of unimpressed disdain didn't falter in the slightest as she cracked their skulls together, effectively removing Aun from her space as he clutched at his throbbing head.

He hissed through his teeth as he felt for blood. "Aaah! Zifeara, what the *fuck!?*"

Leaning back against the wooden wall and crossing both her arms and ankles, she tried to fight the spike of smug satisfaction trying to work its way out of her. "Don't you act like I'm the one out of line. I know you'll realize you were an ass tomorrow when you stop being drunk and apologize, but you should know better by now. Don't fuck with the dragon if you can't stand the heat of the fire."

Grumbling and glaring out of one eye, Aun squared himself back up. Apparently bonding time was over tonight and he was thrown into the deep end of the unsavory pool. "Seriously, what is it? What is keeping you from fucking me? 'Cause I have half an idea of what it-"

Pushing off the wall and grabbing his face, Zifeara forced Aun to meet her cold stare and it shut him right up. "I swear if you even try to say 'Fang', I'm going to knee you in the balls. The reason is that I'm a *fucking demigod* and I don't do anything I don't want to. When you aren't being funny or amiable, you're a selfish, smarmy brat and I wouldn't let you touch me with a ten foot pole. The reason I let Fang so close to me, no matter the time of day, is because he's proven to be a good man that I can trust, and you are *leagues* away from laying a finger on me, little boy. Try to remember this tomorrow."

Shoving him backwards, she was content to leave Aun to his own devices. He would either follow her back to their room or he would get lost in the city. Which it was she currently didn't care. Based on the soft sound of his bare feet on the stone of the city's streets, he made the smarter choice, as well as the one to remain silent the entire way.

Throwing open the door to their room revealed exactly what she had imagined they'd come home to; Fang sitting up in bed, skimming through a book. He seemed more than happy to see Zifeara back to normal, opting out of asking how her night was and instead launching into questions about the book he'd been reading. She was going to have to remember his reluctance to deal with Zephyr. It was... intriguing.

CHAPTER 32

There's Something Wrong With Everyone

Tracing her fingers from one edge to the other, Zifeara turned an ear down. The Tiger's Eye, the Inferno Ruby, the Heart of Ruuta... which is the next closest? Scanning her maps, she knew it had to be very a strong elemental stone, not just any old rock. The only other stones she could think of with that kind of significance were the Forest's Heart - in the deep Rulata jungles, the Dragon's Soul - guarded by the most powerful dragons on Drakk Sivik island, and the Galaxy Opal - atop Mount Shisvrik. None of those were terribly close, but for someone who could fly... the opal might be their next best bet.

"Qet for your thoughts?"

She hadn't noticed Fang come back into the room, but turning revealed him to be leaning in the doorway, arms crossed, watching her with a soft smile.

"Enjoy your bath?" Zifeara went back to her papers, keeping a finger on the mountain to remember where her train of thought had been headed.

He moved into the room, coming up behind her and resting his chin on her shoulder. "Mhm. What do you have here?"

She kept her voice down since he hadn't put his headphones back on yet. "Maps. I'm trying to figure out what exactly Torvak is after now that we've ruined his day a little by getting to the Terra Quartz first. The next stone has to be something just as elementally charged, but since I haven't been in the habit of keeping track of such things... There's only so many magic rocks I can think of that he'd be going for."

Looking slightly to the side, she watched Fang's eyes scan the maps strewn about the table. She knew he couldn't tell up from down on these things without a clear compass drawn for him, but it wasn't his obvious curiosity that held her attention. No matter how many times she was a mere breath away from him like this, Zifeara had always found his eyes stunning. It was easy to forget, especially since she'd been having to leave him in the future so often lately, but now... In the dim light of their room, his ruby eyes seemed to glow. She knew very well they didn't, but that never broke the illusion.

Now that she was thinking that way, Zifeara's gaze trailed further down, lingering over Fang's minute freckles. If his skin were even two shades darker you'd never see them, but pale as he was they were everywhere; lazily draped over the bridge of his nose and just the tops of his cheeks. She'd always thought they were endearing on him as a child and he hadn't grown out of them as an adult. Speaking of growing out of things...

Watching his mouth move, she was still surprised he hadn't grown into his teeth. She may not have been any sort of expert, but she knew that as a Vampyratu, his canines were the one thing besides his ears tying him to the feral form of his race. As human as the rest of him was, Zifeara had expected them to grow in proportionally once he lost his baby fangs, but they only got bigger. She almost laughed remembering the agonizing week he'd spent without both upper canines at once and how little sleep he'd gotten from the pain his larger teeth caused while pushing the rest out of their way. At least his jaw was large enough now that they didn't slightly protrude anymore like they had when he was still so small. His mouth said 'killer' but every other thing about him said 'yeah right.'

"-over here?"

Oh jeez, he had been talking to her and she was *not* listening. "Huh?"

He turned his head ever so slightly, meeting her stare. There was the briefest instance where neither of them drew breath, frozen in place. Zifeara wanted to think she wasn't imagining it when his eyes widened slightly as if he was just now learning what color hers were. Fang had been acting sort of oddly for a while now and she was starting to think it had something to do with her.

There was something he wasn't saying - something he was keeping from her and they simply didn't *do that* with one another. He'd been in her space like this time and time again ever since she took him in, but lately he seemed reluctant to keep her close. She wasn't understanding whatever was going on in his head and she needed to, but she didn't know how to ask without making him uncomfortable. She would never get it out of him if she made him embarrassed about it.

"I- I..." His volume was already low, but now it was little more than a whisper. "I asked... what was over here?"

Zifeara could swear that with the way his eyes darted between hers, he was *looking* for something. *He doesn't trust me with whatever is troubling him...* In a way, that hurt; they didn't have secrets from each other- they never had. There was unbreakable trust between them and she couldn't fathom what could be so important that it sullied such a bond.

She was first to break the trance. Looking where he had his fingers on the map, she nodded. "That's where we're going, at least where we need to end up eventually. That's Terravak."

The small island was nearly invisible on the map he had chosen. Zifeara wasn't even sure how he'd seen it. Not without the upgrade on his headphones.

He gave a shaky sound of affirmation and moved away, turning back to their bed and digging through the bag to find something to occupy himself for the night. Just before she could get back to what she'd been doing, the footsteps in the hallway became louder and their final teammate made his appearance.

Zifeara had been pointedly ignoring Aun since last night, and that seemed to be suiting the tiger just fine. Then again, she was fairly certain he had a hangover and wasn't talking to *anyone*. She knew he'd gone down to the baths with Fang and she could smell the fancy soaps on him when he wrapped his arms around her waist, laying all his weight on her back. He made a dejected noise and she carried on like she hadn't even noticed him.

He huffed. "I have no self-control."

Straightening a bit, Zifeara almost laughed. She had been waiting for this. "I know."

"I'm an asshole."

"I know."

"You're too good to me and I don't deserve it."

She could feel his tail slowly curl around her legs. If Fang hadn't been sitting on the bed, the book he dropped would have hit the floor. Zifeara peered over her shoulder to meet Aun's eyes, barely visible from where he had his nose buried in her shirt. He was trying to be cute and she'd be a liar if she said it wasn't at least somewhat working.

"I know."

"I'm sorry." His tone was serious and his ears dipped back. He looked like he meant it.

Zifeara reached over and roughly pat his head multiple times, more thumping him than petting. "Better be. Don't wanna have to murder you in your sleep, cub."

Aun chuckled and she could feel his chest shake. "No, I wouldn't want that either. Especially considering the threat about the spiders. Pretty sure I don't want to find out if you were serious or not. Or how you'd collect that many spiders."

She could nearly feel the daggers Fang was shooting since they had neglected to tell him about the previous night's incident, but she wasn't planning on sharing now. It was irrelevant, and causing trouble in paradise was something Zifeara saved for special occasions.

¤ ¤ ¤

He wasn't sure how he'd gotten here. One minute he'd been comfortably settled into bed and the next... he was in this hellscape. The thing about nightmares is, no matter how much you logically know you're only dreaming, you can still be scared to death if what your mind conjures is bad enough. Tonight, it was indeed bad enough.[19]

The room was completely bare; white walls, no furniture, couldn't have told up from down were it not for gravity. This was his own personal hell. Fang had been here before... many times before. It had been a long while since his last imprisonment, but that never made the experience any less terrible. He knew there was nothing in here- no way in or out, but that never stopped him from trying. He *despised* this place and at least his own blood on the walls was one speck of color in the blinding white. Any color but white.

The room was infinitely vast and completely restricting all at the same time. If he sat still it stretched for miles, but the second he moved it was no larger than the average bathroom. He couldn't tell which was worse. He had thought that he was done with this place since the first time, but it just kept coming back for him. He didn't have footsteps. The only sounds were the scratching of nails across whatever the walls were comprised of, the thudding of flesh against solid mass, and the rapid rush of air from panicked lungs. There was never anything else, no indication that anything even existed outside this space. No warning if he would be here for hours or days this time. No... anything.

Gods, he hated it. Nothing scared him as much as this one room. He hated being **alone***.*

It seemed like forever before he opened his eyes, hands frantically skimming the rest of the bed for its other occupant. He felt nauseous. His vision was blurred beyond useful with the tears in his eyes, and trying to stop himself from breathing didn't work. It was bad this time. He could feel it getting worse. He gripped uselessly at the empty sheets, pitifully whimpering at the cold air. *Zifeara wasn't here.*

As soon as Fang tried to stand up, his legs gave out, nearly sending him right to the floor. He was shaking everywhere and *goddamnit* he hated that nightmare. Every single time he had it, he became a child again; cowering in a dark room in a strange house, people mere feet away, but so *alone*. He'd gotten over it to a degree, but once he'd been turned immortal, that process brought it all back and had the added bonus of adult anxiety. He'd never known what a panic attack was until that night, and now he wished he could at least stop having them, even if he couldn't banish the dream itself. His brain was thinking a mile a minute, not bothering to devote the attention it should to moving his muscles correctly or retaining control of simple actions like blinking or breathing or stopping himself from dry-heaving.

---

[19] "Nightmares" – All Time Low

Every single sound was louder than even his ears should have made them, meaning it was hard to differentiate the noises coming from the other bed from the ones spilling out of his own mouth. Aun must have been dreaming as well, but that didn't matter right now. *Zifeara wasn't here.* Fang had to find her- to get up and get her to make this stop. She could always calm him down faster than he could fix himself.

Find Zifeara. The thought alone forced him upright again, knees of cooked pasta and eyes rapidly giving up. He couldn't see much anyway, but being completely blind was now a problem. He very likely wouldn't even be self aware for much longer, let alone be able to recall how echolocating worked. He was up but doubled over, locking his joints and planting his face into one of the pillows on the bed. Thankfully it was the right one. Zifeara's scent was now mixed with all the other things in this place, but that helped him remember.

Find Zifeara. If there was ever a time to pray to the gods he knew couldn't hear him, this would be it. Just let his brain work enough that he could seek her out. Forcing himself to breathe rapidly through his nose at least, Fang could tell she hadn't been gone long. If there was anything he could find with his poor excuse for a sense of smell, it was her.

Find Zifeara. Make those legs move. No one else matters, just go. They don't smell just right, fuck 'em. Keep moving. You go until you collapse. You go until you're safe. You go until you're home.

¤ ¤ ¤

"Ow..."

"Oh stop being such a baby." Zifeara had that teasing tone to her voice, indicating he was probably just being dramatic.

She was dabbing something on his face and it stung a bit, not to mention that she was somewhat scrubbing. A cut. He had a cut. As soon as she stopped, Zifeara grabbed a scrap of cloth from her bag and dribbled something clear on it. It had a strong smell that burned his nose.

"Alright, I need to get at the bigger one now. Take your shirt off for me."

Aun could feel the heat rush to his cheeks and he laughed nervously. Everything the wolf guy did and felt seemed natural to him, as though it were his idea despite the fact that they had different personalities. By now, Aun had seen enough that he had a theory or two about who the wolf was. He was starting to think that this man might be the reason Zifeara was so closed off when it came to more romantic situations. She definitely liked this guy- got red in the face and clumsy around him- but nothing had come of it yet. Hell, he knew he felt the same about her, but he seemed to be too much of a wuss to do much about it.

As it was, he swallowed and did as she asked. *She'd never seen him bare in any regard.*

235

Watching Zifeara's eyes widen comically as they drifted over his chest made him thankful he'd kept himself in such good shape all these years. He'd had doubts whether she found him at least somewhat attractive until now, but that was reassuring. He sat up a bit straighter, making himself a little taller. It was difficult not to be self conscious, but even turning his head slightly away didn't manage to tear his eyes from her incredulous expression. He held his breath involuntarily as she reached a hand towards him, clearly intending to touch something that had nothing to do with treating his injury. Oh Farrah, he didn't know what he'd do if...

The instant her fingers hit his skin, he shuddered and it made Zifeara recoil, face quickly coloring. She pressed that rag of hers over the scrape on his side fast enough that the burn made him hiss and he couldn't even say anything.

"Ha-how did you get your scar? The- the one on your face?"

He had a feeling this was to distract him from what had just happened more than anything, but he wasn't about to bring it back up. Zifeara was shy when it came to such things and the last thing he wanted to do was to make her uncomfortable enough to stop seeing him. He'd been so smitten from the first moment he'd seen her, he would do whatever he could to keep her with him. If Zifeara wanted him to be slow and patient with her, hell, he had the rest of his life.

"Oh, this? Well, that's quite a tale!" Now he puffed his chest out and put on the storytelling voice he used with the younger pups. "So, four years back I was out tracking game. It was dark and foggy, dreadful weather for hunting, but we needed the meat."

As Zifeara cleaned and dressed his wound, he regaled her with the epic tale of running into a bear cub. The thing had looked wounded and alone, but the instant he'd moved to help the poor creature, its mother burst from the underbrush and charged him. He hadn't smelled her because of the damp weather, nor had he heard her. The mother gave him no choice but to try and escape. Unfortunately, she was fast and strong, pinning him to the ground and choking the air from him. Just as she rose a paw to strike, his brother lunged from the bushes, firing a volley of arrows into her neck and face. She still swung her paw but it merely grazed him, giving him his scar. He had gesticulated wildly during the entire story, earning him several giggles and a few rolled eyes.

"Is that where Kumah comes from?"

Smiling broadly, he nodded. The town's friendly bear was usually a mystery to most. "Yep! Helped raise her myself since it was somewhat my fault she lost her mother. Can't complain though, no one has ever forgotten my name since I've had this on my face. Stands out."

He liked to be optimistic about most things and Zifeara seemed to appreciate that. He would have to remember that she liked stories. And he may have to see if she was willing to touch him again once she'd settled.

¤ ¤ ¤

Sleep was not coming easily to her tonight. Zifeara had set their course, but her mind continued to wander, and sitting still wasn't agreeing with her anymore. Both boys had long since passed out and she found herself, as per usual, tucked under one of Fang's arms. If she tried hard enough and moved slowly, she could more often than not get up without waking him. It took five minutes, but she was free.

Quietly slipping out of their room, Zifeara decided to meander around the spa grounds. The staff would be making preparations for tomorrow, but it should be calm in the gardens and this side of town wasn't nearly as plagued as the rest of it. Usakara may be a pit, but at least Ming-Da liked to keep things in order in her own personal corner of debauchery. She hadn't made it very far down the hall before something caught her eye.

The figure that had just crossed the hallway perpendicular to hers looked *strikingly* familiar, though he didn't even glance her way as he passed. Her brain screamed at her about the impossibility of what she'd seen, how if that was really who she thought it was, it was likely some sort of illusion trap. Zifeara's feet were moving even as she was trying to talk herself out of it. Chasing phantoms and the shadows of dead people only ever got you hurt, but who could have known to make their trap look like *him*? If it wasn't an attempt on her life, souls did sometimes manifest before they reincarnated to say goodbye. Ghosts existed and it wasn't that extraordinary. Maybe...

Hallway after hallway, turn after turn, this apparition of hers led her out of the main building and outside. Zifeara never seemed to be able to put herself any closer no matter how many times she almost slipped on the freshly polished floors from trying to speed up. Every new glimpse of him she got further assured her that no, he did look exactly like who he thought he did. If this was some sort of trick, someone was going to pay and this stunt would prove *costly*.

She lost sight of him as soon as she stepped out the door that led to the gardens. Zifeara circled the large fountain just in front of the main garden before putting her hands on her hips. She didn't see or hear anyone who might be messing with her and honestly didn't know who could have known her well enough to fabricate a person that had been dead for 142 years. At least not anyone who was still alive.

She was just about to call out to him in case it really was his soul wandering, but the brief flash of long black hair swishing around a tree made her hesitate. Sighing, she made her way to said tree.

"Is this payback for always winning stealth tag, K-?"

Zifeara half expected to be met with solid mass when she ducked around the tree, but coming up with nothing was perplexing. It kind of hurt. If it wasn't an attempt on her life and it wasn't his soul manifesting to see her again, why was she seeing him out of nowhere like this? After so many years of...

Hearing someone else come outside wasn't a huge deal, but the fact that it sounded like they were on their deathbed was. Even from across the patio, the distress in their breathing and unsteadiness of their steps was audible. Oh gods, if someone was actually going to expire out here, she'd need to report it to staff so that they could-

"Ha- ha- Zi-Zifeara...?"

Oh no.

"Fang!?"

She was around that tree and halfway across the courtyard before he'd even made it more than a few feet out the door. If he'd left their room not long after she did, he'd probably been able to track her by scent; at such close range, he did have a better sense of smell than a gifted human. He looked like hell. Fang's entire body was shaking, sweating, his eyes seemed unfocused and were pouring tears, the *second* he heard her he was flailing in her direction...

Grabbing his hands and placing them on her shoulders, she lifted him up enough to fold his legs and drop them to the ground. It didn't matter where they were, he rarely worked himself in to such a state or held her so fiercely. The last time he had, he'd managed to bloody his fingers clawing at the floor. He had the nightmare again, Zifeara would have bet money on it.

"Hey, hey it's alright, I'm here, Mortichai. I'm right here, you aren't there anymore. I'm real, I am. Touch."

She knew from experience that Fang tended to completely lose his sight in his episodes, meaning she'd developed a system for convincing him that he was awake beyond just hoping he was. Zifeara pressed a single finger to the tip of his nose. Past a few unstable breaths and almost poking her in the eye, he raised one of his own hands to mirror her action. It might seem silly to an outside observer, but it helped him focus and come back down. The pattern in which she touched various parts was never the same either, so he couldn't just memorize it.

As the mirrored contact points moved from cheek to forehead to collarbone to heart, Fang was starting to breathe in a normal rhythm again. She was one step closer to getting him sorted. Elbow to chin to hip to sternum was more varied and required him to pay closer attention, causing him to at least see a little past the never ending flood of emotion. Now they were getting somewhere. He lost it for a moment when moving from stomach to ear since those were in different places for them, but repeating the word 'touch' again a couple of times snapped him back. If anything, Fang was always eager to please and that worked in her favor in times like this. Twice more through the cycle and he was done. Now it was just letting it all out and they could go back to bed.

As far as she could remember, this had been a recurring nightmare Fang had ever since he'd become immortal. He didn't like talking about what he had experienced when he took the elixir, and the first time she'd found him like this, she hadn't known what to do. It made her heart ache to think they had a system for it now. Zifeara couldn't help but wonder if he would ever outrun this thing, though she doubted it.

Fang feared one thing above all else, enough to completely destroy himself to seek out a solution if he was too far gone - literally any other sentient being. He *needed* to hear someone talk to him. Sometimes he was cognitive long enough to find her since she could help him faster, but other times he wasn't that lucky. Being autophobic was the thing that hurt him in ways she couldn't completely protect him from no matter how hard she tried.

Zifeara still didn't know what her long lost friend had been doing prancing around on the edge of her sight, but it didn't matter anymore. She had a living, excessively distressed friend to care for now and few things mattered more to her than Mortichai did.

CHAPTER 33

Family Reunion

It was far too early for her mother to have another task for her. They had left Usakara mere days ago and not even Lucifer was fast enough to find another immortal in the same area yet. Zifeara opened her eyes to what could have been any tea room in the region, soft moonlight filtering through the closed paper screens. There was almost an ethereal glow to the space, making her think the room couldn't be anywhere real. The difference between this and other times Zifeara dreamt of her mother, however, was the utter silence hanging over everything. It was oppressively quiet.

Even pivoting her ears to pinpoint the smallest sound didn't help Zifeara pick up on the other presence in the room until he spoke.

"Over here, love."

Whipping around to face him, she gave her brother a confused yet excited grin. "Mortis? What... how are you here? Surely you're too busy to..."

Offering his always easy smile, he moved into the center of the room, taking Zifeara's hands into his own. "Special occasion. Time is in stasis right now."

Her ears tilted. As far as she knew, their grandfather never enforced a stasis upon the world unless something went terribly awry. Mortis must have felt the tension seep into her grip.

"We all thought it best that *I* tell you what was happening, so time had to stop if I was to see you tonight."

Now she was downright *afraid*. They knew damn well she could never be mad at her brother and was always far more inclined to see him than anyone else in their family.

He rubbed his thumbs softly across the backs of her hands. "Zifeara, it's been seventeen years. They want to meet him. Tomorrow."

Her eyes widened and immediately, a protective anger overtook her. She tore her hands from her brother's hold, taking a step back. "No! I know what you're doing! They want to turn him back and they sent *you* so that I would just offer him up!"

"They do not. You knew they expected to see him eventually, we could only put this off for so long."

She wasn't buying it. Her uncle was going to throw a massive fit, demand that order be enforced, and that would be the end of it. They would repossess Fang's immortality - would take him away from her. Mortis stepped back into her space, moving slowly as he placed one hand on her cheek.

"Hey. I understand you're scared, but trust me; I know every soul on this planet and Mortichai is a good man. *Good* good. His soul is radiantly pure and they have no reason to take him."

"...Is it still?" Zifeara hadn't seen Fang's soul since the day she watched it leave his body. She was positive she had tainted it by now.

"Mhm." Mortis' infallible calm and gentle gaze were making her feel the tiniest bit better. "If I dare say, I think it's grown even brighter in the last few years."

She wasn't certain Mortis was capable of lying, but it was hard to believe that being around her hadn't taken its toll on her best friend. She was damned in a way few others were; the container for a true monster and mostly unconcerned with the welfare of others. Zifeara had centuries of blood on her hands and there was no redemption for her. Her own murky soul had to have corrupted his in some way, even minutely.

Her brother always knew her a bit too well, but this time he touched upon something she hadn't even connected yet. "Sweetheart, put a little more faith in Mortichai. He's done nothing wrong. I know you're still hurting from the last time you got too attached to a mortal, but he's one of us and he's going to stay that way."

Her breath caught in her throat. While he was here, she had a chance to ask him about the oddity of a few nights prior. "Mortis... have you seen him? I think I did the other night and I don't know why."

He let his hand fall and took a deep breath, becoming still as the room itself. His eyes remained open, subtly vibrating as he searched for evidence of a mobile soul. His resting expression pulled into a rare frown and he knit his brows. Turning back to meet her nervous gaze, he appeared no less concerned.

"He's... he's already been reincarnated. I can't tell you what you saw, but you aren't going to find him that way, Zifeara. You know as well as I do that the dead are best left alone. You dwell too much in the past and it may come back to haunt you."

She couldn't stop her ears from drooping. She let her gaze fall to the woven rug beneath their feet. "It already does. You said it yourself - I can't let it go. It was my fault and... I cared too much. I didn't *ask* for all these emotions, they just happen and _"

Picking her chin up so she looked at him again, Mortis' unwavering stare was unsettling and vacant to most, but Zifeara could see sorrow roil behind his cloudy eyes. "Do not regret feeling, Zifeara. Emotions are powerful, important things. You're better for having them- they make you stronger just as much as they wound you. If anything, that's what will save Mortichai. He makes you *feel*, and not much does that."

While he wasn't entirely wrong, she couldn't help but think that maybe Fang made her feel *too much*, especially as of late. The last time she had felt too much came at a terrible price.

"I'm not so sure about that, Mortis. I can be more dangerous when I feel strongly- you're well aware what happened last time. If something happens to Fang, I don't know what I'll do. I can't handle losing someone like that again... Not him."

"You won't. They have an expression for that you know; better to have loved and lost?"

She couldn't stop herself from rolling her eyes. "Yeah, right. You know damn well I can't feel love. I was born just like you; not an emotion to my name, and that one in particular doesn't seem to have come through."

Chuckling softly, Mortis shook his head. "Zifeara, of all the people you lie to, yourself shouldn't be one of them." Taking in the confused tilt of her ears and raised eyebrow, he continued. "Every person ever born is slightly different. We all experience love uniquely. Just because you don't have the romance movie experience doesn't mean you've never loved. You have. You *do*. Fiercely and unfathomably deep. You love Mortichai, Zifeara, in a way that only you can. Don't ever take your own emotions for granted; they are far more important than you give them credit for. Trust me."

She could feel herself just on the edge of tears. She really wished she could stow those emotions about now. "I... This was all so much easier before. Why is this so hard?"

"Hahaha, I don't think I've ever known *my* sister to back away from something because it was difficult. My life has been watching people lose the things most important to them. Families they worked hard to build and provide for. Loss never gets easier, hun, we simply become stronger. We never forget and we shouldn't. It will always be hard, but your favorite activity seems to be spitting in the face of adversity, no?"

Zifeara genuinely laughed. She couldn't claim he was wrong, nor could she resist the urge to tell him to fuck off. Their family had been right to send him. There was a strong reason she loved her brother above all else. *Oh...* she... *did* love her brother. He was right.

Mortis perked up as if he heard something before setting his hands on her shoulders.

"My time is up. You have 'til the sun sets to get things squared away and come home. I know it isn't much comfort, but..." He held her close and it was easy to see the family resemblance now. They were even the same height. "Mother wouldn't give up that soul without a fight either. It's one glaring thing to hold over Uncle's head and you know she'd rather take a vow of eternal silence than let him feel vindicated."

He smirked and it was slightly reassuring. She mirrored the sentiment and he gave her a light kiss to her forehead before dropping his hold. Zifeara should have been thankful for the longest moment she'd had with her sibling in years, but it was difficult to feel anything past the heavy pit of dread that was currently sucking the fire right out of her. She had to make a good case for Fang in front of the only things that could manage to separate them.

¤ ¤ ¤

He might have been able to sleep all the way through the night were it not for the claws digging into his chest. It wasn't particularly painful, but Fang was adapting to the need to be alert in another time. The source of his discomfort was no great mystery; Zifeara lay across his chest and whatever it was she happened to be dreaming of couldn't be good. Her distress was apparent in not only the prick of her nails, but also in the curl of her tail around one of his legs and the tilt of her ears. As much as he felt for her, this was one of the few times he was allowed one of his guilty pleasures.

Fang raised the arm he had slung over her shoulders, slowly and delicately running his fingers through Zifeara's hair. There was a small divot behind her ears and if he brushed just right... Softly rubbing at the back of her right ear, he felt the familiar rumble of her chest and it brought a silly grin to his face. Her ears swiveled back to their resting position as she relaxed into him. He could never get away with this if she were awake; Zifeara was always too proud to take the simple pleasure of being petted and Fang was willing to bet she'd deny the fact that she purred.

He took a deep breath in and continued the steady back and forth, melting into the contact himself. The soft, silky fur just at the base of Zifeara's ears was one of the nicest things he'd ever touched and he forgot from time to time how much he loved being able to do this. Considering all the things she always did to keep him level, Fang was grateful he could be of some comfort, even if she wasn't aware of it.

Gazing up at the myriad of stars above them, he couldn't help but imagine their current situation as something a little different. Their campfire had long since died out, but he could still hear the crackle, feel the warmth, picture the heated glow reflecting off every spot he knew by heart. Zifeara's hair was always mesmerizing with the way it shimmered and revealed its secret pattern, each rosette distinct and special. This sound he was drawing from her wasn't just from the motion of his deft fingers across these spots, but from a general sense of contentment and ease. He was her happy place just as much as she was his, and the moments of calm by the fire like this were equally cherished.

Fang had almost let his eyes drift shut again when Zifeara stirred, making him freeze. She *could not* catch him petting her. The slight, almost sad sigh she emitted pulled at his heart. He didn't have long to wonder if she'd had another late night visit.

Zifeara sat up, hovering over his chest, seeming surprised he was already awake. "Couldn't sleep?"

"Woke up and haven't drifted back off yet. You okay?"

The slight droop in her ears suggested she wasn't. "I... Tomorrow... we have to do something vastly different."

"Oh? What happened?" As much as Zifeara sounded unhappy, it did little to deter his curious nature. If she had another job so soon, it shouldn't sidetrack them too terribly.

"I don't like this, but we're going home."

"As in our time, home? Why wouldn't you be happy about taking a break?"

"Because this isn't for a break." She laid her head back down, sighing again. "We're putting Aun and the horses up at my house. We've been summoned."

All his curiosity distilled into dread. If she wanted to bring not only the tiger but their mounts to the present, something big was happening. "S-summoned where?"

Her hands fisted in his shirt and Fang was well beyond concerned over how nervous Zifeara was acting. As far as he knew, nothing in this world scared her.

"My... It's time to pay the piper. We must enter the god realm and go see my grandparents."

He wasn't entirely sure why this was a problem and she must have known as much by his lack of response. When she met his confused gaze, her indigo eyes were wide and held a delicately restrained panic.

"They're about to determine if I'm to be punished for giving you your immortality. If they think you're a liability, I..."

He could practically feel his heart stop. "Wh-what do you mean? I thought Lucifer's deal stopped them from-"

The waver in Zifeara's voice scared him more than anything else in this world ever could. "They're *gods*, Fang - masters of this world and everything in it. If they don't like something, they change it. I stole from literally the highest authority there is. I-I can't stop them from..."

The unfamiliar shimmer in her eyes was only as worrying as the implication that tonight could be his last as an immortal. There was only one thing he knew how to do in a situation like this. Reaching around Zifeara to pull her more solidly onto him and smothering her into the crook of his neck, Fang kept all his own emotions on lockdown. If one of them was going to lose it, it wouldn't be him.

"Then I guess I'll just have to be on my best behavior, huh?"

She started squirming, trying to impress upon him the severity of the matter, but if he saw the impending breakdown in her expression again, he wouldn't be able to keep this facade up. The struggle to avoid his consoling wasn't something he was going to let her win easily.

"Zifeara, what threat am I? I almost cried the first time I killed a deer, I'm sure I'm not that big a deal in the grand scheme of things, right? It'll be alright. Even if I am a problem, they'll have to take it out on me and you'll be–"

"I don't care what happens to me!"

Being that she was stronger than him by far, it was impossible to keep her where he wanted her. Zifeara pushed herself up, still threatening tears but now for a reason completely different from what he had expected. The way she was glaring at him kept Fang quiet.

"They can do any damn thing they want to me, but they can't have *you*! I'm important to the order of this world, so there's only so much they can punish me with. Whatever it is, I can take it. They need me, but I'm the only one who needs you..."

There was no forthcoming response to that. Fang knew he was important to Zifeara, but she never *needed* him. She never needed anyone. His stunned silence gave her long enough to snap out of being emotional and back into a guardian.

"I don't care what happens, I *will* find a way to keep you safe. Mortis thinks you'll be alright, but neither Lucifer nor I will let them take you. Your soul is important to her and you're important to me. This isn't going to stand."

"Zifeara, calm down." She was starting to work herself up and Fang was worried they'd wake Aun at this rate. As much as he appreciated her consideration for his life, he was starting to think all this fuss over him was unnecessary. He wasn't worth her stressing this much and definitely not worth fighting *gods* for. He reached up to slip his fingers into her hair and coax her back down.

"Listen. We'll deal with it tomorrow, just settle. I promise you that we can handle this, one way or another. You can handle *anything* and if they think I don't serve a purpose, then I know you can convince them otherwise. Especially now that I'm here with you instead of just milling around in our time. Relax and try to go back to sleep."

Zifeara huffed and stopped fighting to be upright. She had her ear right over where his heart was and she lost steam fairly quickly. Fang was tempted to throw reservation to the wind and resume stroking her hair, but thought better of it. If he irritated her with it, he'd undo any progress he'd made in calming her down. She scooted herself further up his torso to bury her face back in his shoulder and he honestly couldn't recall the last time she'd been so... *clingy* with him.

From so close to his ear, her whispered words were loud enough that he caught the unfamiliar desperation in them. "They can't have you... not on my life."

Softly rubbing between her shoulders, he decided that if he couldn't risk comfort in his favorite way, he might want to try Zifeara's method. His voice was hushed and warm as he started to sing the first song[20] that came to mind. She never seemed to grasp any of the hints he was throwing her in the songs he sang, but that wasn't important at the moment. He wouldn't let himself get distracted from his current task by the thought that he could be running out of time.

Zifeara was thankful that from where she was laying, Fang couldn't have seen nor felt the tears dribbling down her face, only exacerbated by his song choice. She knew he was trying to soothe her in the way she always did him, but what she wanted more than anything right now was to just tuck tail, run to the nearest cliff, and scream like only a wolf was able. Wolf song could speak of sorrows unshared in ways impossible in other languages. Its haunting tone turned even the most heart-wrenching anguish into a majestic aria, smelting pain into something beautiful. As it was, however, there was nowhere else in the world she'd rather be right now.

---

[20] "Lover's Eyes" – Mumford and Sons

CHAPTER 34

Preparing For The Worst

With everyone briefed on the plan, Aun was practically bouncing in place. He'd been curious about the future ever since he had started believing Zifeara wasn't making things up. Watching the humming, blue portal opening and closing as Fang and the horses passed through it only made him impatient. Just as the soft azure light consumed the last of Orro Heme's tail and the mystic doorway closed, Zifeara placed herself in front of him.

"Alright, look here; you need ground rules before I allow you into a completely different time." He opened his mouth in protest, but she cut him off. "Rule number one: you are not to leave the grounds of my house. I have twelve fenced-in acres of land for you and the horses to roam, you'll know if you're about to leave. Rule number two: I am about to have my maid babysit you so that you don't destroy things you don't understand."

Aun could feel his ears perk up slightly. "Is she cute?"

Zifeara didn't even glare at him for that one, instead offering the most deadpan tone she had at her disposal. "I had a feeling you'd jump straight to that. She's at best fairly naive, at worst somewhat of an idiot. Not to mention in the future, we have rules about when you are an adult and when you're still a child; Lola is *underage*. If I find out you so much as ogled her a little too long while I was gone, I will personally rip your dick off and choke you with it. Are we clear?"

He kicked at a rock. "Killjoy."

"Rule number three: please don't make a general ass of yourself? My poor butler works hard and I do not need you giving him any grief. You go to the future and are welcomed as a guest in my house, you behave. I promise you can come back for something more fun later, but right now Fang and I have an important matter to attend to. Fair?"

Putting a hand on her shoulder and patting a few times, Aun let an easy smile settle on his lips. "Fair. Don't worry Zifeara, I *can* behave, I just usually chose not to. It's more fun to be a hellion, but I'll reign it in for you."

For the first time that morning, she returned his grin and rolled her eyes. "Oh gee, aren't I special."

"To me you are."

For a fraction of a second, he could tell Zifeara didn't think he was serious and had expected a snarky comment. As soon as she properly registered what he said, her ears tilted and she scanned his face for any indication he'd been kidding. When she didn't find it, the slight dusting of pink across her cheeks was exceptionally rewarding.

"C-come on."

She dropped her crystal once more and ushered him through the portal. Aun expected that casually walking between two different time periods would have felt odd in some way; maybe a bit like falling or stopping too suddenly but still moving. It felt exactly like stepping through any other doorway. He almost slipped on black polished marble of the floor, but it was the accusatory outcry from somewhere on his right that really set him on edge.

"What the devil?!"

Just as the tiger fixed his eyes on the older man gawking at the excessively large *horses* inside the lavish building, Zifeara herself passed through the portal, faint sheepishness to her tone.

"Sorry Graham, I did send Fang in first to try to warn you, but we're on a bit of a time crunch. You wanna open the doors and get these guys outside, love?" She jerked her head towards what Aun could only assume were the front doors, prompting Fang to grab Treble's reigns and start moving.

The shriek from the other side of the foyer made everyone jump. "OMG, *ponies!*"

Oh that's the maid. Allowing himself at least a once over of the girl he'd be spending all day with, Aun could see why Zifeara was worried considering his personality, but the avian was nothing to write home about. She was cute, but in more of a childish way than he'd consider fair game.

Lola ran right up to Thrush, immediately fawning over her despite the surprised snort. Aun almost stopped her, but his mount settled quickly once she realized the small person meant no harm. He couldn't help but think Lola was lucky she picked the most amiable horse to accost; she very likely would have gotten kicked if she'd done that to either of the other two.

"Lola, they are *not* ponies. They can understand every word you say. They're travel mounts and friends." Zifeara reprimanded as she helped urge the steeds out the door, "Now leave poor Thrush alone. You're stupid lucky you spooked the one Airneir least likely to hurt you."

Aun stopped paying attention to the sorting of the horse situation, instead letting his gaze travel the room. Even counting the spa in Usakara, he'd never set foot in somewhere so expensive-looking. The black walls were paneled, accented with red inlays rimmed with gold. The stairs that led upwards were of a black wood as well, shined just as the marble underfoot, a deep purple runner snugly blanketing the middle. The chandelier hanging from the upper levels gleamed a bright silver, shedding light across the space by some magic he was unfamiliar with. He'd seen pictures drawn of palaces less opulent than this.

Just as he was about to wander off, Zifeara finished what she was doing and laid a hand on his shoulder. Turning to meet her gaze, he found her grinning. "One more thing? Stay on the first two floors. The only thing above that is my room and I don't want you in there. I don't know how long we'll be, but make yourself at home and don't break anything. We'll probably spend the night here before we go back too. Lola will tell you which room is yours."

With that and a quick pat, she stepped away from him and made her way back out the door. "Let's go, Fang! No point putting this off. Besides-"

Zifeara's voice trailed off, leaving him to stand there alone in this strange new world. Well, almost alone.

"Hiya, I'm Lola! Zifeara told me look out for you today, so what do you want to do first? Oh, and how do you say your name? Zifeara didn't say it earlier, but I kinda heard Fang do it. Is it more like ow-n or ah-oon?"

The younger girl seemed to have no concept of personal space, standing just shy of their toes touching, staring up at him with wide eyes.

"Uh, ah-oon. What... how does that light work?"

Lola furrowed her brow before looking above them, pointing to the large fixture. "What, that one?"

He nodded, still unsure as to why she had to be this close and took a step back. Lola talked fast enough that the explanation of how modern electricity was generated took barely a full minute and Aun had to pay very close attention or he'd have missed most of it. It was equal parts fascinating and disturbing that current could be produced by something other than the sky or an elemental, but then again, there were an awful lot of things his futuristic friends had that he couldn't quite wrap his head around. Asking about the room he would be staying in produced more noise and endless questions as he was lead upstairs.

As they passed a few closed doors, Aun was quick to observe that Zifeara's favorite color was likely either black or purple. While the walls here mirrored the ones downstairs, the royal carpet on the stairs had taken over the floor and was impossibly soft. Lola opened one of the doors down the right hallway, holding an arm out to welcome him in. This room looked nothing like what he'd seen so far. The walls were painted a deep navy, perfectly matched to the carpet and sheets on the large bed in the center. The flowing drapes covering the expansive bay window on one wall were equally as dark, though they made the scarlet sashes tying them in place pop.

"Lola, is everything in this house one color or the other? Because if every single room in this place is a different shade of something, I might lose it."

Giggling, the girl shook her head. "Oh no, of course not. Most of the house is purples and blacks, but Zifeara won't change the guest room. This used to be Fang's when he lived here and she let him decorate it however he wanted. Blue is his favorite color."

Great, he was stuck in *Fang's* room. Of course he was. He made a face at the area in general before stalking back out, convincing her to show him the rest of the house. There had to be somewhere he could spend his time here that didn't ring of the Great White Wimp.

¤ ¤ ¤

Stepping through the portal for the last time, Zifeara had never known Hell to feel so unwelcoming. The general sense of dread firmly lodged in her stomach was only growing heavier the closer they got to crunch time. She couldn't shake the feeling that things were going to go terribly wrong, or that a decision was already made and she had no chance. She was well aware that she couldn't hope to win a physical fight against a god, but the nervous tingle under her skin told her she wouldn't hesitate to *try*. Calm on the outside, entirely prepped army on the inside.

She and Fang didn't even have time to talk out a tentative plan before Lucifer was upon them. Today the devil had chosen to appear far more casual; plain black turtleneck over equally plain slacks, simple dress flats, I-want-to-speak-to-your-manager haircut. Her gnarled horns seemed shorter than usual. Zifeara thought she kind of looked like a lawyer on their day off.

There was always something subtly hilarious about the way all six feet of the literal Queen of Hell insisted on lifting Fang off the floor every time she greeted him and Zifeara couldn't help the tiny smile it brought her.

"Mortichai! Oh, it's been far too long love, how are you? Enjoying yourself?"

He shrugged as soon as he'd been put back down. "Never better. The time difference was a bit hard to adapt to at first, but I think I've got the hang of it now. Nothing's eaten me yet, so I consider that a win."

"Hahahaha, I would say so!" Turning to glance at her daughter, Lucifer's demeanor remained stable. "Are we ready?"

Zifeara nodded solemnly, seeing no point in putting this off. They had all day to show up here and she'd considered taking Fang somewhere to have fun first, but that felt a bit too much like spoiling a dog before putting it down. She *refused* to think that way for more than a few seconds at a time. He was *hers* and they couldn't have him.

"He isn't going anywhere, you know." Her mother's even, assured tone made Zifeara jerk her head up from where she'd been inadvertently been watching her nails cut into her clenching palms. Lucifer leaned over and pinched Fang's cheek. "Mortichai has been such a good boy, I can't fathom how your uncle would be able to justify terminating him. Besides, ever since you stole that vial, Father has been second guessing himself as to how he treats us. Mother gave him an earful about his insensitivity and he's been in the proverbial doghouse ever since."

Zifeara knew she was still scowling and her tilted ears weren't adding anything positive to her expression. It was difficult to step away from the hard edge her emotions were on right now and she almost let herself wish she could just turn the damned things off again. What Mortis had told her last night rang in her skull but she snorted. She couldn't claim having feelings had really made her better. She could think of several times it had cost people their lives. She had a tendency to become a *real* monster when she was angry enough.

Lucifer clapped her hands before gesturing towards her room. "Shall we go get this over with?"

Zifeara was seconds away from spitting embers but as her mother started off down the hall, Fang followed closely, lacing their fingers together and pulling her with him. She was honestly dumbfounded as to how he was handling this so well. To the best of her knowledge, Fang had never been the one to turn to in times of crisis- that was always her. Yet here they were, traversing the endless reaches of space and he was marveling at the distant stars as opposed to... what she was doing. Zifeara sighed. She may pretend to be calm on the outside, but she was no good like this.

Focusing on the warmth traveling up her arm from where she was connected to her best friend, she refused to let herself think about what she'd do if that heat wasn't there anymore. Instead, she let her mind drift to the last time she had legitimately no stress whatsoever.

¤ ¤ ¤

The day had been exhausting in the best way possible. The weather was warm and all her closest friends had a day where they could all relax together, Todd suggested that they head to the beach. She hadn't been near the ocean simply for fun in a long time and they had all agreed it sounded like a good time. After an entire day of building sand palaces, diving for neat shells, chasing about the local wildlife, catching fish to eat, and trying to teach Fang how to surf, Zifeara was happy to lounge about in the soft sand by the fire she'd made. Now happily drunk just as all her friends were, she couldn't think of anywhere more appealing than right here in this moment.

"Uh... Nagaris?"

"Mm-mn. Wrong time of year. Try again."

Sighing contentedly, she leaned further into the warmth against her back. She could feel Fang's chest rumble as he growled in frustration. She was trying to teach him all the constellations, but it was a work in progress, especially since he couldn't see most of the stars without difficulty. It had taken her a while to be able to effortlessly pick out the correct shapes amidst the stars littering the night sky as well, more so just after the seasons had changed. His arms were crossed over her knees and she had removed her chin from them, now more committed to being comfortable.

"Am I allowed a hint? You know I'm still bad at summer stars, not to mention they all look the same."

Craning her neck to look up at him, Zifeara couldn't help but grin. "They do not, you just don't have it yet. You started learning barely a month ago from a book that had all the lines drawn for you. Try again."

He gave an exasperated huff, hunching forward a bit more to squish her as best he could. Training his gaze skyward once more, she didn't stop herself from watching the firelight play off his crimson eyes as he tried to discern which of all these twinking dots comprised recognizable shapes. Zifeara knew this would be hard for him, but she admired his tenacity.

Todd and Loli were across from them, giggling about something or another, but the jackalope spoke up, stealing their attention. "C'mon, dude..."

Fang raised an eyebrow at him and Todd dipped his head and shook it slowly, making his lowered ears flop about. Even Sara was laughing as Fang narrowed his eyes, attempting to pick up on what his friend was telling him.

"Zifeara, show me again."

Raising her hand, she pointed to the stars in question for him, slowly this time so that he could follow her finger more easily. The mercury coursing through her veins was tempting her to snicker at him too, but that would likely put him off trying. "I know you know which one this is, Todd was trying so hard to help."

She felt Fang jump a little, realization practically smacking him in the head. "Oh, oh, oh! The hare! The- the- bloody what was it? The leporidon!"

"There we go! That's the one!" She knew he would get it eventually; he literally couldn't forget for long.

With more drinks, a few stupid games between them, and Todd passing out, she and Fang decided to do one last walk along the shore before they all piled into his car and went home. They were both a bit unstable, but letting the cold ocean water wash over their feet as they walked and giggled about silly little things together hadn't ended in tears yet. She couldn't remember when she'd taken one of Fang's hands, but he was swinging them as they walked, making an exaggerated arc in the air like a child strolling with their parent.

"No, he just fuckin' glared at me the whole time an' had to suck it up! He knows his manager'd *kill him* for kickin' me out! Petty lil' shithead."

"Fang, you're *exactly* as petty if not worse than Dewford. Vhans has instructions to punt Dewy down the block on sight!"

"The SoundCave's a safe place- I can't *willingly* let him anywhere near you! 'Specially not since I-"

Turning to meet his eyes, she was somewhat surprised that Fang had stopped walking and was starting to color as if he'd said something he shouldn't have. Zifeara didn't find that to be an odd direction for the conversation and expected his next words to be 'can't stand him' or something similar. She raised an eyebrow, curious as to why he seemed to be having some sort of internal crisis.

"Fang? Where's the rest of that sentence?"

"Uh, I kinda..."

His expression was bouncing between reservation and sheer panic, further making her question what in the word had just happened to him. She was beyond aware that no one liked Dewford, but this was straight up bizzare. He shook his head, visibly swallowing.

"Sorry, got kinda dizzy for a sec. Maybe we should go back? 'M not feelin' great."

If she were honest, he didn't sound too well either. The first thing Fang lost when he started heading past just 'drunk' and into 'truly hammered' was his ability to form coherent words and he'd been slurring for at least an hour. She was better on that front, but then again, she was rarely ever *that* intoxicated. It was dangerous for someone with as much power as she had.

"Yeah, okay. C'mon, you can lean on me if you need to."

His physical coordination was always next to go. He didn't seem too keen on the idea and let go of her entirely, even as he swayed slightly. "No, 'm fine! Totally-"

Falling over. Being that she was always taller than she should be around Fang, it was easy enough to grab his waist and pull him forward. While it stopped him from landing himself in the surf and getting an unpleasant mouthful of sand, the move did unfortunately shift his momentum enough that now he was falling towards her. Fang grabbed her shoulders out of reflex, meaning that between his hold and the way she had to use her other hand to push back on his chest, they were now in an officially awkwardly position.

Out of all the hundreds of times she had been this close to her very best friend, this one in particular was... off. Something was wrong and it made her ears tilt. Fang being inches away from her face wasn't the problem, nor was it the light, breathy noise from his lungs that she could feel across her skin. It wasn't the tensing of the muscles in his chest that she could feel under her palm or even the look in his wide eyes that she couldn't place. The *problem* was the tight coil forming somewhere in her abdomen. It was constricting her organs and generating heat, maddening though not painful.

Zifeara knew what embarrassment felt like. She was well acquainted with fear, shame, and dread. This didn't feel like *any* of those things- not even close. This had never happened before, most definitely not around Fang. As her brain scrambled to make sense of when she'd ever felt that way, her friend seemed hellbent on not letting her get that far.

Raising one of his hands to rest it along her jawline, he too looked as though he were confused by what was going on. "I... 'm awake right now... right?"

"U-uh, yeah, Fang. You're really, *really* drunk though and..." *And I'm **something**...*

He huffed, brushing his thumb over her cheek. "Wish I weren't. Could've..."

Zifeara was fairly certain the water around her feet was steaming. She felt unnaturally hot and it wasn't helping her think clearly. She needed all of her reasoning power to figure out what it was Fang was even *doing* right now much the less where he was going with this. He was always clingier when he was intoxicated, but this was bordering on highly unusual.

Before she could back up and enforce some sort of logic upon the situation, he yelped, jumping away like she'd burned him. Now with nothing to keep him upright, Fang hit the sand and his most pressing issue made itself known in the form of aggravated gurgling. The large Qeyl crab now clamped onto Fang's leg made it known that they were far too close to its den and that blood was the only penance for this intrusion. It would have given him quite a scar if their bodies didn't heal as well as they did.

Grabbing onto the claw holding her friend hostage with one hand and using her weight to trap the rest of the snapping beast as best she could, Zifeara started forcing its grip loose. Fang was likely making the appropriate amount of noise for how much this had to hurt, but she did somewhat wish he'd tone it down. The colorful selection of swear words leaving his mouth was concerning.

The crab was slowly but surely weighing the options of letting go and losing a claw, wisely deciding to give up just before the crushing point of chitin. Once they'd gotten him up and back to the car so she could do something about his leg to help it heal faster, Fang was quiet - too quiet to be normal. Something big had just happened and Zifeara hadn't a clue what it was. Nor could she seem to get it out of him.

CHAPTER 35

Of Gods and Grief

E ven after all this time, she still couldn't seem to puzzle out what that feeling had been. As much as she'd learned and experienced since then, it still didn't make any more sense.

Snapping her attention back to the present, Zifeara heaved a sigh. They were here. The door to the god realm had never looked so foreboding before, but it was too late to do anything differently now. They were here and everything would be *fine*. The hand holding hers squeezed, only once and very briefly before he let go, helping her steel herself. A thought occurred to her at the last minute and Zifeara almost slapped herself for the sheer carelessness she'd just displayed.

Leaning over to reach Fang's head, she all but hissed at him. "*Fetka*, I'm so sorry, I can't believe I didn't tell you. The god realm is stupidly white. I'll make them change it before you even come in, just stay here."

Lucifer glanced over her shoulder at the two of them. "Hmm? Do we have a problem?"

Zifeara could feel the growl threatening to leave her chest at her mother's feigned ignorance. "You know damn well what's going to happen if we let him go in right away. He is not setting foot in there until it looks less like the barren *hellscape* it always does."

"Ah, but helplessness in the face of something benign always bodes well for the pity vote. Shame." The devil chuckled softly, letting herself into her parent's home and closing the door behind her.

"Zifeara, what did you mean? It's white like the spa in Usakara or..."

"No, love. White like you aren't going to sleep for a week. Gods, I can't even fathom how I forgot to warn you, I'm such a mess." She pressed her face into his shoulder, leaning all her weight into him. "I'll look in the door before I let you through, just to make sure it isn't bad anymore, okay?"

He nodded and smiled, allowing her to move away before poking her head through the large door. It opened directly into the study, multiple plush armchairs arranged neatly around a burning hearth.

Mother Nature caught sight of her first and waved. "It's alright, my dear, he should be safe here. Bring him in."

Taking a deep breath, Zifeara held a hand out behind her. Feeling Fang slip his back in was all she needed to harden into the confident wall of defiance she'd meant to be now that they were here. They were not having him. He was hers.

Stepping into what could only be described as perhaps an excessive amount of library, Fang could feel all eyes on him and he inadvertently fisted the hand in the pocket of his silks. He forced a smile, only faltering as something bright forced itself inches from his face.

"Good to see you again! Maybe we'll actually get to talk this time! There have been so many things I wanted to ask you!"

Blinking a few times to refocus his eyes, Fang soon recognized the chipper mass as an angel. *The* angel. Zifeara's warning tone helped confirm this to be true.

"Gideon..."

Darting a glance to his cousin, the boy shrank back to a reasonable distance for carrying a conversation. "He-hey Zifeara. How's your friend?"

She narrowed her eyes, tension still present in her pitch. "He's much better, thank you. Will you please get out of our way so we can come in?"

Gideon's own eyes widened a fraction as though it hadn't occurred to him that he could even be in the way before he ducked to the side. Fang smiled at him as they passed and made their way to a chair. These appeared far too large for a regular person, meaning he had to somewhat scramble onto the thing. He had assumed Zifeara would move onto her own chair, but she jumped up once he was settled, firmly gluing herself to his side.

"Now then," Father Time began, "I'm sure you know why you're here. It's been quite long enough since we've been brought the recipient of our latest vial and we wish to evaluate him. Should he prove detrimental to the order of your world, we'll have to intervene."

Taking her own seat, Mother Nature tutted. "You make it sound so harsh, dear. We've only heard good things about Mortichai. We just want to make sure nothing has been upset and get to know the newest member of our family."

Fang already liked her. Her soft smile seemed genuine, as though she was entirely at peace, inside and out. The disgruntled sigh from the other end of the row of chairs, however, was abrasive and spoke of a deep-seeded irritation.

"'Member of the family'. He's only here because of Lucifer's petty rules and Mother's insistence on allowing this to continue for far too long!"

Fang had to assume by the faint glow of the man and general appearance that this was Dios. He had his arms crossed over his white robes and not a hair in his golden beard was out of place. The ivory horns adorning his skull were reminiscent of deer; delicately curved and an even number of tines. His amber eyes were sharp and fixed on his sister. It was easy to see Gideon as his son so long as you imagined a mother contributed all the boy's softness.

"Dios, be kind or I am sending you home. Mortichai hasn't said a word yet and you're being unfair. First warning." Mother Nature's gentle voice didn't so much as waver.

"He prefers to be called Fang." Zifeara was sitting rod straight, one ear slightly cocked, "And you could talk about him more like a sentient being and less like a pet, you know. You may be family and you may be gods, but he can *hear* you."

Lucifer's eyebrows were nearly to the ceiling. Her daughter had never spoken back to her grandparents before in her 10,000 years of life and she was finding it *interesting*.

Nature and Time took it in turns to ask Fang questions of every kind, ranging from his daily life to where he'd come from, sometimes sprinkling in something that forced a bit of his moral alignment into his answer. Zifeara hovered like an angry ghost, but the more Fang answered and the more disgruntled Dios seemed to become, the more she relaxed. This was going... rather *well*. Maybe Mortis was right. Maybe she hadn't ruined Fang's soul yet.

It was as Gideon was hanging off the arm of their chair asking Fang if he liked having to sit around on a horse all day that she noticed Dios was thoroughly eyeing them. It was clear he was trying to puzzle out whether this was all just an act they were putting on or not. Zifeara returned his hard glare, refusing to back down from this. Nothing he had asked so far had turned up anything damning about her best friend and she wasn't going to return to her state of nervous jittering yet.

"She's just so sweet! I mean yeah, she isn't very good about defending herself since most things scare her, but that's what she has us for, right? Treble is a good girl; I've never had an animal I connected to so much before. I mean, I suppose it helps that she understands me when I talk to her, though, hahaha." Fang was now much more relaxed in this massive chair. The situation was almost what he imagined an Einrit family dinner to be like with a new girlfriend or something, not a life or death interrogation.

Mother Nature stood from her chair and clapped her hands together. "I think I'm just about ready for some tea and maybe a little... game of sorts. Let's move to a different room." She saw Zifeara about to protest and shushed her. "No white walls, I promise."

The hallway they entered appeared as though it were made of stone like a castle, innumerable wooden doors on either side. Fang wondered how anyone knew where they were going in this place, but then again, these were gods. Maybe all the doors were for show. Maybe they led to alternate realities where everyone wasn't themselves. Maybe they were just for storage.

The door Nature did open for them led into what looked somewhat like a movie theater; large screen on one wall and nicely arranged couches. Tea was already waiting for them on a long table and they helped themselves. Before Fang could ask what this room was for, Time spoke up from his place next to his wife.

"Zifeara, dear, do you remember a man by the name of Geralt VonDelvo?"

She stared at the cup in front of her in thought, scanning its contents as well as her memory banks for the answers. "Yes. Wealthy man, lived in the early five thousands, loved lavish parties. He owned large tracts of land though he was merely a viscount. Why?"

"Because Fang has said that he's been helping you with your task and I would very much like to see that. Actually, I'm sure we'd all like to watch you work and see exactly how it is you keep order in your way."

¤ ¤ ¤

"Okay, okay, tell me again? Slower this time; it's impossible to understand you when you talk so fast."

They had been sitting there for almost an hour, unable to move beyond the game room. Aun had nearly jumped out of his stripes as Lola turned the television on and once she had convinced him that the people weren't real nor could they hear him, he demanded an explanation. She had been trying, to the best of her knowledge, but he always seemed to have more and more questions that she didn't know the answer to. He'd come just shy of attempting to *open* the TV to determine how it worked, but she had at least prevented that by introducing video games. He forgot most of his inquiries once he got absorbed in figuring out how to drive a car and asking how *those* worked.

Lola was rather thankful Zifeara had an expansive collection of games for every system imaginable, considering the tiger only spent half an hour on each title before wanting to see a new one. Watching the endless wonder shimmering in his eyes and hearing the unreserved glee in his tone every time he got excited for completing a task was beyond cute. She didn't mind having to switch the disks all the time, plus this was kind of like a day off.

Aun found that it was less fun being taught how bathrooms worked than learning how the mystical screen in the game room functioned, but he was pretty set to never go back to his own time ever again. Once Lola had accepted that he would need a minute to marvel at the 'bathtub' thing Fang had told him about once and left, the tiger could go about his business and maybe... disregard *one* rule.

Shifting into a small tabby so that his ascent wouldn't be heard, Aun made his way up the stairs until he hit a small landing with only a single, deep red door. The molding that comprised the frame was intricate, all hand-carved dragons and flourishes, while the silver knob boasted its extensive polish. Yeah, this seemed to be perfectly Zifeara's style. It was easy enough to just wedge himself under the door as a lizard, so no one would be any the wiser he was in here. Standing up from the floor, he gawked at the space.

The walls almost reminded him of home. They were black paneling like most of the others, but instead of being inlaid, they had what looked like screen between the slats. Hand-painted dragons sprawled across the room, drifting over forests and streams, small waterfalls and running deer. Some coiled up the walls and onto the very ceiling where they danced among stars and the colored dust of the cosmos. Aun wasn't sure until he reached out to touch one of their hides, but the texture of it sent vibrations up his spine. This wasn't paint. These were *real* scales affixed to painted backgrounds.

Just near his face sat a shelf on the wall, littered with small things he didn't know the name or purpose of and that he knew better than to attempt to find out. Trailing his eyes along the surface, he hit something he did recognize. While not a sketch or painting, as he would have encountered in his own time, this was very clearly an image of Zifeara. It took him a moment to realize, but the small child she was holding couldn't have been anyone but Fang. His bright eyes and crooked smile were both the same- albeit missing teeth- but he couldn't have been more than a few feet tall. Tilting his head and looking further down, Aun was surprised to find more of these portraits.

The next one he ran into was different only in that Fang was bigger. Bigger by far to reasonably be held, but Zifeara had him up nonetheless. They were hovering over what he knew to be cake, though the treat was somewhat on fire. The image after that, Fang had grown at least a foot and was holding the guitar Aun had always seen him take out on their trip. One more picture down and Fang had to be his regular size if Zifeara was anything to go on, lazing on some sort of fine soil near water. He was making an odd symbol with one of his hands, though the tiger's eyes lingered elsewhere a while. Whatever Zifeara was wearing didn't cover up much and he was starting to wonder why she never wore *that* for swimming as opposed to turning into an animal.

Tearing his focus away and looking around, he realized there were several more of these images around the room on various surfaces and in different frames. Zifeara had *a lot* of pictures of her and Fang and it was making him itch. Snorting and wandering elsewhere, he traced one of the columns holding the sanguine canopy up over her bed. The wood was carved to resemble a polished version of a decrepit tree, barren branches holding aloft delicate ravens and the columns at the head of the bed sported two more dragons with metal rings in their mouths. There was something unsettlingly real about how long Zifeara must have been accumulating the wealth to afford to make her house this way; how many man hours had been devoted to crafting each and every intricate thing she owned.

Aun felt his ears start to swivel back. He wanted something like this someday. Nice things just because he *could* have them. As it stood, he wasn't even a second-class citizen in his own town- more like third-class. Maybe he could convince Zifeara to just... let him stay. He could find something to do here to be of use to her. Even if she wouldn't have him as a mate, she did say they were friends and he could find some purpose in this house. Maybe he could find a cute tiger with a muddied bloodline like his since they were supposedly more common here. Get his own house, start filling it with amazing things he wasn't allowed back home, have cubs, die happy. He existed in the wrong place and time.

¤ ¤ ¤

Tucked away behind the hedge wall to the VonDelvo estate, Zifeara and Fang were attempting to form even half a plan as to how they could make this work. Her grandparents idea of a 'game' was just giving a repeat performance of a job she'd done before, meaning this should be easy enough in theory. Now in a time period she'd rather not linger in, she was hoping they could make this fast. She hadn't done this era twice yet.

"The first time I was here..." Zifeara had a hand over her mouth, eyeing the fancy marble mansion with contempt. "I came as someone else. Baroness DeChangue hates these parties and didn't RSVP, but if a lady shows up unannounced, it would be majorly rude to turn her away. With you here, I don't know how viable my old scheme is now."

Zifeara was thankful that great and powerful universal magic could produce the dress she had stored in her bag for this time. The bright violet of it had always been appealing to her, though it did mean that she stood out anywhere she went. This era was more about pastels, but there was only so much she could make herself fit in without also ignoring her personal comfort. If she had to dress this way, she was going to do it in style.

An entirely new outfit had to be conjured for Fang. The clothes she wore as Zephyr weren't well fitted to him and as such, would not fly in high society. He looked rather handsome in the navy suit and its silver accents were an amusing choice. He could complain about the tight fit until he saw the sun rise, but this was a good look for him, uncomfortably sharp shoes and all. She had almost giggled at the face Fang had made when he saw how many layers he would have to put on just to be considered decent, but that all paled in comparison to the sheer amount of dress she had to squeeze into. He hadn't been sure what a petticoat was or why she needed so many, but thought it sounded complicated.

"Isn't it going to be super obvious I don't belong here? I know absolutely nothing about how classes work or what is and isn't socially acceptable with the people in this time- I mean, I have no clue how your *dress* even works. I can't answer questions about anything happening in the world right now. How am I supposed to hold a conversation with anyone?"

"You aren't." She shushed him with a hand on his shoulder. "You can act sheltered and polite so long as we present you correctly. You're dressed too nicely to be a footman of any sort, so dignified acquaintance might work. With my title here, you being rather quiet would be expected."

Fang raised an eyebrow. "Am I even supposed to be talking to *you*, your grace?"

Zifeara looked him up and down before smirking. "Honestly? Probably not. Either way, we're wasting time. Do you remember a million years ago when I taught you how to dance to swing and you rolled your eyes the entire time?"

"Uuuh, yes?"

"Okay, well go fuck yourself because I told you you'd thank me someday. Let's go. Hold your arm out like this and stand up straight."

Zifeara moved Fang where she needed him to be in order to properly escort her, at least ensuring they looked like they were supposed to be here. She rarely showed up at these events either, though she'd never brought company before. Scaling the marble steps while managing her dress reminded her why she never wore clothing she couldn't properly move in if she didn't have to. Zifeara honestly hated having to be all tarted up for anything. If she couldn't kick someone without tearing some form of garment, the outfit was not for her.

Approaching the doorman checking his list for invited parties, Fang was quick to notice that this was a period so old, history books didn't even spend that much time here. This was the era of powdered wigs, carrying handkerchiefs in breast pockets, and heels designed for men while women had sensible shoes. This just also happened to be when most well-off civilized people learned to party. His music history class in high school was particularly fond of this period thanks to the sheer number of strange instruments invented. This was considered the major musical revolution of Marien.

The doorman nearly dropped his scroll when Zifeara approached him and stated her title, though Fang was uncertain how high on the fancy-people-scale she was. He couldn't have told the difference between Grand Duchess and Baroness, yet he would imagine her name carried just as much weight here as it did anywhere else. That and the word 'grand' tended to mean you were important. Once allowed in and past the foyer, he could immediately see why Zifeara talked about coming to this party with no small amount of disdain in her tone.

The mansion was what could only be described as a shimmering cream and off-white *nightmare*. This place was like a strange mirror world; exactly opposite Zifeara's own home in every way. The walls were still lavishly paneled and held a similar pattern, yet the gold inlays failed to stand out against the soft eggshell color of the base. The matching chandeliers shone so brightly against the white marble floor that every single thing in the ballroom seemed to radiate the light of a bright summer day.

Zifeara's house was always pleasantly dark, not dim per se, but welcoming and snug in the way it swallowed light as opposed to amplified it. The vaulted ceilings made for impressive acoustics, bouncing both the noise of the happy crowd and the live band off its intricate molding. Fang expressly hoped no one asked about his headphones as he turned the dial up a few ticks to make himself more comfortable.

As if reading his mind, Zifeara spoke next to him as they moved to a somewhat isolated corner of the ballroom. "If anyone asks about your headphones, tell them they're an accessory from a foreign land, delicately painted to glow. They'll buy that, people are starting to be into glowing stuff now."

Looking down at her, Fang's first question had nothing to do with the task at hand. "Zifeara, why are you so short still? Like, I know that's how tall you really are, but... it's hard to reach you from up here."

Giggling, she just shook her head. "Listen, there are plenty of people who don't know I'm a shifter. It usually makes my job easier for them not to. I can manage a couple of inches without anyone saying much, but when all you do is lounge about and socialize, you tend to notice when someone has gotten taller. Not to mention humans aren't as tall as they can be yet. Look around."

Darting his eyes around the room, it was plain to see that most human females hovered around five feet, five and a half for males. Man, he really stuck out.

Shifting herself maybe three inches more, Zifeara stuck her tongue out. "Now stop complaining. Alright, I haven't seen VonDelvo yet, so we need to mill about until he pops out of whatever dark recess he's crammed himself and some harlot into. The great thing about offing this guy the first time was that it was really easy."

"Cool, how do we do that?"

Zifeara looked at him as though he had subpar intelligence and Fang was quick to become sheepish. "Oh right... Shut up."

Throwing him the grin that meant she was up to no good, she took a step back. "Aren't you going to ask me to dance, Marquis DeNict?"

Cocking an eyebrow, he offered one of his hands as he gave a short bow. "Only if you tell me what you just called me."

Laughing once more, Zifeara settled into the proper position for them to dance and began maneuvering towards the open floor behind them. "Well I can't call you by your name here; not only is that uncouth since you are a man and I am a woman, but neither of your names make *sense*. If I've gathered you as my guest from somewhere in my providence, that gives me free reign to make things up. You need to remember your new name and title for me, it's important."

Focusing more on where his feet were going while resisting the urge to look down since that would appear silly to everyone around them, Fang picked just the tip of Zifeara's ear to watch. "Alright, but does that mean anything?"

"Of course it does. Nict is Drakonic for 'night' and damn near everyone has 'De' in front of their last name right now. Means 'of'. Your here-name is close to the real thing. Start turning us more; I'm trying to find this guy."

He obliged, starting to remember how to dance. It'd only been eighteen or so years since he'd first learned, before he'd even become immortal, though he could recall Zifeara brushing him up on this a few times 'just for fun'. Realistically it wasn't too difficult, Fang just had to be very careful not to either step on her or run them into anyone else. He knew Zifeara's attention was legitimately everywhere else, so he could be in charge of where they were headed. He should be leading anyway by this time's standards.

Once he had the hang of the waltz well enough to focus on something else, he eyed the band to discern how they were making noises that sounded like they could be coming from his era more than theirs. The assembly of a dozen or so musicians was impressive by itself, but their wide selection of oddly bent metal and other indecipherable materials was purely awe-inspiring. It may have been the music nerd in him taking over, but Fang was entranced by the way they shifted instruments between songs to produce such an odd variety of sounds. He'd never appreciated what in his time was called electro-swing before he'd seen technologically lacking people play it. [21]Not only that, but the female singer was doing a hell of a job, her voice carrying a soulful tone he didn't often hear in modern music.

The clearing of a throat and tap on his shoulder snapped Fang's attention back to the current situation. A rather finely groomed gentleman, human by the look of him, stood next to them. His curled moustache had enough wax in it to line a beehive and his garish pastel blue suit could probably make a robin jealous. Fang supposed the blond man was attractive enough for his time, but that was likely irrelevant as it all came down to status. The harsh, whispered swear he was lucky to have even heard past his headphones made it clear that this was someone Zifeara would rather not deal with.

The man bowed low, smile looking a tad bit restrained. "Might I borrow the Grand Duchess for a dance?"

Fang wasn't sure how to properly tell someone to shove it in this era's language, but Zifeara took care of that for him. "You may not. I am occupied for the evening."

The other man scowled, dropping his amiable facade. "And may I ask why not? For as rarely as one has the pleasure of being in your presence, may we not take advantage of it?"

---

[21] "Ended With the Night – Caravan Palace

"I simply do not wish to be parted from my betrothed tonight, if it's all the same to you, Alonse."

Fang wasn't sure which of them was the first to choke on their own tongue, but he was a pretty good bet. He at least managed to disguise it as a cough so that the other man could stutter out some apology and leave. He wasn't sure how he could look Zifeara in the eye since he definitely couldn't form real words, but she was quick to reassure.

"I'm sorry, it's a pain in the ass in this time to be a rich, single woman - you sort of give me an out I can use for a really long time. Men talk to me about marrying them at least a dozen times a night. It's a huge reason I never *do* these damn parties unless someone needs to die."

Alright, this was a whole new thing he didn't need weighing on him. She had her ears tilted back in a way that suggested she really hadn't wanted to do this to him, but if this was helpful to her...

"It's - it's fine, whatever. I, uh -" *Have no idea what to do about this now.* "Let's just find your guy, yeah?"

Smiling and returning to their interrupted dance, Zifeara nodded. "Thanks. You don't have to act the part or anything since people don't really do that kinda thing in public. Man, news like that is going to spread like *wildfire* and this is going to make my life so much easier. Gods, they hear I'm getting married and-"

Fang did not hear a single other word she said past *married.* The number of things he'd give for that to be fact and not a convenient lie were innumerable. He was sure Zifeara kept talking to him about the social boon this would grant her amidst more scattered praise for his willingness to play along, but his mind checked out for as long at it took to cool off. This was something he was unprepared for as an assistant to Zifeara's work; dangling the one thing he'd go the to ends of Marien to earn right in front of his nose as a ruse. Should he be given even half a reason why he had to prove that this was no charade, he might completely lose it and that would be one hell of a way to explain that he'd been head over heels for years.

"Hey, are you gonna be alright?" When his eyes focused again, Zifeara was staring at him, concern blatant. "If it really makes you so uncomfortable to be used like that-"

"Am I going to have to kiss you?"

If there was ever a time he legitimately wished he was dead, this was it. Not only was that not supposed to even remotely be said aloud, but it fell out of his goddamned mouth like it was a *bad thing.* If sheer force of will didn't drop him dead right here, right now, the clear hurt that flashed across Zifeara's face would have. It was brief before settling into what looked mildly apologetic, but her ears were as flat as they could get.

"Would that be the worst thing to happen to you today?"

He felt like *such an ass.* "Gods, no, I-" Dropping his dancing pose to grab both her hands and bring them to his chest, Fang willed himself to say what he meant to, just for once. "I didn't mean it like that, I swear. You do so many things you don't want to just to get your jobs done, I shouldn't be contributing to it. I don't care if it ruins the plan, I will *never* make you uncomfortable like that."

CHAPTER 36

Damage Control

L ucifer, did you do as I asked?"
Smiling broadly, Lucifer tore her eyes from the large screen. "Of course, Father."

She rose from her chair, now at the same height as her parents since it was more comfortable. As much as she hated to miss anything happening now that Fang was finally serving his intended purpose, she had something important to prove. She reached into the pocket of her pants, pulling a small amount of space manipulation to produce the vial that contained Fang's soul. Its brilliant silver shone softly, accompanied by the erratic hum she'd become accustomed to so long as he was even remotely near her daughter.

"By the stars..." Dios stared in awe, no doubt dumbfounded by the rarity of color. The fact that it was still so high was to be applauded.

"Auntie, why's it making that noise? I didn't know souls could do that!" Gideon was curious as ever, following the vial as it was handed to his grandfather for inspection.

"Because Fang is quite fond of Zifeara. Their souls have bonded in a way few ever have the joy of experiencing. I've noticed that his soul gets louder if they are physically near each other." Lucifer was having a hard time keeping the smugness from her tone in front of her parents. Her brother was practically foaming at the mouth from seeing Fang's soul in pristine condition *and* knowing such a pure being had bonded to the legitimate harbinger of evil.

Time had his eyebrows raised to his hairline as he turned the vial over repeatedly, Mother Nature grinning over his shoulder. Her tone of voice suggested she was just about as excited as she ever got. "Then it would be cruel to part them. You know what happens when you break a soul bond, dear."

That Time did. When souls were this attached to each other, severing that bond would prove fatal. Removing either one would slowly break the other down until the soul itself fizzled out. Not only was it a painful process, but the high-pitched keening a soul often emitted at the loss of its mate was enough to drive a person insane.

Looking back to his daughter, Time sighed. "And she's bonded as well? I just can't picture it; Zifeara has the blackest soul to ever have existed."

Lucifer couldn't stop her teeth from showing as she pulled the second vial from her pocket. "Not anymore."

Gideon and Dios both made an audible sound of distress upon seeing the color of the soul that could only be Zifeara's. The blue flame within the purple writhed as though in pain, but the rest danced to its own rhythm, loosing its embers like any other did. Gideon was quick to recover, darting forward to marvel at the change in his cousin.

"I *knew* she was getting better! Oh, there's hope for her yet, Father!" He hefted himself off the floor, hovering closer to where Lucifer held the vial in order to hear it better. "Oh, listen! It sounds so happy!"

The noise emanating from the glass jar came in pulsing waves, less like the intricate song from its partner. Gideon cocked his head, clearly trying to hear both and understand why they weren't synched.

"Auntie, what wrong with them? Why aren't they the same? Is Zifeara's broken?"

Lucifer gave a hearty laugh before handing the small boy the vial and sitting back down. "No child, her sound is different because she feels differently. Her emotions come and go, just like the noise from her soul. Mortichai feels constantly and strongly, thus his soul mirrors it. Nothing is-"

Mother Nature jumped slightly as the vial she had since taken from her husband to admire began to *sing*, prolonged aria sputtering more notes and melding more sounds than Lucifer had ever heard it manage before. Quickly shifting her gaze back to what Zifeara and Fang were currently doing, it surprised her to see another man standing impatiently next to them.

"And may I ask why? For as rarely as one has the pleasure of being in your presence, may we not take advantage of it?"

"I simply do not wish to be parted from my betrothed tonight, if it's all the same to you, Alonse."

Ooh, *that* was why Fang was so excited. Lucifer cackled out loud, earning confused looks from her family. Wiping a tear from her eye, she couldn't bare to drop her attention from the scene unfolding, waving a hand at the rest to sit back down and enjoy this. "Come on, you'll miss the best part! That little soul is about to *scream!*"

Watching his cousin and Fang interact had never confused Gideon more. He was certain that even someone *blind* could see how deeply the other immortal loved her, so why couldn't she? The angel smacked himself in the face at how patient and sweet Fang was being but... gods, how could Zifeara not know?

¤ ¤ ¤

The list of things Zifeara had done to serve her purpose was indeed a long one. The kitsune she'd recently killed came to mind, though to her it was all just work. Nothing was ever personal and she always got her man before things went much too far for her liking. This outburst Fang was having brought a light haze to her cheeks. She, of course, had considered that they might need to solidify this ruse they had going, but this was *Fang* they were talking about; her best friend, the one she trusted implicitly, probably the only person she could expect to be cool about this. If she had to be stuck in this very situation with someone, she would have picked him. The only issue she would have had along the way was his reluctance to participate, especially with whatever awkwardness was hanging between them as of late. Zifeara hadn't considered the possibility that he would hesitate because of *her* feelings, even though that sounded exactly like something he would do.

"Fang, don't... don't worry about me so much. The job is more important than-"

"No it isn't!" He squeezed her hands, the deep ruby of his eyes holding a fire she rarely saw. "Not to me. I didn't sell my soul to put other things before you and I damn well am not going to start now. Getting the bad guy is *your* job, taking care of you is *mine*. If you're unhappy or uncomfortable, I'm doing something wrong or I need to fix whatever the problem is. You didn't drag me all the way back in time to make your life harder."

There was absolutely something wrong with her. All this nonsense with her grandparents had broken whatever fickle device that regulated her emotions and now it was out of control. No one took care of her; Zifeara was a force of nature not to be trifled with that could kill a man in a hundred ways. Her ears were already low thanks to the direction of their conversation, but she could feel them trying to fuse with her skull. She was feeling too much all at once- everything melding together into something she couldn't name with any certainty. All of it *hurt* and Fang wasn't giving her the chance to catch her breath.

"You trust me with everything you have, I need to be worthy of that confidence. Besides, you're far too important to me to let you be someone you're not when we're together. I *know* you Zifeara, better than anyone else and..." He raised a hand to cup her jaw, setting his own in determination. "I wish you would let me help you more- stop sheltering me so much and *tell me* things."

She swallowed harshly, entirely transfixed by the split-second transformation in him from her soft best friend to this steely warrior ready to fight her himself. "L-like what...?"

"You won't tell me about your dragon, won't tell me about what it is that makes you so misty-eyed when you talk about people you used to know, won't tell me *anything* about how you feel when it isn't something favorable- *fuck*, Zifeara! You're borderline invincible but you act like showing me any fault in your armor will be the one thing to break you."

If she were being completely honest with herself... it might. There were so many things she did to protect Fang from everything unsavory in the world like he deserved to be after his terrible start to life that she couldn't tell where the line drawn between protecting him and protecting herself was. She was wholly unprepared to have this discussion and the realization jolted her into remembering that they were supposed to be *doing something.*

They were in the middle of a job. This was neither the time nor place to focus on this. People were probably staring.

Fang hadn't quite finished with her, his voice adopting a ragged edge she was unaccustomed to. "I would never do anything to hurt you- not on purpose anyway- you know that. I'm not a child anymore; you can put weight on me, lean on me, bend me. I'm not going to break. I can hold us both, I swear. I'm not stronger than you, faster than you, or nearly as brilliant as you are, but I think I'm just as resilient. You don't have to do this alone, Zifeara. I can *be* the strength you need when you run out, just *let me.*"

"C-can we maybe... have this conversation later?"

Blinking a few times, Fang sounded even more agitated at first. "Why?"

His combative mood only lasted until the first tear from her eyes hit the hand he still had on her face. "Because I'm sup-supposed to be doing something right now. This isn't the best..."

The change in his demeanor was instantaneous. His shoulders relaxed as if he hadn't noticed he'd let them become so tense and the hard line his brows formed smoothed back out. Then the flustered panic set in as soon as he realized he'd just made her cry. He had *never* seen her cry.

"Shit, I- I didn't mean to..." Fang wiped at the moisture clinging to her face, trying to backpedal from the damning cliff they were about to tip over. "Okay, please don't... do this? Just promise me we *can* have this conversation later?"

Choking out a curt laugh, Zifeara nodded, bushing a hand over her other cheek. "You are so goddamned lucky I'm not wearing makeup right now or I'd kick your ass for ruining it in front of all these stuffy people."

"You know what, I'd let you. I feel bad for, uh, doing this *now*. I guess... I had all of this in me for a while and it just kinda spilled out. I mean it, though. This is what I'm here for; the whole reason I wanted to be immortal at all was to be there for you however I could. Let me get my money's worth for my soul, huh?"

She could tell he was saying that just to make her feel better, but she laughed anyway. All of this must have been what he thought he couldn't bear to tell her recently, and now that he'd finally said it, Zifeara felt like a layer of dust had just been blown off her. Whatever grit had built up between them was gone, completely cleaned out and no longer a wrench in the cogs. Plus... Fang was right. She had to stop babying him at some point and from what she'd seen on this trip, that point had come. He was going to be with her until the end of time itself- she might as well start acting like it.

Fang could hardly believe what had just happened. He'd always wished Zifeara would stop withholding things from him like she had, but he'd never wanted to push her too far. It was obvious he had done *exactly that* since he was trying to prevent the meltdown she was about to have, yet he could only feel so bad for finally getting things off his chest. He hadn't realized how much it had weighed on him; he'd often felt a bit useless since she wouldn't share her most personal thoughts with him when he was all but an open book to her. Well, almost open. The last few pages of his story were stuck together and he was trying to let her read them without ruining everything, but it was taking time.

Before he could attempt to banish the residual sadness from the situation, Zifeara's eyes widened at something over his shoulder. Fang almost got to turn and look, but she stopped him.

"Don't. He's here. I need..."

She removed both his hands from her, holding them near her mouth, thumbs tapping at his knuckles. Zifeara was thinking, but the way she was doing it was starting to make him fidget. She snapped her eyes back to meet his, smile slowly forming.

"What's the most difficult, impressive to watch classical piece you remember how to play on a piano?"

Tilting his head, Fang had to seriously think about that one. There weren't many classical compositions he'd bothered to learn after he drank his vial, mostly because he found he had little interest in them. The few he did know were much slower and...

"Uh, this is going to sound super lame, but probably the Alla Turca. I'm not big on the classics, Zia."

This didn't seem to put a damper on her plans as she nodded towards the massive grand piano in the corner near the band. "Work your magic, love. Be flashy and put on a good show. It's what you do; you've got this."

She clapped him on the arm before gathering up her dress to catch up to their target. Alright. He'd been given a task and he had to perform to high standards. At least this was something that should be easy enough, all things considered.

Making his way through the still dancing crowd of people to reach the band, Fang was fairly certain he should ask if it would be acceptable to borrow the piano a moment before just doing it. The musicians seemed thankful for the break and were more than eager to let him steal the crowd for a short while.

The piano bench was about as uncomfortable as the stiff, shiny fabric upholstery suggested it was, but there were worse things in life, like remembering how to play the one very old composition he knew flawlessly and in an instant. Lifting the key cover and taking a deep breath, Fang closed his eyes for just a moment as he positioned his fingers. He could hear the tune in his head and could just about see his own hands darting over the keys in perfect time. He was really hoping his immortal memory wouldn't fail him now, of all times.

A few people had gathered around the piano before he'd even struck the first key, but once those first few notes flew from the instrument,[22] Fang attracted a real audience quickly. Zifeara had always told him he had the perfect hands for piano, and she'd been right, in more ways than one. While all his time spent mixing music on his soundboard had been a good way to learn how to manage two things at once, being mildly ambidextrous didn't hurt either. While his left was his dominant hand, Fang could switch to his right almost seamlessly unless he was trying to write something.

He tried to do as Zifeara asked, putting a bit more flair into the movement of his fingers and adding some flourish to finishing off notes before moving to the other end of the keys. If he had as many people watching him as it felt like he did, Fang was confident he'd done his part. He was almost surprised by the way his body moved on its own, much like running a program as opposed to actually having to recall how the song needed to be played. It let his mind wander.

Unfortunately, his mind immediately chose to remind him that he had essentially just yelled at Zifeara for being a closed off mess and made her cry. Gods, if only he could stop being so nervous. This was worse than not being able to shoot her and having no good reason for it. *Wait...* this was exactly like that! Fang had to resist the urge to stop what he was doing and stew in his own asinine revelation. Both the aiming problem and his new unease around Zifeara stemmed from the *exact same thing*: he was trying too hard. He was making things far more difficult than they needed to be.

The absolute best part of his relationship with Zifeara had always been how easy it was to simply exist around her. She was never judgmental about something unimportant, she never expected anything of him that he wasn't already rolling over to give, she never pried into anything too personal. He was well aware that he was his own greatest obstacle when it came to telling Zifeara that his feelings were starting to overflow from the closet he'd jammed them in, but this was positively, mind-numbingly *stupid*. He was coming at this all wrong. He needed to behave as he always had and just... let it happen. Stop being so wound up and trust that she would adapt.

Gods, he was starting to think that he might be some kind of idiot.

As the song he played drew to a close, Fang snapped his attention back to the real world, glancing around as he struck the last few notes. The railing of the upper floor was just as light as the walls of the house, making Zifeara's hair stand out against it as she leaned over to observe the scene below. Her arms were crossed over the

---

[22] "Alla Turca" - Mozart

banister, a smile on her lips as she licked them. The brief flash of red revealed by licking her lips told Fang he had done what she needed him to.

While the small crowd around the piano clapped as he took a bow, he watched the band resume their positions out of the corner of his eye. Excusing himself from any attempted conversations, Fang made his way to the bottom of the staircase as quickly as he could. He was very ready to get out of this time.

Calm as ever, Zifeara eased right back into his hold as if they'd never stopped dancing. "You, my dear, are the perfect distraction for this time period. That was excellent."

Smoothing over his hair, there were a lot of things he wanted to say, but enacting the 'holy crap just chill dude' plan was probably going to take some form of meditation first. Fang settled on something to satisfy his curiosity. "Thanks. Where's buddy friend? Closet or something?"

That sly grin overtook Zifeara's face once more. "Please, closet is amateur work. No one looks under a bed until the smell starts up. We have time to spare."

You know you're starting to become a horrible person when the thought of a man crammed under his own excessively frilled bed makes you laugh. He couldn't help it and he knew he certainly wouldn't get any flack for finding morbid things funny around *Zifeara*. She gave a grand flourish of her hand and a mock bow herself before she eyed him in that way that made him nervous.

"I did say we had time, do you think we could squeeze in one more dance before they drag us back to judgement central? It's the one thing from this time I actually enjoyed."

Knowing he'd have to make up for snapping at her earlier, Fang sighed and offered himself up. "Probably. Though we could do this at home, you know."

Cocking a brow, Zifeara settled as the last notes of the current song faded out.

"And pass up the full experience? I'm not wearing this dress in my own house and it'll be centuries before I have to put it on again, a few more minutes won't be the death of either of us. Besides," she brushed some unseen lint off his shoulder before resting her fingers there, "you best appreciate the tight pants while you still have them. I didn't forget my threat to put you in a kimono, Fang. I'm just waiting 'til we get a good festival."

Scowling, he knew there was no hiding the color he could feel tinting his cheeks, yet he also didn't entirely care. There were worse ways to embarrass yourself than donning a period accurate dress. Fang recognized the next song[23] as one he knew Zifeara loved, making it even harder to deny her request.

---

[23] "Violente Valse" – Caravan Palace

There were also worse ways to end a night you thought would turn out disastrously than pressed close to the love of your life whispering about how absolutely hideous some of the people surrounding you had managed to make themselves.

CHAPTER 37

Spooks and Dragons

S tepping through the portal into her foyer, Zifeara could barely hear herself think. The music[24] pouring from her house-wide sound system was absurdly loud and she was surprised the windows weren't shaking. Fang nearly toppled over as he shot a hand to his headphones and it made her thankful she could legitimately shift herself deafer.

"You've been letting Aun listen to your MP3 again, haven't you?"

Fang shrugged as they both made their way into the game room, finding the source of the cacophony. The small music player connected to the stereo looked strikingly familiar, while the perpetrator of the disturbance himself was standing atop a couch, singing at the top of his lungs.

"Aun, what in Hell's name are you doing?"

Whipping around, the tiger's face brightened as he continued to shout the words to the song, hopping down from his perch. Zifeara had to admit, for someone not from their time who had to have learned how to dance from watching TV all day, Aun wasn't half bad. He took one of her hands, twirling himself around her, and she could *feel* Fang's eyes roll. She knew exactly what Aun was up to, though she couldn't say she wasn't tempted. There was a female part to this song and today had been favorable in the end.

"You don't even know who this song is about!"

That hardly seemed to matter. Aun persisted, constantly moving around her and pointedly ignoring every condescending thing out of Fang's mouth. Heaving a sigh, Zifeara gave up; there was only so long she could resist light-hearted tomfoolery with the good mood she was in. Besides, if Aun wanted to test her with the unsubtly suggestive song he had playing, it was only fair to prove that he had no clue what he

---

[24] "Moves Like Jagger" – Maroon 5

was getting himself into. Even without using a fraction of her powers, Zifeara was betting she could turn the tiger on his head.

Their impromptu dance party ended up lasting an hour before Graham put a stop to the excessive noise with a summon to dinner. It would forever be entertaining to introduce Aun to more new food, though pizza and ice cream were up there as the most confusing for him. He was disappointed to learn that ice cream didn't stay cold for forever, but that was short lived when he discovered how many flavors it came in and that he could try four of them *right now.*

Once they were all full, Zifeara announced that they would definitely be spending the night in her house before returning to the past. She figured one night of complete comfort and no fear of danger was overdue and with the stressful nature of the last two days, she was dying to relax.

Aun wasn't quite ready to end his obsession with all things future, which was how they ended up on the couch in the game room, colossal TV displaying a house so stereotypically haunted that it had cobwebs in every corner. While Zifeara was comfortably in the middle of both boys, Aun was practically tucked under her. He didn't seem to understand the concept of movies being works of fiction and certainly wasn't on board with the idea of some ghost taking over his body. Fang was trying his hardest not to laugh out loud at every single jump scare purely because he was watching the tiger as opposed to the movie, and Zifeara couldn't claim she was in any sort of hurry to inform their friend that possession wasn't a thing real ghosts could do. She nearly came to regret that choice by bedtime.

Instead of turning towards the room that had been designated as his, Aun caught Zifeara's hand before she could reach the stairs to her own. Scratching the back of his head, he didn't manage to keep embarrassment from tinging his request.

"Uh, do I... have to stay down here? There's strength in numbers and you're probably a good deterrent for spectral evil... right?"

Cocking her hip to the side, she raised an eyebrow at him. "Aun, are you saying you want to come sleep with us? Like we're your parents or something?"

Fang was the first to decide this had gone far enough. "Dude, calm down. You'll be fine sleeping by yourself - possession isn't a real thing that can happen; ghosts can't even mess with the living."

The tiger's eyes widened and his posture grew rigid before whispering, "They actually exist?"

Zifeara passed her free hand over her face. There were times it wasn't worth the fight and now was definitely one of them. She was too tired for this. Keeping hold of his hand, she made for her room again. "Fine, c'mon you baby."

"Wait, seriously?" Fang's indignance wouldn't dissuade her.

"You don't have to be included in this; him sleeping with me leaves your room open. I'm going to bed either way, you do you."

Leading the way up the stairs and pushing her door open, Zifeara strode right up to her bed, let go of Aun, and flopped face first into the blankets. She'd get under the covers in a second, but being horizontal really brought out the exhaustion settling into her bones. She may have been able to go through life without sleeping, but some things could only be fixed by true unconsciousness. She could feel the bed dip before Aun vaulted over her, burrowing into the sheets on her left. Rolling just a bit to the side, she cracked her eye open to either watch Fang leave or push him into laying down.

Hovering with his arms crossed, the scowl on her best friend's face indicated that he'd need persuading to make a decision. Realistically, Zifeara couldn't see the problem with all of them sleeping in her bed; she'd be the buffer between the boys, she and Fang always slept together, and Aun had more than likely learned his lesson about getting fresh with her.

"You know you don't really want to sleep by yourself when we're in the same house. Lay down, Fang."

His noise of protest said 'You're right and I hate you,' but he wisely remained silent as he lifted the covers on her other side and climbed into bed. Zifeara turned all the way over and got in with them, stretching out until she was comfortable. She almost got to tease Fang for being so grumpy, but the sudden movement in front of her made her jump.

Aun surfaced from under the blankets, wrapping an arm around her waist and cramming himself beneath her chin, ears flat and tail tightly wrapped around his legs. He molded every inch of himself to her and it made her giggle. He looked like he believed that if he couldn't see anything, they couldn't see him either. Of all things, she hadn't expected a B-grade horror movie to be so unsettling to a boy who grew up in a world of far scarier things than angry spirits.

Fang sighed behind her, grumbling about how stupid this situation was and trying to settle into as normal a position as he could with a plus one. It didn't escape her notice that he laid his arm over both of them, nor that there was a distinct lack of protest from the tiger at the action. Who knew all it would take to make everyone get along was for something to spook Aun.

¤ ¤ ¤

Somewhere in the back of his mind, Fang knew something was off. He wasn't entirely awake yet, still groggy and mind struggling to remain asleep. He knew they were safe, he was nice and comfortable, and the familiar weight against his chest told him all was as it should be. *It still felt wrong.*

Minutely shifting his weight, his arms closed around the warm mass clinging to him. He smiled in his bleary haze; the tail around his legs and fingers desperately clutching at his shirt were an all too common occurrence. Zifeara was dreaming and

276

it wasn't about anything pleasant. With the kind of day they'd had, he wasn't surprised. Fang absentmindedly raised a hand to relax her as he often did anymore, instantly finding the point of contact between skull and ear and rubbing softly.

It only took a few passes before the deep, droning rumble started, but something about the sound set him on edge as opposed to soothing him back to sleep. Willing himself more awake though not stopping his motions, Fang slowly forced his eyes open. Blinking once or twice, the thought occurred to him that he should have been able to see Aun over Zifeara. He looked down the length of the bed, but didn't see any small, furry mammals, meaning their third bedmate was either somewhere *in* the blankets or altogether absent. Fang couldn't remember the inconvenience of having to get up to use the bathroom in the middle of the night, but that didn't mean it didn't happen to everyone else in the world. His eyes almost shut again, convinced he was just being paranoid. Almost.

The purring just under his chin faltered a moment as the ear he was petting flicked, brushing across his skin. Fang was awake in a flash, cold chill down his spine. That... *felt* wrong. That was too broad and completely the wrong shape to be what it should have been. Unwinding his arms and leaning back, he almost screamed when he saw stripes. It came out as more of whine, but thankfully, the disturbance caused Aun to yawn and turn over, leaving Fang to escape. He was glad he didn't know where Zifeara was because she never would have let him live that down if she'd seen it. He mostly just wanted to wash his hands.

Creeping to the bedroom door, he made his way down the stairs and checked the spots he most often found Zifeara when she couldn't sleep. She had to have been wiped out, but that was usually prime time for insomnia to strike. He became more and more worried for his friend with each empty room, but she had an awful lot of places to go. Since he couldn't find Zifeara anywhere in the house, Fang assumed she had to be outside. Exiting from the door in the kitchen, he had a decent idea of where she might have ended up.

It wasn't any mystery why Zifeara loved her koi pond; the moonlight reflecting across the ripples caused by the roiling waterfall was a magical sight and the constant sound of flowing water was calming. The reeds surrounding the large slab of slate she was seated on formed a sort of alcove and Fang might not have even seen her had he not discovered her there many times before. The verdant fortress lacked a roof and she often found peace stargazing to the sounds of her personal corner of nature.

Knowing she had to have heard him approaching, Fang stopped just before parting the stalks. "Can I come in?"

"Mhm."

Moving the plants out of his way and breaching their protective ring, he wasn't surprised to find Zifeara on her back, arms behind her head, tail softly thumping by her side. She turned to meet his stare as the vibrant light of the night shimmered green over her eyes. There were times like this that Fang couldn't help but shudder; her gaze was soft and almost sad, but eyeshine was a big tell to the predator she truly was. He had rarely noticed it until he started following her to older times, though he supposed they had always been that way. Putting the thought aside, he sat down and let his own eyes skim the water masking its occupants.

Zifeara sat up next to him and for just a moment, the tension in the air was palpable. Fang didn't dare look at her just yet, afraid of what he'd find. It was only once she emitted a heavy sigh that he turned towards her. She had her gaze trained on the water, something just as deep and unseen playing behind the thick veil of indigo he'd become obsessed with.

"It hurts every single time."

Before he could ask her to clarify, she continued. "Each time I turn into that...*fucking thing*, I can feel every snap of my bones, each muscle tear, and every scale stab through my skin. It's the only time I have no control over my shifting and it's agony."

Fang felt his stomach churn as bile fought to the back of his throat, hot and acrid. His mouth went dry and he was locked in place.

"Normally when I shift, it's a fluid motion; every piece of me works in tandem to become something else and it feels no different than just... slipping on a jacket and stretching. But when the It comes out, it feels like I'm exploding from the inside. I'm fireproof but I swear nothing has ever felt more like burning alive. It breaks everything I am to fold me up and store me away for later, just like the vessel I was meant to be."

His hands shook and tears sprung to his eyes at the waver working its way into his best friend's voice. Her fists clenched, her nails likely making holes in the knees of her pajamas.

"If that wasn't bad enough, when it gets what it wants I'm almost... trapped inside. I can see through its eyes as if I'm held prisoner in its skull. I have to watch everything it does as I'm powerless to stop it. I've tried a few times, but I have no control of its actions. I *hate* being helpless against it, *hate* that I have to pick who to unleash this thing on, *hate* that I can't just fight it myself. I'd battle it all night if I could keep it from doing what it does."

Zifeara finally looked up, though not at him. The moon hung high overhead, bright and somehow more ominous than ever before. "Once I get you two back to where we belong, I'll have to go again. It's coming."

The light breeze that picked up only served to highlight the wet trails racing down his face. The taste of his own stomach acid was growing stronger and more potent, urging him to retch. Fang couldn't imagine something so terrible, much the less that Zifeara- his world, his strength, his *everything*- had to go through this every single month and there was nothing he could do for her.

"I never wanted to tell you about it because there are some things I wouldn't wish on anyone else, no matter how terrible a person they are. I've been dealing with this for almost as long as our planet has existed; I know what to expect and how to plan for it. For the most part, the rest of my life is whatever I want it to be- it's just that *one night...*"

Swallowing was a monumental task but he managed, forcing down every physical reaction he was having to being trusted with details surely no one else had. He had to at least try and handle this well or Zifeara would go right back to keeping all her problems pent up. Fang had asked for this and he knew it.

Scooting closer, he placed himself behind her, reaching his arms around to make her lean back. "If I know anything about you, you don't want me to say I'm sorry. I really, *really* want to because..." Fang had to take a deep breath before he could finish his sentence. "Because I can't imagine what that's like and I'd give *anything* to take even a fraction of that pain from you."

Zifeara's chest rose and shuddered, a clear indication that even revealing this much had taken a toll on her. Fang bent over, pressing his nose to the soft spot where neck meets shoulder and murmuring into her exposed skin. "But I'm not going anywhere, Zifeara. I know that thing isn't you and there's nothing in this world or any other that could stop me from wanting to be by your side. I'm glad you finally told me. You can *always* turn to me."

There was a prolonged lull where the only sounds were the rush of water, the steady pumping of blood, and the unseen crickets populating the yard. They had both stopped breathing as if the drag of air through their lungs would cause a shift neither were prepared for. Zifeara was the first to regain her faculties, bringing a hand to cover one of Fang's larger ones. She didn't speak, content the simple touch could communicate far better than her words. It was another several minutes before he broke the spell.

"Can... can I see it?"

She whipped her head around to shoot him a look that suggested he was insane for wanting to be that close to such a monster, but Fang ran his fingers down her back to illustrate his point. Zifeara blinked a few times before her eyes narrowed and her brows pulled up in concern.

"Okay..." she whispered.

Facing forward yet again, she leaned away from him, pulling her shirt up and over her head. The faint purple lines streaking their way across her shoulders and down her torso stunned the embarrassment right out of him. The marks resembled bruises but were too neat; lacking the bleeding spread a regular blemish would show. They formed the perfect outline of bones, seamlessly mirroring a medical illustration for the structure of wings.

Fang traced a line from the connection to her spine all the way out, following it as far as it would go across her shoulder and right down the majority of her back. If these didn't signify the worst time of Zifeara's life, he would have found them hauntingly beautiful.

"They keep getting darker until the very moment I turn, entirely black by sunset. It even... feels like there's something under my skin by then, too- like I've got actual bones just below the surface. It's... it's kinda weird."

"Promise I'm not being insensitive?" Zifeara gave him an odd look before he grabbed the shirt from her hands and held it up for her to slip back into. "You have the most badass tattoo I've ever seen."

Her mouth hung open for a moment before she laughed, raising her arms. "You're lucky I have a twisted sense of humor, Fang. If I didn't go as far as collecting things with the It on them, I might have actually been offended."

Something pinged in the back of his mind and he found himself looking around to see if she'd brought her bag out here for some reason. "Oh hell, I completely forgot! I had something to show you. I have for a stupidly long time now! Where's the bag?"

"I left it in the house, duh. What do you have?"

Fang didn't think he wanted to try and explain it to her, especially not since he'd had such a strong reaction to finding the thing. "It's a necklace. Where in the house? I'll go get it. I think this is something I'd really rather show you and have *you* tell *me* what it looks like."

Retrieving Zifeara's bag from where she'd left it, he dug around until he found the trinket. Sitting back down and handing it over, Fang watched her eyes widen as she inspected the necklace.

"Where did you get this?"

"Picked it up at a stall in Oranda while you were gone. Dude who sold it to me said it came from somewhere far off, though. I swear I've seen something that looked like the thing on it before..."

Zifeara's ears turned down and she met his gaze solemnly. "You have. When you were really little, maybe six or seven, I had something brought into the house late at night. I didn't want you to see it because I didn't know if it would scare you or not. You weren't supposed to be awake, but bedtime was always more of a suggestion with you."

She shook her head and turned the necklace over once more, now inspecting the back of it more carefully than was really necessary. "It was a slab of stone with a painting on it. A painting of *this*. Do you remember?"

Bringing a hand to his mouth, Fang couldn't say he did. Realistically, his memory of everything before high school was pretty crap, much less when he was *that* young. Still, her question prompted one of his own. "No, but where did you put it? I've lived in your house my whole mortal life and I've never seen anything in your collection."

"I... It's like that on purpose. There's a vault under the house; it's hidden past a secret door so no one could find it without knowing exactly where to look. I keep my most prized possessions and everything I've been collecting for millennia down there. The vault is lined with the strongest materials on Marien and holds irreplaceable objects. You've never seen it because I've never taken *anyone* down there."

Looking back to him, she held the necklace out for him to take. "This is going to need to be put with the others. Hang onto it and I might let you do it yourself one day."

Fang wrapped the cord of the pendant around his fingers, inspecting the dragon on it once more. As much as he wanted to see the vast and varied depictions of this horror, he knew better than to protest being made to wait, or worse yet, try and find the room himself. There were so many places it could be hidden, but if Zifeara wasn't ready to share, he was not going to be the one to find it.

"Is this really what it looks like?"

Minutely nodding, Zifeara leaned back on her hands. "Close as anything ever is, yeah. The It isn't a pretty sight and there's only so many details you can gather about it and live to tell the tale..."

Fang didn't have a response to that and he was fairly certain Zifeara was ready to let the topic drop anyway. Instead, he stood, holding a hand out to help her up. "Let's go back to bed. You're going to need the sleep for tomorrow."

Softly sighing, she accepted the offer and held tight once she was upright. "Fang? Thank you. You were... right. It sucks to talk about some things, but having someone else who knows about some of my bullshit is sort of nice. In a weird way."

"You know, Zia," He smiled and brushed his thumb over her knuckles, "A long time ago, someone taught me that expressing my feelings didn't make me weak or any less of a man. That being vulnerable wasn't any kind of personal shortcoming. That needing *help* didn't mean I'd failed. Maybe you should start listening to yourself when you talk. You've got some good ideas knocking around in there with all the sarcasm."

That lopsided grin of hers over took her face. "Oh really? Well then maybe *you* should stop giving me lip while I teach. You learned all your sarcasm from me buddy boy, don't test the master."

"Would 'the master' like me to carry her upstairs out of respect for her amazing skill? Perhaps tuck her back in?"

Maybe it would be easier to just relax around Zifeara than he thought. He hadn't felt the least bit embarrassed to say that directly to her face and the color it brought to her cheeks didn't make him want to disappear into the pond. *This was getting easier.*

Tilting an ear back and shoving him as she moved towards the house, Zifeara was back to her usual self. "Fuck off!"

Fang couldn't have been any happier unless he could prevent what would come to pass as the full moon arced into the inky night sky.

CHAPTER 38

Bad Things Are Coming

S ire, news from the wizard!"

Sighing, Torvak looked up from the maps spread across the heavy wooden table. If this was about to be like the last time his courier had 'news', he was going to make a new cape out of the man's hide.

"Yes, what is it?"

"My lord, Nagarae arrived in the region safely, but..."

Narrowing his eyes, Torvak could feel the fire in his chest straining to escape. He *detested* bad news, even more so when it was bad news due to incompetence. He'd thought that by employing demons as opposed to enslaving them as he did his human workers would have done some good, and yet...

The man straightened up, gripping the end of his scaled tail to prevent it from betraying his nerves. "She's had to relocate to a different town. Tiyang was destroyed before she got there."

"Destroyed? How so?" Torvak had a rather good idea of what had happened, but he wanted to be certain.

"It seems to have burned down. From what Nagarae's message said, it may have been attacked by something, maybe a dragon."

At least Torvak knew with greater certainty where Zifeara was now, give or take a few miles. It was worrying that she was so close and that she seemed to be moving to intercept him. It would appear that she'd caught on to his plans and that was highly inconvenient.

While his minion hovered, Torvak thumbed the stones on the table. The one closest to him shone a brilliant sapphire, something deep inside cycling through various greens and blues. It was only the size of a plum, but the Ocean's Heart hadn't been easy to obtain, and he knew better than to underestimate its power. This one small gem could wreak untold oceanic havoc, but he needed it for greater purposes. The three stones in front of him were worth several times their weight in gold, even before he repurposed them.

Waving a his hand in the direction of his courier, Torvak dismissed the man, needing to be left alone to further plan his next move. Sending one his most adept wizards after the shifter's merry band of misfits would buy him time to crest Mount Shisvrik and take the Galaxy Opal. He was willing to bet he could reclaim the stones he was missing by prying them from Zifeara's cold dead hands when the time came, but staying one step ahead of her could only make things easier.

Dragging his claws across the parchment, he smiled to himself. This was still going well. Sure, Zifeara had two of the stones he needed, but he had more. He was winning this war and had much more at his disposal than a kitten with inferior blood underneath a bad haircut and a blind, emotionally compromised branch. He had the upper hand and he would be the first man in history to achieve immortality and kill a demigod to preserve it.

¤ ¤ ¤

It wasn't hard to figure out he was dreaming this time, yet Fang wasn't in control of the events at all, nor was this something that he could recall from his past. He was in his own house, sitting on the edge of his bed, wearing only a pair of jeans. He was staring at the doorway to his unused bathroom, listening. Waiting for something. Electricity surged under his skin, betraying an anticipation he hadn't felt in a long time, but he was still. *Good things to those who wait.*

There was something odd about the silence hanging over his space, though that could just be a product of the dream. It was far too quiet, yet... he almost felt as though someone was watching him; hunched in the corner of the room, observing the twitching of his ears as he strained to discern what it was he felt excited for. The presence didn't feel entirely benevolent, either. Just as he was about to turn his head to find out what had stowed away in his unconscious mind, the object of his rapt attention made itself known.

Zifeara leaned into the doorway, every inch the very definition of perfection, though in clothes he was positive she didn't own. Not only would she never wear shorts *that* revealing, but she definitely didn't have a single crop top to her name, especially not one that said 'BITE ME' in bold, red lettering across the front. He could feel the current in his blood sparking, close to igniting a fire he couldn't hope to put out. He was not ready for another one of *those* dreams, but this was always the best train wreck he couldn't tear his eyes from.

Fang watched each muscle flex beneath her exposed skin as she sauntered towards him and he was fairly certain that simple observation had already set his own body down a path he was all too familiar with. As much as he was working on achieving the

DEMENTED: DESTINED DERANGEMENT

relaxed state around her that he used to settle into effortlessly, Zifeara turned him on without trying at the best of times. He was willing himself to wake up before this got out of hand again, but something was keeping him here. A haze settled over his mind, causing his eyes to lose focus and draining him of the ability to think.

Zifeara ran a finger under his jaw, lifting his gaze from her midriff to her entrancing smile. Just that brief contact was enough to push him over the edge, blood boiling in his veins and no longer able to back away from the cliff he perched upon. Reaching his hands out, his fingers brushed the expanse of tantalizing flesh, drawing a deep hum from its owner. Her skin was warmer than usual, as if she'd been lying the sun just moments ago. The familiar scent that always hung over Zifeara flooded his lungs and Fang knew he was lost to this.

Slowly sinking down, Zifeara placed herself in his lap, straddling his hips. The turn this was taking was already far worse than his last; he'd dreamed about *doing things* with her before, but they very rarely involved her being this forward. It was getting him riled up faster than it should have. Somewhere in his last bastion of logic, Fang remembered that something about the room was off and had unsettled him before he became nothing more than a sentient sex drive. He tried to look towards the disturbance one more time, but he didn't quite make it.

Huffing, Zifeara slipped her hands under his jaw and turned him back, destroying any fragment of sense he had left by insistently pressing her lips to his. The fog that had begun seeping into his consciousness completely consumed him, sending a harsh shudder down his spine and overwriting everything he wanted. Fang's body moved without him, sending his palms up and under her shirt and opening his mouth to allow her tongue inside. *She tasted divine, like stardust dipped in honey.*

He was given precious little time to enjoy the flavor of pure bliss before she retreated. Something about being denied such pleasure so quickly made him irrationally angry. He wanted that back. He wanted *more*. A growl reverberated deep in his chest, a guttural sound he'd never heard himself make. There was a price for Zifeara's coy behavior in this one place where he could have what he wanted and Fang was about to lay down the law. This was his dream, his mind, *she belonged to him here*.

He was lightning fast to tear the flimsy shirt over her head, letting it fall wherever it may as he tangled his fingers into the base of her hair. Now with firm control of her head, Fang tilted it to the side, giving him unrestricted access to the column of her neck. The second his lips touched skin, Zifeara squirmed, creating a maddening friction as she moved her hips. The sudden pressure to his crotch caused him to jerk, accidentally dragging his teeth a bit too hard. The tang of blood filled his mouth and he could feel his nostrils flare as they took in the scent.

Fang was instantly someone else. He no longer wanted to be gentle with his lover in any capacity as his usual MO demanded; this was the most intoxicating thing he'd ever tasted and he needed to keep the blood flowing. His canines were always made to serve one very specific purpose and for the first time in his life, he was ready to use them as nature intended.

Yanking the fistful of hair he held further back, the new angle gave him plenty of room to sink his fangs into the meat of Zifeara's shoulder, burrowing ever closer to the source of liquid euphoria. The whine spilling from her mouth might have been the most erotic sound he'd ever heard her make and it spurred him onwards, sucking at the wound to gorge himself. Fang wasn't sure when he started rocking his hips upwards to meet her own, but between the taste on his tongue and rub against his cock, he was going to get off from this and *quickly.*

Blood dribbled from the corners of his mouth as he messily gnashed his jaws to prevent the punctures from closing, easing the slide of their bodies. He was starting to get full but he couldn't have cared less; all he wanted was to keep going until he exploded. He was pretty sure his stomach would outlast what was about to be the absolute best orgasm of his life. He might have gotten to find out had the body above him not stilled.

Jolting awake, Fang's eyes darted about, attempting to discern his position and how immediately in danger he was of having to explain a wet dream. His stomach flipped as he moved, warning of his impending need to vomit. Sitting up in the sleeping bag, he found Zifeara where she always was; on his right, sound asleep, unaware of the utter disaster he was right now. Thank gods.

Easing himself out and into the woods, Fang leaned on a tree to catch his breath. He kept his mouth open in case he really was going to be sick. In all the dreams he never dared to admit he succumbed to from time to time, he had never *once* been even remotely rough, much less...

He wasn't like that. He didn't want to hurt *anyone* he had ever cared about in that way to such an extent. Hell, the worst he'd ever done was leave perhaps an excessive amount of hickies on Bridget's neck once, just because she was being a brat and teasing him about being so soft with her.

Fang wanted to flay himself. He was somehow *still hard* and *still* about to hurl at the same time. His body was having two completely different, opposing reactions. He wanted to just curl up into a ball and cry over both until he forgot. There had to be a reason these dreams, these urges, were presenting themselves. Zifeara had told him once he became immortal that the elixir could change his body- bring out things over time that otherwise would not have happened. She couldn't tell him when or even if it would occur, but he so desperately hoped that he wasn't changing for the worse.

While his gut was no closer to settling, he started moving further into the trees, intent on doing something to calm himself down before dawn. They'd need to get going again to make it up the mountain before night fell like Zifeara wanted them to.

¤ ¤ ¤

Traveling at a steady clip, the Arneirs were extra spry due to their extended rest in the future. They hadn't taken a break since they'd set out from the outcropping they'd slept under and it was already midday. The terrain was getting more and more sparsely planted as they surged onwards, further indicating that they were constantly climbing.

As ill as the thought still made him, Fang needed to know if his dream might have had something to do with what he was. "Zifeara? I was, uh, hoping you could teach me something more specific on the way up the mountain. I wanted to know about... my race."

Glancing back at him, her brow furrowed and a lilt of concern crept into her tone. "Fang, I taught you everything there was to know about the way you work and you're fairly normal for your breed. What else could you want?"

Gods, he was not looking forward to this. "You taught me about *modern* Vampyratu, sure, but I want to know about the primal kind; who we were before we became civilized."

Aun chimed in from where he'd been lounging atop Thrush's head, voice diminished by his tabby form. "Oh, that sounds fun! Did his race always suck at being demons or is that just him?"

While they both glared at the cat, Zifeara was the first to speak again. "Actually Aun, Vampyratu used to be devastating hunters. They had a wide range of tools in their arsenal and it was only their tendency to prey upon humans that altered them in the end."

She sighed, instructing Orro Heme to slow down and move off the trail, urging them to rest now since they wouldn't be stopping again today. While the horses drank and grazed on the last patch of grass they'd see until the journey up Mount Shisvrik was complete, she motioned for the boys to huddle up around her.

"How... in depth do you want this lesson to be, Fang? There were some fairly unsavory things your ancestors engaged in and I'm not sure what benefit it would be for you to know all of it..."

This meant there was likely a very good reason for his unnatural behavior in the dream. Now he *had* to know. "Tell me everything, Zia. No species is without it's unfortunate history, and besides, we aren't monsters anymore. I know I'm not like they were." *In theory.*

Rubbing at her temples, Zifeara relented. "Primal Vampyratu were ambush predators. That means they sat around and waited for a good opportunity to seize prey. They often lived on the outskirts of human villages or in abandoned buildings near well-traveled paths to give them more foot traffic to choose from. They looked very different than you do now."

Rummaging in her bag, she produced a tome and flipped through chapters until she found what she was after. Turning the book around and presenting it to him, Fang swallowed hard at the image before him. The creature depicted had a humanoid body but large, bat-like wings, each with a wicked claw at the apex. Its grey skin made it appear anemic, clinging to its delicate bones. The nose formed almost an upside down heart, comprised of several folds and was a bit too large to be proportional. It had no hair, meaning its familiar ears were exposed, though Fang could tell they were slightly wider than his own. It had oddly long, clawed fingers and it wore very little clothing.

Tearing himself away from the large, rounded eyes, he handed the book to Aun and posed his question in the safest way he could think of. "So how did this thing, hideous as it is, manage to reel in something to eat? It doesn't look particularly strong..."

"Oh big surprise there. Farrah, a human *fucked that*!?" Aun had an ear turned down in disgust, but that didn't stop him from studying the thing.

"Well..." The hesitance Zifeara approached this with put Fang on edge. "Yes and no. Inbreeding with humans was a direct result of how they functioned socially. Vampyratu males patrolled a territory, fighting for the best access to humans since they were the weakest and therefor easiest prey to catch. Females, however, wandered place to place as a way to keep themselves and their young safer. If a female got spotted passing through a male's territory, he'd mate her and then she could move on."

"Oh, since they could fly, the courtship must have been fun! They have an aerial dance or something like that?" Finally something positive about his race! Fang's joy was short lived as Zifeara grimaced.

"Afraid not, love. I said he *would* mate her if she was seen, not that she had a choice. Vampyratu would have been classified a tier three intelligence level at best; males were brutes and females only cared for their young until they were strong enough to fly and then left them on their own."

"What do you mean a tier three?" Fang thought Aun was picking the wrong thing to focus on, but then again, the tiger did live in this time and such barbarism was commonplace here.

"In the future, we have different classes sentients are sorted into based on how self-aware they are and how well they can communicate their thoughts and feelings with others." Zifeara pointed at the Arneirs. "Heme and the girls are a class two species; they can understand the common language and react appropriately, but they can't speak and lack more intensive problem solving skills. Wicked smart as they are, some abstract concepts are wasted on them. The three of us are obviously tier one, highest on the scale. Anyway."

She waved the tiger off and continued. "Vampyratu started up a nasty habit of... playing with their food. Male and female alike. They almost never killed the humans they fed from anyway, they just took it one step further and before you know it, they started ending up with bat babies that weren't quite right."

"Okay, but how do you get a human to hold still long enough to do all of that without them calling for others? It's what humans do and they can't all be on a deserted stretch of road at night, right?" Aun handed the book back to Zifeara and she nodded.

"Look at you trying to problem solve like a predator. There were a lot of things Vampyratu were good at, one of which was immobilizing other creatures through sheer intimidation. They could exert a force on weaker beings, rendering them too scared to move; one reason why they favored humans was because it worked especially well on them."

The tiger snapped his head in Fang's direction, tone highly accusatory. "Wait, can you still do that?"

Grinning sheepishly, Fang shrugged. "I mean, yeah. I try not to though, unless someone's in my face and really pissing me off. It has its uses."

He was well aware Aun had just connected the dots and realized this had happened before. The first time Zifeara left them alone together, they had not been on good terms nor had he really meant to let himself abuse his powers like that. It got Aun to shut the fuck up and leave him alone for a while, but it was still slightly uncalled for.

Unfortunately, this explained a lot. Fang had dreamt of going primal. The desire to feed from warm bodies was in his nature and he'd ended up with stronger Vampyratu traits than his siblings, maybe he was just starting to feel the effects of going his whole life without feeding from a sentient. That, or the elixir was finally altering him and this was part of the repercussions. Whatever it was, the mere thought of blood in any form still made him ill, meaning he'd steer clear of it for as long as he could manage. Blood may have been akin to water for his kind, but there was a definite time in which he could go without.

Once back on the road, their progress up the mountain didn't falter in the slightest. The winding path meant that the Arneirs had to stack single file to fit, but it seemed well-maintained so there was little issue. Zifeara had mentioned that their current destination was a small village only a fourth of the way to the summit, the highest anyone dared live on Shisvrik. The wildlife and climate generally deterred most from even venturing higher, aside from the handful of brave souls that guarded the Galaxy Opal. Fang assumed Zifeara had a plan for traversing the rest of the mountain, likely one that would allow them to avoid trouble.

Though the day was warm, the air grew crisp from the altitude and the breeze blowing through the rocky crags delivered a faint chill reminiscent of the snow-dusted peaks. The few pines that had managed to take root here were laden with new cones and the small antelope skipping across the rocks kept their new calves close to their sides. Birds darted to and fro, each merrily screaming to the world about their day as they carried on. The hills were strangely serene despite the many large predators Zifeara described living here.

While the peaceful ascent was a nice change of pace from being beset upon by unfriendly creatures, it gave Fang too much time to think and he could not put last night out of his head. Not only was feeding from a sentient such a primal, vulgar urge, but the fact that it had been Zifeara was more than a little worrying. From what she had said about Vampyratu, sex and food had always been closely linked, but he knew for a gods given fact that he would *never* hurt her.

Watching Zifeara as she laughed while talking to Aun, Fang could feel that queasy sensation stir again. *I'm not a monster, I'm not a monster, I'm not a monster...* He could think it all he wanted, but it wasn't helping. *Nothing could make me hurt her, not a goddamned thing in this world. I love her more than life itself, I could never.* Recalling how her body had stilled as he reached his climax caused him to bury his face into Treble's mane lest he try to vomit again.

Playing the dream over and over, he had a nagging feeling that he was missing something. Every time he attempted to focus on it, however, it slipped away into the recesses of his consciousness. It was like trying to grab an eel that had stolen your wedding ring; he needed to catch it but was failing miserably. Fang grappled with his own mind until they reached the small town they were headed for, straining to sift out the one thing he wanted from the active torture that plagued him. He never got any closer to finding it, but he had a bad feeling about the whole ordeal.

He never wanted to hurt Zifeara... but maybe there was something close at hand that did. Fang had sworn to lay his life down over and over to save her even the slightest amount of grief, so whatever it was would have to go through him to get to her. He dreaded the thought that something could be trying exactly that.

SONGLIST

These lists are to provide some extra listening immersion while reading. These are all songs to fit the mood of the scene or that helped the author feel connected to a character. A superscripted number will denote when a song should be played from this list and will be shown in the body.

Recommend listening by chapters:

Chapter 1
1 "Sugar" by Robin Shultz

Chapter 2
2 "Let's Go" by Joe Ghost
3 "Jetfuel" by Joel Fletcher and Uberjak'd

Chapter 4
4 Ho Hey by The Lumineers

Chapter 5
5 "Learn To Be Lonely" by Andrew Lloyd Webber and Charles Hart
        (from The Phantom of the Opera)
6 "Hate Me" by Eurielle

Chapter 7
7 "The Munsta" by SCNDL

Chapter 10
8 "The Girl" by City and Color
9 "Little Talks" by Of Monsters And Men

Chapter 11
10 "Thistle and Weeds" by Mumford and Sons

Chapter 13
11 "I'm Gonna Be" (500 Miles) by The Proclaimers
12 "Six Weeks" by Of Monsters And Men

Chapter 14
13 "Sabotage" by Kura
14 "La Da Dee" by Cody Simpson

Chapter 15
15 "True To Me" by Metro Station

Chapter 19
16 "Lisztomania" by Phoenix

Chapter 28
17 "Wanderer's Lullaby" by Adriana Figueroa

Chapter 31
18 "Primitive" by Richard Vission

Chapter 32
19 "Nightmares" by All Time Low

Chapter 33
20 "Lover's Eyes" by Mumford and Sons

Chapter 35
21 "Ended With the Night" by Caravan Palace
22 "Alla Turca" by Mozart
23 "Violente Valse" by Caravan Palace

Chapter 37
24 "Moves Like Jagger" by Maroon 5

Character Theme Songs:

Fang
"The Music In My Headphones" by Telepathic Teddybear (Note: The singer's voice in this song is the closest I've heard to how I hear Fang's voice in my head.)

Zifeara
"When You're Evil" by Voltaire

Aun
"Animal" by Mike Snow

Zifeara's Dragon
"The Animal" by Disturbed

The Sound Cave anthem
"We Own The Night" by the Wanted

Mortis
"Oh Death" by Jen Titus

Torvak
"Don't Mess With Me" by Temposhark
"Supervillain" by Powerman 5000
"King of the World" by Porcelain Black

Lucifer
"Inside the Fire" by Disturbed
"Call Me Devil" by Friend in Tokyo

Gideon
"Human" by Ellie Goulding

Songs in general by person:

<u>Demented as a Story</u>
"Freak" by Steve Aoki, Diplo, Derro
"Raise Hell" by Dorothy
"Where the Lonely Ones Roam" by Digital Daggers
"Raise Your Glass" by P!nk
"Wolves" by Sam Tinnesz
"This Is The Hunt" by Ruelle
"Freaks" by Timmy Trumpet

<u>Fang and Zifeara</u>
"Immortals" by Fall Out Boy
"Give Me Your Hand" by The Ready Set
"Issues" by Julia Michaels
"Feel Invincible" by Skillet
"We Hold Each Other" by Great Big World
"Of the Night" by Bastille
"This Beating Heart" by The Score
"Young Forever" by The Ready Set
"I Wouldn't Mind" by He Is We
"Carry You" by Ruelle

<u>Zifeara</u>
"Battle Cry" by Beth Crowley
"One Woman Army" by Porcelain Black
"Built For This Time" by Zayde Wolf
"The Storm" by Blackmore's Night
"Lady in Black" by Blackmore's Night
"Just Like Fire" by P!nk
"No Rest for the Wicked" by Godsmack
"Hustler" by Zayde Wolf
"Out of Hell" by Skillet
"Killer Queen" by Queen
"Back From the Dead" by Skillet
"Monster" by Beth Crowley
"Battlecry" by Beth Crowley
"Blood On My Name" by The Brothers Bright
"Cry Wolf" by Bebe Rexha
"New Kind of Animal" by Ghost Machines

Fang

"Hiding In My Headphones" by Reel Big Fish

"Good Grief" by Bastille

"Headphones On Your Heart" by Leeni

"Oh Oh Oh Sexy Vampire" by Fright Ranger

"Wish You Were Here" by Blackmore's Night

"Take Me To Church" by Hoizer

"Love Like Woe" by The Ready Set

"Become the Wind" by Adriana Figueroa from The Cat Returns (2002)

"Somebody To Love Me" by Tryon

"All My Life" by WILD

"You're My Best Friend" by Queen

"Believer" by Imagine Dragons

"Genghis Khan" by Mike Snow

"I'm Bad at Life" by Falling in Reverse

"Back to Back" by The Ready Set

"Moments" by Gabrielle Aplin

"I Like It Loud" by Cash Cash

"Tightrope" by Michelle Williams from The Greatest Showman (2017)

"Born to Be Yours" by Imagine Dragons

Aun

"Girls" by AJ Mitchell

"Zero" by Imagine Dragons

"Everyone Else Is An Asshole" by Reel Big Fish

"Goodbye" by SR-71

"HandClap" by Fitz and the Tantrums

"Watch Me" by The Phantoms

"Wild Target" (feat. LIZ) by Henrik The Artist

"Freak Show" by Set It Off

"Hated" by Beartooth

"Never Going Back" by The Score

"Bad Reputation" by Joan Jett

"The Man" by Aloe Blacc

"Am I Wrong" by Nico & Vinz

"Nothing Wrong With Me" by Unlike Pluto

"Big Cat" by Wild Beasts

<u>Zifeara's Dragon</u>
"Kill Everybody" by Skrillex
"Monster" by Skillet
"Fear the Fever" by Digital Daggers
"Monsters" by Ruelle

Made in the USA
San Bernardino, CA
18 August 2019